An Irish Country Courtship

ALSO BY PATRICK TAYLOR

Only Wounded
Pray for Us Sinners
Now and in the Hour of Our Death

An Irish Country Doctor
An Irish Country Village
An Irish Country Christmas
An Irish Country Girl

An Irish Country Courtship

PATRICK TAYLOR

A Tom Doherty Associates Book

New York

AN IRISH COUNTRY COURTSHIP

Copyright © 2010 by Patrick Taylor

All rights reserved.

Maps by Elizabeth Danforth

A Forge Book
Published by Tom Doherty Associates, LLC
175 Fifth Avenue
New York, NY 10010

www.tor-forge.com

Forge® is a registered trademark of Tom Doherty Associates, LLC.

ISBN 978-0-7653-2174-9

First Edition: October 2010

Printed in the United States of America

0 9 8 7 6 5 4 3 2 1

To Dorothy

Acknowledgments

Once more I must pay tribute to my friends, without whom this book would be but a shadow.

To Simon Hally, who nurtured O'Reilly from his first appearance in *Stitches: The Journal of Medical Humour.*

To Carolyn Bateman and Paul Stevens. No author could ask for more superb editorial skills.

To Patricia Mansfield Phelan, copy editor par excellence.

To Alexis Saarela, who works as an unsung heroine in publicity.

To the artist Gregory Manchess for his superb rendering of the cover, and to Irene Gallo for yet another lovely concept.

To Tom Doherty, without whose faith in my work this and its predecessors in the series might never have seen the light of day.

To my British agents, Rosie and Jessie Buckman, who are tireless in selling foreign rights.

To Natalia Aponte, who acquired *An Irish Country Doctor* for Tom Doherty and Associates and who now, as my agent, has resolutely championed books three, four, five, and six.

And to Doctor Tom Baskett, now of Halifax, Nova Scotia, but who in the sixties was a fellow student of Queens University Belfast Medical School. He confirmed my belief in how a twin delivery might be conducted in the patient's home.

I offer you all my admiration and my deepest gratitude.

Author's Note

If you are reading this you may be new to the *Irish Country* series or you may be reentering the little village of Ballybucklebo in County Down, Northern Ireland, at the turn of the years 1964–1965. Welcome to the world of Doctor Fingal Flahertie O'Reilly, young Doctor Barry Laverty, and their redoubtable housekeeper, Mrs. Maureen "Kinky" Kincaid.

I hope you will enjoy your time here in their company and among the villagers, to say nothing of Arthur Guinness, a dipsomaniacal Labrador; Lady Macbeth, a homicidal white cat; and the remarkable women in the lives of the two doctors, Caitlin "Kitty" O'Hallorhan and Patricia Spence.

I don't want to keep you from the story, but if you could spare a moment to permit me a few words of explanation I would be grateful.

Since the appearance of the first book in the series, *An Irish Country Doctor,* many readers have written and often they have posed some pertinent questions. The most frequent of these are: What is Ulster, and how is it related to Northern Ireland and the Republic of Ireland? How were rural GPs of the time paid? How different were the way of life in rural Ireland and the practice of medicine forty years ago from the way things are today? Where *exactly* is Ballybucklebo, and who was Doctor O'Reilly? Is the vernacular of the characters true to life, or are you, Patrick Taylor, not entirely at ease with the English language? And finally, how do you pronounce "Siobhan"?

That last is easy. In Irish, *s* preceding an *i* or *e* is pronounced *sh*, and *bh* is pronounced as a *v*. The *a* is long, so Siobhan is "shivawn."

If you want the preceding questions answered before you delve into the story, you can find the answers on page 425, along with some comments on grammar and syntax. In addition, you will find a glossary of unfamiliar words and expressions on page 439.

And that's enough from me. Doctor O'Reilly and the usual suspects are waiting and are eager to greet old friends and meet new ones. Please have fun together.

PATRICK TAYLOR
Cootehall, Boyle
County Roscommon
Eire

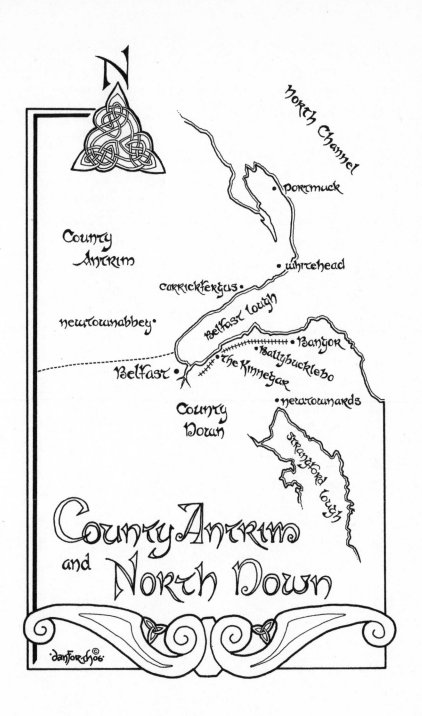

N

North Channel

• Portmuck

County
Antrim

• whitehead

carrickfergus •

Belfast Lough

newtownabbey •

• Bangor

• Ballybuckleho

Belfast • the Kinnegar

• newtownards

County
Down

Strangford Lough

County Antrim
and
North Down

danforth'06

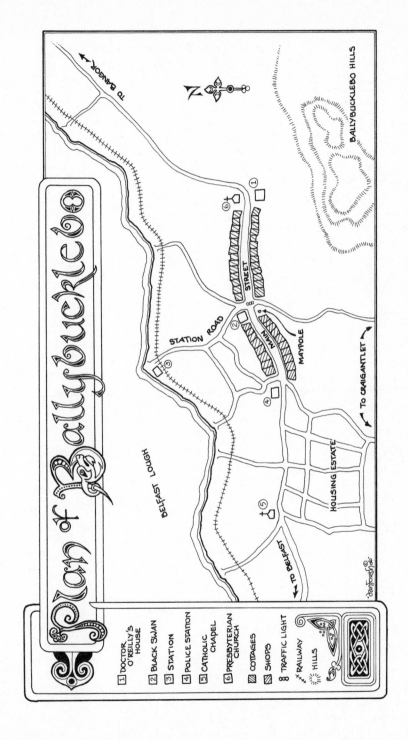

Plan of Ballybucklebo

TO BANGOR

BALLYBUCKLEBO HILLS

STREET

STATION ROAD

① ⊕⁶

② MAIN MAYPOLE

③

④

BELFAST LOUGH

TO CRAIGANTLET

HOUSING ESTATE

⊕⑤

TO BELFAST

1 DOCTOR O'REILLY'S HOUSE
2 BLACK SWAN
3 STATION
4 POLICE STATION
5 CATHOLIC CHAPEL
6 PRESBYTERIAN CHURCH
⫘ COTTAGES
⫙ SHOPS
8 TRAFFIC LIGHT
⊢⊣ RAILWAY
☼ HILLS

An Irish Country Courtship

1

A Crowd Is Not Company

Barry Laverty—*Doctor* Barry Laverty—stood in a jam-packed drawing room where the sound level was as intense as the racket of riveting guns in Harland and Wolff's shipyard. Over the noise of many conversations the gramophone blared.

How much is that doggie in the window?

Barry smiled and squeezed Patricia Spence's hand. Having her back home in Ulster was wonderful even if she had left it to the last minute to get here. He looked at her deep brown eyes, bent to her, and tried to make her hear. "Somebody *really* likes Patti Page. She made that one a hit in 1953. I was thirteen."

Patricia shrugged.

So did Barry—and he smiled. Bertie and Flo Bishop's 1964 version of their annual Boxing Day hooley was not a place for more than shouted small talk, and if Patricia hadn't heard Barry, so what? It wasn't as if she'd been disinterested when he told her how much he loved her, how he wanted to start planning their future here in Bally-bucklebo. Och, well, a couple more hours of this wouldn't matter, and then he would have her to himself and could tell her exactly what was on his mind. And damn it, this *was* a party.

"I don't suppose," he shouted into her ear, "Bertie thinks much of the Beatles or the Dave Clark Five, but I thought he might have a recording of Roy Orbison's 'Pretty Woman.'"

She raised an eyebrow.

"I'd ask him to play it for you." He squeezed her hand again. Her return was feeble.

Barry sighed. Was he boring her? He couldn't put his finger on it, but this morning she had seemed different from the laughing girl who'd headed off three months ago to study civil engineering at Cambridge University. She was more distant. More detached. He shook his head. She'd still be tired from travelling, that was all.

He looked around for space, somewhere he could talk to her, ask her if everything was all right, but it seemed the entire population of Ballybucklebo and the surrounding townland was in attendance. It was de rigueur to come to this party. No one refused an invitation from Bertie, and indeed Barry was pleased to have been asked after only six months as an assistant to Doctor Fingal Flahertie O'Reilly. Being here was a mark of how well he was fitting into the little community in the north of County Down. Being accepted by the villagers was important. He'd only six more months to go until he became a partner in the practice.

Patricia inclined her head toward the door. Her raven hair fell away from her neck in a rippling wave. By watching her lips he thought he could understand what she was saying. "Let's see if it's quieter next door." She tugged his arm and began to force her way through the throng.

He followed Patricia into the hall, loosening the knot of his tie. He reckoned the anteroom to hell was probably kept at the same temperature. It *was* less noisy, but they were brought up short by a knot of people.

Barry recognized the carroty thatch of Donal Donnelly. He was fond of Donal, the first denizen of Ballybucklebo Barry had met last July while on his way to his interview with Doctor O'Reilly. Julie Donnelly, née MacAteer, stood beside her husband, who had a tress of her hair firmly clasped between his right thumb and forefinger. Not for the first time, Barry was struck by the beauty of her long, cornsilk locks.

"I'm for having none of it. The brass neck of the man." Donal abruptly released Julie's hair, and the scowl on his usually cheerful face seemed odd at a party. "I'm for telling him to run away off and chase himself, so I am."

"But Donal, it's only a few snaps." Julie sounded calm.

"Huh. For everyone to gawp at? I'm not having it, so I'm not."

The couple had been married for three weeks, and if this was going to develop into a spat Barry would rather not become involved. But it was too late. Donal swung to him.

"We'll ask Doctor Laverty, so we will."

"Ask me what, Donal?"

"Do you see thon man over thonder?" He pointed back into the lounge to a tall, slim, immaculately coiffed individual of about thirty who wore a red velvet jacket and was smoking a cigarette held in an ivory cigarette holder.

Barry nodded. He was aware of Patricia standing at his shoulder.

"He's a cousin of Bertie Bishop, so he is. Big photographer, like. Has a studio up in Belfast."

"Like Van Buren's?" Barry asked, remembering the society photographer who took photos of couples at formal dances. They also did graduation portraits. His mother was very proud of one of Barry in his academic robe.

"I'd not know about that, sir. I'm not much of one for having my snaps took, but thon eejit wants Julie to pose for him." Donal bared his buckteeth. "It's not on, so it's not. Does he think she's the Venus de Millisle?"

"Milo, Donal. Venus de Milo. Millisle's a village on the Ards Peninsula down past Donaghadee."

"Aye. Like enough you're right." He glowered at his wife. "But she's not posing. Not for nobody."

Barry stole a glance at Donal's wife. He could understand why Bertie's cousin wanted her to model. She looked even more stunning than usual. Perhaps it was because—as only she, Donal, Barry, and O'Reilly knew—she was pregnant again.

"What kind of poses?" Patricia asked.

"Ask Julie," Donal snapped.

Julie smiled. "Mr. Hunter introduced himself, admired my hair, and asked if I'd think about letting him photograph me."

"Next thing she'll be in *Spick and Span* or *Men Only*, one of them smutty magazines," Donal said.

"It's not like that, Donal," Julie said patiently. She turned to Patricia for support. "Mr. Hunter says one of the big English shampoo companies is having a competition for their next shampoo girl. He thinks I could win it."

"You might well," Patricia said. "Your hair is lovely."

"I've said no." Donal stood legs astraddle, arms folded over his chest. "I'm saying no more."

"Donal," Patricia said, "I'd like to hear a bit more about this."

Donal sighed and inclined his head. "Go on then," he said to Julie. "You tell Miss Spence."

"He'll pay me ten pounds each for two sessions. He's only interested in my hair. He'd pay for hairdos too."

Donal put one hand against his chin. "Ten pounds?"

"Yes. And if I get into the last five when they start the judging, the company guarantees fifty pounds, even if I only come in fifth. It goes up the better you place. If I come in first, they'll pay me five hundred pounds and I'll be on all their advertising and on their labels. I might even get to do a TV ad."

"Five hundred pounds?" Donal nodded to himself. "That's a powerful wheen of do-re-mi, so it is."

It's more than Donal would make in a year, Barry thought.

"That's all well and good," Donal said with a frown. "But nobody does nothing for nothing. What's in it for him?"

"If my photos win, he gets a prize too and a contract to take pictures for the company," Julie said. "That's only fair."

"It is. You should both think about it," Patricia said, "but it must be Julie's decision."

Donal shook his head. "Not at all. She's *my* wife, so she is."

"It's Julie who's going to be photographed," Patricia said firmly.

Donal looked from Patricia to Julie, back to Patricia, then turned to Barry. "I'm blowed if I know what to say, Doctor. What do you reckon?"

The name's Laverty, not Solomon, Barry thought. And yet wasn't resolving dilemmas as much a part of rural medicine as treating coughs and colds, sniffles and sneezes? "I think," Barry said, "I'd be inclined to leave the choice up to Julie."

"Would you, sir? Honest to God?"

"Yes. I would. Cross my heart."

Donal frowned. "I'll need to think on that for a wee while, sir." He brightened. "And I'd need a jar to help me."

"You'll see Patricia's right," Barry said.

"Aye. Likely. Thank you, sir." He turned away, then back. "Can I get you and Miss Spence one while I'm at it?"

"No thanks, Donal." Barry glowed. In Ulster the offer to get somebody a drink was a sure sign of fellowship.

Donal set off, pulling Julie by the hand. " 'Scuse me, Cissie," he bawled at a heavy woman in a floral dress.

Barry guided Patricia past where Cissie Sloan stood talking, not to, but *at*, Alice Moloney, the dressmaker, as well as Mrs. Brown and Gertie Gorman. He thought Gertie looked very well for a woman who had delivered a breech baby only ten days ago.

Alice, on the other hand, looked—he struggled to find a good term—ashen. Mind you, she had only just begun treatment for her anaemia. It was probably a trick of the light.

He made a note to pop around to visit her in the next week or two. He liked that aspect of practice here, seeing patients not because they had called, but because you had a notion they might need you. Doctor O'Reilly had taught him that.

This party was not the place for impromptu consultations. He would definitely go to see Alice, but not this week. Patricia was only home for a few days. Tomorrow O'Reilly had agreed to hold the fort so Barry could run her down to her folks' place in Newry, and he was hoping she'd be back up in time for him to take her to the New Year's Eve dress dance at Queen's University. He'd ask her—once he got her on his own.

Barry noticed that Donal, with a pint in hand and Julie by his side, was now in deep conversation with the velvet-coated Mr. Hunter.

"Patricia," Barry said, "you'll be going back to Cambridge soon. Why don't we nip up to Van Buren's? I'd love to have your portrait."

"I'll see, Barry. I'm . . . I'm going to be a bit busy."

Barry frowned but decided to let the matter drop until later. The more he thought about it, the more he liked the idea of having her picture on his bedside table to wake to every morning.

They went through the door and into the hall where Mr. Coffin was explaining something to his friend Constable Mulligan.

The undertaker munched on a sweet mince pie. "Oh yes, Malcolm, I assure you there is quite a bit of alcohol in embalming fluid."

And by the way Mr. Coffin was swaying in him too. At a party in August, Constable Mulligan had slipped the undertaker a mickey.

He'd got a taste for the vodka in his tea, and now Mr. Coffin had forsaken his allegiance to the Pioneers, a teetotal organization. The poor man had rhinophyma, a condition of the sebaceous glands of the nose, and his nose seemed even more bulbous and scarlet than it had been when Barry first met him. It was unfortunate that the music suddenly brayed, "Rudolph, the red-nosed reindeer . . ."

Barry grinned, smiled at the two men, and moved toward the bar in the kitchen. Where there was drink to be had, the odds were good that there also would be Doctor Fingal Flahertie O'Reilly.

Even before Barry had steered Patricia through the door he heard his senior colleague. O'Reilly was declaiming in tones that must have stood him in good stead when HMS *Warspite,* the battleship he'd served on in the war, was smashing her way through the Mediterranean gales, "There's not enough in that glass to give a gnat an eyewash, Willy Dunleavy. Top it up." O'Reilly stood in front of a counter where Willy Dunleavy, publican of the Black Swan, known to the locals as the Mucky Duck, served his customary function, ably assisted by his chubby daughter, Mary.

Laugh lines fanned from the corners of O'Reilly's deep-set brown eyes. His untidily trimmed black hair hung in shaggy fringes over his cauliflower ears. He scratched the side of his bent nose. No respecter of formality, he stood there, the sleeves of his now collarless striped shirt rolled above his elbows. The red braces that held up his tweed pants were taut across his ample stomach.

O'Reilly accepted the brimming glass of John Jameson and Son's Irish whiskey. "And a glass of—?"

"White wine," said Kitty O'Hallorhan, who stood near O'Reilly.

"You heard that, Willy?" O'Reilly yelled.

The senior nursing sister from the Royal Victoria Hospital in Belfast waved at Barry, who waved back.

She had supposedly been going home after dinner yesterday, but the snow that had fallen for most of Christmas Day had made the roads impassable. Getting back to Belfast for her regular shift in charge of the neurosurgical ward at the Royal was not an option, so she had telephoned to arrange for a friend to work for her. She had spent the night at O'Reilly's home at Number 1, Main Street. O'Reilly had been insistent she come to this hooley before she went back to town.

Kitty was talking to the host and hostess, Bertie and Flo Bishop, who because of their stoutness always reminded Barry of John Tenniel's illustrations of Tweedledum and Tweedledee.

Kitty, who was in her early fifties, did not. She was slim and chic tonight in a black, knee-length pencil skirt over mulberry stockings and patent-leather pumps. It amazed Barry that any woman could stand for hours in stiletto heels, but it didn't seem to bother her.

He glanced at Patricia, who was speaking to O'Reilly, and doubted she had noticed Barry's appraisal of Kitty. The heels accentuated the curve of her calves, and Kitty O'Hallorhan had a very well-turned leg.

Her ivory silk blouse was open at the neck, revealing cleavage. Her nose was a little too large, her lips too full, but her eyes, grey flecked with amber, shone with the laughter that was never far beneath the surface of the woman who had known O'Reilly when they were both students in Dublin. She had come back into the big man's life five months ago. It would be interesting to see how matters evolved between her and the widower O'Reilly.

"Here you are, Kitty." O'Reilly handed her a glass and slipped his arm around her waist. "So *there* you are, Barry. Have you a drink?"

Barry showed his glass of sherry. "I'm fine, Fingal," he said.

"Patricia?" O'Reilly asked.

"Fine, thank you."

"Right," said O'Reilly. "We'll get away from the bar so other folks can get in." He let go of Kitty and roared, "Coming through." O'Reilly, like a bluff-bowed tug, moved ahead and parted the waters.

It seemed miraculous to Barry that the four of them fetched up in a relatively quiet backwater. Kitty and Patricia were already deep in conversation. He was pleased by how the two women had become friends in the short time since they'd met last summer.

O'Reilly lifted his glass and said, "*Sláinte.*" He drank.

"*Sláinte mHaith.*" Barry sipped.

"Quite the ta-ta-ta-ra," O'Reilly said. "Are you having fun?"

Barry nodded and said seriously, "And not just at this party, Fingal."

"Oh?"

"You know what I mean."

"Do I?" said O'Reilly with a smile. "Now there's a thing. Mind reader, am I?"

Barry smiled. "Fingal, sometimes you can be a tad infuriating."

O'Reilly guffawed. "Indeed I can be, when it suits me."

"You do know perfectly well what I'm talking about," Barry said.

"Fair play to you, Barry. I'll not tease you anymore. You're having fun here in Ballybucklebo, aren't you? That's what you mean?"

"It is." Barry nodded. "And in the practice with you, Fingal."

"Me working you like a Trojan, threatened lawsuits, competition from Doctor Fitzpatrick in the Kinnegar just up the road notwithstanding?" O'Reilly raised one eyebrow.

"You never promised me it would be all plain sailing. I just wanted to thank you for taking me on last July and to tell you, before we go back to full-time work in the new year, I'm going to do my very best in the practice and have every intention of . . ." He was distracted by a look on Kitty's face. Her eyes were wide, her brow wrinkled, as she mouthed a single word that, despite his inability to hear above the racket, Barry could lip-read as "No." Her mouth stayed open.

And as is often the way at cocktail parties, as if on cue everyone stopped talking. Everyone save Patricia Spence, whose voice Barry heard distinctly above the music. "I mean it, Kitty, but I don't know *how* I'm going to tell Barry it's over."

"It's what?" He whispered and swallowed. He couldn't move.

He saw her looking at him. Her hand covered her mouth. She must know he'd overheard. He stood as if paralyzed. It's over? Over? She can't mean it. Drops of sherry splashed onto his hand that held the glass. He looked down. His hands were trembling and he felt chilled.

Barry shook his head and tried to go to her, but Constable Mulligan was yelling at the top of his voice, "Doctor O'Reilly. Doctor Laverty. Come next door, quick. Mr. Coffin's choking, so he is. He's terrible blue looking. Come quick."

2

Nothing but to Choke a Man

Barry thrust his glass at a bystander and tore after O'Reilly. Kitty, trained nurse as she was, followed.

"Out of my light," O'Reilly bellowed. "Let the dog see the rabbit." He knelt beside Mr. Coffin, who lay on the drawing room carpet making guttural noises, struggling to breathe. His boot heels drummed on the floor. A half-eaten sweet mince pie was clutched in his right hand. The left clawed at his throat. Spittle flecked his lips, and his lips and cheeks were turning blue.

O'Reilly hauled the man into a sitting position and with a hand the size of a soup plate whaled him on the back with seemingly sufficient force to drive his spine against his breastbone. O'Reilly clouted the man again.

Mr. Coffin's eyes rolled up into his head, but his breathing did not improve.

"Bugger," said O'Reilly, laying the patient flat. He turned to Barry. "He's choking. He's got mince pie stuck in his trachea. Those thumps didn't get it out." He rummaged in his pocket and produced a large penknife. "We'll have to do a trachy."

Barry flinched. He knew it was possible to make an emergency incision in the trachea—a tracheostomy—to save a life, but he'd never seen it done.

The gramophone blared.

I've got the world on a string, sitting on a rainbow—

"Turn off that music," Barry called.

Click. Silence.

"Kitty," O'Reilly yelled, "get Flo to give you one of those things she uses to hold up the crust of a steak-and-kidney pie. If she has a kettle boiling, scald the thing and bring it back here, give it to Barry, then phone for an ambulance."

"Right."

"Somebody bring a bottle of whiskey." O'Reilly glared around. "I need four men. Donal . . . Fergus Finnegan . . . Archie . . . Bertie."

They stepped forward.

Typical O'Reilly, Barry thought. Not a moment's hesitation when it comes to deploying his troops. Barry wasn't sure he could have found the courage to act as O'Reilly was about to. He was glad his senior colleague was here.

"You." O'Reilly pointed at Bertie. "Lie over his legs. Keep him pinioned."

The councillor did and the heel drumming stopped.

O'Reilly's voice could be heard over the noise of Mr. Coffin's gasping. "Donal, Fergus, take a shoulder apiece and hang on like grim death. He'll thrash like all bedamned when I cut." O'Reilly opened the knife. The blade reflected the light from the overhead fixture. "You, Archie, when I tell you, take hold of his head and push it as far back as it will go to expose his neck. Barry, kneel down by his other side. Kitty's going to get you a steel tube. It's about two inches long and an inch wide at one end and tapers to about half an inch at the other."

"I'll be ready."

"Good lad." O'Reilly smiled at Barry. "And don't worry. I've done dozens of these. They had a diphtheria vaccine in the thirties, but a lot of mothers, the superstitious eejits, wouldn't get their kids immunized. If a child got the disease, it was often a trachy or the kid would die with all that clabber in its wee throat."

Barry stripped off his sports jacket. This could get bloody. He understood why O'Reilly hadn't time to explain things to Mr. Coffin. Getting things organized, making sure Barry was able to play his part, and operating must take precedence and had to be done within four minutes or the undertaker would start to suffocate.

But although Mr. Coffin could not speak, he could hear. The man must be petrified. To be thankful for small mercies, he had a good skinful taken. The alcohol would dull his senses.

Barry knelt and looked him straight in the eye. There was naked fear in the man's gaze.

"Mr. Coffin. Can you hear me?"

The slightest nod.

"We're trying to help you."

Another tiny nod.

Barry put his hand on the man's shoulder. "It's going to hurt." Mr. Coffin's eyes widened. "But it'll be over quickly and then you'll be able to breathe. You're not going to die. I promise."

It wasn't much, but it was the best he could do.

Barry snatched a look around. Most of the partygoers had moved away, but the morbidly curious were still craning forward. "Come on, folks," Barry said. "You heard Doctor O'Reilly. Let the dog see the rabbit. Move back, please."

"Here's the whiskey," a voice said.

"Pour it over my knife, my hands and Doctor Laverty's, and save a taste for your man's throat." O'Reilly held his hands out. "It's not such a terrible waste of the craythur," he remarked. "Luckily it's only Scotch, not Irish."

Barry held Mr. Coffin's gaze with his own and gave his shoulder one last, he hoped, reassuring squeeze. "You'll be breathing in just a minute," he said.

The fumes of the neat spirits stung Barry's eyes, but alcohol was antiseptic.

"Right, Archie," said O'Reilly. "Push his head back."

Barry was glad he didn't have to stare into Mr. Coffin's eyes anymore.

O'Reilly knelt at the victim's right side. He put his left index finger on the bottom of the Adam's apple, and his thumb and middle finger on either side of the trachea. "He's going to lepp," he said. "Hold him." He put the knife's blade between his finger and thumb and sliced down.

The patient tried to buck but was restrained. Judging by the grunts and sounds of heavy breathing coming from the four men it was taking a great deal of effort to hold him.

The wall of the trachea was visible, red muscle with white rings of cartilage.

Blood ran from both sides of the wound over the man's neck and onto the carpet.

"Barry . . . Barry." Kitty tugged at his shoulder. "Here." She handed him a warm metal tube.

O'Reilly glanced at Barry. "Ready?"

"Yes."

O'Reilly cut into the trachea. "Get the tube in."

Already the patient's chest had inflated, and Barry could hear some air being sucked in. He could see anxiety in Fingal's eyes. Barry shuddered. It took courage and a good deal of compassion to slice into an unanaesthetised man. He wondered for a moment if he was going to be able to push the steel tube into the hole O'Reilly had cut. Damn it, this was no time to let his friend down—or the patient.

"Sorry, Mr. Coffin," he said, gritted his teeth, placed the tube over the tracheal incision, and pushed. To his delight it slid into place.

He felt a current of air on the back of his hand as Mr. Coffin sucked air into his oxygen-starved lungs, then exhaled a great shuddering breath. A fine spray of blood sprinkled the back of Barry's wrist. He looked at the man's face. Already his colour was improving. When Barry was a student, it had been a standing suppertime joke for one student to ask another, "And how many lives did *you* save today?" What O'Reilly had just done *had* saved a life. "Well done, Fingal," Barry said quietly.

"Aye," said O'Reilly. "Kitty, did you call for the ambulance?"

"I did. They'll try to get through, but it might take a while in this snow."

"Fair enough." He got to his feet. "Your man'll survive until they get here. I've morphine in the car. I'll fetch it because he's going to be sore. Barry, go and get yourself cleaned up. Kitty, keep an eye on Mr. Coffin. He should be fine until I get back."

Kitty nodded.

O'Reilly stood.

It seemed incongruous to Barry, but nevertheless well merited, when he heard a muted round of applause.

"I'll tidy up in a minute," Barry said. He'd decided he'd keep an eye to the patient for a little longer. "Do you hear that, Mr. Coffin? You're going to be all right."

The undertaker's breathing came in short gasps. His eyes begged for help, but although his lips moved, no words were formed. The air that usually made the vocal cords vibrate to produce speech was going to and from his lungs through the metal tube *beneath* the larynx.

"It's all right, Mr. Coffin," Barry said. "I know you've a sore throat, but Doctor O'Reilly's gone for morphine. He'll be back very, very soon."

Some of the fear left the undertaker's eyes.

"Can you lie still?" Barry asked.

The man's lips moved and he tried to nod.

"Fair enough," Barry said. Then to the men holding the patient he said, "You can let him go, and thanks a lot for helping." For a moment he had a vivid mental image of the orlop deck of one of Nelson's warships, with tough, tarry-pigtailed sailors letting go of a rum-befuddled man. They'd been holding him down as the ship's surgeon amputated a leg.

Donal, Fergus, Archie, and Bertie Bishop stood. Barry noticed how pale the councillor's usually ruddy cheeks were and how his hands trembled.

"Boys-a-dear," said Donal, the wonder in his voice clear. "See that there what Doctor O'Reilly done? I would not've had've believed it if I had not've would've been here."

The other three nodded in solemn agreement.

Ulster as she is spoke *and* comprehended, Barry thought, trying to hide his smile.

He stood. God, but he had a crick in his back. And damn it, his new trousers were covered in blood. O'Reilly's housekeeper, Mrs. Kinky Kincaid, would kill him. He'd lost track of the number of times in the last six months she'd had to clean or mend a pair of pants for him.

He looked around. The other partygoers were huddled together at the far end of the room like a flock of animals needing the nearness of each other for comfort and seeking guidance from the lead animal.

"Ladies and gentlemen," Barry said, "may I have your attention? Please?" Every eye was on him. He smiled at Maggie Houston, née MacCorkle. He'd not noticed her before. She was hanging onto Sonny Houston's arm. "For those of you who don't know me, I'm Doctor Laverty, and the gentleman who did the operation is Doctor O'Reilly. I'm sure most of you know *him*."

There was a murmur of assent.

"Mr. Coffin got food stuck in his gullet and he was suffocating." Maggie's mouth fell open. She was wearing her dentures.

"Doctor O'Reilly made an incision into the windpipe so Mr. Coffin can breathe. It looked messy, but actually he lost very little blood and"—Barry glanced down—"most of that seems to be on my pants."

He noticed one or two flickering smiles.

"Let me by." O'Reilly's voice rang out and the little crowd parted, much, Barry thought, as the Red Sea had done for Moses.

O'Reilly, panting from his exertions—he must have run to and from the car—knelt beside Mr. Coffin, preparing a morphine injection. Barry wondered if the senior practitioner would exhibit the same lack of attention to ordinary routine Barry had witnessed his first week on the job in Ballybucklebo while watching O'Reilly inject his patients with a tonic. Sure enough, O'Reilly dabbed a cotton ball soaked in methylated spirits on a trouser leg and rammed the needle through the serge and into the patient's thigh muscle.

Still kneeling beside the patient, O'Reilly said, clearly enough for everyone to hear, "When the ambulance gets here, Mr. Coffin, they'll take you to the Royal. The surgeons there will give you an anaesthetic, clear out your throat, and sew you up."

Mr. Coffin's eyes widened. He sucked in a great breath.

"You're going to be fine," O'Reilly said, laying a hand on the patient's arm. Even as he did so the morphine started to take effect, and Mr. Coffin's eyes fluttered and closed. His breathing was steady and slow. O'Reilly stood. "I'm going to get cleaned up," he said. "He'll be grand. Just fine."

Barry saw heads nodding in agreement.

O'Reilly headed for the bathroom.

The atmosphere was less tense. "Mr. Coffin will be home in a day or two, and all he'll eventually have to show for his troubles will be a small scar where the incision was," Barry said.

"The poor oul' eejit was half cut already before Doctor O'Reilly finished the job," a voice remarked.

There was a communal chuckle. "Half cut," along with "tore," "legless," "paralytic," "flootered," and "stocious," was one of the many Ulster euphemisms for "drunk."

"I hope he gets better soon," the voice said. "He's the only undertaker we've got. His business is the dead centre of Ballybucklebo, so it is." The words were delivered with absolutely no inflection.

Someone else said, "It's a good thing we have our doctors too, so it is. They're two learnèd men."

Barry grinned. He noticed the sounds of conversations beginning. He distinctly heard Cissie Sloan's hoarse tones as she said, ". . . and hasn't Doctor O'Reilly been known to do that wonderful operation where they remove the whole brain, clean it, and put it back? I heard about it at Sonny and Maggie's wedding."

There was a chorus of amazed "oohs" and "aahs" from her audience. "Sure cutting somebody's throat is only wee buns to a doctor like him."

Barry laughed and as he did he felt a presence at his shoulder. It was O'Reilly and Kitty.

"Your coat," O'Reilly said, handing Barry his sports jacket.

"And your drink." Patricia, who had come into the room, gave Barry his sherry. She did not meet his eyes.

Barry's smile fled as he shrugged into his jacket and accepted the glass. The intensity of the medical emergency had, for the moment, made him forget the words he had heard Patricia say to Kitty. Now the warmth he'd felt because he'd successfully helped O'Reilly in a life-or-death situation turned to an icy chill. He couldn't bear to look at her.

He wanted to go home.

"Now," said O'Reilly to the little crowd, ignoring the approving noises, "all the excitement's over. I'm sure Doctor Laverty here has explained that the patient's going to be fine." He took a swig from what must be a recently refreshed glass of whiskey. "I see no reason to let this ruin an otherwise wonderful party."

"Hear. Hear," Bertie Bishop said. "I'll open another bottle."

"Ah," said O'Reilly, raising his voice. "Of Jameson, Bertie?"

"Aye, surely," said the councillor.

O'Reilly grinned and lowered the level of the liquid in his glass considerably. "I'm sure Mrs. Kincaid can wait twenty minutes more so we can have just one more wee wet." He positively beamed at Bertie Bishop and looked down at the now somnolent Mr. Coffin. "I'll need to stay to keep an eye on him until the ambulance gets here."

Barry looked down at his bloodstained pants. "You stay here, Fingal, but I want to get washed, then go home, change, and get these pants in the wash." He glanced at Patricia, but she would still not meet his eye. He did want to go home, and not because he gave a tinker's damn about his bloody pants.

"Go on then, Barry," O'Reilly said. "Go and wash. But there's no need to walk home. As soon as I've finished my jar and seen Mr. Coffin off to Belfast, I'll drive you and Patricia back to Number 1." He looked directly at Barry, then said very quietly, "I'm sure you need to have a chat with Patricia."

Barry nodded. The big man had heard her too.

"When I've dropped you, I'll take Kitty straight home. It's no night for her to try to get to Belfast in her wee Mini. . . . And I'll get your car up to you, Kitty, as soon as the snow's thawed a bit. If I give Donal a few bob, he'll drive it up and come back on the train."

"I'd appreciate that," Kitty said quietly, "but when you've had your 'just one more' whiskey, Fingal Flahertie O'Reilly, *I'll* drive your Rover."

"Fair enough," he said.

Kitty O'Hallorhan certainly had the measure of O'Reilly. Barry doubted if anyone, other than a senior officer when O'Reilly'd been in the navy, could order the man about the way she had. Perhaps Kinky Kincaid, but no one else. Barry swallowed a large mouthful of sherry and set the glass on a nearby table. Kitty understood Fingal all right. He wished he could fathom Patricia. Her "It's over" was crystal clear, but why? Why?

He headed for the bathroom. He washed his hands, then bent and splashed cold water over his face. The icy sting of it matched the chill in his heart.

Perhaps he'd misheard? Perhaps she hadn't really meant it? He headed back to the party. Once he got home, Mrs. Kincaid, who had stayed behind to answer the surgery phone, would take her turn at the Bishops' party. And with O'Reilly on his way to Belfast with Kitty, he and Patricia would have Number 1, Main Street, to themselves.

Perhaps he could still straighten all this out?

3

Flee from the Cruel Madness of Love

Barry sat stiffly beside Patricia in the back of O'Reilly's Rover. They did not speak or touch, but her faint perfume whispered to him. He stared out the window. On the trip along the Shore Road where the Bishops lived he'd seen that the drifts on the verges were at least two feet deep. They'd returned the car's headlights with a flat white glare studded with the glinting of icy sequins. It was dark by four thirty in December in Ulster, and beyond the twin beams and their reflections the evening was pitch black. Sombre as Barry's mood.

Kitty drove under the single-arch railway bridge and along Station Road to the left turn at the traffic signals—the only ones in the village—onto Main Street. The sign at the Black Swan wore a topping of icing-sugar snow. The thatch and the slate roofs of the low terraces of cottages lining the road were frostily glistering in the glow of the few streetlamps.

On the way to the party Barry'd thought of the snow as a winter wonderland. He'd imagined walking through it with Patricia, laughing with her, kissing her, but now it was a cold barren place.

He said good-bye to O'Reilly and Kitty, held Patricia's arm, and walked slowly to accommodate her limp as they stepped along the slush-covered footpath to the front door of Number 1, Main Street.

Barry pushed the door open. No one would dream of locking a

house here. Then he stood aside, letting Patricia precede him into the well-lit hall. By the time he'd hung his overcoat beside her duffle on the hall clothes-stand he'd warmed up. At least his fingers and toes had. Inside he was numb.

"I'm going to change these trousers," he said. "I'll be down in a minute." Barry climbed slowly to his attic bedroom, pulled off his stained trousers, made sure his legs weren't bloody too, put on a pair of corduroys, and headed downstairs with the soiled pants. As he passed the upstairs lounge, he noticed Patricia sitting in an armchair. It seemed so natural to see her there. Why, Patricia? Why is it over?

In the hot aroma-filled kitchen, two saucepans steamed on the stove. Mrs. Kincaid had her back turned to Barry. She was wearing her overcoat and her best green hat. Grey rubber galoshes, large and lumpy, covered her shoes. Wisps of silver hair strayed from her chignon. She patted the escapees with a beefy hand, then turned and saw him.

"I never heard you. Is it home you are, Doctor Laverty?" She glanced at the bloody trousers he held. "Jesus, Mary, and Joseph, have you done it again?" She tutted. "Maybe we should get you a set of dungarees—or oilskins."

"I'm sorry. It was an emergency. Nothing too serious. Everything's OK now." He knew his voice sounded flat.

Kinky gave him a long look. "They'll have to be soaked before I go to the Bishops' or I'll never get them clean. There's cold water in the sink, sir. Could you put them in?" Her native Cork brogue was soft against his harsher, northern accent.

He dropped the pants in, watching the blood drift out into the water to swirl, and thin, and vanish like smoke in the air on a windless day—or as love when it has flown. His hands shook.

"I'll wash them later," she said, fussing in a cupboard, then closing the door. "I'll finish up here; then I'll be off."

He did not want to ask, but courtesy demanded. "Can I give you a lift?"

"Not at all, bless you, Doctor Laverty. It's no distance. Only a wee doddle. I've walked further back home in County Cork on much worse nights, in deeper snow than this, so. The exercise'll do me a power of good." She paused, looked straight at him, and frowned. Then she said, "Excuse me, sir."

"Yes, Kinky?"

"If you don't mind me asking, are you all right?"

"Why?"

"You've a face on you like a Lurgan spade, and I hear dry rot in your voice."

"Sorry, Kinky, but I'm fine. Honestly."

"If you say so, sir. But it's not like you to be down, so. Is it something to do with the emergency?"

Barry shook his head, took a deep breath, and then exhaled. "Go on, Kinky. Go and enjoy Flo's hooley. I'll be grand." Of course I will be fine. And apples will grow on a cherry tree.

She inclined her head. "I'll be off then"—she pointed to the stove—"and don't worry about the lentil and the turkey-vegetable soups I'm making. They'll come to no harm for I'll be home soon. So if you're sure you're all right, sir, you go upstairs and see to your young lady. There's Christmas cake and meringues on the sideboard in case you get peckish, and I'll go and see what the *craic's* like over at Flo's."

"Thanks, Kinky." He followed her into the hall and climbed the stairs, trying to decide exactly what he should say to Patricia.

It was cosy when he went into the lounge, and the fire's cherry-red clinkers and ebony anthracite pieces were blended colours on an abstract painter's canvas. Arthur Guinness, O'Reilly's black Labrador, snored on the hearth rug. Patricia sat in an armchair with Lady Macbeth on her lap, stroking the little cat's white head.

He saw Patricia's raven-wing hair glossy in the light from the overhead fixture, her deep, peat water–brown eyes soft in their almond-shaped settings, her cheekbones those of a Slavic princess, her lips full and kissable. And he was enraptured by the loveliness of the young woman, the golden girl who'd stolen his very being in a train compartment riding down from Belfast on a soft starlit night.

He swallowed the lump in his throat. He heard the front door close below. "Kinky's going to the Bishops'," he said. Then he stood there, tongue-tied.

"Will you sit down please, Barry?" Her words were clipped. "Please?"

"I'd rather stand," he said. "Would you like a meringue?"

"No, thank you."

"A drink?"

She shook her head.

"I will, if you don't mind."

"Go ahead. Of course I don't mind."

The conversation was stepping along as formally as a Restoration minuet. I know you don't mind if I have a drink, he thought. After all, it's over. Why would you care about anything I did? He poured himself a Jameson and drank. The spirits caught in his throat. He coughed. His vision blurred. When it cleared, he saw her looking at him, but the warmth he sought in her eyes was not there.

"We need to talk, Barry," she said.

"I know. I heard what you said to Kitty."

"I'm sorry. You weren't meant to."

"I'm sorry too." Lord, man, what are you apologizing for? "But I did hear. You said—"

"I know exactly what I said." She was sitting stiffly, knees together, hands clasped in her lap. "Barry, I'm sorry. I'm awfully sorry."

"But you meant it." Say no. Say, Barry, you were mistaken about what you thought you'd heard. Please, Patricia, say it.

He set his drink on the sideboard and knocked over half a dozen Christmas cards. He couldn't be bothered to straighten them up. "Why?" he whispered. "Why?"

"Why did I tell Kitty?"

Barry shook his head. "I don't care about you telling Kitty. I want to know why it's over. What did I do wrong?" Before she could answer he carried on, the words tumbling, unstoppable and burning as molten metal from a blast furnace. "I should have guessed when you almost didn't make it home for Christmas. I should have known. You'd plenty of time, but you wanted to go bird-watching, to London, to carol services. Excuses. That's all excuses. You never wanted to come back to Ulster at all. Did you? You never wanted to see me again. Never."

She looked down.

"Why not? Why the hell not?"

"Please don't get cross, Barry."

He felt his fists clench and took a deep breath.

"Barry, I'm sorry."

He tried. He really tried, but he could not stop himself from saying with an edge in his voice, "Don't get cross? You're sorry?" His lips pursed; his eyes prickled. "Sorry? How the hell do you think I feel?" He moved two steps toward her, and she held up one arm in front of her face as if to ward off a blow. She looked so vulnerable. His voice softened. "Patricia, I still love you. I'm trying to understand, that's all."

She lowered her arm and looked up at him. Little tears trickled down her cheeks. "Barry," she said, "I thought I loved you—"

"But?" He tried to keep the bitterness away. "But you didn't."

She looked at the carpet and said in a little voice, "It would have been all right if I hadn't gone away."

"No, it wouldn't. You know I love Ulster and this job here in Ballybucklebo. It's too small for you, Patricia. You want the world. Ballybucklebo's not Cambridge."

"That's right. There's always something going on there. It's . . . it's alive . . . vibrant. London's only an hour away." Patricia stared at the carpet. She held one hand in the other in front of her skirt. The fingers of the left entwined with the right and she brought her locked hands up and rested her mouth on the knuckles for what seemed to Barry like an eternity. Finally she lifted her head and looked him in the eye. "Barry, I couldn't live here. I'd get claustrophobia. And I've seen how O'Reilly and you work. The village owns you both. You'd have no time for me."

"I'd have every other night off, one weekend in two."

"And be coming home too tired to do anything but sleep. Barry, I'm not cut out to sit at home knitting, waiting for my man."

"I see." He was at a complete loss for words. Surely there must be some compromise they could both accept?

"It's not just that. And I had to tell you to your face. That's why I came home. I couldn't tell you over the phone." She swallowed. "Can you please sit down?"

He came close to saying, "Why bother?" But he nodded and sat.

"Well?" Barry let the word hang. "I'm listening."

"Barry, I thought I was in love with you. I did all this summer. It was wonderful."

Indeed it was. "But once you got to Cambridge you started having second thoughts?" he said. "You've just told me."

"There's more—"

"More?" His voice rose.

"Barry, please, don't get angry. Please, just listen." She held her hands outstretched to him, palms up.

"Go on."

"Phone calls and the odd letter weren't enough," she said.

"They were for me. They had to be."

"You never saw anybody else?"

Barry pushed back into his chair. He looked away, then back at her. "I was angry because you were meant to have come home, but you kept putting it off. I went to a nurses' dance with my friend Jack Mills." He shrugged. "I drove a girl home. It was on the way here anyway, nothing happened, and I'll not be seeing her again." He forced a weak grin. "Ships that pass, that's all."

"I see." She pushed Lady Macbeth away and stood. "It's not just about how small this place is." Her face screwed up. She picked at a nail bed.

He knew. He absolutely knew what she was trying to say. He'd make it easier for her. "There's someone else, isn't there?"

She nodded.

Barry rose. He stood beside her. "I don't want to hear any more. I understand."

"Barry, how can you be so calm?" Her voice broke. Tears flowed.

He ached to comfort her but did not move. "Because I'm trained to understand," he lied, but he'd not tell her that he could not bear to see her cry. "It really is over, Patricia? There's no hope?"

She nodded.

"I love you. I always will."

"I'm sorry."

"I wish you well with your career and—" He didn't want to think about another man.

She whispered, "Thank you, Barry," and pecked his cheek. "I'll miss you."

He raised both arms, thinking to hug her to him, but let them fall limply to his sides.

"I'm not hungry," she said. "I'll go and read in my room."

"All right."

"I'll phone Dad first. Ask him to come and get me tomorrow."

"Fine." Barry's world had collapsed. He was shrouded in confusion as dense as the dust from a blast, shattered like a jumbled pile of bricks. Yet here he was discussing practicalities like getting her home to Newry.

"Good-night, Barry." She moved toward the door. "I'm sorry," she said, and then she was gone.

Barry sighed. Blinked back all but one tear. There wasn't much point going to bed. He'd not sleep. Supper? He shook his head. The room was colder since she'd gone. He picked up his whiskey and flopped in a chair.

A cinder rattled as it fell through the bars of the grate and the embers settled. Barry stared into the hearth. The fire was only a red glow. Fires, like feelings, needed attention if they were not to go out, so he rose, told Arthur to move, and waited until the big dog stepped aside. Then Barry put on lump after lump of coal from the scuttle, and each made a pleasant, crackling noise as it fell into the hot embers.

"You can go back," he said to the dog. You can, but I can't.

Arthur settled down on the rug again. In a moment, the little white cat had snuggled up against Arthur's tummy.

A comfortable room, a warm fire, contented animals, a small whiskey, and a pleasant glow. It was the kind of domesticity Barry had been sure was going to be in his stars once he had secured the job here. But now? Dear God, what about now?

He swallowed the remaining whiskey in one gulp and relished the way the spirits burned. If only he could cauterise his soul. Make it empty, but he couldn't because he knew she'd always live inside him, the way O'Reilly's dead wife, Deidre, dwelt in him.

Barry inhaled very deeply. Perhaps Kitty could exorcise Deidre's spirit, make Fingal whole again.

But—he sighed and hunched forward, elbows on his knees—who could do that for Barry Laverty?

4

Tired with the Labour of Far Travel We Have Come unto Our Own Home

O'Reilly didn't want to talk while Kitty drove to Belfast. He knew he might have seemed to the onlookers to be completely in charge back at the Bishops'. Inside he'd been taut as a tightly sheeted sail in a stiff wind. Now he was happy to sit alone in his thoughts and let the tension ease.

Barry had been his competent self. That boy had the makings of a great GP. How was he getting on back at Number 1? O'Reilly had nearly choked on his Jameson when he'd heard Patricia say, "It's over." The statement had burst from the calm waters of the party as violently as the great plumes hurled up by an exploding depth charge. Lord knew he'd seen enough of those in the Med.

Kitty braked at a red light. "You're quiet, Fingal," she said.

He didn't want to talk about Barry. "I'm not used to being driven," he said. "You're doing a great job, Kitty. Thanks."

"You did a good job yourself on Mr. Coffin." The light changed and she turned onto May Street.

"Aye," said O'Reilly, "with your help—and Barry's."

"I was proud of you."

He heard the breadth of her Dublin accent where "I" was "Oi" and "proud" was "perowud." He was glad it was dark inside the car because he could feel warmth in his cheeks and he didn't want her to notice. "Did you ever see a TV program, *Tales of Wells Fargo?*" he asked. "I enjoyed it when the hero, Jim Hardie, would shrug and say, 'Sometimes a man's gotta do what a man's gotta do.'"

"And being complimented would give you heartburn, wouldn't it, Fingal?" She let the back of her hand touch his thigh. A small familiar gesture.

Her nearness was pleasant. Very pleasant.

"Mr. Coffin owes you his life. I know it—and you know it."

"Sure if I'd not been there young Barry would have coped." O'Reilly wriggled in his seat.

"Do you think so?" Kitty crossed to the Grosvenor Road and drove steadily. The traffic was light.

"I know so. I'm lucky I'm going to have him as a partner."

"And he's a nice man." He heard her taking a deeper breath before asking, "Will he stay with you, do you think?"

"By God, I hope so."

Kitty sounded thoughtful. "You overheard what Patricia told me?"

"I did." And he could understand how smashed Barry had felt. O'Reilly had only to close his eyes to recall, word for word, how Admiral Cunningham had broken the news to a young Surgeon-Lieutenant O'Reilly of his new wife's death, and his numb, disbelieving shock. "Poor Barry . . . but he's young yet."

"You think he'll get over it?" She indicated to turn left. "We'll take a short cut through the grounds of the Royal Victoria Hospital."

That was typical of Kitty O'Hallorhan. He'd given her a golden opportunity to remark that he, Fingal O'Reilly, had had long enough to get over his wife's death. Instead she'd changed the subject.

He watched as she drove past the almost completely empty parking lots and familiar, red brick buildings of the venerable teaching hospital. Could Kitty be right to hint that a brokenhearted Barry might decide to leave Ballybucklebo?

She parked outside Broadway Towers, the subsidized housing for nurses from the Royal Group of hospitals. "Here we are. Come on in."

He held open the front door and felt the rush of heat from the small foyer. O'Reilly immediately helped Kitty out of her coat and took off his own. "Bloody hot," he said.

Kitty pushed the lift's call button. "I'm on the tenth floor."

"Here we are," she said again, when the lift had carried them up. She opened a door and flicked on a light. "*Chez* O'Hallorhan. Give me your coat, then go on into the living room. I need to powder my nose." She vanished through a door to the left.

O'Reilly, fumbling in his pocket for his pipe, wandered down a short hall. The room ahead was partially illuminated by the light from the entrance. He could half make out a couple of oil paintings and assumed Kitty was the artist. He remembered how she'd been painting back in the thirties.

The curtains were open at the far end of the room, and he walked over to stand by the window. From high over the city he saw the heart of Belfast, a sea of shining brightness from the streetlights, store lights, and their reflections from snow-covered rooftops. Church spires and the bulk of the Albert Clock stood darkly above the other buildings, their outlines limned by the glow.

In the centre of the glare the dark serpent of the River Lagan wound its way out to the wider blackness of Belfast Lough, whose margins wore a twinkling necklace of the lights of towns and villages along both shores. Somewhere on the lough's right side was the glow from Ballybucklebo. On the horizon the lighthouses at Black Head and Mew Island sent questing, ghosts' fingers over the navigation lights of a ship heading to the Port of Belfast.

"It's a pretty sight, isn't it?" Kitty's voice was low.

He hadn't heard her coming up behind him. "It is."

"I often sit here at night with the lights off and the curtains open, just staring out. It's a great cure for those days when the ward's gone daft, half my staff are off sick, a patient you've grown fond of dies—"

"And 'The world is too much with us.' "

"Exactly. Well put, Fingal."

"Willie Wordsworth said it first."

"Look at that," she said, pointing to where a plane drew green, white, and red lines of light across the dark night as it made its descent into Aldergrove Airport.

He watched, but his thoughts were of this Kitty O'Hallorhan, the girl he'd loved when he was a student, the woman who had resurfaced in his life this August and who he'd been seeing regularly since.

Kitty, who'd been in love with him before he'd married Deidre, had said that she could care for him again. If he'd let her, she'd give him a second chance; she'd wait for him to decide, but she'd not wait forever.

"Penny for them, Fingal?" Kitty moved closer.

O'Reilly swallowed. *Tell her how you feel, you great eejit,* he thought. "Kitty, I . . ." O'Reilly turned, saw her face in the glow of the city lights. He put a hand on each of her shoulders and looked down into her eyes. It was too dim to make out the amber flecks in their grey. "That is . . ."

He dropped his arms from her shoulders and fumbled for his pipe. Filling it always allowed him time to marshal his thoughts when dealing with a patient.

If you don't tell her now, you never will. Get on with it.

O'Reilly let the briar fall back into his pocket.

"Kitty, I've been giving a great deal of thought to something you said."

She inclined her head to one side; one eyebrow rose, but she did not speak.

O'Reilly swallowed again, cleared his throat. "You told me you could care for me again if I'd let you."

Her eyebrow rose higher, but she offered not one word of encouragement.

He glanced at her lips, but there was no beginnings of a smile. *Was she going to tell him he'd kept her waiting too long?* O'Reilly felt as if he were sixteen, trying to pluck up the courage to ask the captain of the girl's hockey team to go with him to the rugby club dance. No. It was more like being fifteen, standing on the edge of the ten-metre board at the swimming baths. Once you jumped there was no turning back.

"Kitty, I could fall in love with you all over again." His palms were sweating.

She was smiling now with her lips and her eyes.

"Will you let me try?"

She reached up and kissed his lips softly.

O'Reilly tingled.

"I will, Fingal."

"Bless you."

"And I understand about Deidre. I always have done."

O'Reilly held Kitty in a gentle hug. Poor Deidre, married to him for six months, then snuffed out by a German bomb in 1941 when the Luftwaffe blitzed Belfast. Part of him had died then too. "Thank you."

She moved back a pace. "No. Thank *you*, Fingal. I know how hard it's been for you to let go of her memory. I'll try to make it worthwhile, I promise."

O'Reilly, although he felt at home here with her, realized he was trembling.

Kitty touched his hand. "I'm glad you came up here, glad you've finally started to open up, Fingal. I know it's not easy."

Her touch, her words, warmed him. "I have to tell you . . ." He struggled to find the right sentences, but could only manage, "Kitty . . . thank you."

"My pleasure." To his relief she did not press him about what he had been trying to say.

He looked down at her upturned face and put a hand on her shoulder. She turned her head to the side to hold it between her cheek and shoulder. "It's not too many men my age get a second chance," he said, and he felt the pressure increase as she moved her head against his hand. She put her arms around his waist and held her face up to be kissed.

O'Reilly lowered his lips to hers, feeling them warm and open, the tip of her tongue on his. He tingled and the memories flooded back. He broke the kiss and held her tightly to him, her head on his chest.

O'Reilly saw himself at Belfast's Ravenhill rugby grounds in 1935, kissing a twenty-three-year-old Kitty when Ireland beat Wales by a score of 9 to 3. The pair of them whirling like dervishes under star-speckled skies, on the soft grass at a summer *céili* in the Wicklow Mountains outside Dublin.

The old slumbering feelings stirred, roused themselves, blinked sleep from their bleary eyes. He was holding her hand, walking Kitty to the nurses home after a student dance. He . . .

He was kissing Deidre on their honeymoon night in 1940. He could taste her, smell her perfume, feel her soft warmth, hear her laughter.

O'Reilly moved away. Coughed. Swallowed. Cleared his throat. "Kitty . . . I . . ." He was in the admiral's day cabin of HMS *Warspite* refusing compassionate leave. Where the hell would he go to? And he realized that then, and now, work had been an anodyne of sorts. It had occupied his mind.

She looked up at him. "I understand, Fingal. It's all right. Honestly."

O'Reilly felt close to tears. Whether it was because his memory of Deidre had been so vivid or because Kitty's willingness to understand had touched a nerve deep within him, he could not say. Kitty'd certainly aroused feelings that he'd been able to keep at bay for twenty-odd years. He thought he'd be better on his own for a while. He took a very deep breath and said softly, "Kitty, I do have to go now. I'll get Donal to see to your car, and I'll phone you tomorrow. I know Barry and I will be busy once the holidays are—"

"I've time to make up myself, remember? Jane Bingham's working my shift for me today. And I'm on duty on Sunday, I'll do her work on Monday, and Tuesday's my own turn again."

Was she hinting that perhaps she didn't want to see him after all? O'Reilly frowned. Damn it all, he bloody well wasn't going to let her slip away. Not now. "How about the weekend? I'll give Barry time off."

"I think he'll appreciate it. Be kind to him, Fingal, when you get home."

"I will. If he lets me. Barry's a very private young man."

"He's going to need a friend."

O'Reilly nodded. "I'll do what I can, but I want him to get away this weekend. Why don't you come down to Number 1 on Saturday or Sunday?"

She hesitated. "I'm going to a painting workshop."

"Bugger," he said, and because he knew his usual strategy for getting his own way by simply overriding objections wasn't going to work, he lapsed into silence.

Her laugh was musical. He felt her hand take his. "Fingal, you look like a little boy who has lost his mummy in Woolworth's."

O'Reilly harrumphed.

"I'll postpone the workshop. I'd love to come down."

He grabbed her in a great bear hug. "Bloody marvellous," he

roared, "and I'll give Kinky a couple of days off too. If you don't mind cooking?"

"Not a bit. I enjoy it—but how will Kinky take to another woman in her kitchen?"

"She's a heart of corn, that woman. She'll not mind one bit."

"Fine." She kissed him again. "Now, Fingal Flahertie O'Reilly, get your coat, home with you, never mind tomorrow, and phone me tonight to let me know you're safe. I'll be down at the weekend and—"

He kissed her.

"Drive carefully, do you hear?"

O'Reilly stared into her laughing, amber eyes flecked with grey and said, "I will because, Kitty, I do want to see you again."

"And you will, Fingal." Her voice was soft. "You will." One more kiss. "And don't forget to phone me when you get home."

5

I'm More Than a Little Sick

Barry heard the phone ringing below. The last thing he wanted was to go to work, but he took a deep breath, got out of his chair, and left the lounge. He yelled down from the landing, "It's all right, Kinky. I'll take it," and started downstairs.

Barry caught a glimpse of Mrs. Kincaid retreating to her kitchen. What she was doing in there at seven o'clock at night was a mystery. She'd come home half an hour ago. He guessed that other people at the party must have overheard Patricia's outburst, and if Cissie had found out, it would have been the first thing she would have said to Kinky, followed swiftly by a point-blank question about how things were back at Number 1. Kinky would have said nothing, but still the rumour mill would be at work.

Kinky, sensitive woman that she was, had not come upstairs since her return, and for that Barry was grateful.

He picked up the phone. "Doctor Laverty."

"Doctor? It's Gerry Shanks. Sorry to bother you, but can you come quick?" Barry heard the fear, the edge in the man's voice. "It's wee Siobhan, so it is."

"What's wrong with her, Gerry?"

"She's had a sore head and she's awful hot now and she started throwing off there about an hour ago. She near boked her ring up, so she did."

"Is she awake, Gerry?"

"Aye, but she says she feels sleepy, you know. We have her teed up on the sofa in front of the fire. Says her wee neck's awful stiff."

Barry flinched. A stiff neck could be a symptom of irritation of the meninges, the membranes that covered the brain. "I'll be straight out. What's your address?"

"We've a wee red-roofed bungalow out the Belfast Road. First house on the left past the Catholic chapel. You can't miss it."

"I'm on my way," Barry said and replaced the receiver.

He ran to the surgery, grabbed his bag, and pulled his overcoat from the hall coat stand. With coat half on, he ran toward his Volkswagen. As he pulled away, he reckoned he had a good idea of what would be waiting for him at the Shanks house.

He'd made a tentative diagnosis. Certainly it was the right time of the year. Winter and early spring were infectious meningitis season, and if an examination confirmed his suspicions, the sooner he got the child to hospital and the treatment started, the better were her chances for a complete recovery. Bacterial meningitis, a killer of children before the war, was now readily treated with antibiotics.

Barry tried to remember what else he knew about Siobhan Shanks and her family as he waited for the town traffic light to change. Why was the thing always against him when he had an emergency to attend to? The Shanks family had moved here recently from Belfast. Siobhan was four and had an older brother, Angus. Gerry, their dad, was a plater at Harland and Wolff shipyards.

The light turned green. Barry drove on.

Mairead, Gerry's wife, had coppery hair. The couple were trying to have another baby and had consulted O'Reilly for a second opinion about Doctor Fitzpatrick's treatment for infertility.

Oh, yes, Gerry supported Glentoran Soccer Club, and his best friend, Charlie Gorman, husband of Gertie whose breech baby O'Reilly had delivered, cheered for Linfield.

All that had little bearing on Siobhan's case, but it pleased Barry that like O'Reilly, who had had years of practice, Barry was getting to know his patients, to recognize them as people, not simply as their diseases. Hospital specialists rarely had that privilege.

He parked the car on the verge and picked up his bag from the passenger seat. The spire of the nearby church looked sharp, like a needle scratching the sky. He knew the tower was an example of Early English detailing because Patricia had explained it to him when they'd walked together past it hand in hand shortly before she'd left for Cambridge bloody University.

Barry's grip on his bag tightened as he walked up the path.

Gerry greeted him. "Thanks for coming, Doc. Gimme your coat."

In the narrow, carpeted hall, two black-and-white photos of Gerry dwarfed by the steel ribs of a ship under construction hung on one wall.

"That's me and the *Canberra*," Gerry said. "Launched her in 1960, a day before Saint Paddy's Day, you know."

Barry heard the pride in the man's voice fade. "Pay no heed to that. Come you away on through, sir, and take a keek at our wee girl." Gerry's voice cracked.

The parlour was small and warmed by a coal fire burning in a black metal grate. A print of the slopes of Slieve Donard in the Mourne Mountains hung over the mantel, where ranks of Christmas cards were flanked by two brass candlesticks.

A Christmas tree stood in the far corner. The acrid smell of vomit overpowered its piney scent. Its needles were turning brown, but it wouldn't be taken down until January sixth, Little Christmas.

Mairead sat on a straight-backed chair in front of a sofa, where Siobhan lay under a tartan blanket. Mairead didn't look up when the door opened. She supported the girl's head as the wee one puked into a baking bowl.

"See what I mean, Doc?" Gerry stood beside his wife and put a callused hand on her shoulder.

"Doctor," Mairead said, giving Barry a weak smile. " 'Scuse me." She stood and headed for the door. "I need for to give this here an empty and a wee wash."

Barry nodded, then said, "Hello, Siobhan." He knelt beside the child and took her wrist so he could feel for the pulse. Her skin was burning. No need for a thermometer to tell him she had a fever.

Her voice was weak. "I don't feel good."

He looked into her eyes. They were dull. Her pulse was 120 instead of the normal 88. He was convinced he was right about what was wrong with her. "When did it start?" he asked.

"About two in the morning," Gerry said. "She said her head was main sore."

Barry felt someone behind him.

"Here," Mairead said, handing him a clean bowl. "Just in case, like."

"Thank you, Mrs. Shanks."

Gerry sighed. "We thought it would all get better soon"—he looked Barry right in the eye—"and it's your holidays, like. We didn't want to annoy youse doctors."

Barry understood that annoy didn't mean "to anger." It meant "to inconvenience." Country patients. Salt of the earth. "That was very considerate, Gerry." Don't, Barry told himself, say, "I wish you'd called me sooner," even if it were true. How many times when he'd been in training had he, without thinking, scolded, "I wish you'd come to us sooner"? He'd not realized then that what he was really saying was "Let me help you feel even guiltier than you already do."

"It wasn't until she told us her wee neck was stiff and she started to throw off that I told Mairead, no more mucking about," Gerry said. He put his arm around his wife's shoulder. "I says to her . . . I says, 'I'm for getting himself or your man Laverty, so I am.'"

"You did the right thing, Gerry." Barry looked at Mairead and saw the moisture in her eyes.

Barry saw the father nod to himself. His shoulders seemed to sag less. The mother swallowed, rubbed her eyes with the backs of her hands, and managed a weak smile.

"I'm pretty sure we'll get her right as rain in no time." Proper treatment *should* effect a complete cure, but there were risks of complications. Cases of subsequent blindness or deafness sometimes occurred. Water on the brain, epilepsy, and muscular spasticity happened, and very rarely a patient died. "I just need," he said, "to take a wee look at you, Siobhan."

The little girl gave him a grave, old-womanish look. "That's all right," she said.

He set the bowl on the chair. Barry's examination was thorough, and as he worked he asked more questions of Gerry and Mairead. They told him that Siobhan had not had any rigors or seizures. Good.

Clearly she was not in a coma, but her neck was stiff, and light hurt her eyes. To his relief there was no purple rash or skin haemorrhages, which were invariably present if the germ had invaded the bloodstream and caused septicaemia—blood poisoning—which had a lethal potential.

Barry stood, shoved his stethoscope into his pocket, and inclined his head toward the hall door. It wasn't customary to discuss children's illnesses in front of them.

Gerry followed Barry into the hall. The moment the door was shut he asked, "Is it bad, Doc?"

"It could be better, Gerry. I'm pretty sure Siobhan has bacterial meningitis." He saw Gerry frown. "It used to be called brain fever and—"

"My God." Gerry put a hand against a wall to steady himself. "That sounds ferocious bad, sir."

Barry shook his head. "Once we know what germ's causing it, the right antibiotics'll see to it."

"Honest?"

"Honest to God." The odds were very good that the child would recover, but they had to act fast. "We'll have to get her up to Purdysburn in Belvoir Park on the far side of Belfast."

Gerry frowned. "The looney bin? Is her brain that bad?" His voice rose.

"No, Gerry, no. Siobhan's not going mad. There *is* a psychiatric hospital there, but Purdysburn's also where the fever hospital is. That's where she's going."

"Oh. That's all right then."

Where Patricia would have been in 1951. Barry pursed his lips. He shouldn't be thinking of her now, but pieces came back to him of the first night he'd met her and he'd walked her to her flat in the Kinnegar.

He'd asked about her limp, thinking it might be from a field hockey injury.

"I didn't hurt it," she'd told him, quite curtly.

"What happened?"

"Nineteen fifty-one."

"The polio epidemic?"

"My left leg's a bit short. I suppose I won't be hearing from you now? Men don't like women who aren't perfect."

"I don't give a damn about your leg, Patricia. I don't care at all."

Gerry's voice broke into Barry's reverie. "Will we need the ambulance, sir?"

"Sorry, Gerry, I was thinking." About the stars in Orion's belt that night, and how their light sparkled like burnished silver from a tear on a young woman's cheek. And how in that instant Barry Laverty had lost his heart to a girl with a limp.

"Thinking's your job, Doc." Gerry managed a small smile. "Don't let me interrupt."

Barry forced himself back to the now. "Where's your phone?"

"Thonder." Gerry pointed to a small table.

Barry dialled. Come on. He pulled his fingers through his hair. *Come on.*

"Ambulance dispatch." The voice was impatient.

He heard phones ringing, other voices in the background. "It's Doctor Laverty in Ballybucklebo. I've a girl with meningitis—"

"Jesus, Doc. It's like a friggin' zoo here tonight. It'll be hours before I can get an ambulance out to you."

"But I need one now."

Barry heard the irritation. "You and every other bloody doctor in County Down that's having too good a Boxing Day to be bothered to see patients. We get nights like this. There's bugger all I can—"

"Just a minute." Barry let an edge creep into his voice, exactly as O'Reilly would have. "I'm here, in her house, with a girl with meningitis who needs to get to hospital *now*."

The dispatcher snapped. "And I told you you've not a snowball's chance in . . ." The voice softened. "Hang about. Did you say Laverty?"

"Yes."

"The fellah that runs patients to the Royal in his own wee German motorcar?"

"That's right."

"How's about ye, Doctor? It's Danny here, so it is. Sorry I was a bit short, sir, but I'm run off my feet, so I am." His tone was friendly now.

Danny? Barry had no recollection of the man.

"I was having a smoke when you brung in a wee girl with the miscarriage in August; then I showed up at a road accident and you'd a sodger with a broken leg and a fellah dead in a sports car—"

That Danny. "I really do need an ambulance, Danny," Barry said.

He heard an in-drawing of breath. "Like I said, it's a wee bit tricky, like. They're all out, and the roads is—"

"I've a very sick kiddie here. I have to get her to the fever hospital. Is there nothing you can do?"

"Gimme a wee minute, Doc. I've a half-notion. Might be able to help you out, seeing it's you and all."

It was just as his father used to say about how things worked in Ulster. "It's not *what* you know, son, it's *who* you know that counts." He was getting to know people, and not just in Ballybucklebo.

Barry heard Danny say, "Over," and realized the man was using a radio-telephone. "Roger that, Joe. Out."

"Doc, I've Joe McSorely coming in from Helen's Bay. They're not far from you. He says he'll pick up your wee one, go to the Royal with his patient, then on to Belvoir. Would that work?"

"Marvellous. She'll be ready to go. The address is 11, Belfast Road. Just past the chapel."

"They'll be there soon."

"Thanks, Danny."

"That's all right, so it is." Over the line Barry heard phones ringing in the background. "Jesus, it's a right Paddy's market. Gotta go. Bye, Doc."

"The ambulance is coming?" He heard the relief in Gerry's voice.

Barry nodded. "Tell Mairead to get Siobhan ready. Clean nightie, wash bag, a favourite toy. I'll phone Purdysburn."

"Right, sir."

Barry redialled and waited to speak to the registrar on duty. He knew the proper treatment for bacterial meningitis was usually a combination of sulphadimidine, with the antibiotics benzylpenicillin and chloramphenicol. Once in a while the infective organism was not one likely to respond to that combination. Getting a sample to culture before starting drugs had its place.

It would require a lumbar puncture to get at the fluid that bathed the brain and spinal cord. Barry shuddered. The prospect of slipping a needle between two of a child's lumbar vertebrae, even if the skin had been anaesthetized, made him squeamish. He simply could not be a paediatrician. Better to be a country GP and let somebody else do the job, somebody like the registrar he was trying to talk to.

He reckoned he had been waiting at least five minutes when a woman finally answered. "Sorry to keep you. We're very busy."

"That you, Irene?" He thought he recognised a classmate's voice. "Barry Laverty here."

"Hi, Barry. What have you got for us?"

"Meningitis. Wee girl called Siobhan."

"That'll be the sixth tonight." He could hear Irene's tiredness.

Barry asked if he should start the antibiotics, but was told not to. He should give Siobhan's brother, Angus, a prescription for sulphadimidine—half a tablet in milk every four hours for three days. He might have been near whoever infected Siobhan.

"Thanks, Irene." Barry put the phone down just as the front doorbell rang.

The ambulance attendant had dark rings under his eyes, his navy-blue uniform mostly hidden under an army-surplus greatcoat. "Wee girl wi' meningitis?" He carried a blanket.

"Come in." Barry led the man, who Danny had called Joe McSorely, to the parlour. "Gerry . . . Mairead. The ambulance is here."

Gerry bent and picked up a tearful Siobhan. She clutched her teddy bear and whimpered, "I want my mammy."

"It's all right, dear," Mairead said. "Mammy's coming too." She looked at Barry. "I can go, can't I?"

"Joe?" Barry asked.

"Aye, certainly. We've another patient on board, but we'll make room. The wee button'll be scared shi . . . scared witless without her ma, so she will. Here," he said, giving Gerry the blanket. "Wrap her in that there."

"Can you carry her, Joe?" Barry asked.

"Aye, no trouble." He reached out to take the little girl.

"It's all right, Siobhan," Gerry said. "Mammy's going with you. I'll need to stay at home to keep an eye to your brother."

"We'd best be going, Doc," Joe said.

"Thanks for coming, Joe."

"Sure isn't it what we're here for?" Joe, with Siobhan cradled in his arms, started to move past Barry. Siobhan took a deep breath, made a whooping noise—and vomited all over Barry's clean pants.

"My God," Gerry said. "I'm sorry about that, Doc."

Barry shrugged.

"Could we get them dry-cleaned for you?" Gerry asked.

Barry shook his head. "It's all right." He started to lift his coat from the rack. "I'll write you a prescription for Angus—just a precaution—then I'll be running along home."

Running? It was a figure of speech. Why should he rush? What was there to hurry back to Number 1 for?

6

Put the Car Away

O'Reilly was looking forward to getting home. He chuckled and would have rubbed his hands together had he not been steering. He drove past Palace Barracks and into Holywood, the only Irish town other than Ballybucklebo to have a Maypole. Not much farther to there now.

And Kitty would be coming down on . . . damn it all, why not ask her to stay for the whole weekend? He grinned and let go a blast of smoke from the pipe he'd lit only seconds after getting into the car. He would ask, by God. As an old bachelor—well, old widower—he had forgotten until five months ago how enjoyable it was to be in the company of a woman, and a bright, feisty, bloody good-looking woman at that.

He'd tell Barry to take the weekend off, and would give Mrs. Kincaid a few days as well. She had a married sister, Fidelma, and nieces and nephews down in County Cork. Fidelma's husband, Eamon, farmed near Beal na mBláth. O'Reilly'd speak to Kinky tonight. By God, he would.

He sang to himself:

> Oh love is pleasing and love is teasing
> And love is a pleasure when first it's new . . .

He accelerated, knowing he should stop thinking of Kitty O'Hallorhan and concentrate on his driving. The traffic was light, but the roads were still slippery despite their having been salted and sanded.

On the far side of Holywood he hit a right-hand corner and felt the back end of the Rover start to go. O'Reilly wrenched the steering wheel into the skid, hoped to God nothing was coming the other way, and by brute effort forced the car back on course. He grunted and muttered, "Bloody slush."

The spire of the Ballybucklebo Catholic church loomed to his right. O'Reilly turned into a sharp left and headed for home, where he'd get his supper and a Jameson. He'd settle down in front of a big fire, get stuck into a plate of cold ham and turkey, see how young Barry was, and . . . *"Christ Almighty."*

He wrenched the wheel to the right, slammed on the brakes, and rammed the heel of his hand on the horn. Someone was wheeling a bicycle across the road in front of the car. He hauled the wheel back left, but this time nothing could bring the big car out of the skid. An unstoppable juggernaut, it crabbed ahead, missing the cyclist by inches. The crunching as the car's nose slid into the ditch underscored the horn's blaring. Steam hissed as it jetted from the radiator. O'Reilly sat rigidly now that the movement had stopped. "Bugger," he muttered.

Ignoring the steam, he put the car in reverse and floored the accelerator. Perhaps he could get the old Rover to limp home. The engine howled, the back tyres screeched, and the stink of burning rubber filled his nostrils. He decelerated, then tried again, with exactly the same results. "Bugger," he said again, switching off the engine and pounding his fist on the steering wheel. "Hellfire and damnation."

O'Reilly grabbed a torch from the glove compartment and climbed out. The Rover's nose was well into the ditch, and the rear tyres had dug muddy trenches and thrown twin plumes of darkness onto the skid marks behind. "Blue blazing buggery." He'd have to leave the car and walk home. When he got his hands on the buck eejit with the bike—

"Excuse me, Doctor sir."

Donal Donnelly stood in front of O'Reilly. Donal's duncher was pushed back over his carroty hair, and he scratched his scalp. His other hand held his self-decorated bike of many colours by the handlebars.

O'Reilly roared, "Donal? Donal bloody Donnelly, you great glipe, you unmitigated *amadán*. What in the name of the sainted Baby Jesus in velvet trousers were you doing crossing the road? You've put me in the fornicating ditch."

"Makes a change," Donal said.

"You impertinent—" But O'Reilly had already seen the funny side. He'd lost track of the number of times his driving had forced cycling locals, including Donal, off the road. He cleared his throat and tried to scowl at Donal, but then he said, "Fair play. Touché. You're all right, Donal? Not hurt?"

"Och, I'm grand, so I am, sir, but when I came to see how you were, I took a quick gander up front. There's a brave dent in the bonnet of your motor; I think the radiator's banjaxed. She's stuck in thon ditch too. I doubt we'll no' get her out the night."

"I'll have to leave her, get someone to bring a tractor round tomorrow and drag her out."

"I'll get hold of Charlie O'Hara first thing," Donal said. "He's got a big Massey-Harris. Charlie's a good head. He'll see you right in the morning, sir."

"Thanks, Donal." O'Reilly remembered his promise to Kitty. "I need another favour too."

"Fire away."

"If the road's better tomorrow could you drive Miss O'Hallorhan's car up to Belfast?"

"Aye. In soul, I could. Me and Julie's going down to Rasharkin to see her folks. It would save us the train fare to Belfast."

"Pop round about nine. I'll give you directions—and a couple of quid."

"I'll be there, sir." Donal fidgeted. "Would you like a lift home now, sir?"

"You've no car."

"No, but I've the bike, so I have. You could sit on the crossbar, like."

O'Reilly roared with laughter. He'd not been transported sitting sidesaddle on a bicycle since he was a chiseller, but why not? "You're on," he said, and with very little effort the archtrickster of Ballybucklebo was soon trundling along the road with the village's senior medical practitioner clutching the bike's crossbar.

"Home, James, and don't spare the horses," O'Reilly roared. "I want to know the state of play at Number 1."

Donal wobbled near the snowy ditch, but regained his balance, and Doctor Fingal Flahertie O'Reilly threw back his head and in his mellifluous baritone belted out, "Daisy, Daisy, give me your answer, do . . ."

He and Donal were finishing the final chorus, "But you'd look sweet upon the seat of a bicycle built for two," when Donal stopped, put one foot on the ground, and said, "Here y'are, sir. Home sweet home."

"Good night, Donal. Thanks for the lift."

"Doctor O'Reilly?" Donal asked quietly.

"Yes, Donal."

"It's dark and it's cold and this is no place for a chat, but I'm sore troubled by a wee money matter."

"Julie and the photographer?"

Donal shook his head. "No. It's to do with a horse."

"A horse?" O'Reilly pricked up his ears. When Donal was involved with racing greyhounds or horses, there was usually a bob or two to be made. "Tell me more."

"It's too long a story, sir. I promised Julie I'd be home—"

"Tell me when you pop round tomorrow."

"Would Friday suit, sir? Like I said, Julie and me's going down to Rasharkin to see her folks for a few days." He lowered his voice. "She'll be with me tomorrow and I'd rather not talk about it in front of her."

O'Reilly laughed. "Fair enough. Friday morning it is. I'll be waiting with bated breath." He leaned closer to Donal and lowered his voice. "I hope it's a good story, Donal."

"Huh. It is not, so it's not. It's all about shares in a horse, you know."

"Shares?" O'Reilly frowned. "In a horse?"

"Aye. And Councillor Bishop. My boss."

"Donal Donnelly, come inside this minute. I want to hear all about—"

"Saving your presence, Doctor O'Reilly, I really need your advice, sir, but I promised Julie—"

"All right, all right. Go on home, but I'll expect you tomorrow at nine and at ten on Friday."

"I'm your man, sir. Thank you. Good-night, sir."

O'Reilly stood for a moment chuckling and watching Donal's departing back. Shares in a horse *and* Bertie Bishop? He'd look forward to hearing *that* story.

When he let himself in, he could hear Kinky clattering about in her kitchen. Off with his overcoat and down the hall he went. "How are you, Kinky?"

She turned from the counter where she'd been rolling out pastry. "Grand, so. And yourself, sir?"

"I could be better. I've bent the Rover."

She made sympathetic clucking noises.

"Och, sure it could have been worse. There's not a scratch on me."

"Praise be."

"And how was Flo's?" he asked.

"The *craic* was ninety." She chuckled and her three chins wobbled. "Cissie Sloan could make a cat laugh when she gets a head of steam up." She wiped her hands on her apron. "She was very interested in what I knew about Doctor Laverty and his lady friend too."

"What did you tell her?"

"Not a word. Sure what I knew was no more than what Flo told me. Poor young man."

O'Reilly sighed. "Aye."

"And it's all over the village by now."

"At least," O'Reilly said, "it's unlikely to be malicious."

Kinky nodded. "He's liked well enough, so."

And that, O'Reilly thought, coming from Kinky, who had a firm grip on the pulse of Ballybucklebo, is praise indeed. "You're a sound woman, Kinky Kincaid," he said. He nodded up to where two pairs of Barry's pants were hanging to dry on the bars-ropes-and-pulley device, then pointed at her cooking. "And you work too hard." He smiled. "How'd you like a few days off this weekend? See your family?"

She put a hand on her hip. Her eyes narrowed. "Would Miss O'Hallorhan be coming down?"

O'Reilly felt the blush start. "She would."

Kinky turned back to the counter and with a fine brush began to paint egg yolk onto the pastry. "I'd need to leave on Wednesday, sir, to travel all the way to Cork and get back by Sunday, but I'd like to see Fidelma and Eamon and theirs. I'd have to phone her to see if it's all right."

"You know where the phone is. Go on and ask your sister if it'd be all right for you to go on Tuesday. Make a decent holiday of it. I know it's a fair stretch of the legs from here to Beal na mBláth. Train to Belfast. Change stations. Train to Amiens Street Station in Dublin. A different station for a train to Cork City, another to Clonakilty. Then what?"

"Eamon'd pick me up in his motorcar."

"Great. Barry and I can manage." He stepped behind her and gave her a pat.

She spun round. "Don't you be taking liberties, sir," she said, but her grin was ear to ear. "And you'll not need to worry. I'll leave this turkey pie and plenty of other stuff in the fridge and instructions for heating them. And I've tonight's cold supper ready in the dining room, so."

"You're a marvel. Thanks, Kinky." A thought struck. "Has Barry eaten?"

Her smile fled. "He has not. That boy is sore wounded."

"Has he told you himself about Patricia?"

"Before I left to go to the Bishops', I asked him what the matter was. He was very low." Kinky looked O'Reilly straight in the eye. "But he did not have to tell me. Nor did Cissie. I already knew."

Fingal felt goose bumps start, as he always did when Kinky exhibited her uncanny ability to know things she had no way of knowing. Mrs. Kinky Kincaid was fey.

"I did see it coming, the poor *garsún*."

"Is he upstairs in the lounge?"

"He is not. Nor is Miss Spence. He was there when I came home, but he got called out. When he came back, he gave me another pair of pants to wash, apologized for that, and said he was going to bed." She sighed deeply. "I think he's in his room licking his wounds."

O'Reilly sighed. "I wanted to talk to him after I'd had my supper. I could have taken him up a bite too."

"I think, sir, if you'll take a woman's advice, you'll leave him be tonight. I think Doctor Laverty is the kind of man to bottle things up. A private sort of a kind of a person, so. I do think he will want to talk to you, but not until he does be good and ready."

O'Reilly pinched his nose, considered Kinky's opinion, and then said, "You're right, Kinky. I'll let him come to me." He patted his tummy. "And I'll go and see what's in the dining room."

7

To Comfort All That Mourn

Barry was in no hurry to go to the dining room for breakfast. He'd had no appetite for days—three days to be exact. He finished shaving. The tuft of fair hair was, as usual, sticking up from his crown the way it had once in a railway carriage and she'd said, "Your hair sticks up like a little boy's." His hand had flown to it then, and he'd made some weak joke about it. Now he couldn't be bothered to smooth it down. The blue eyes that looked back from the mirror were bloodshot and had dark circles beneath. He'd not dropped off until two in the morning. Since Saturday's disastrous conversation with Patricia, sleep had been hard to come by.

By the time O'Reilly'd come home that night, Barry had already retreated to his attic room, where he tossed and turned into the small hours. He'd stayed there on Sunday morning until he'd heard a vehicle draw up and Patricia's voice saying good-bye. An alto bell tolling the death knell for a lost love. She might as well never have existed, but for the memories and the ache.

Fingal had come home again later that morning from having his car towed to a garage. He'd made no mention of Patricia. His conversation had been confined to explaining about his crash. The mechanic had said it would take a week to repair the Rover.

O'Reilly'd suggested that they split the work for the week between Christmas and New Year's. Whoever was free would see any patients who came to Number 1, and the carless O'Reilly would walk to visit any who lived nearby. Barry was to go by car to the more distant ones. If he was willing to let O'Reilly drive the Volkswagen in the evenings, which he was, they'd split night call.

They had not been overly busy. The Shankses weren't the only ones conscious of "annoying" their doctors during the holidays when the surgery was officially closed. Only those who considered their complaint to be urgent came to the house or asked for a visit.

At least when Barry was working, his mind was occupied, and he was grateful for it. And he was thankful that although he couldn't quite put his finger on it, the patients seemed to be more concerned for his welfare than usual.

His spare time dragged. An aunt had once told him that no matter who hurt him his books would always be his best friends. He'd tried one, but somehow *Catch-22* didn't seem as hilarious as when he'd first read it three years earlier. The television news on BBC1 was full of gloom. The Americans, led by their president, Lyndon Johnson, were getting more deeply mired in Vietnam. BBC2, the network's second channel, had been launched in April by Denis Tuohy as a niche channel, but Barry could find nothing on it to interest him.

He'd tried not to, but he couldn't stop thinking about her. Sunlight reflected from a cup of black coffee and he saw her eyes. A flicker of a bird's wings and she was telling him what kind of bird it was. She spoke to him at any time, day or night, but he had spoken to no one.

The memories and the pain in him grew like the pressure in a boil. Perhaps it was time to lance the sore? Maybe it was time to talk about Patricia to Fingal?

Barry left the bathroom and went downstairs to find O'Reilly sitting in the lounge, booted feet up on a stool, briar belching, the *Times* clutched in one hand.

"Morning, Fingal."

O'Reilly lowered the paper and looked over his half-moon spectacles. "Morning. Sleep well?"

Barry pursed his lips. His shoulders twitched.

"Aye," said O'Reilly quietly. "Aye." He pointed to a headline. "They're still picking up after the December twenty-third cyclone in Ceylon. Thousands dead. Terrible."

"It is. Awful." Barry walked to the window. "What's it like out?"

"Not a bad day for the time of year it's in."

The snow had gone, but the sky was a sullen grey, flat and dull as an ancient ploughshare. The church steeple opposite presided over a dejected-looking group of yews, silent bowed mourners for those in the graveyard beneath. In the distance, across Belfast Lough, the Antrim Hills merged with the clouds as if the darkness of a charcoal sketch had been finger-smudged to blur the distinction between the sea and shore, hillcrests and heavens.

Barry turned and took a deep breath. "Fingal?"

"Yes, Barry."

"I'm sorry I've not had much to say lately."

O'Reilly let go a puff of smoke.

"I think you understand why."

O'Reilly set the pipe in an ashtray. "I do. You're sorely hurt. I'm sorry."

"Thank you." He felt a lump in his throat. "I miss her, Fingal."

O'Reilly rose and wandered over to where Barry stood. "I understand about that too. You know about my wife?"

Barry nodded. "I only *knew* until Saturday. Now I'm beginning to understand." He looked into O'Reilly's brown eyes. Damn it, Patricia had brown eyes you could drown in.

"It's hard," O'Reilly said. "Very hard."

Barry nodded. "What can I do?"

O'Reilly folded his arms across his chest. "Would you be disappointed if I said I don't know?"

Barry held his hands palms up, blew out his breath.

"Well, I don't," said O'Reilly. "Did they teach you anything at medical school about how to help someone hurting like you?"

Barry shook his head.

"Nor me," O'Reilly said. "Come on." He put a hand on Barry's shoulder. "Let's sit down."

When they were both seated, O'Reilly relit his pipe.

Barry glanced at Lady Macbeth, drowsing by the fire. Seeing the cat brought a picture of Patricia sitting here on Saturday, stroking the animal, and saying, "We need to talk, Barry."

O'Reilly coughed. "I suppose," he said, "you could do what I did. Throw yourself into your work. Refuse to have anything to do with women. It wasn't hard for me on a bloody great battleship."

At that moment the thought of isolation on a ship at sea appealed to Barry.

"I've seen men in the navy and here climb into the bottle." O'Reilly shook his head. "I don't recommend it."

"You needn't worry about that with me."

"I know." O'Reilly laughed. "Sure don't I take enough of the craythur for both of us?"

Barry had to smile.

"But it's not to make me forget, Barry." He held Barry's gaze and lowered his voice. "I'll never forget."

Hearing the older man's sadness eased Barry's own. He nearly stretched out a hand to lay on Fingal's, but Ulster boys from Barry's boarding school had been trained to shy away from physical signs of affection.

"You won't forget, either. I promise you that," Fingal said.

Barry sighed.

"The trick, as I see it," O'Reilly said, "is to get through the first while." He stared deeply into the fire, then turned back to Barry. "That took me twenty-three years."

And it could take me longer, Barry thought. Oh, Patricia.

O'Reilly puffed. "I found the work a great solace. It's never dull, and if you repeat this to anyone, I'll kill you, Barry Laverty, but if you need some kind, any kind, of love, you can get it from your patients."

Or a bloody great Labrador, Barry thought. But it's not that kind of love I need.

"I hope," O'Reilly said, "you do get through the next 'however long.' I'm here if you want to talk. I'll try to keep you occupied. I did before, when you and she seemed to have split up shortly after you met, and when she was in England. I worked you hard when you thought you were going to be sued."

Barry remembered suspecting what Fingal had been up to at those times. He'd not expected the man to confess it. And he had to admit it had worked. Being slack now over the holidays didn't help.

"And you need a safe home. This house, Ballybucklebo, and surrounds are your home now, Barry Laverty," O'Reilly said. "Think about it."

Home? Barry shifted in his chair. This upstairs lounge was as familiar to him as his old bedroom in his folks' house in Bangor. He'd not lived with his parents since he'd moved into the Queen's Elms Halls of Residence in Belfast in his third year as a student. He and his old school friend Jack Mills, now training as a surgeon, had managed to stick together as they moved from one service to another. In the succeeding years and when they were housemen in their final year of training, they'd lived in student and junior doctor quarters in the teaching hospitals of Belfast. A gypsy existence, but a time for friendships to grow.

Everywhere he'd lived had been temporary. Number 1, Main Street, Ballybucklebo, could be permanent, at least until he got a place of his own. He smiled. He was in no rush for that. He couldn't cook like Kinky.

"Thank you, Fingal. You're right," he said, but there was an ache around every corner. In a glen he might see himself wearing too-big pants, borrowed from Fingal, helping a girl across a bridge. On the shore he'd remember her dark hair, wind-tossed by the half gale that had churned the waters of the lough to foam and blown to tatters the black smoke from a coal boat's funnel. Her joy in little things: a perfect fuschia blossom, wind shaking a field of ripe barley, her first-ever Chinese dinner, the "Rose Duet" from *Lakmé*.

"And," said O'Reilly, bringing Barry back to the lounge, "when we get you through, one day . . . one day there'll be another girl."

"I don't think so."

"Ah, but . . . you never know." O'Reilly stood, went to the mantel and leaned against it, raised a bushy eyebrow, and said, "Kitty's coming down for the weekend."

"I'm happy for you both, Fingal."

"Do you know, Barry, that's very gracious of you? Particularly now. Especially now."

Barry pursed his lips, turned his head to one side, and raised that shoulder.

"So," said Fingal, "I'm going to give you the weekend off. I told you Kitty's coming. Kinky's going down to Cork today—"

"And you'd like me out of the house too?" It didn't matter one way or the other to Barry.

"I'm not sure I'd put it *exactly* that way." O'Reilly's grin gave the lie to his words. "But I thought you might like a weekend off. Saturday and Sunday." O'Reilly's voice was guileless.

"I'll call Jack Mills. He always has room in his Belfast flat."

"Thanks, Barry. I'll do next weekend."

"Fine."

"Now," said O'Reilly, rising. "You've had no breakfast, and I could go another slice of toast and a cup of coffee. What do you reckon?"

"I'll come with you," Barry said, and to his surprise he did feel a tiny pang of hunger.

8

My Kingdom for a Horse

"You'll not go hungry with me, Barry Laverty." O'Reilly waved his fish knife in his assistant's direction. "I like to ring the changes at breakfast so it's a brace of kippered herrings this Friday morning, and being the day it is, a Happy New Year to you too."

"And to you, Fingal."

O'Reilly inhaled. The aroma filled the dining room. He noted that Barry was finishing the second of his smoked fish. The lad's appetite wasn't single-handedly going to drive Ireland back into *An Gorta Mor,* the Great Hunger, but he *was* eating again. A good sign.

Last night, New Year's Eve, had been a bit tense at Number 1. Barry, clearly suffering from the added stress that festive events put upon those who are grieving, had turned down Fingal's offer of a trip to the Mucky Duck to bring in the New Year. The lad had muttered something about having two tickets to the New Year's Eve formal dance up at Queen's that O'Reilly was welcome to if he wanted to take Kitty. Pity she'd been working, so after trying once more to persuade Barry, Fingal had left him on call and gone down to the pub where in good company he'd sunk a few pints and roared out "Auld Lang Syne" with the other eejits when midnight struck. He'd even let them persuade him to sing "The Parting

Glass" before he'd headed home at one. Officially, singing was illegal in Ulster pubs, but it was New Year's Eve.

Now with the jollifications behind them, it was business as usual. The surgery was closed, but emergencies could crop up. And there was another matter outstanding.

"Can you make home visits this morning?" O'Reilly asked. "Donal's coming to see me at ten, and before you ask, it's not about a dog. It's to do with a horse." He looked at his watch. "He should be here in fifteen minutes."

"Sure," Barry said.

"Thanks." O'Reilly waited to see if Barry would show any curiosity about Donal's doings. Instead Barry said, "Mrs. Brown phoned earlier. She wants me to have a look at Colin. It's probably just a heavy cold, but I had one case of meningitis already. On Christmas night."

Kinky had told O'Reilly that Barry'd had a call, but with the whole Patricia business upsetting the lad he must have forgotten to discuss it with O'Reilly. "Who was it?" he asked.

"Siobhan Shanks. I sent her up to Purdysburn."

"What about her brother?"

"Angus? I started him on prophylactic sulphas and told Mairead to let me know if he showed any symptoms. I've not heard from her."

"Good lad." For a second O'Reilly marvelled at modern medicine's ability to prevent diseases by such a simple measure as giving a few pills. Changed days from when he'd started in practice. O'Reilly set his fork on his plate and said, "Now pass up the toast."

Barry rose and carried the toast rack to O'Reilly. "Here you are," he said. "I'm going upstairs to get my jacket; then I'm off." He turned to leave, got halfway to the door, then asked, "What's Donal Donnelly doing with—or is it to—a horse?"

O'Reilly paused from buttering a slice of toast. Good lad, he thought. He's starting to take an interest in things again. "Damned if I know," he said. "It's something about shares in the beast—and Councillor Bertie Bishop's involved."

"Bertie?"

"Uh-huh."

Barry managed a second smile. "Good luck, Fingal."

As Barry left the room, O'Reilly heard the front doorbell ring and Barry in the hall saying, "Good morning, Donal. You're early. Doctor O'Reilly's expecting you. Go on into the surgery."

"It's all right," O'Reilly yelled. "Tell him to come in here."

O'Reilly watched Donal, duncher in hands, creep into the dining room. He looked around, wide-eyed, much, O'Reilly imagined, as a peasant might regard the Hall of Mirrors at Versailles. "Morning, Donal."

"Morning, sir." Donal's tone was hushed. "Happy New Year."

"And to you. Come on in. Sit down. Would you like a cup of tea?"

"Me, sir? Tea, sir?"

"Aye, you, Donal. Would you like a cup of tea? You're not in the presence of royalty."

" 'Deed I would, so I would." He dusted off a chair with the palm of his hand. "Can I sit here, sir?"

"Course you may." O'Reilly stood, poured, and gave a cup to Donal. "Sugar and milk's there. Help yourself." He waited until Donal had poured in some milk and put in three spoonfuls of sugar. "Now," said O'Reilly, "what's all this about?"

Donal sipped his tea. "Money," he said. "You see, me and Julie'd like to buy a house. Just a wee one, like"—he looked around— "nothing grand like this. Just wee. We have some money saved up."

O'Reilly smiled. He knew where it had come from but was not going to tell Donal.

Donal sipped again. "Doctor Laverty's Miss Spence . . ." He hesitated, then said softly, "I'm sorry for his troubles, so I am."

"Thank you, Donal."

Donal sucked air past his buckteeth. "Anyroad, Miss Spence was dead-on, so she was, with her advice. I left it up to Julie to decide. She went up to see your man the photographer on Tuesday. We got the first tenner and the snaps is lovely. Just lovely. I'm for having some framed, so I am. She's a dead cert to win the five hundred pounds." Donal smiled. "That and our savings would make a brave down payment.

"That's where your man Bishop comes in. I'd been thinking about a house even before Julie and me finally did get married. Back in October the councillor comes up to me and Billy Brennan, like, seeing as how we were working for him and all. How'd we fancy making a few extra bob? How'd we like to own shares in a horse and race it for a while?" Donal's face lit up. "It's great *craic,* the racing, and it would be even more if it was your own horse running."

"And you'd sell it when, as you'd hope, the value goes up?" O'Reilly knew it was a common practice among the horsey fraternity, but he said, "Bertie Bishop, a man who's usually too mean to spend Christmas, wanted to let you and your mate in on a moneymaker? A horse?"

"Not just us, sir. He was going to let a few smart lads in, so he was, chippies, sparks, and brickies that worked for him."

Carpenters, electricians, and bricklayers were involved? O'Reilly could understand how flattering it would be for workingmen to be asked by their boss to come into the syndicate.

"How many of you are there?"

"Billy, him and me, and six other lads."

"And you eight own the whole horse?"

"Not quite, sir. We've ten percent each. Councillor Bishop has two shares. Twenty percent, like. He called them controlling shares."

That's my Bertie, O'Reilly thought. Controlling. Gurrier.

"He understands things like that, so he does. We just have

shares. We agreed to that." Donal set his teacup in the saucer. "She's a right nice wee filly, too. He called her Flo's Fancy."

"Jasus." O'Reilly snorted. "For one-fifth of its value Bertie Bishop's got a controlling interest in your horse?"

Donal grimaced. "It's not as unfair as it sounds, sir. He'll be swallowing the cost of tack, pasturing, stabling, training, the jockey, and all."

"All right. I'll accept that. You're not being asked to pay for any of that?"

"No, sir. Mind you, Mr. Bishop owns plenty of pastureland and a stable. He can save a brave bit there. And when it comes to prize money, he's dead decent too."

"How?"

"If she wins, all of us is to get ten percent of the purse each."

"And if she places?"

"Them prizes is pretty wee, so they are. We agreed he could keep them to help pay the expenses."

O'Reilly thought hard. He couldn't quibble with Donal's assertion that Bertie was paying money for upkeep, and as such his distribution of any prizes was fair. Place money wouldn't cover Bertie's expenses. It seemed that he, owning pasture and stable notwithstanding, was going to be spending a lot of cash without much chance of making a big profit. But with Councillor Bishop, worshipful master of the Ballybucklebo Orange Lodge, things were rarely what they seemed at first sight. Particularly where money was concerned.

"Aye," said O'Reilly, thinking harder. Money could certainly be made by selling the animal if the racehorse performed well. Some owners did sell shares to defray the initial cost of purchase, but at sale time their profit was reduced accordingly. The big money came to people who owned the animal outright. Owned the animal outright. "Aha," O'Reilly said, "I think I'm beginning to understand." His frown was so tight his eyebrows made each other's close acquaintance. "Donal, tell me again what Mr. Bishop calls his shares."

"Controlling."

That was the key: control. He'd bet twenty pounds to a hazelnut that Bertie Bishop did have plans to own the whole animal. "I don't like the sound of that control, Donal. How much was a share?"

"She cost a thousand pounds. We put in a hundred pounds each; Mr. Bishop, two hundred. And if we didn't have the money to start with, he was happy to put in our share and stop a bit of it each week out of our wages until it was all paid off. He'd only charge five percent a year, so he would."

So Bertie had the horse, and he held their loans at a rate one and a half percent higher than a house mortgage, but about the same as that of a bank loan. That surprised O'Reilly. He would have expected Bertie to be charging usurious rates.

Donal went on. "I didn't think we could lose. Likely we'll make a big profit when the horse's sold."

"What if the horse doesn't do well?" O'Reilly asked.

Donal shrugged. "Then we're up the creek without a paddle. Julie'll kill me, so she will. A hundred pounds doesn't grow on trees." He managed a weak smile. "I've seen the wee animal run on a training track. I've had a stopwatch on her." He lowered his voice to a whisper. "You ever hear of a Yankee horse called Seabiscuit?"

"That beat War Admiral in 1938 at Pimlico?"

"Aye. Well, Flo's Fancy is faster against the watch."

O'Reilly whistled and nearly relaxed. "If she's that good, I'd not worry too much, Donal. You're a hell of a judge of horseflesh."

Donal blushed. "Thank you, sir. I just wish I was a good judge of business."

O'Reilly did not like the sound of that.

"That's why I come to you, sir, you being a learnèd man and all." Donal lowered his voice. "I . . . I know what I said about her being a good wee horse and all, but I still think we're getting rooked, like." He glanced around. "You'll not tell nobody?"

O'Reilly shook his head. He could understand why Donal, archfinagler, wouldn't want anyone to know he'd been conned.

"Sure didn't I know that?" Donal said, smiling. "Youse doctors take the hypocritical oath—"

"Hypoc*ratic*, Donal. Hypoc*ratic*."

"Aye, him. Your man. Hippy-whigmaleery. I'm the right looper when it comes to them foreign names, so I am, but I'm no eejit about betting." His face fell. "At least I wasn't. Not until now."

"Tell me about it, Donal."

"Councillor Bishop said he knew how to make a bit more money on the side while we waited for the animal's price to go up."

O'Reilly's eyes narrowed. "How?"

"Betting on her. And he's been right decent the way we do it. He decides when to bet, puts up our stake money out of his own pocket, and if we win we're quids in. He keeps the stake money— it's his after all—but we all share the winnings. And because she's so fast he only ever backs her to win. He doesn't waste money betting to place."

"What if she doesn't come first?"

"That's where it gets tricky. He doesn't ask for money from us to cover the lost stakes. He just takes a bit of our share of the horse."

As far as O'Reilly was concerned, the stench of rodent suddenly overpowered the smell of kipper in the room. It seems he'd guessed correctly that Bertie was going to try to own the whole horse. "So he just takes a bit of your share of the horse. And you lads together own eight hundred pounds of her?"

"We did, sir."

"Did? *Did?*"

"Aye. Last time she was out, Mr. Bishop put ten pounds for each of us, on the nose. We'd have won a hundred pounds apiece."

O'Reilly heard the flatness of Donal's voice. "But?"

"She came second by a nose."

"So the eight of you lost eighty pounds between you."

"I know," said Donal sadly, "and it's not the first time. Our share of the horse is down to five hundred and sixty pounds." Donal sighed. "We'd do all right for a win, but we're bollixed if the horse loses or places."

"Jasus, Donal. A few more races that she doesn't win and none of you'll have any share at all. And Bertie—"

"I know, sir. He'll own the whole bloody horse." Donal sighed again. "When we started setting this up, we thought we'd a great chance to make a bit betting, and with every win the value of the horse goes up so our shares increase in value."

"I understand," said O'Reilly. And, he thought, I also understand that the secret of a good con artist is to play upon people's greed. There was something he *didn't* understand about the betting, something that was niggling at him.

Donal continued. "At the very start, when he asked us if we approved"—Donal stared at the tablecloth—"me and the rest took a vote on it. We were dead certain we were on to a sure thing, so we were."

"You agreed to Bertie's conditions? How he bets? The prize money?"

"We did."

"Jasus," said O'Reilly, "I think you *are* bollixed. He's gradually bleeding you dry."

Donal hung his head.

"I have the hang of it," O'Reilly said. "Unless the animal wins, Bertie'll end up owning the whole horse and making the entire profit when he sells her." O'Reilly snorted. "That's iniquitous. Bloody disgraceful. The gobshite."

Donal forced a weak smile. "If the wee thing doesn't start winning soon, it'll not matter about us losing our shares. She'll be worth nothing at sale. Who'd want to buy a racehorse that can't win?"

O'Reilly scratched his chin. "Good point." And Bertie Bishop was astute enough to see that too. Bertie was up to something. But what? O'Reilly needed to think. "Give me a minute, Donal."

Donal nodded.

O'Reilly made a series of rapid calculations. On the last bet Bertie had put up one hundred pounds: the men's communal stake and his own of twenty pounds. He used his money, was now out of pocket one hundred pounds, and in return had acquired eighty pounds worth of shares in the horse. "Jesus," O'Reilly said, unaware that he had spoken. "I don't believe it."

"What, sir?"

O'Reilly took a very deep breath. "Donal, by my calculation Bertie Bishop is certainly doing you and your mates out of your shares, but he could do it cheaper by simply buying you out. Look . . ." It took little time to convince Donal that O'Reilly was right.

"What do you think it means, sir?" Donal asked.

"I'm damned if I know . . . yet. But he's up to something that'll make a big profit for Bertie Bishop unless, Donal, we can find out *what* he's about and put a stopper in it." O'Reilly grinned. Sorting this out could be fun.

"Can you, sir?"

"I think the first thing to do is to persuade him to stop placing bets until we've worked out what he's up to."

"Stop him betting, sir?" Donal asked. "How? We all signed a paper that said he could bet whenever he liked." He hung his head. "And when someone holds your job in his hand, and me with Julie and a wean coming on to support . . ." He sighed. "I hope to God she wins that five hundred pounds for her pictures." Donal looked at O'Reilly. He'd seen that supplication in Arthur Guinness's eyes.

"I hoped, sir, when I come here maybe I could get yourself to have a wee word with him."

"Did you ever hear of an English king, Canute, telling the tide not to come in?"

Donal shook his head.

"Doesn't matter." O'Reilly looked to the ceiling, then back to Donal. "Donal Donnelly, I think you and your friends have taken leave of your senses."

"I think maybe we have, so we have." Donal hung his head. "I just hoped, you know, maybe you could see a way out of it, sir."

"I'll be blowed if I can right now, Donal. Not if you've signed a piece of paper. Not just at the moment—"

"I see, sir." Donal's face crumbled.

"But—"

"But what, sir?" Donal looked O'Reilly right in the eye. "What?"

"I'll think on it. There must be a way. At least we have something to start with. Bertie's so mean he'd wrestle a bear for a ha'penny. He's got *something* going, and I'm going to ferret it out."

"Thank you, sir. Thank you very much." Donal tugged his fore-lock.

O'Reilly was aware of Barry appearing in the doorway, saying, "Happy New Year, Donal."

"Thank you, sir, and to you."

"Fingal," Barry said, "I'm off. The Browns live quite near. I'll leave the car. I'll not be long."

Donal rose. "Are you walking into the village, sir?"

"I am."

"I'll come with you. Bit of company, like." Donal turned. "Thank you very much, Doctor O'Reilly. I know you'll sort everything out. Youse doctors always do."

9

No Man Gets a Full Meal

Jack Mills was not going to be able to sort things out between Patricia and Barry, he knew that, but it was good to be in his old friend's company. Now Barry had someone other than Fingal to tell his troubles to, even if, at the moment, Jack was taking his time, clearly waiting for the opportunity to bring the subject up—or for Barry to do so.

They sat at a Formica-topped table in the University Café, an establishment known universally as Smoky Joe's. The smell of deep frying permeated the very structure of the place.

Barry had slept late this Saturday morning and being in a rush had settled for a cup of coffee for his breakfast. He'd had time to tell Fingal about the cases he'd seen yesterday. The senior man had laughed when Barry explained that Colin Brown's "cold" was more likely a severe case of I-don't-want-to-go-back-to-school-itis, a singularly prevalent condition near the end of the holidays.

"Silly boy," O'Reilly remarked. "He'd be missing the chance to see that teacher—the one we met at the Christmas pageant." He looked straight at Barry. "What's her name?"

Barry immediately understood what O'Reilly was trying to do. "Miss Nolan," Barry said. "Sue Nolan . . . from Broughshane."

"Pretty girl. Marvellous hair."

"I'm sure you're right, Fingal. I didn't really notice." Of course, he hadn't missed the schoolmistress's single plait of waist-length copper-coloured hair, but he didn't want to talk about her. Not now. Barry looked at his watch. "If I don't go, I'll miss the 11:27 to Belfast. I'll see you on Sunday night. Have a great weekend."

"I will." O'Reilly chuckled. "Now you run on. I'd not want you to miss the train."

Barry had got off at Queen's Quay Station, where only six months ago he'd waited for a girl with a limp to catch the night's last train to Bangor. A girl called Patricia Spence.

Trying and failing to stop dwelling on her, he'd gone by bus from the station to Jack's flat on Camden Street near the university and Smoky Joe's.

Now Jack sat opposite him and spoke to the waiter. "Right, my good man." He had to raise his voice to make himself heard above the occupants of the other seven tables. He mimicked the drawling aristocratic tones of Hercules Gritpype-Thynne, a character played by Peter Sellers in the BBC's wildly popular *Goon Show*. "As the caviar's off and the chateaubriand'll take the chef far too long to prepare"—he scrutinised a blackboard where the all-day menu was scrawled in chalk—"I'll have the . . . um . . . the sausage, egg, and . . . uh . . . chips. Yes. Chips."

The waiter, a man with a cast in his left eye, licked the tip of his pencil and scribbled on a notepad.

Jack continued: "The sausages medium rare; the eggs, as our American cousins say, sunny-side up, peculiar expression; and just the merest, the merest soupçon of coriander on the French-fried potatoes."

"Away off and chase yourself, Doctor Mills. They'll come the way we always do them, so they will."

Jack sighed. "I suppose a properly infused cup of Earl Grey is completely out of the question?"

"You'll get your tea stewed, same as usual, and in an enamel mug."

Jack curled his lip. "Have you *no* Dresden china?"

The waiter laughed. "Jesus, you're a gas man, Doctor Mills, so you are. How many years have you been coming in here, acting the lig? Trying to take a hand out of me?" He shook his head. "Pull the other leg. It has bells on it, so it has."

How many years, Barry thought, since Jack and he'd shared a room in Queen's Elms just up the road? On nights when the institutional food had been worse than usual, they'd have come to Smoky's. The waiter, who never seemed to age, had been here as long. "Pay no heed to him, Brendan," Barry said. "I'll have the bacon and egg. No chips." He didn't need to look at the blackboard's menu to know that no matter how the combinations of sausages, eggs, bacon, ham, potato cakes, black pudding, and tomato might be worded, every single dish ended with "and chips."

"Right. You want toast?"

Barry shook his head.

Jack played with his fork until the man was out of earshot. "So," he said. His Cullybackey accent was its normal self. "She blew you out? I'm sorry, mate. I really am. I was shocked when you told me on the phone."

"Aye," Barry said. "So was I when she told me." He looked at Jack and saw concern on the red-cheeked face of his friend. "This time last week I thought I knew exactly where I was going. Where *we* were going. And now?"

Jack put the fork down. "You know me. Love 'em and leave 'em. But she was special for you, wasn't she?"

"Very."

Jack leant forward. "You reckon you've no mission?"

"Not a snowball's. You've met her. You know once she's her mind made up. And she says there's another—" Barry swallowed. He didn't want to say it out loud.

"Shite," Jack said. "That's ferocious."

Barry's friend's words put everything in a nutshell.

"So what are you going to do?" he continued. "Have you phoned her? Are you going to?"

"Not at all. I'm—" Barry swallowed, felt prickling behind his eyelids. "I'm hurting enough. I'm not going back for seconds."

Jack nodded and said seriously, "You're probably right letting her be."

Barry sniffed.

Jack sat forward. "So what *are* you going to do?"

"What can I do? I'll have to try to put her behind me"—fat bloody chance, he thought—"get on with my life."

"And you can start with this here." Brendan stood beside the table. "I'm sorry, Doctor Laverty. I wasn't listening in. Honest." None too gently he set down two chipped china plates, one for Barry and one for Jack. "Here y'are." He put a trefoil wire condiment holder on the table. One set of rings held vinegar; one, HP Sauce; and the other, Heinz tomato ketchup. Brown lumps of the dried ketchup clung to the cap and neck.

Jack unscrewed the cap, upended the bottle, and waited. Nothing. He shook it repeatedly until a gout of ketchup spewed out. "God," he said, " 'shake and shake the ketchup bottle. None'll come out and then a lot'll.' "

Barry couldn't be bothered to try to identify the source of the quotation. He just wished he could pour out all that was in him—the ache, the longing, the disbelief, and yes, the anger, red as the bloody ketchup. But he couldn't. Not here. Not in Smoky Joe's.

He cut up one of his rashers and took a bite. The bacon was

undercooked, salty, and had been fried in lard that should have been changed. His eggs had scruffy, burned, brown bits in the whites. He prodded a yolk, and the yellow contents oozed across the plate.

Jack tucked into his breakfast.

Barry sat, elbows on the tabletop, chin on his clasped hands, and looked around at the familiar pale-green painted walls and the fading posters tacked to them. Take the Boat to Heysham. Come to the Isle of Man. The beckoning girl in that one wore a rubber bathing cap and a swimsuit that had been out of date when his father was a student at Queen's. A student of structural engineering, the same sort of courses Patricia was taking at Cambridge. Damn it, even a couple of ratty old posters reminded him of her.

Looking across his empty plate, Jack said, "I can go and call the cows home now." He used the last bit of his toast to mop up some remaining egg. "Yours not up to scratch?"

"I'm not very hungry."

"More tea?"

Barry put his hand over his mug.

"Fair enough." Jack finished his tea. He looked at his watch. "Sun's over the yardarm, and Doctor Mills's prescription for those with classical, crushing, cardiac collapse, tending to chronicity—"

Barry was only half listening. "What?"

"A broken heart that could go for a long time unmended."

Barry wished the lump would leave his throat.

"The Doctor Mills's symptomatic cure is a pint—or two." He rose. "Brunch's on me, the Club Bar is open across the street, and the first pint's on you, mate."

10

We Have Drunken of Things Lethean

Jack pushed through the bat-wing doors of The Club. Barry followed. It was dim inside and smelt of beer and stale tobacco. The simple room had a planked floor and a few tables surrounded by wooden chairs. Not long ago there would have been spittoons and sawdust. This, the public bar, was where workingmen and male university students drank. No women allowed. That law was ages old and had been aimed at preventing fights over prostitutes who might have tried for custom inside.

In term time, The Club, the nearest bar to the main campus, would be packed, but it was quiet today. High stools were ranked in front of a straight bar. Three were occupied by men drinking pints of Guinness. Each man had a whiskey chaser beside his glass of stout. There were at least two empty places between each solitary patron. I suppose, Barry thought, I'm not the only one with troubles to nurse. It was small comfort.

He walked up to where beer pumps on the counter stood to attention, waiting to dispense Younger's Number Three, Harp Lager, Smithwick's Ale, and Strongbow Cider. At the back of the bar, bottles of spirits were arranged along a shelf beneath barrels of Guinness, each with its spigot firmly hammered into the bunghole.

"Barry. How's about ye? Long time no see. You too, Jack.

Happy New Year." Mick Agnew, the pub's fire hydrant–squat, silver-haired, ruddy-cheeked proprietor, stood in his accustomed place.

"And to you, Mick," Barry said.

"Usual?" Mick asked.

"Please." Barry didn't have to give more detail. The Club public bar was where he and Jack had had their first drink together in September 1957, and it had become, as Jack had described it, an extension to their living room.

Next door in the adjoining lounge bar where women were welcomed, the room was better lit and much more fashionably appointed. Of course the drinks were more expensive there too. It was where Barry and Jack had entertained their dates before Saturday hops at the Students' Union and formal dances at the Whitla Hall in the grounds of the university. Like the one he'd *not* gone to on Thursday night. Formal dances where Van Buren's took your photo, Van Buren's where he'd wanted her to have a picture taken to put by his bedside. At least, he thought, he'd never brought her to The Club. No real memories in every nook here.

He heard Jack say, "Anyone in the tunnel, Mick?"

The tunnel was reserved for Mick's favoured customers when they wanted privacy.

The owner turned from where he was drawing pints from the Guinness barrels. "Harry Sloan's in with a wee blonde."

Damn. Barry had wanted to talk in private.

"I'll just go and say hello," Jack said.

Mick lifted a flap at the end of the bar counter and held it up until Jack passed through. He returned in a minute and with perfect mimicry of a Belfast docker announced, "Harry says to me, so he does, 'Happy New Year. How's about ye, oul' hand?' says he. 'Rightly are yiz? Dead on. Come away on on on in.'"

"I'll bring your pints through," Mick said.

Barry smiled and ducked under the counter. He turned left into a narrow space where, against one wall, crate upon crate of beer and soft drinks were piled and barrels of Guinness were stored. Upended half-tuns served both as seats and tables. A single shadeless sixty-watt bulb hung overhead. In the tunnel, Jack was already seated, and Harry Sloan, a classmate and trainee pathologist, perched on another half-tun. Harry's silver hair glinted in the bulb's light. A petite blonde sat beside Harry. Barry recognised her as Jane. He couldn't remember her surname, but she was a nursing student at the Royal Victoria Hospital. She and Harry both said, "Barry."

"Harry . . . Jane." She'd been the object of Harry's pursuit at a nurses' dance before Christmas. Things must have progressed.

"Grab a pew," Harry said. "We're off in fifteen minutes."

"Harry's taking me to the matinee to see *Zorba the Greek*." Jane's voice was little-girlish.

Barry parked himself.

"It's been a while since we were in here," Jack said.

"The night we got our finals results," Harry said.

"And you three lads got full as goats," Mick remarked, setting two pints on a makeshift table. "You, Doctor Mills, kept yelling, 'I deserve it all,' until you passed out."

"You never did," Jane said, eyes wide.

"And precisely how many nights in a man's life does he qualify as a doctor?" Jack asked. "And I *did* deserve it all. Always did. Always will."

"Here, Mick." Barry paid. "Cheers." He lifted his glass and drank.

Jack raised his pint and put on a Scottish accent. "Here's to us, wha's like us? Damn few—and they're mostly deid." He sank a swallow.

Jane giggled.

Barry managed a smile and took a pull. A deep pull.

"So," Harry said, "what do you reckon about the Irish rugby team this year, Jack?"

Barry was happy enough to let the conversation flow around him. He drank.

"Honestly?" Jack said. "I don't know. They beat Scotland, but took awful pastings from England, France, and Wales."

"That fly-half Gibson's a hell of a player," Harry said.

"Aye," said Jack. "Barry and I were at school with his older brother Peter, and do you two remember a fellah called Kennedy? He was at Campbell College with Barry and me too."

Barry, who certainly remembered the lad, took a drink.

"Nyeh." Harry frequently prefaced his remarks with that noise. "Dark-haired lad? Ken Kennedy? A couple of years behind us?"

"Aye. He'll get an Irish cap this year or my name's not Jack Mills." Barry could hear the disappointment in Jack's voice. He and Kennedy both played in the same position. If the younger man got the spot and proved his worth, Jack's hopes of being selected to represent his country must be close to nonexistent. "Still," Jack continued, "we need all the very best men we can get, and Ken Kennedy's a bloody fine hooker."

That was typical of the farmer's son. Big Jack Mills didn't have a selfish bone in his body. Barry looked at his glass. Empty. That had gone down well. "Anyone for another?"

"Pint," Jack said. "I'll call them. Harry? Jane?"

"Not for us," said Harry. "We'll finish these up and be running on."

Jack called to Mick, then went right back to discussing with Harry the merits of two other Irish players, Willie John MacBride and Syd Millar, both from Ballymena.

Ballymena, Barry thought, isn't far from Broughshane. He was wondering why that had suddenly popped into his mind, when he heard Jane saying, "Nice to see you again, Barry." She rolled her eyes at Harry. "He's rugby daft, that one."

Barry smiled.

"Did you never see anything more of Peggy?" she asked.

Barry shook his head. Peggy Duff. The girl he'd driven home after that dance.

Jane leant over.

He found her perfume strong and cloying.

"Two pints," Mick announced.

Barry reached for his and took a healthy swallow from it. The fresh yeasty smell in the mouth of the glass overcame the scent of Jane's Midnight in Paris.

Jane leant closer. "I see Peggy every day, so I do. We're nursing on Twenty-six."

Ward 26, the metabolic unit that dealt with hormone disorders.

"I think she fancies you, Barry. She told me a couple of times she'd not mind seeing you again."

If you get tired of your girl, you know where I live. He could remember Peggy saying that outside her flat only a few weeks ago. He didn't know what to tell Jane, so he drank. He noticed her rummaging in her handbag.

Barry was distracted, then heard Harry announce, "Nyeh . . . your man Anthony Quinn's not going to wait for us at the cinema. Kickoff of the film's in twenty minutes." He spoke to Jane: "Get that down you, dear."

Jane finished a coloured drink that, by the fruit around the rim of the glass, Barry assumed had been Pimm's Number One Cup. He felt her pushing something into his hand. "If you want to get ahold of Peggy, that's her number," she whispered.

He stuffed the paper into his pocket. "Thank you," he said.

When the couple left, it was quiet in the tunnel. Barry didn't feel much like talking, and he reckoned Jack understood because he held his peace for quite a while. Finally, when Barry had almost finished his second pint, Jack said, "Come on, I know you're hurting, lad, but back in Smoky's you mentioned getting on with your life."

Barry sipped. "Aye . . . I suppose."

"Aye . . . I suppose," Jack said. "Jesus, Barry, you can do better than that. I'm going to ask you the tough one. How? How are you going to get on?"

Barry set his glass on the half-tun. "O'Reilly says it'll take time to get over things. I know that. It took me six months to stop moping over the nurse who went off and married a surgeon."

"So there's light at the end of the tunnel? Six months isn't long."

"I don't know." Barry picked up his pint. "I didn't feel about her the way I did—still do—about Patricia." He took a swallow. "Two more, Mick," he yelled. Barry turned back to Jack. "O'Reilly says one trick is to chuck yourself into your work. It takes your mind off things."

"And can you? Get really immersed?"

"At the moment we're pretty slack with the holidays."

"Me too. Only emergencies right now, but it'll be pretty hectic once we're back to normal."

Barry sighed. "Sometimes all the trivial stuff can get boring."

"I know," Jack said.

"Specialist training takes a lot of your time, doesn't it?" Barry asked.

"Bloody right." He looked up. "Just set them down, Mick." He proffered five shillings. "Here."

Barry lifted his third pint.

Jack hoisted his own and said, "Come on. Drink up. Like the old joke says, 'Get it down you, Paddy. It'll do you good.'"

"Aye, and the punch line, after twelve pints, and your man outside with his head bent over the gutter: 'Get it up you, Paddy. It'll do you good.'" Barry took a deep swig and asked, "But, overall you really enjoy the work, don't you?"

"I do," Jack said, "but don't tell anybody. I'd not want people to think I was dedicated or anything like that."

"But you do enjoy it, don't you?"

"Between you and me? Yes. I like working with my hands."

"We don't get much chance for that in GP. Lance the odd boil, sew up cuts . . . that's about it." He brightened for a moment. "Midwifery's fun. I delivered a face presentation last summer."

"Rather you than me."

"I like obstetrics. A lot."

Jack frowned, scratched the back of his head, started to speak, but cut off the words.

"What?" Barry asked.

"I was going to ask if you'd think about packing up GP. Doing obs and gobs."

"Obstetrics and gynaecology? Me? A specialist?"

"Why not? You always got better marks in it than me. Had a knack for it."

"Nah. I like Ballybucklebo." I do, but I hate how everywhere there reminds me of her. He took a long drink. Barry shook his head. "I like working with O'Reilly."

"You think about it. Being a gynae. registrar would certainly keep you occupied, and don't think training's all work and no play," Jack said. "I've still time for girls, like your old friend Mandy." A good quantity of his drink vanished too.

Mandy. The brunette ward clerk with the big smile and great legs. She wore short skirts and didn't mind giving young doctors a flash of her thighs. "You can keep her, Jack." Barry's head felt fuzzy. He realised he'd barely eaten today and wished he'd made more of an effort with the eggs and bacon back at the café. "You can keep the whole bloody lot. The whole 'monstrous regi . . . regiment' "—he realised he was stumbling over his words—". . . 'women.' " He swallowed beer and coughed.

"Fair enough," Jack said. "I understand what you're saying. You don't give a tinker's damn about girls—yet. But she's only gone a week, remember."

"Seems like a bloody lifetime." Barry sank the last of the pint in one swallow. "I miss her, Jack." He heard his voice crack, then rise. "I miss her. Why did she do it to me, Jack? Why?"

"I don't know, mate," Jack spoke quietly.

"I hate her." Spit it out, Paddy, it'll do you good, he thought, but it wasn't helping. He still loved her. "What'll I do, Jack?"

"You can feel sorry for yourself, if that's what you want."

Barry shook his head.

"In that case I'm only giving you a month."

"And then what? Then what?"

"We're going dancing. You and me."

"Jack. I don't wanna go dancing with you." Barry frowned. "We'd look silly together."

"Not us, you eejit." Jack was laughing. "I meant we'd go to a dance together—looking for girls."

Barry shook his head. "Let that hare sit for a while. Let the hairy hare sit." That line struck Barry as wildly funny. He giggled.

"I will for a while, but I'll not let you go broody on me. I bloody well won't."

"I'll go dancing when I'm good and ready." Barry's voice was cold. He stood, then shuffled a few unsteady steps. He looked at his glass. There were four dirty-white tidemarks on the sides of the glass and the remnants of the froth of the head on the bottom. Where the hell had the stout gone? "You fancy a wee half?" he asked Jack. Why was Jack smiling like that?

"No. Not for me, but I'll call one for you."

And why was Jack putting on that funny slurred voice? At least, it sounded slurred to Barry.

Barry found a glass of whiskey in his hand and by the weight of it knew it must be a double. He sipped. It didn't taste like the occasional Jameson he'd learnt to drink. He held the glass at arm's length and squinted at the amber fluid. "Wass is it?" he asked.

"Bushmills," Jack said. "Black Bush."

"Bushmills whiskey? And you bought it? The special Black Bush? You're a good man, Jack Mills. A sound man. You're a good friend to me." He sipped. "I wish Patricia had been a good friend too. I do so. I still love her." His voice cracked. He peered at Jack. "It's time you were home, Mills. You're pissed. Your face is getting blurred."

Barry sat heavily on a half-tun and finished half the whiskey in two swallows. "Your face is all right. It's my fault. *I'm* seeing things in a haze," he said, "because you always do when you're crying." He dashed tears away with the back of his hand, sniffed, and swallowed. "I want her back, Jack. I love her." He felt the glass being taken from his hand.

He heard a voice from somewhere so far away it seemed to be coming from the top of Malone Road. "All right, Barry. You've had the first half of Doctor Mills's cure. Let's get you back to my flat for part two—"

"A little shleep, a little sl . . . slumber, a little folding . . . folding of the hands . . ."

11

Your Name upon the Soft Sea-Sand

"Did you sleep well, Kitty?" Fingal left his accustomed place at the head of the dining room table. In the distance, he heard the 10:30 Sunday bell of the Catholic church. For more than two hundred and fifty years, its chimes had called villagers to mass, tolled the Angelus thrice daily, announced weddings, christenings, and funerals. In 1945 its bronze voice had sung out, "Victory"—in Europe in May and in Japan in August—just as it had hailed the armistice in November 1918, Waterloo in 1815. Timeless. The bell. The village. Home.

"I've been up and doing for an hour," he said, as he pulled out the chair beside his. "I heard you clattering about upstairs for the last forty-five minutes."

"Takes a girl a while to put her morning face on," Kitty said.

She looked stunning in a simple, polo-necked, white cable-knit sweater and black slacks. She wore very little makeup. She didn't need any, he thought.

"I slept like a log until Lady Macbeth decided to give me mouth-to-nose artificial respiration."

"Bloody cat."

Kitty sat and said, "She's just being affectionate. Like other people in this house." She blew him a kiss.

O'Reilly grinned. He was delighted that he no longer blushed when she teased him. He went back to his place. "Coffee?"

"Please." She held out her cup. "What's on the agenda for today?"

"After sitting round the house all day yesterday waiting for calls—"

"Which never came."

"Apart from Colin's mum phoning to say he was all right. Bloody good thing too. You never know. Barry's had one case of meningitis already." And selfish as he knew it was, he wasn't only glad for Colin and the other kiddies. Because there'd been no calls he'd had Kitty to himself from the time she'd arrived, shortly after Barry had dashed off, until eleven at night when she'd gone to her bed, leaving him to finish his last pipe.

Kitty all to himself. And the hours had flown by. O'Reilly squeezed his elbows against his sides, a personal hug, and smiled. "I was in no rush to stamp out disease anyway, but we were in here all day. I think we need a bit of fresh air. And Arthur could do with a run. Let's take him down to the shore."

"Fair enough."

"But before that I'm going to make us breakfast."

"You've been up for an hour and haven't eaten anything? Nothing?"

"There's no need to sound incredulous. I thought I'd wait for you. That's all." You're worth waiting for, he thought.

"That's sweet, Fingal, but you must be starving."

I have been, he thought, and not only for food. "I could force a bit of grub down. I'm going to cook us up a great big fry." He felt his mouth watering.

"No you're not. Too much fatty food's bad for you. You should know that."

"Women," he said, with the tiniest edge in his voice. "First it's Kinky telling me I'm too tall around and serving me rabbit food for lunch."

"Salads are healthy."

"Now you want to cut me off my Sunday fry, and I'm a grand man for the pan. Is it a conspiracy?"

"Not at all," she said, "but Mrs. Kincaid and I *do* have something in common."

"I know. You're bloody well bound and determined to starve me to death." He tried to stop the frown.

"Fingal Flahertie O'Reilly, don't sulk. We are doing no such thing." She stretched out one hand, put it on his arm, and lowered her voice. "But we are both fond of you."

The frown stopped. A smile started.

"Very fond." She squeezed his arm and looked him in the eye. "And neither one of us wants to lose you."

This time he did blush.

"And to show you I mean it, if you'll give me the run of Kinky's kitchen, I'll make us pancakes."

"Kitty O'Hallorhan"—O'Reilly stood, hauled her to her feet, enveloped her in a great hug, and planted a firm kiss on those slightly-too-large lips—"for buttermilk pancakes, and another kiss, I'll give you the run of the Kingdom of Heaven and I'd chuck in the Pearly Gates as a bonus."

She kissed him again and he savoured her. "Now," he said, a little breathlessly, "kitchen." Holding her hand and feeling eighteen, he led her out of the dining room.

O'Reilly's tummy was happily distended by buttermilk pancakes sweetened with Tate and Lyle's Golden Syrup. He helped Kitty into her coat.

"Are you sure it's all right to go out? There'll be no one here if there's an emergency," she said.

"I don't leave the shop unattended often," he said, "but when I do, if it's not really serious the customers call back later. If it is urgent they'll assume I'm out making a home visit—I very well could be—so they'll send for the ambulance to take them to hospital. That's probably where they'd be going anyway."

She nodded.

He handed her a thick woolen muffler. "Put that round your neck. It'll be nippy out." He couldn't bear the thought of her getting cold.

"Thank you." She wound the scarf around her neck and tucked her grey, black-streaked hair under a woolly toque.

"Come on. We'll go out the back to collect the lummox."

Kitty hesitated in the kitchen and pointed to where the breakfast dishes were piled in and beside the sink. "Fingal, we really should tidy up before we go."

"They'll not run away, and I want to be out before it gets colder."

"All right, but I'll do them the minute we get back."

O'Reilly held open the back door.

Arthur came bounding from his kennel, his bottom swinging from side to side as he thrashed his tail. He skidded to a halt in front of Kitty, had a good sniff, and grinned his great Labrador grin.

O'Reilly thought the dog was saying, "Nice to see you back, old friend." "Heel," O'Reilly said to the dog. He grabbed Kitty's gloved hand and strode through the back garden. The apple trees were leafless. Their thin branches waved good-bye to the breeze as it sped to the Ballybucklebo Hills, carrying to them a mixture of the scent of sea salt and seaweed and the plaintive voices of curved-beaked curlew. The short grass underfoot must have felt too tired to grow. Overhead a watery sun played peekaboo through strips of high clouds that patched the pale sky like gauze dressings.

"You're not too cold?" he asked.

"I'm fine."

They didn't meet a soul until they'd crossed Main Street at the traffic lights and were heading down to the railway bridge.

Gerry Shanks came out of the tobacconist's, a copy of the *News of the World* under one arm. He stopped and smiled at them. "Happy New Year, Doctor . . . Miss." Gerry lifted his duncher to Kitty.

O'Reilly stopped, dropped Kitty's hand. He felt like a kid who'd been caught writing a note to a girl in Sunday school. "And to you, Gerry. This is Kitty O'Hallorhan, an old friend of mine."

"Pleased to meet you, Miss. Gerry Shanks," he said. "Grand day, for the time of year it's in." Social niceties discharged, he turned to O'Reilly. "Will you be seeing Doctor Laverty, sir?"

"I will."

"Will you please say thank-you to him for me? Our wee Siobhan got home from Purdysburn yesterday, so she did. Your young lad was spot on, so he was."

"He'll be happy to hear that."

"And he was right civil to me and the missus the night he come round for to see her." Gerry slipped one hand into his raincoat pocket. "I hear tell he's only temporary here?"

"He'll be my assistant until July."

"I hope you don't think I'm being too forward, like, asking, sir, but will he be staying after?"

"That's up to him, Gerry." O'Reilly had learnt early on to keep important matters to himself.

"There's a brave wheen of folks here hoping he will stay, so there are."

They could count Fingal O'Reilly among them. "I'll tell him, Gerry. I'm sure he'll be pleased."

Gerry turned back to Kitty. "I seen you at the rugby match, Miss, the Gallowglass game. Not to speak to, you know, but I seen you there with himself here."

"Did you?"

"Aye."

O'Reilly couldn't be sure, but he thought Gerry's left eyelid had flicked shut and as quickly reopened before he said, "My Mairead's of the opinion we should be seeing a lot more of you, too."

And your Mairead's right, O'Reilly thought. Then, smiling to let Gerry know he wasn't cross, he said, "That, Gerry, is for me to know—and you and Mairead to find out." He sought Kitty's hand, held it in his.

"Right enough, Doc," Gerry said, and this time there was no mistaking his wink. He touched his cap. "Got to be trotting. Enjoy your walk."

O'Reilly set off at a brisk pace. Kitty must have sensed he wasn't feeling talkative, for she strode along at his shoulder saying nothing. Enjoy your walk. How could he not? He had Kitty's hand in his, and he was pleased by how much sympathy was forthcoming, unasked, for young Barry. Gerry's words should bring comfort to him, and Fingal hoped Jack Mills, a very solid citizen, would be helping the young man too.

He had to smile at the way the villagers were matchmaking. Tongues were wagging. That was no different from the way things were in every village in the thirty-two counties. He was well used to it. And if his seeing more of Kitty was what Mairead Shanks wanted, he'd be happy to oblige.

He took the path through the dunes. It provided shelter from the onshore breeze, which was strong enough to blow streamers of yellow sand from the crests and whisper to the marram grasses. He stopped, forcing Kitty to. It was private among the dunes. She made no demur when he bent his head and put his lips to hers. "Thanks for coming down, Kitty. It's been a wonderful weekend."

She put her arms around him and kissed him again. "It's not over yet. And I hope there'll be more."

O'Reilly's laughter was so loud it startled a flock of tern. The birds sprang scolding from among the grass and flew away on narrow wings, their forked tails twisting this way and that as they coasted down the wind's path.

"There'll be more, all right, Kitty O'Hallorhan. A lot more. And more of these." He kissed her. "Now come on," he said. "We'll take Arthur down to the water. Give him a swim."

O'Reilly opened the back door and immediately heard the rattling of dishes. Kinky stood at the sink, beefy forearms half submerged in soapsuds. "Kinky, Happy New Year. How was Cork?"

"It was grand, so. Fidelma and hers are all well." She sounded tired.

"Long journey?"

"Long enough. I went up to Dublin last night and stayed with a school friend so I could get the early train back up here today." She scrubbed a bowl fiercely. "I'd not want to leave things unattended for too long, so."

Kitty said, "Mrs. Kincaid, Happy New Year."

"I do hope so." She set a mixing bowl on the draining board. "I'd not expected to be tidying up the minute I came home."

O'Reilly inhaled deeply. "I'm sorry. That's all my fault, Kinky."

"I didn't know you could cook pancakes, sir, for that was the mix left in the bowl." She stared at Kitty.

"You're right," O'Reilly said. "Kitty's the cook. And a—" He was going to say, "and a very good one, too," but bit off the words. Kinky rarely got irritated, but already O'Reilly had grasped the reason. Another woman in *her* domain, cooking for *her* doctor . . . there was no need to rub salt in an open wound by praising Kitty's cooking. "And I'm the one who left the dishes. Kitty wanted to wash up. I wouldn't let her until we'd had our walk."

"It would not have hurt to soak them at least." Kinky sniffed. "It's only a shmall little job." She lifted out two plates.

"I'm truly sorry, Mrs. Kincaid," Kitty said.

"Aye, so." Kinky scrubbed the frying pan.

Kitty looked at O'Reilly, who shrugged.

"Doctor O'Reilly, sir, go you and Miss O'Hallorhan on up. I'll bring coffee and biscuits in a while, so."

O'Reilly glanced at Kitty, who mouthed, "Say, yes."

"Thanks, Kinky, we'd like that," he said. Then he jerked his head toward the hall.

Kinky was reaching for a towel as O'Reilly led Kitty into the hall.

Once up in the lounge, with Kitty ensconced in one armchair and O'Reilly in the other, she said, "I'm sorry if I've upset Kinky."

"Och," said O'Reilly, "maybe she's just tired. It takes a lot to bother her."

"She was pretty sharp."

O'Reilly sighed. "Leave it to me. I'll get her calmed down."

"Please try, Fingal. I like her. I really do, and I want her to like me. I'd not want any friction if I come down again."

"Not *if*, girl, *when*. And I will pour oil. Kinky's had her rough patches in this life. I'll not see her have any more if I can help it. Damn it, Kitty, for more years than I care to remember, she's been like a mother to me."

Kitty pursed her lips. "And do you think Kinky's like lots of other mothers?"

"In what way?"

"Frightened of losing her boy to a woman—any woman?"

O'Reilly cocked his head. He thought about that. Maybe Kitty was right.

"And is she going to?" she asked.

O'Reilly looked deeply into those amber-flecked grey eyes.

"She might very well, Kitty O'Hallorhan," he said softly. "She might indeed." He fished out his pipe, lit it, and puffed out a cloud. "But I'd like to have my cake and eat it too." Please don't tell me, he thought, that I'll be healing a rift between Kitty and Kinky, never mind sorting out whatever pickle Donal Donnelly's got himself into, *and* worrying about Doctor Barry Laverty's love life—or lack of same. He said slowly, "We'll just have to see what the rest of 1965 brings, won't we?"

12

My Bones Are Out of Joint

Barry showed Cissie Sloan out. She'd come in to have her prescription for thyroid medication renewed. The writing of it took two minutes. Dealing with Cissie's well-meant enquiries about Patricia had consumed a good five minutes more. Another easy-to-deal-with patient who put the first few working weeks of 1965 in Ballybucklebo into perspective. Plenty of work, but very little in the way of interesting cases. "Bye, Cissie."

"Bye, Doctor Laverty, and you just keep your chin up. My cousin Aggie says—you know, the one—"

"With the six toes. Bye, Cissie," Barry said and shut the front door. Shaking his head, he walked along the hall to the waiting room. The first weeks of 1965 might have been dull for him, he thought, but they'd brought their own drama to the world stage. Sir Winston Churchill, aged ninety, had suffered a stroke the previous week. He was not expected to survive. On a more positive note, on the same day Churchill fell ill—January 15—there had been an historic meeting in Belfast between Captain Terence O'Neill, the Northern Ireland prime minister, and the *Taoiseach* of the Irish Republic, Sean Lemass. This was the first time two Irish premiers had met since the country had split asunder in 1922. The hopes raised for cross-border cooperation had been a glimmer of sunshine in an otherwise politically grey climate.

The month's weather had been unremittingly gloomy, the days short, the nights long, and for Barry the time dragged. The usual winter ailments in droves, one broken leg, and a case of whooping cough. It was all very well O'Reilly saying there was solace to be found in the work. There was boredom too.

He collected another mother and her child with a cold, examined the child, recommended fluids, rest, and aspirin, showed them to the door, and headed back to the waiting room. How many coughs and colds did he have to see? Where was the challenge in another old patient with creaky joints? Maybe Jack Mills was right, that a specialist's work was more fun.

O'Reilly was making home visits. It was Barry's turn in the surgery today, Thursday. He opened the waiting room door. By this point in the late morning, the rows of plain wooden chairs were almost empty. The awful, bright, blooming roses on the wallpaper mocked the downpour he could hear outside. "Who's next?"

A man who must have been in his eighties rose clumsily to his feet. He pulled off a damp duncher, shook it, and said, "Me, sir." His pate was shiny-smooth as an egg. A thin, grey, circumferential trim could be seen above his two large cauliflower ears. Yellowed by tobacco, his moustache had all the attributes of a walrus's; and half a century earlier, it would have been called an Old Bill.

"Come on then." Barry led the way back to the surgery and sat in the swivel chair. "Please have a seat, Mr.—?"

"Gamble, sir. Shooey Gamble."

Barry had lived in Ulster long enough to recognise that Shooey meant Hughey. In fact, there was a popular children's riddle about the name.

What do you call the window cleaner's son?

Wee shammy [instead of Sammy, for the chamois leather used to wash panes].

And the cobbler's son?

Wee Shooey.

"And what can I do for you, Mr. Gamble?" Barry asked.

Shooey unbuttoned a long raincoat, rolled up his right trouser leg, and pointed to his knee. "I've been getting a ferocious stoon in her, so I have."

"Pain? For how long?" More rheumatism. All right, he told himself, get on with it.

"Do you mean how long does it last, or when did it start, like?"

"Both."

The old gentleman thrust out his lower jaw. Barry saw one single fang sticking up into the hairs of Shooey's upper lip.

"It started coming on, I don't know, about three years ago, just after I turned eighty-five, and it's there pretty much all of the time now, so it is. Gets worser after I walk a bit, especially on a bucketing-down day like today."

"Do you a lot of walking, Mr. Gamble?"

"Och, I did. I used to be a shepherd. I'd go for miles, so I would." He shook his head. "It's all I can do today to get to Bangor and back, and it seizes up something fierce when I sit down for a wee minute."

Barry whistled. That was a round-trip of twelve miles, far enough for a youngster, never mind an old man whose symptoms, responsivity to low pressure, and postexercise seizing-up, sounded very like osteoarthritis.

"And it's just the one knee?"

"Aye." He pointed. "That's the boy there."

Gout could afflict a single joint, often a small one, but usually came on at night and was excruciatingly painful. Rheumatoid arthritis was unlikely. It afflicted many more women than men and usually appeared before age fifty-five.

Psoriasis could cause single-joint arthritis, and dull as the man's case was, Barry was not going to treat it lightly. "You've not had any rashes?"

"Aye, I did."

Barry leant forward. Psoriatic arthritis was a rare condition. "Where?"

"Where? Here in Ballybucklebo. I've lived here near all my life."

Barry had to chuckle. "No, I meant where on your body?"

"All over. I'd the chicken pox when I was six and the German measles when I was twelve. Oh, aye, and I had trench foot in 1916."

That would account for the old soldier's moustache. "Nineteen sixteen? You were at the Somme?" Barry was impressed—and interested. The bloodiest battle of World War One. He did a quick subtraction. "But you'd have been nearly forty then."

"Aye." Shooey leant forward and lowered his voice. "I was with the Thirty-sixth Ulster Division at Thiepval Wood. I lied about my age to get in, so I did." He winked and Barry saw the *arcus senilis*, the pale rim of age, around the pupils of a pair of startlingly blue eyes. "We couldn't let that Kaiser Bill bugger get away with what he did in Belgium, you know, or with what he did to Nurse Cavell. He should never have shot her for a spy."

Barry heard the intensity in the old man's voice. Barry shook his head. It was hard to believe he was sitting here with a survivor of the Great War, a man who'd been born in 1876, the year the first telephone call had been made, the year of Custer's Last Stand at Little Bighorn. Shooey'd been nine when General Gordon was killed at Khartoum, and probably could remember hearing about it.

Barry wished he could afford to spend more time with Shooey Gamble to hear more of his story. It was all fascinating—but it wasn't going to help with the diagnosis.

"Mr. Gamble, you know I sometimes have to ask personal questions."

"Fire away."

"You were in the army. Did you ever have a . . . a dose?" Both gonorrhoea and syphilis could cause joint damage.

"Nah. I never did." He took a deep breath and stared at the carpet. "I was married. She was a lovely wee girl. I met her when I was sixteen. I never looked at another woman. Not in sixty-three years." His voice softened and he looked at Barry. Shooey had the sagging lower eyelids of the old. They glistened, brimmed, and tears rolled. He dashed a hand across his eyes. "Sorry about that, Doc," he said, "but I still get a bit choked up. My Dora's gone nine years in June. I miss her yet." He hauled in a very deep breath.

"I'm sorry," Barry said. "I really am." And even if it is only a few weeks for me, I know how you feel, he thought. Or perhaps I don't. Your generation, much more than mine, was raised not to show emotion in public. And yet Shooey could openly shed a tear. "Don't worry about the odd tear," Barry said. "It's good to let things out." I only wish I could, he thought. He rose, abruptly facing the window before turning back to his patient.

"Thanks for that. I get a bit embarrassed, like, but you being a doctor and all, you understand. I know that." He smiled at Barry. "I'm sorry for your troubles, too, Doctor Laverty. When we were sitting in the waiting room earlier today, Cissie Sloan told me you'd lost your wee girl. I don't mean to be too personal, like"—Shooey cocked his head—"but I hear tell being there, feeling things yourself that your patients suffer, like, makes a fellah a better doctor. Maybe that's why you just said what you did? Here I've just met you, and I'm telling you about Dora. You're an easy man to talk to, Doctor Laverty."

"Thank you. That means a lot." Barry turned back, cleared his throat, and tried to make light of things. "Mind you, if you're right about feeling things your patients feel, I'd better work out how a man can have a baby."

Shooey smiled. "True on you, sir."

"Can you come over to the couch, Mr. Gamble?"

"Och, Doctor, it's Shooey, so it is. Everybody calls me that, sir."

Barry completed a thorough examination of both knees. The left one seemed to function perfectly; the right, although cool to the touch, moved stiffly. He'd been able to feel a grating under his fingers.

"Let me help you down." Barry took his seat. "Shooey, my best bet is that you have osteoarthritis. It's a wear-and-tear thing."

"Is it?"

"It is."

"And what would bring that on?"

Barry tried to be tactful. Older folks could be sensitive. "Age, I'm afraid." He was surprised when Shooey burst out laughing.

"Do you know about the Vikings, sir?"

"I know they gave Ireland a terrible time until Brian Boru beat them at Clontarf in 1014."

"Aye. And they gave me my name."

"Shooey?"

"Not at all. Gamble. It's from the Norwegian, Gamball."

Barry waited.

Shooey chuckled. "It means old, so I'm old Shooey Old—and I *am* eighty-eight."

"Fair enough, but it doesn't mean you just have to put up with it."

"Can you do something, sir?"

For such an interesting man Barry wished he could work a miracle, but he had to say, "I can't cure eighty-eight years of wear and tear, but I can try to make it a bit easier for you."

"How?"

"I'll arrange for you to see a physiotherapist, who'll give you some exercises. We'll get you a heat pad for the cold days, and you can buy a liniment at the chemist. Deep Heat's pretty good. Maybe a walking stick?" Barry looked straight at his patient. "I know folks have lost faith in it, but aspirin really does help."

"I believe you, Doctor." Shooey's grin exposed the tooth again. "Mind you, I'm sure thousands wouldn't."

Barry had to smile at the old Ulsterism.

"Boys-a-dear," Shooey said, "I thought I was just going to have to thole it, but you say we can do things? That's grand, so it is. Sticking out a mile. You're not going to have to shoot me like a sick horse?"

"Not yet, Shooey." The resilence of the country patients. It was humbling. "And if it gets really bad, there is an operation." Giving steroids, Barry knew, while useful for rheumatoid arthritis, didn't help osteo.

"Aye. I'm sure there is, you know, but I think we'll cross that bridge when we come 'til it, sir."

"All right, but I will get a note off to the physiotherapy department in Bangor Hospital. They'll send for you. And if you just hang on—" Barry scribbled a note. "Take that round to the chemist's and they'll give you the heat pad."

"Thanks, Doc. Thanks a million." Shooey headed for the door, then turned. "I've one more wee question, like."

"Go ahead."

"You said it's all because of eighty-eight years of wear and tear." Shooey chuckled. "D'you know, Doc, I've had the other bloody knee for eighty-eight years too. Why doesn't it hurt?"

And Barry Laverty couldn't help join in with the guffaws of Shooey Gamble, whose surname meant "old" and who had a wit sharp as a tack. O'Reilly had a point. The work could take your mind off quite a lot.

13

And Green-Ey'd Jealousy

"So," asked O'Reilly, "how was the work this morning? 'The daily round, the common task.' "

" 'Should furnish all we ought to ask.' I know, Fingal." Barry took his usual place at the dining room table. "I know the hymn and I know I should be satisfied with my work. I should be."

"And are you not?" O'Reilly looked closely at his assistant.

Barry shrugged. "It was pretty run of the mill this morning."

"You get days like that," O'Reilly said, hoping this wasn't the first symptom of the young man falling out of love with rural general practice. "Not one single interesting customer in the whole lot?"

"The patient before the last. Hughey Gamble."

"What's wrong with old Hughey? I hardly see him from one year to the next. He's tough as an old boot."

"His knee's not. He's got osteoarthritis."

"Hardly a diagnostic conundrum to baffle the late great Sir William Osler," O'Reilly said.

"It wasn't. It was the man himself who interested me."

O'Reilly was going to ask Barry to elaborate, but Kinky's arrival interrupted. "I've lentil-and-ham soup here," she said, setting her tray on the sideboard. "Made from the hambone. There's butter. I used to churn the milk myself when I was a girl but, och . . ." She shrugged. "That's my own wheaten bread, a wedge of Cheddar, and a wedge of Cheshire." She handed a plate to O'Reilly. "I know, sir, 'tis something more substantial you'd be wanting, but the festive season is gone by and loss of a bit of—" She glowered at his waist.

"It's all right, Kinky," O'Reilly said. "I understand. When Kitty was here she explained. She said it's because . . . because Kitty thinks I should lose a bit too." O'Reilly realised that if he said Kinky was watching his weight because she was very fond of him, he might embarrass the undemonstrative Corkwoman.

"Does she now? There's a thingeen." Kinky folded her arms and pursed her lips. O'Reilly could practically hear what Kinky was thinking. And it's my job to look after you, not hers. He knew that the addition of the suffix "een" in Irish made something into "a little something" and was pejoratively diminutive. He said quickly, "And she told me to thank you for looking after me. Says she doesn't know how I'd get on without you."

Kinky's lips relaxed, but she did not smile.

"She'll tell you herself next time she's down." Kinky had mentioned nothing more about Kitty being in her kitchen, and as Kitty had been gone these past three weeks, O'Reilly had thought the matter was closed. Apparently he'd been wrong. "She's coming on Saturday."

"And will she be cooking, sir?"

"No, she'll not." O'Reilly shook his head. "It's the marquis' pheasant shoot. Barry'll be covering here. Kitty'll get her breakfast before she comes down, and His Lordship will give us lunch," O'Reilly said.

"And dinner?" Kinky asked. "Will Miss O'Hallorhan be wanting to cook dinner?"

"Not at all. I'm taking her out," O'Reilly said and waited, hoping to God Kinky wasn't going to ask if her cooking wasn't good enough.

"So I'll have Doctor Laverty?"

"Aye."

"Grand, so. I'll see he doesn't starve." Kinky left, saying, "I'll bring you coffee later."

"What was that all about, Fingal?" Barry asked.

O'Reilly served the soup. "Help yourself to bread and cheese," he said.

"You didn't answer my question."

O'Reilly swallowed a mouthful of soup. "A couple of years back a fellah, Robert Ardrey, wrote a book called *African Genesis*. He reckons humans are primates and have all the primate behaviours. One is establishing pecking orders; another is protecting their territory. I think Kinky's feeling her territory is threatened by Kitty."

"Oops," Barry said. "What are you going to do?"

O'Reilly lifted his soup spoon. "I don't know. Step one will be to keep Kitty out of Kinky's kitchen."

"Makes sense. And step two?"

"I think," said O'Reilly, attacking the Cheddar, "Kitty might have an answer; she's a woman after all. But as for me? That's a bridge we'll cross when we come to it."

Barry nodded. "That's exactly what Shooey said when I told him if his knee didn't respond to simple measures we could think about an operation."

"What did you make of him?"

"I think he's absolutely amazing."

O'Reilly finished his soup. "He always was. He once rowed a boat from here to Portpatrick in Scotland and back—for a bet."

"Good Lord. That's at least fifteen miles one way."

O'Reilly nodded. "And did you know he was in the army?"

"He told me."

O'Reilly buttered another slice of bread. "I'll bet he didn't tell you he won the M.M."

"The Military Medal. For bravery?"

"Aye. If the hand grenade under the steel helmet he was lying on to protect the rest of his platoon had gone off, he'd have been awarded the Victoria Cross—posthumously."

Barry whistled.

"And do you know, en passant," said O'Reilly, "only three men have won the V.C. twice, and two of them were army doctors?"

"I didn't know."

"Men called Chavasse and Martin-Leake." O'Reilly finished his soup and refilled his bowl. "His Lordship collected a D.S.O. during the Arnhem battles at the Meuse-Escaut Canal. He's like Shooey; he never mentions it."

Barry cocked his head. "Fingal, did you win any medals?"

O'Reilly cleared his throat. He had been awarded a Distinguished Service Cross at the Battle of Crete when his ship was badly damaged by German Stukas. He'd carried on treating the wounded despite fires raging outside his sick bay. He too never spoke of it. The medal was collecting dust at the bottom of his sock drawer.

O'Reilly shook his head and changed the subject. "I'm very fond of John," he said, using the marquis' Christian name. "I'm looking forward to Saturday at the estate and not just for seeing him and a bit of shooting. I need to get a chance to have a word with Donal Donnelly. He'll be beating." O'Reilly saw Barry smile. "No. It's not because he's on the fiddle. This time Donal's getting conned, and I promised to help."

"You didn't tell me."

"I thought you'd enough on your plate." O'Reilly spent some minutes explaining Bertie's shares-in-a-horse scam. "What baffles me is that Bertie seems to have set up a scheme that is *costing* him money."

"If I understand what you've just told me," Barry said, "when she fails to win, Donal and his mates forfeit a piece of their share in the horse to Bishop."

"You've hit the nail on the head, Barry. That's exactly right," O'Reilly said. "Donal and his mates can't afford to be swindled out of that much money. You're a doctor and it would take you three months to earn a hundred pounds. Imagine how long a carpenter would have to toil." He popped the bread and cheese into his mouth. "I've got to stop Bertie," O'Reilly said. He looked at Barry from under knitted brows. "I'm not sure how, but I'll work on it."

"If you like, Fingal, I'll help if I can."

"Will you?" O'Reilly had expected no less from the young man, and it suited Fingal to keep Barry involved in every aspect of the practice.

"Of course, and I've had a half-notion." Barry put both forearms on the table and leant forward toward O'Reilly. "Who do we know who really knows horses?"

O'Reilly thought. "The marquis, me, Donal—"

"And Fergus Finnegan. The jockey who had—"

"Acute ophthalmitis that you fixed. Laverty, you're a genius. I might even see him at the shoot. He often beats for His Lordship."

"He might have heard of this kind of swindle before. Maybe he'll have some suggestions."

O'Reilly frowned. "I promised Donal I'd not tell anybody."

"Come on, Fingal. You don't have to. Tell Fergus it's me who's in trouble. Everybody here knows I wouldn't know a cannon bone from a crupper."

"You wouldn't mind?"

Barry laughed. "If it lets us put one over Bertie, I'd be delighted."

"You're on, Barry—if I need to," O'Reilly said. "It'll be interesting to see how this works out."

"It will indeed." Barry laughed.

O'Reilly was delighted.

"You know, Fingal, it wouldn't be Ballybucklebo if you weren't up to your neck sorting out Bertie Bishop."

"With your help, lad. With your help."

Barry shrugged.

O'Reilly heard the phone ring. He waited. Kinky stuck her head around the door. "It does be Aggie Arbuthnot. Could she have a word?"

"Coming." O'Reilly rose. "I hoped I'd finished the calls this morning. I was going to put my feet up this afternoon." He headed for the door.

"Why don't you? If she needs a visit, I'll go," Barry said. "I want to pop in and see Alice Moloney anyway. I've been meaning to since the Bishops' party."

And it quite slipped your mind. I understand, O'Reilly thought. "Fair enough," he said. "Give Alice my regards."

14

Tread Safely into the Unknown

Barry'd been able to answer Aggie's question on the phone and so had gone straight to the Ballybucklebo Boutique.

"How nice to see you, Doctor Laverty." Miss Alice Moloney smiled as Barry entered her dress shop. There were no customers in the little establishment. Sally, the eighteen-year-old assistant, smiled at him. He'd seen her last month for acne. She still had an angry-looking pustule on her chin, but her cheeks looked much better.

"Good afternoon, ladies," he said.

Sally bobbed and blushed.

"And Doctor O'Reilly sends his regards, Miss Moloney." Barry noticed that Alice's pepper-and-salt bun was not as tight and tidy as usual. Her skin really did look pallid. It had been no trick of the light at the Bishops' party. She wore low-heeled brogues and a maroon, knitted, midcalf-length skirt. The way it sagged at her hips was a marker that she had lost weight. Her hazel eyes seemed dull, but there was no yellow tinge in the whites. That discolouration would be the first hint of jaundice, so at least he needn't worry about that. "I was passing and wondered how you were getting on," he said.

"Thank you." She sighed. "To tell you the truth, Doctor, I could be doing better. I was going to come and see you. I'm not altogether at myself."

"I thought you looked a bit peakèd last time I saw you."

"Very observant."

Barry looked around. This was not the place for a consultation. "I'd like to take a look at you."

"We'll go upstairs. Take care of things, please, Sally."

"Yes, Miss Moloney."

Barry followed her through the shop to her upstairs flat.

"Please sit down."

He sat in a Queen Anne armchair and waited as she shooed away a spherical tortoiseshell cat and perched herself on a Victorian side chair.

Billie Budgie, her budgerigar, screeched, "Who's a good boy then?"

Not you, you little twerp, Barry thought, stroking the finger the bird had bitten last month. The place looked exactly the same. Antique furniture and souvenirs of Miss Moloney's life growing up in India were arranged precisely. They rubbed shoulders with cheap mementos of her solitary trips to London, the Isle of Man, and the Highlands of Scotland, holidays taken since her return to Ulster. On the walls, prints by Degas and Monet kept company with framed dried flowers and an embroidered sampler of the Lord's Prayer. Barry noticed that the sampler hung slightly askew, and there was a fine layer of dust on the surface of the table.

"Tea?"

"No, thank you." Barry had to stifle his urge to straighten the sampler.

She cleared her throat. "Before we talk about me, Doctor Laverty, and I do not mean to pry, I have been told that Miss Spence and you are no longer keeping company. I try to disregard gossip, but if it is true, I am deeply sorry. I think I understand a little of how you must feel."

"I'm sure you do, Miss Moloney," he said. If anyone understood, it was Alice Moloney. She'd been in love—once. "I thank you for your concern." He stole a glance at a photo of a handsome young man in the uniform of Skinner's Horse. He hoped she wasn't going to dwell on Patricia.

She inclined her head. "I told you, it's Alice, and I believe you came because you are interested in the state of my health."

Thank you for changing the subject, he thought. "Yes, Alice, I am." Barry looked straight at her.

Her lips narrowed. "I was so relieved when you diagnosed my anaemia and I've been taking the iron treatment and trying to eat properly, but I don't seem to be getting any better. I'm tired all the time—"

While she was speaking, Barry started fitting the pieces together. He knew she was fifty-two, childless, menopausal; she'd had piles treated by Fingal; and there was nothing else of importance in her history. Tired? It was early yet for her anaemia to be responding dramatically, and tiredness was a symptom. He studied her pale face. It was a pasty off-white colour. What did that mean? Anaemic people were pale.

"I'm irritable. I'm ashamed to say I yelled at Sally twice this week, and sometimes I sweat at night—"

Irritable? Wasn't he that way himself at the moment? Night sweats? She was menopausal.

She sat more primly in her chair. "I get periods of colic and . . ."—a wry smile played on her thin lips—"I've been farting like a cavalry charger." She leant forward. "A stallion at that."

Barry sat bolt upright. Farting? Alice said, "Farting"? Like a stallion? He chuckled—he couldn't help it—but why shouldn't she say it? She was familiar with cavalry regiments. The expression must come naturally to her. "Colic? Wind? I see," he said, but he didn't. He couldn't make her symptoms add up, no matter how picturesquely expressed. They could be associated with diseases of the lower bowel, like diverticulitis or ulcerative colitis, but she'd had a barium-enema X-ray recently and it was entirely normal. Those symptoms often simply meant the complainant had eaten something that, in common parlance, disagreed with them.

Contrary to popular belief, he, like all doctors, rarely made a diagnosis by examining a patient. Rather they'd sift the history, and by the time of the examination would be seeking confirmation of a strong suspicion already formed. Was there something she was not telling him?

"Have you any pain anywhere? Diarrhoea?" She had grown up in India. "Have you ever had dysentery?"

"No pain. No diarrhoea. Everyone had Delhi belly once in a while out there, but I was never in hospital with it." She grimaced. "I do remember in forty-six there was an outbreak in troops coming home from the Far East. Several *sowars* and one *daffadar* actually died. Very sad. The medical officer said it was amoebic dysentery."

"I'm sorry . . . *sowars? Daffadars?*"

She smiled. "Sometimes I forget I'm not talking to an old India hand."

Barry heard India as "Injah."

"In the Indian cavalry, a *sowar* was a private and a *daffadar* a sergeant. Poor chaps. None of us Europeans was affected, thank goodness."

"I see." Another blind alley. Barry frowned. He'd examined her last month and found nothing. Her skirt was loose at the waist now. Weight loss could be due to advanced cancer, but really advanced cancer was often accompanied by tightness of the waistband. The belly was distended because it was full of fluid called ascites.

So. Paleness, weight loss, tiredness, irritability, colic, wind, anaemia?

Barry did not know where to go for corn. He was stumped. "Can we use your room, Alice? I have to examine you." He did have to, but it was going to be a fishing expedition.

And it was angling without so much as a nibble. Apart from the paleness, he found nothing physically abnormal. He did notice the flock wallpaper, the pink canopy over the bed, and a large, battered, and obviously much-loved teddy bear propped up on the pillow of Alice Moloney, spinster of this parish. The sight brought a lump to his throat.

He went back to the drawing room and was admiring a photograph of Alice's father standing with Mahatma Gandhi when she reappeared.

"Well?" she asked.

"To be honest, I simply don't know."

"I see." She looked crestfallen.

"But it doesn't mean I can't try to find out."

"More tests? I didn't like that enema."

He shook his head. "Not yet. I'll get a second opinion from Doctor O'Reilly, and I'll go back to my books, see if they can help. If that doesn't work, we'll send you to see a specialist."

"I'd appreciate that, Doctor Laverty."

"We'll get to the bottom of it, Alice."

"I know you will."

Her confidence pleased him.

"If you don't mind," she said, "I'll let Sally look after things. She's quite able. Can you see yourself out?"

"Of course."

"Thank you. I'd be grateful. Climbing the stairs is a burden."

She was sitting in a chair when he left, shoulders drooping, her face . . . her face that peculiar alabaster tint that afflicted the tip of Fingal's nose when he was furious.

Barry was still thinking about Alice Moloney as he let himself in through the front door of Number 1. He really was at a loss, but perhaps he might find a clue to the nature of her illness in one of his textbooks.

He hung his coat, then shuffled through the mail on the hall table. He could tell the contents of most envelopes just by looking at them. Lab report, lab report, bill for car insurance—blether. More expense. Something personal for O'Reilly. An envelope from Purdysburn, probably a report on Siobhan Shanks's meningitis. It usually took this long to get reports from hospitals.

The last envelope bore familiar handwriting. Barry froze. His hand shook. He didn't have to look at the postmark to know the letter had come from Cambridge. He swallowed, tried to reread the writing, but the words had blurred.

The surgery door was open. He crossed the hall, closed the door behind him, went to O'Reilly's desk, and stood staring at the letter. Why now? Not a word for a month. Now this. Why would she write to him now? He still hurt, but after the initial awful moment, then the numbness, his pain had slowly settled to a steady background grumbling. But little things could produce sudden surges, sharp as the spikes of an electrocardiograph tracing. It was like a toothache that was bearable until a careless bite sent shock waves.

He groped for O'Reilly's letter opener.

Had she had a change of heart? Was she apologising, asking for another chance? Barry felt a smile start. It had to be that. Had to be. She'd seen sense. She must have. He chucked the bone-handled paper knife aside, ripped the letter out, and unfolded the single page.

Dear Barry,

I am finding this difficult to write, but felt that because of the abruptness of our parting I still owe you an explanation. I know you were in love with me. I know I have hurt you terribly. I don't think you will ever be able to forgive me—and I don't think you'll ever understand . . .

Barry let the arm that was holding the letter drop. Patricia, if you walked through that door this instant, I'd forgive you. And I do understand. I wasn't good enough. You found someone else. It's as simple as that. He pulled the chair out from the desk, sat, and for a moment simply cradled his head in his hands. Then he lay the letter on the desk and began to read again.

Barry, I made a mistake. You did nothing wrong. You are a dear, sweet man, and I know you'll be a wonderful country GP. But I'm not suited for country life. I'm sorry. I need a wider horizon. I hope one day you will be able to forgive me and look back fondly as I do on our few months together. I'm not sure how to finish this, so I'll ask your forgiveness once more and tell you I wish everything good for your career and you.

Patricia

Barry's hand fell to the desktop. He let the sheet of paper slip from his grip and leaned back in the chair. Forgive her? Of course I forgive you, Patricia. You do that if you love somebody. I forgive you. I'll grieve for you, and I'll never forget "our few months together." He let his head loll until he was staring with tear-filled eyes at the ceiling above. It was painted a gloomy shade of hospital green, flat and featureless. As flat as his prospects for happiness.

15

Thaw Not the Frost That Binds

O'Reilly scratched his nose, screwed up his eyes, and inhaled deeply. His sneeze made the decanters on the lounge sideboard rattle. He dragged out his hanky and snorted into it.

"Bless you, Fingal O'Reilly," Kitty said. "I hope you're not getting a cold."

"Divil the bit." He sat back in his chair and shoved his handkerchief back in his pocket. "Just a nose tickle."

Kinky brought in a tray of coffee. "I thought, sir, you and the lady would enjoy a hot cup before you left for His Lordship's shoot."

"Indeed we would," O'Reilly said.

"Good morning, Mrs. Kincaid," Kitty said. "Lovely day."

Kinky set the tray on the sideboard. She sniffed. "You never can tell in late January if it will last, so." Without another word, she left.

"Oops," said Kitty, moving to pour the coffee. "I think I'm still in the doghouse, and it's not only because we didn't soak the pancake dishes last time I was here." She handed Fingal his cup and went back to pour her own.

"'Fraid you're right on both counts," O'Reilly said. "It's not like Kinky to bear a grudge for so long." He sipped his coffee. "It's been nearly three weeks."

"I told you back then, Fingal, I think I have her worried about her position here." Kitty sat in the other chair.

"She needn't be."

Raising an eyebrow, Kitty smiled and said, "I know. You've not asked me to marry you yet."

O'Reilly choked on his coffee, hacked, and spluttered. He was grateful to feel Kitty slapping him on the back.

"And I'm not in a rush for you to," she said, looking him right in the eye.

"Phew," he said. "Well . . . that is . . . I—"

Kitty sat again. She reached across and squeezed his arm. "I love being with you, Fingal Flahertie O'Reilly."

He looked at her and saw softness in her eyes.

"You make me feel like a teenager," she said.

She had the same effect on him.

"I told you I'd not rush you. And I'll not," she said.

"Thanks, Kitty."

"There's been a void in your life since Deidre died. I know that."

"And in Kinky's since she lost her husband," O'Reilly said, grateful for a cue that let him change the direction of the conversation. "She was widowed very young. Never remarried. The day she took the hump with you she'd just come back from visiting her married sister in Cork."

Kitty frowned and put her half-finished cup on the saucer. "And you wonder if seeing her sister, with all the things Kinky never had—husband, children, house of her own to call home—made her sad?"

"More than sad. Number 1, Main Street, is all the home she's known for nearly forty years, I'm her only family here, along with Arthur and Lady Macbeth, and I suppose Barry now. I think you have her terrified."

Kitty rocked in her chair. "I understand. I'll have to see how I can make her feel more comfortable with me." She stood and walked over to stand in front of O'Reilly and kissed his forehead. "Because I've no intention of not coming here again."

O'Reilly stood to hug her, giving her a resounding kiss. "Nor I of not asking you down again." He glanced at his watch. "Eight o'clock," he said, kissing her again. "I'd like to continue this"—he cleared his throat—"this . . . discussion, but we'd best be off. The marquis expects punctuality. You didn't mind getting up early to drive down here?"

"Not at all. I'm looking forward to today." Kitty put their cups on the tray and picked it up.

"Leave it," he said. "Kinky'll—"

"Appreciate it, I hope, if I save her having to climb the stairs."

Kitty had a point. O'Reilly let her precede him. She suited the midcalf tweed skirt and thick woollen stockings that vanished into a pair of laced, brown brogues. Not the rig for a ballroom, but sensible wear for an Irish winter's day out of doors.

The kitchen was pleasantly warm. "We're off, Kinky," O'Reilly said. He heard the rattle as Kitty set the tray on the counter.

"Thank you, Miss O'Hallorhan," Kinky said stiffly, "but I am able to carry a tray myself, so."

Come on, Kinky, O'Reilly thought. Can't you see Kitty's trying to be friendly?

Kitty's tone was soft. "I'm sorry, Mrs. Kincaid," she said. "I did not mean to give offence. I brought it down because I'm a nurse."

Kinky sniffed, then said, "And what has that to do with carrying trays?"

"When we make ourselves a cuppa in the ward kitchen there's a printed sign over the cooker—"

"And what does it say?"

O'Reilly detected a hint of curiosity in the way Kinky frowned and leant a bit closer to Kitty.

"It says, Your Mother Doesn't Work Here. Tidy Up after Yourself. That's all I was doing."

Not trying to usurp your place. O'Reilly understood clearly what Kitty was implying.

Kinky cocked her head, frowning. "Your Mother Doesn't . . . I see. It was only helpful you were being?"

"It was. Why else?"

"Miss O'Hallorhan? A moment ago you said you meant no offence. None is taken." But her words were formal.

"Thank you," Kitty said. "And I'll say it again. I'm sorry about the pancake dishes not getting soaked the last time I was here."

"Och," said Kinky, "least said, soonest mended. Now if the pair of you will excuse me"—she looked pointedly at O'Reilly—"as you will be out tonight, sir, I've only Doctor Laverty to see to. I've a nice piece of filet steak for his tea, and I thought I'd start him off with a prawn cocktail. The Marie Rose sauce for the cocktail won't make itself."

"Begod," said O'Reilly, feeling his mouth start to water. "And are you doing your béarnaise sauce for the steak?"

"I am, so."

"Kinky Kincaid, if I'd not promised Kitty her dinner out, I'd stay home. There's not a woman in the Six Counties—six, bedamned, there's not a woman in all thirty-two, from Cork to Donegal, from Dublin to Galway City, the whole length and breadth of Ireland—who can cook a steak to match yours." You're laying it on with a trowel, he thought.

Kinky grinned. "Get away on with you out of that, Doctor O'Reilly, sir. You'd turn a poor countrywoman's head with your flattery." She turned to Kitty. "Miss O'Hallorhan, just you watch that tongue of his, or he'll feed you cotton wool and have you believe you're eating smoked salmon, so."

"I will, Mrs. Kincaid," Kitty said.

The mutual lack of Christian names was not lost on O'Reilly. They were still sniffing round each other and time was wasting. "Come on, Kitty . . . Ballybucklebo House. The car's out at the front."

"Have a good day—the pair of you," Kinky said, as they left.

"I think," he said, as he closed the front door, "your bringing the tray, your apology—"

"And your going on about her cooking—"

"Have started a thaw. But we're not there yet. We'll keep up the good work. She's daft about hats—"

"I'll get her one in Belfast."

O'Reilly thought about that. Recently Barry and he had given Kinky a new hat. "On second thought," he said, "I've noticed her handbag's getting a bit worn." He opened the passenger door of the Rover to be greeted by a series of delighted yips from the back. "Settle down, Lummox." As Kitty got in, he said, "Alice Moloney knows what Kinky really likes, but she'll not be open until Monday."

"I'll be back in town. Would you pick one, Fingal?"

"I will. I'll buy one before the next time you come down," he said. Then he put the big car in gear and roared off along the Bangor-to-Belfast Road.

16

Ηυρηκα *(Eureka): I Have Found It*

"I'm sure, Doctor Laverty, you'll enjoy this." Kinky replaced Barry's cereal bowl with a steaming plate. He'd come down for breakfast after O'Reilly and Kitty had left.

A delicate aroma of smoked haddock teased his nose. "Thanks, Kinky."

"Don't let it get cold now."

"I'll not." He tasted hard-boiled egg, rice, and a spice he could not identify. Their flavours and texture perfectly complemented those of the flaked fish.

"Will I pour your coffee?"

"Please."

"I hope himself and Miss Kitty are enjoying themselves," Kinky said, as she filled his cup. "They've a brave morning for it." She inclined her head to the window.

Barry looked over as a small cloud rolled back, and like customers at a New Year's Day sale, sunbeams jostled into the room.

"Fine day, indeed," he said. The sun was well risen, and the day looked set fair. He lifted another forkful, but stopped before he put it into his mouth. "This is delicious, Kinky. What is it?"

She smiled. "It's only a shmall little thing. Kedgeree. Scottish troops took the recipe to India with them more than a hundred years ago. My da met Indian sodgers in the Great War, had some with them, and got one to write it out for Ma so she could try it in Cork. She showed me how to make it, so." Her look was far away. "We used to get a lot of fish from a little harbour called Ring, near Clonakilty."

"Scotland to Ballybucklebo by way of India, France, and Beal na Bláth, County Cork. Small world," Barry said and finished the forkful.

"It was not shmall when I was a girl," she said. "Anyone who'd been twenty miles from home was looked on like a world traveller. I'd a brother Art went to Philadelphia with his wife. We never expected to see them again in this life, so."

"Did you?"

"Och, indeed. Didn't he and Emer and all of theirs come home in 1960?" She chuckled. "And him, a man of sixty-two, wearing mustard-coloured pants, a checked jacket, and a porkpie hat. He'd a Yankee accent you could cut with a knife layered on top of his natural Cork speech. The way he said, 'aend,' down his nose when he meant 'and' set a body's teeth on edge."

Barry smiled, then frowned. "Kinky," he said, "all this talk of India and people going away and bringing things back has put me in mind of a promise I made yesterday and haven't kept." Since he received Patricia's letter, all thoughts of looking at his textbooks and asking Fingal's advice had fled. Had Alice Moloney brought something back with her from the subcontinent? Some odd disease? He'd told her he'd try to work out what was wrong with her, but so far he'd neglected to do so. That he'd said he would had simply slipped his mind. He'd been too wrapped up in trying to decide if he should reply to the letter, and if he did, what would he say?

Kinky cocked her head to one side. "That's not like you, Doctor Laverty, sir, not at all, at all, but I suppose"—she sighed—"I suppose you've had a lot on your mind since Saint Stephen's Day."

Barry stopped in midswallow but managed to get the fish down. He stared at his plate. "Aye," he said quietly. "I have. A lot." And all Kinky's talk about people not straying far from home? That was him. He'd thought he'd be happy settling here in a village. He'd failed to meet Patricia's expectations. If he'd told her he'd come and study at Addenbrooke's in Cambridge, that once he'd qualified as a specialist he'd be willing to look for work somewhere exciting, would that have made a difference? *You did nothing wrong,* she'd written. But perhaps he had. Perhaps he'd not tried everything. Dad's philosophy was always, If you want something really badly, it's up to you to work hard enough to get it. Barry hadn't worked hard enough.

He looked up. "Sorry, Kinky," he said. "I was woolgathering."

"Aye, so," she said. "I wish I could see the way ahead for you," she said softly, "but for some reason—"

"It's all right, Kinky. I understand." Barry was determined to finish the kedgeree and took more from the serving dish. "When I was a schoolboy, that American actress Doris Day had a big hit with a song called 'Que Sera, Sera.' "

"I remember it well, and I've often wondered would that 'kay' be a pier in America? Like Derry Quay in the song 'Star of the County Down'?"

"No." Barry stifled a smile. He'd not want to hurt Kinky's feelings by making her feel uneducated. "It means, What will be, will be." He polished off the last mouthful. "And I suppose it will." But I wish it had turned out differently. I wish everything would come all right again. And somehow, somehow he must be to blame.

" 'Tis a wonderful thing, you knowing words in those foreign languages," she said. "With your head so stuffed with the learning, it's no wonder you forget the odd promise."

Barry looked at her face. Her expression was forgiving. It was a neat excuse, but it wasn't the truth. He'd better concentrate on his patients. His heartbreak must not compromise their care. "Thanks for reminding me, Kinky." Barry picked up his coffee. He had no qualms about breaching patient confidentiality with Kinky. "I'm worried about Alice Moloney."

"I'm not surprised," Kinky said. "When I saw her at the Bishops', there was not as much on her as would dust a candlestick, so."

"And she's a very funny colour."

"I noticed that. Even with a bit of rouge on her cheeks, I thought she looked pale. Did you ever see fuller's earth, sir?"

Barry sipped his coffee and shook his head.

"It's a special clay. You use it to get the lanolin out of cloth spun and woven from sheep's wool. Funny, pasty grey–looking stuff. I remember a neighbour-friend of mine in Cork, a fellah called Connor MacTaggart, using it. Poor Alice's face would have matched it."

Barry scratched his head. He'd no idea about treating wool, but somewhere, somewhere he'd seen that description of a patient's earth-coloured face. It was a sign of some obscure tropical ailment. What the divil was it? "You're a genius, Kinky," he said. "I think you've given me the clue I need." He finished his coffee. "I'm off to look at a textbook."

"Go on then with you, sir. I've a béarnaise sauce to make."

As Barry climbed the stairs he could hear her singing happily.

The future's not ours to see . . .

Considering Kinky was fey, it wasn't what he'd hoped for from her. But she'd made it clear that this time she couldn't tell what lay in store for him. He wanted her to promise him that Patricia would have second thoughts, drop whoever *he* was—the man in England—and come back to Belfast to finish her studies and be near Barry again. But Kinky hadn't seen that, and so Barry deduced that Kinky couldn't see it because it wasn't going to happen. Ever. Because he,

Barry Laverty, village GP, could never hope to be able to provide the sophistication a girl like Patricia Spence would need.

He trudged up the final flight of stairs.

When he reached his attic bedroom, he put the coffee on his bedside table and pulled down *A Short Textbook of Medicine* from the bookshelf. Barry flipped to the index. *Tropical diseases, 452–465.* Fourteen pages. In Ireland there wasn't much call for knowledge about such conditions. He scanned the print, trying to match at least some of Alice's symptoms with the descriptions in the book.

Malaria, trypanosomiasis or sleeping sickness, leprosy, cholera, plague, yaws, bilharzia, and typhus didn't fit the bill. Neither did acute amoebic dysentery, but as he read on, the description of "chronic bowel infestation with the causative parasite" piqued his interest. Alice had said there had been acute cases in Indian soldiers near where she'd lived, so she might have been exposed to the protozoan *Entamoeba histolytica,* the microscopic animal that brought on the disease. She was tired, irritable, losing weight, and flatulent. That all matched, but she hadn't complained of recurrent bouts of diarrhoea or tummy pain.

He sat on the bed and read on. Diagnosis? According to the text, the parasite itself could be identified from a sample examined under a microscope. But here was the rub. It could be done "only by an expert." Looking directly into the lower bowel with a sigmoidoscope might be of value. He tutted. How many rural GPs could use this hollow tube illuminated by a small bulb to peer into the colon?

Turning the page, he read that the organism could affect the liver, but the patient usually had a fever and abdominal pain. The liver was tender and enlarged. That certainly wasn't Alice's situation. Her liver had been perfectly normal when he'd examined her.

In the next short section, Amoebic Abscess in the Liver, he found an intriguing sentence: "Such an abscess may develop many months or years after the original infection." Alice said she'd had

Delhi belly on a number of occasions. Could she have been misdiagnosed? "It may be clinically silent until a late stage." Interesting, but that was all the information he could glean.

He replaced the book on the shelf and took down *A Short Practice of Surgery*—all 1,389 pages of it. He well recalled Jack Mills's remark when they'd bought their copies in third year. "Blimey, mate, if this is short, Lord preserve us from the long version. We'll never get this lot read." Fortunately, a fourth-year man had tipped them off to a much more concise work, *Lecture Notes on General Surgery*, which had given them enough knowledge to satisfy the examiners. He was glad now he'd kept the larger tome too.

By the time he'd devoured the chapter, he'd learnt that although liver abscesses more frequently attacked men, women could also be afflicted. On rare occasions, the disease had been diagnosed more than thirty years after someone's return from the tropics. Alice had come back to Ulster from India in the late forties. She could be harbouring a latent abscess.

The early symptoms were—Barry swallowed—anaemia. He'd been treating Alice for iron-deficiency anaemia. Could he have been wrong in assuming its cause was simple dietary lack because she was a vegetarian? He read on. In addition, the patients lost weight—Alice certainly had—and they had earthy complexions. Earthy. That was almost exactly as Kinky had described Miss Moloney. It was beginning to look to Barry as if he had been wrong about the cause of her anaemia, but he was now on the trail of her real disease.

His pride took some comfort when he read that making the diagnosis was tricky. An X-ray might help, not by identifying the abscess, but by showing that the lung on the affected side had been displaced upward. The liver enlargement caused by the abscess could bulge toward the chest cavity rather than down into the abdomen.

In many cases, the final answer could only be found by inserting a needle into the liver and sucking out the typical pus. That was not going to be done at Number 1, Main, either.

The biggest risk was that the abscess could rupture, but according to the author of the text, healed lesions could be found during an autopsy when there was an entirely different cause of death. So rupture wasn't inevitable.

Barry put the book on his bed and picked up his coffee cup. Damn. He'd been so engrossed he'd let it go cold. He'd see if there was any left in the pot.

On his way downstairs he made up his mind about what to do with his newfound information. He was going to ignore the immediate temptation to rush round to see Alice Moloney. If he was right and she did harbour an abscess, she must have had it for nearly twenty years. She wasn't in any immediate danger. She wasn't in pain. Today was Saturday, so he couldn't arrange for her to be seen by a specialist until next week. He'd only worry her more by raising the question.

He'd ask O'Reilly who was the best surgeon to refer Alice to. First thing Monday he'd make the necessary arrangements for her to be seen at the Royal Victoria; then he'd nip around and let her know what he was thinking and what he'd arranged.

He headed for the kitchen. "Any coffee left, Kinky?"

"I'll make you another pot," she said.

"Instant'll be fine."

"Not in *my* house, Doctor Laverty."

"Sorry, Kinky." He should have known better.

She lifted down a bag of coffee beans and the grinder. "And what," she asked, "will you be doing today—that is, if no one calls?"

"I'll do my crossword this morning. Lunch . . . read . . . watch the Irish-Scottish rugby game on BBC."

She tutted. "It's a such a lovely day for you to be stuck inside."

"I'm on call."

"Why don't you go and see a friend? As long as you give me your phone number, I'll take the calls and send for you if it's urgent."

"Doctor Mills is working this weekend and Harry Sloan's gone to Portrush. I phoned him last night."

"And there's nobody here you'd call a friend? You're like Himself. Like all doctors, I suppose."

"How, Kinky?"

"You can't be close friends with your patients. You might know their secrets, but you can never tell them yours. You have to keep a bit of a distance."

"That's true." He had no friends here save Fingal and Kinky. Jack had always been close. Harry Sloan was a good head, and Patricia, she'd been his friend. He could talk to her about anything. She always tried to understand. He missed her kisses, but dear Lord, he missed walking with her, holding her hand, and chatting with her about anything from the death of Ian Fleming last August to laughingly trying, as she called it, to unravel the secrets of the universe. But he had had other friends before medicine became all-consuming. Kinky was right.

"You'd not mind holding the fort?" he asked.

She shook her head. "And sure, Doctor Laverty dear, why would I? Have I not held it for nearly forty years for Himself and Doctor Flanagan who had the practice before?"

"You're a marvel, Mrs. Kinky Kincaid." He rummaged in his inside pocket and pulled out a diary. "I'm going to go down to the Yacht Club after lunch. I was a keen sailor once. I had a fourteen-foot dinghy called *Tarka*, but I had to sell her in my final year as a student so I'd the cash to buy the Volkswagen." He flipped through the diary. "I'll give you the club's phone number." Barry reached into another pocket and found a loose sheet of paper—with Peggy Duff's phone number on it. He stared at it for a moment, then decided he wasn't going to phone her.

"And sure isn't it only twenty minutes in your motorcar if I need you?" Kinky said.

"It is." Barry scratched out Peggy's number and scribbled the number of the Yacht Club. He handed the page to Kinky.

"There'll be plenty of my old sailing friends in. Nice day like today, they'll be getting a head start on their boats' spring refits."

"Aye, so," she said quietly, "there always does come a time when things can benefit from a fresh start, Doctor Laverty." She poured him a fresh cup. "Now," she said, "take that upstairs and do your puzzle."

"Thank you, Kinky," he said, knowing full well he was not just thanking her for the coffee.

Barry headed upstairs and went into the lounge to find Lady Macbeth standing on her back legs, back arched, forelimbs extended, claws raking the curtains.

In a fair imitation of O'Reilly, he yelled, "Get away to hell out of that."

She looked at him balefully and pulled her right paw free, but she clearly had her left one stuck. "*Eeeeeow.*" She struggled, twisting from side to side.

"Hang on." He set his coffee on a table and went and unhooked her claws. "Sometimes, Your Ladyship," he said, "it takes somebody else to get you unstuck."

And as he went back to drink his coffee, he silently thanked Kinky for her concerned advice. He realised he'd been able, for the moment, to stop feeling sorry for himself, and he was actually looking forward to spending the rest of the day at the Yacht Club.

He wondered how O'Reilly and Kitty were getting on with theirs.

17

How Blessed Is He Who Leads a Country Life

Gravel crunched under the Rover's tyres as O'Reilly swung in through the wrought-iron gates of Ballybucklebo House. The paint was chipped, and rust patches marred the black enamel finish. He slowed on the long curved drive.

"Slowing down, Fingal? That's not like you."

"Peacocks and peahens wander all over the grounds. The marquis takes a *very* dim view of anyone who runs one down."

From the backseat came a series of yelps and the thumping of a heavy tail on the upholstery.

"You know where you are, don't you, Arthur?"

"Aaarghow." Heavy panting. "Aaargh."

"Eejit," O'Reilly said, reaching over to lay a large hand lightly on the dog's head, then returning to the steering wheel to swing the car past the Virginia creeper–covered gable-end of the mansion and under a high archway of Mourne granite blocks. The Big House was to the left, stables and outbuildings to the right across a cobbled courtyard. An identical archway pierced the opposite wall.

Two of His Lordship's hunters, ears alert and twitching, looked out over stall half-doors. They surveyed the scene with their limpid brown eyes and snorted steamy puffs from wide nostrils. One horse, a chestnut, shook his mane and gave a ferocious whinny, as if complaining that rather than wasting his time shooting, the marquis should be hunting. The horses would have their day soon, when the Ballybucklebo Hunt met.

O'Reilly stopped the Rover beside cars parked near the house. He heaved himself out. The smell of coal smoke from the mansion's chimneys, along with horse and dog scents, filled the air. He opened the car's back door. "Stay."

Arthur whimpered. O'Reilly took out his shotgun and the gamebag holding his cartridges. "Come, sir. Sit." Arthur obeyed, looked up, and ignored a group of folks standing outside the stables. Some carried ashplants, stout walking sticks made from ash saplings. Others brandished sticks of knobbly blackthorn. Many had dogs held on choke chains. Springer spaniels, an Irish setter, two pointers, and three Jack Russell terriers. These men who would beat the coverts and retrieve fallen birds were listening to instructions from Rory Mehaffy, His Lordship's gamekeeper. "It'll be cocks only," O'Reilly heard him say. A sensible move to protect next year's breeding stock.

Kitty had let herself out of the car. "We've a grand day for it," she said.

"We have. And it's not too nippy." Overhead the sky was porcelain blue, and small clouds hung, holding station like fish idling in a calm sea. There wasn't as much wind as would stir a cow's tail, and although the air was crisp on O'Reilly's cheeks, it had not the bone-chilling rawness of the day last month when he'd been out wildfowling at Strangford Lough.

"Looks like a good turnout," Kitty said.

"Always is here." O'Reilly looked over to Ballybucklebo House, old, solid, timeless, like Ulster itself. The building had been completed in 1799, in the reign of George III, fifteen years after he'd lost the American colonies and a year after the abortive rising of the United Irishmen. And, O'Reilly thought with a grin, forty years after the founding by a Mr. Arthur Guinness of a brewery at Saint James's Gate, Dublin.

"Interesting building," Kitty said.

"It is that," he replied. O'Reilly had always thought that the old building and the newer additions looked as contentedly haphazard as the terrace houses on the main street of the village itself. Successive lords of the manor had built a new wing here, a conservatory there, and pushed out bay windows. He pointed up. "It was the marquis' great-great-grandfather who erected that astronomical observatory. It has a revolving dome with a slot for a telescope."

"My goodness."

"It was about the time Herschel discovered a new planet. He wanted to flatter the king so he suggested the name Georgium Sidus, but by convention the planets got named for ancient deities, so it ended up as Uranus. Comets weren't so grand though, so when the marquis' ancestor discovered a new one it was called MacNeill after the family."

He spotted someone heading their way. "Here comes that other object on an eccentric orbit," he said to Kitty. "Donal Donnelly. He'll want to chat to me about a horse called Flo's Fancy. It's very hush-hush."

"I understand. Mum's the word."

"Good lass."

Donal waved and Fingal waved back before glancing over to where people stood, the marquis among them, between the conservatory and the main building. Wives and members of the guns' families were sharing the shooting equivalent of stirrup cups, probably hot whiskies. The guns would not be drinking. The marquis was strict about that, and rightly so. Shooting and jars did not mix.

"Morning, my lord," O'Reilly yelled to the tall greying aristocrat. "A belated Happy New Year."

"And to you, Fingal. Glad to see you've brought Arthur. We'll talk in a minute."

"You've met His Lordship, and I think you know most of those folks," O'Reilly said to Kitty, pointing to the group.

"I met His Lordship's son, Sean, and Captain O'Brien-Kelly, the Irish Guards officer, at the marquis' open house," she said. "And of course I've met Councillor Bishop."

"The marquis always invites him to the January shoot. A case of noblesse oblige if ever there was one. It's in recognition of Bertie's standing as a member of the village council."

"He looks like something out of an Austrian hunting print."

O'Reilly liked her description. Bertie's green-felt Tyrolean hat was authentic, right down to the drooping pheasant's feather. A tweed Norfolk jacket covered his ample belly—just. Corduroy jodhpurs were wrapped to his shins by a pair of canvas gaiters.

"He takes it very seriously," O'Reilly said. "Years ago Bertie took expensive shooting lessons at the famous English gunsmith E. J. Churchill in Buckinghamshire. He needn't have bothered. He'd still have difficulty hitting a barn with a carpet beater."

Kitty chuckled. "Who's that woman?" She hesitated. "I don't want to sound pass-remarkable, but—"

"Go ahead, Kitty. I'll not think you're commenting unfavourably."

"It's that skirt. Where in heavens did she get it?"

O'Reilly laughed. The garment in question was voluminous, like a small black bell tent, even though the woman was perfectly proportioned for her height of five foot two.

"That's Myrna Ferguson, the marquis' younger sister." Myrna, who was fifty-eight and childless, was under O'Reilly's care for psoriasis. "When she hunts—and she still does frequently—she rides sidesaddle. And she shoots in her riding skirt. She may look like an anachronism, but she's a tough lady, Myrna. Six years ago her husband of twenty years broke his neck in a hunting accident."

"Oh, Fingal. How dreadful."

"Myrna did her grieving, then she got on with her life. She has a D.Sc. in physical chemistry and is a reader at Queen's University—"

"I've a painting friend who's a reader at Queen's in medieval history. That's only one rank below full professor. Good for Myrna." Kitty looked thoughtful. "She'd have been graduating in the late 1920s."

"Got her B.Sc. in '27. Took her another four years for her doctorate."

"Something of a trailblazer."

"*And* she's a crack shot. A regular Annie Oakley." Even though, he thought, because she stood only five foot two, she used a light twenty-bore instead of a twelve.

Kitty cocked her head and gave O'Reilly a thoughtful look. "You seem to think very highly of the marquis' sister. She's obviously a very eligible widow. Did you never consider . . ." She let the words trail off, but O'Reilly had no doubt about what she was suggesting.

"Away off and chase yourself," he said. He chuckled, then shook his head no. "She's a patient"—he noticed three other men in a second loose group, the marquis' neighbouring landowners—"just like those three blokes over there."

There would be ten guns, with himself, the marquis' group, and these three who were dressed for the field in hacking or Barbour waterproof jackets. Two sported Paddy hats; the other, a deerstalker. Each had a shotgun in the crook of an arm, the breeches of the weapons open. The locals would shoot here today, and reciprocal invitations would ensure the marquis had a good pheasant season and a day or two on the Donegal grouse moors in August.

" 'Scuse me, sir . . . Miss O'Hallorhan," said Donal Donnelly. "True day, so it is." Most of Donal's ginger thatch was tucked in under a caubeen. He wore a scuffed, sleeveless, mid-thigh-length, leather waistcoat over a thick woolen shirt. His moleskin trousers were tightened above the knees with nicky tams.

"Looking forward to beating today, Donal?" O'Reilly asked.

"I am that. His Lordship pays us a guinea apiece and gives us a brace of birds each when it's all over. I'm very fond of a mouthful of pheasant, so I am. You ever want a bird, Doc . . ." He winked at O'Reilly, who wondered how many of His Lordship's preciously protected, pampered, and preserved birds Donal came by honestly—and how many were purloined on moon-bright nights. As one of O'Reilly's professors at Trinity College had once observed, "Some questions are better left unasked."

"The grub's good too." Donal picked at his buckteeth with an index fingernail. "After a morning beating the thickets, I could eat a wooden chair. You get a right tightener at lunchtime and a bottle of stout."

Kitty looked puzzled. Dubliners and folks from County Down had different ways of expressing themselves.

O'Reilly spoke both dialects. "A tightener," he translated, "is a very satisfying meal, with lots to eat."

"Aye," said Donal. "Sets you up great for the afternoon drives, so it does. Makes it a grand day out, you know. And"—Donal lowered his voice—"wi' Julie up the spout, the money helps too."

"How is she?" O'Reilly asked.

Donal smiled. "You mind the photographer, Bertie Bishop's cousin, like?" Donal nodded in the councillor's direction, then looked O'Reilly in the eye and sadly shook his head.

Fingal didn't have to ask to understand that there was no change for the better in the horse affair. "I do," O'Reilly said. "The cousin wanted her for a hair model."

Donal nodded. "She's been up to see your man again. He's paid her the second ten quid he promised. The snaps I'd had framed is lovely. Just lovely."

O'Reilly heard the pride in Donal's voice and glanced at Kitty. Julie Donnelly, née MacAteer, wasn't the only gorgeous woman in Ballybucklebo today.

"I'm sure they are, Donal," Kitty said. "Your Julie's a beautiful girl."

Donal grinned. "You're not the only one who thinks so."

"Oh?"

"Mr. Hunter sent in the two best ones to the English shampoo company like he promised, said it was like trying to get her to be the Brick girl."

"I think," said Kitty, "you mean the *Breck* girl."

"Aye, likely it is, but Brick . . . Breck . . . what the heck? Sure it doesn't matter what it's called, what does matter is dead wheeker, so it is. Stickin' out a mile."

"She's won?" O'Reilly asked.

"Not yet, but she's been picked for the last five. That guarantees fifty pounds if she only comes fifth. They'll be picking the winner on the twenty-sixth of February."

"I'm delighted, Donal," Kitty said. "And I'll bet she wins."

Donal's face fell. "Just at the moment I'm not happy about making any bets." He looked sadly at O'Reilly. "Flo's Fancy's running this afternoon."

Damn. Donal and his partners' shares in Flo's Fancy were in jeopardy again. This had to be stopped—and soon. He remembered what Barry had suggested. "Donal, you know Fergus Finnegan, don't you?"

"Is the Pope Catholic? Declan's brother, the wee bandy-legged jockey? Sure everybody knows Fergus."

"Is he beating today?"

"He is, so he is."

"Tell him I'd like a word with him after lunch."

Donal frowned and O'Reilly remembered his promise to Donal of secrecy. "I need to ask him about a horse—but not anything else."

Donal grinned. The message had sunk in. "I'll tell him, sir."

The marquis called over, "Time to go, Fingal."

O'Reilly looked across the yard to see the guns and spectators climbing into Land Rovers. The beaters and their dogs were getting onto trailers pulled by tractors. "Kitty and I'll join the others, Donal, and you run on off with the beaters."

"Right, sir." Donal started to stride across the courtyard. He turned and called back, "I'll talk to Fergus. You have a good morning's sport, sir."

"I'm sure we will. Heel, Arthur. Come on, Kitty," O'Reilly said, following Donal. "I'll ask His Lordship if you can stand beside me in the firing line."

"Not with the other spectators?"

O'Reilly grinned. "I haven't seen you for nearly three weeks. I'll not be deprived of the pleasure of your company this morning."

18

Shoot Folly as It Flies

On the first two morning beats, Rory Mehaffy, the gamekeeper, had shown the guns fine birds. Arthur's coat was muddied and matted with sticky burrs from the undergrowth he'd pushed through. He'd retrieved pheasants, two woodcock, and a wood pigeon for O'Reilly and the neighbouring sportsmen. The Labrador, tongue lolling, sat alertly at O'Reilly's feet as they waited for the third drive to begin.

Kitty, in a gabardine raincoat and a paisley silk headscarf, sat on a shooting stick beside him to his right.

"Having fun?" he asked.

"I'm having a lovely day." She lowered her voice. "It's been better than a pantomime watching some of your neighbours."

O'Reilly chuckled. To his right, two of the locals, a man Fingal did not recognise, and the marquis' son, Sean, held their positions. Five more guns were spread at twenty-five-yard intervals to his left. Bertie was closest, then came Captain O'Brien-Kelly; Myrna was next, followed by one of the other landowners. The marquis stood at the extreme left of the line.

"It's a good thing you're here to mop up after the councillor," she said.

"I think," said O'Reilly sotto voce, "that Bertie might be well advised to reverse his weapon, hold it by the barrels, and use it as a club." He was pleased to see her laugh. "The captain isn't much better. And him from the Irish Guards. I'd expect a bit of marksmanship from a military man. It's a good thing Myrna and His Lordship are here."

"And you, Fingal. I've been watching. You've been shooting very well."

"Thank you."

"That was a beauty the way you nailed that wounded bird."

"Pure luck," he said. The single cock had burst out of a stand of larches. In the bright sunlight, its head had been shining like an emerald as it clawed for height, flying straight in the councillor's direction. Bertie'd given it one barrel to no avail. As the bird fled higher still and curled off to his right side, Bertie'd fired again. To his cry of "Tower bird," the pheasant, true to the habit of its kind when injured, rocketed straight up.

O'Reilly had spun, arched his back, and put his gun to his shoulder with the barrels pointing vertically. He held the bead sight to cover his target. It reached the apex of its flight and stalled as he knew it must, a tiny cross sketched on a limitless sky. In the split second when it hung motionless, he squeezed the trigger.

Feathers puffed loose, as if a pillow had been punctured, and with wings folded, head thrown back, long tail feathers fluttering, the bird had plummeted to the ground.

"It was a good shot, Fingal," Kitty said.

"It was pure luck."

"About as lucky as Maria Bueno winning Wimbledon last year," she said.

O'Reilly glowed to her praise, but said, "She'd certainly have won if she'd played me."

Kitty shook her head and smiled. "You're a hard man to compliment, O'Reilly."

He heard the gamekeeper's whistle, the signal for the third drive to begin. "I'd better pay attention if I'm going to keep up my record," he said, facing front and slipping off the safety catch. He was determined to continue shooting skillfully if the opportunity presented. Inside he knew he was like a boy showing off to the new girl in town, but what the hell? Why shouldn't he?

The line of guns stood on the coarse grass of a wide cartwheel-rutted clearing. Behind it, rowans stood among leafless silver birches. Each of their tops was a filigree of twigs so fine as to seem to be pencil strokes against the sky. The ground beneath the trees was covered by thickets of dead brown bracken and sere, yellow rushes dappled by patches of sunlight and shadow.

Thirty yards in front of O'Reilly and Kitty, the short grass was swallowed by the edge of the covert. Gorse and rhododendrons struggled with brambles, heather, and dead ferns for space. The almond scent of yellow whin flowers mingled with the piney aroma of the spruce and fir trees that lifted pointed heads to the underbelly of the sky.

Until the whistle blew, the only sounds had been Arthur's panting, Kitty's quiet conversation, and the squabbling of a flock of rooks. Now the peace was shattered by the clamour of the beaters as they responded to Rory's signal and advanced through the wood. The staccato rattle of ashplants and blackthorns on tree trunks was punctuated by the crash of feet pushing through the brittle undergrowth and the cries of men urging on their dogs.

"Hi lost, Sally."

"Hey on, Landy. Hey on. Push him out. Push him out."

All along the line, guns waited.

With a hoarse "kek-kek-kek-kek" and the rapid-fire rattling of stubby wings, two birds scorched from the wood to O'Reilly's right. Two guns fired.

Three more cocks flew over Bertie and O'Brien-Kelly. The

men's four shots might as well have been fired straight up in the air, but before the fleeing pheasants could reach the safety of the birch wood, Myrna fired. Twice. Two birds fell. O'Reilly, despite his intention to impress Kitty, ignored the third escaping bird and sent Arthur to retrieve. Funny, he thought, he must be getting old. He'd rather work Arthur now than shoot any more pheasants today.

To his left, a single cock, crouching low, came running from the rhododenrons. It couldn't have known the received wisdom in shooting circles: "No true sportsman would ever shoot at a sitting duck or a bird on the ground." But it must have understood the wisdom of not flying over a line of guns.

The pheasant's neck was outstretched. Its entire being, from the neb of its yellow bill to the tip of its long striped tail, was one long multihued line. O'Reilly admired its bottle-green head, red wattles, white collar, and golden-brown body feathers as it raced to pass between O'Reilly and Bertie Bishop and gain the birch wood and safety.

"Good luck to you, bird," O'Reilly said, as it approached. Then from the corner of his eye, he noticed Bertie Bishop throwing his shotgun to his shoulder and starting to swing on the fleeing pheasant. He'd be aiming at Kitty in a second.

O'Reilly yelled, "Shite," and hurled himself at her, carrying her to the ground out of the line of fire and protecting her with his own body.

Bertie's shotgun roared, not once, but twice. The loads must have passed within inches of O'Reilly. He hoped to God that Arthur, who was returning with one of Myrna's birds in his mouth, was all right.

O'Reilly sat up, the smell of smokeless powder harsh in his nostrils. He was untouched. The cock had vanished. Bertie had missed the bird, and Arthur was sitting at O'Reilly's side with a pheasant in his mouth. O'Reilly pushed himself off Kitty and stood. He was shaking. He gave her his hand and pulled her to her feet. "Are you all right, Kitty?"

"Fine," she said. "I'm fine, but what was all that about?" Clearly not understanding the gravity of the situation, she joked, "I've heard of a fellah sweeping a girl off her feet—but that was some sweep." She dusted off her skirt with her hands.

"Bertie was trying to hit a running bird. He could have shot you, by God. I didn't have time to warn you, so when I saw him swing his gun I jumped and shoved us clear."

"Good thing too by the sound of it. Thank you." She frowned. "But why on earth was he shooting so low?"

"He's hardly hit anything all morning. Being Bertie, he wanted a kill—at any price." Fingal put a hand on her shoulder. "Thank Christ, he missed you."

She cocked her head and looked into his eyes. "He missed you too, Fingal, and you were between him and me." She sucked in a deep breath. "You could have been shot."

"Och," he said, "we're both untouched." O'Reilly's trembling had stopped, but he'd not clenched his fist more tightly since his boxing days. Earlier this morning he'd wrung the neck of a wounded bird. Now O'Reilly struggled to control his urge to run across and strangle Bertie Bishop.

"Doctor . . . Doctor." O'Reilly looked round to see Bertie trotting over. He wasn't carrying his gun. "Are you all right, Doctor?"

O'Reilly ignored him and stooped to take the bird from Arthur's mouth. The big dog had waited patiently at O'Reilly's feet.

Bertie arrived panting and wringing his hands as convincingly as Uriah Heep. His chubby cheeks were flushed. "Are you all right, Doctor? I'm dead sorry, so I am. Don't know what come over me—"

O'Reilly dropped the bird and spun on his heel. "We're all 'all right,' Bertie—but only just," O'Reilly said levelly, but he was thinking how in 1914 the British and the Germans had had a short-lived

Christmas truce on the Western Front. Now in 1965, the festive suspension of hostilities, obtained at the Christmas pageant, the Rugby Club party, and Bertie's open house, was definitely over too.

Bertie, after all, was the man who built appallingly substandard housing, tried to use his position as a councillor to finagle old folks out of their properties, wanted to muck about with village landmarks—and all for profit. *His* profit. Now he was rooking Donal and his friends out of their hard-earned money. His own employees, for Christ sake. Donal had been worried about a photographer taking some innocent photos of his wife, Julie. Donal would murder Bertie Bishop if he ever found out the councillor had made passes at Julie when she worked as a live-in maid at the Bishops' house.

O'Reilly struggled to keep control. He put an arm round Kitty's shoulder and felt her move closer. "We're all right . . . but"—he leant closer to Bertie and spoke icily—"if you'd have put one pellet any nearer Miss O'Hallorhan. One bloody pellet . . ."—O'Reilly knew his voice was rising—"you'd have become the subject of an experiment to see how effective shotgun barrels are as a sigmoidoscope."

"Well, I only made a mistake—"

"Well, you made a mistake? *You made a mistake?*" O'Reilly didn't give a tinker's damn if his roaring could be heard by the beaters in the wood. "It was your mother made the mistake not drowning you at birth, Bertie Bishop. I'm very fond of Kitty O'Hallorhan. *Very* fond. If you'd harmed—"

"Thank you for that, Fingal," Kitty said, pulling on his arm. "Thank you very much."

He looked into her face at her upturned lips, saw the sparkle in her grey, amber-flecked eyes, the smile crinkles at their corners. He felt his anger ebbing like the Strangford Lough tides he'd watch flowing off the mudflats on his days' wildfowling.

"Councillor Bishop *has* apologised," she said.

Bishop snatched off his Tyrolean hat. "Honest to God, Miss O'Hallorhan," he said, "I'm mortified. I'm quare nor sorry, so I am."

"I'm sure you are," she said. "Accidents *do* happen."

"You're absolutely sure you're all right, Kitty?" O'Reilly asked.

"One hundred percent."

He turned back to the councillor. "Just make sure they don't bloody well happen again, Bertie, because if they do, I'll keep my promise." Then, glancing at Kitty and back to Bishop, O'Reilly took a deep breath. He said in a voice that had almost returned to his ordinary conversational tones, "And we'll let that be an end to it." He'd be damned if Bertie Bishop was going to force any more temper loss in public.

"We will, Doctor O'Reilly. We will. Thank you."

O'Reilly grunted and then said. "All right." He was aware that the marquis had appeared.

"You all right, Fingal? Kitty?" His voice was solicitous. "Mehaffy told me what happened."

"Fine, thank you, my lord," Kitty said.

"It wasn't very good form shooting at a running bird, Councillor." O'Reilly saw Bishop visibly shrink. "It'll not happen again, sir."

"I'm sure it won't," the marquis said icily. "Quite sure. Now if you're certain everyone is all right I'll be heading up to the Big House, make sure everyone's being looked after." He turned his back on Bishop. "You and Kitty will be sitting at my table, Fingal."

"Delighted," O'Reilly said. He noticed that the day had become much quieter. The only raised voices were those of dog handlers directing their animals to fallen birds. No guns were firing. The drive was over. The shooting party had already started on the fifteen-minute walk back to the stableyard and lunch, a prospect to which O'Reilly was looking forward enormously.

Someone tugged at his sleeve.

"Excuse me, Doctor sir." It was Donal Donnelly, cap in his hands. "Morning, Councillor."

O'Reilly watched the play of emotions on Bertie Bishop's face. Being civil to the councillor's social inferior won over disdain for a man stupid enough to let himself be conned. "Good day to you, Donnelly." Bertie turned to O'Reilly. "I'll need to get my gun." He walked away.

O'Reilly congratulated himself for getting his temper under control. Quietly pursuing Bertie's downfall in private would be a much more satisfying matter, particularly if it led to financial relief for Donal and his friends.

"Bejizzis, Doctor, your man Bishop near shot you and the lady. I was beating over there fornenst thon birch." He pointed. "When I seen him swing, I yelled, 'Look out,' but you mustn't have heard."

"Thanks, Donal. We were lucky."

"Lucky my aunt Fanny Jane, sir. No harm to you, but I seen what you done to protect the lady." O'Reilly heard the respect. He wanted to change the subject. As far as he was concerned he had done nothing more than circumstances had dictated. "Aye, well," he said. "Did you get a word with Fergus?"

"I spoke 'til him first thing, but he's away at the other end of the beaters' line now, you know. He asked me to ask you, can he see you in the stableyard after lunch?"

"Ah," said O'Reilly. "Lunch." He picked up the pheasant and stuffed it in his gamebag. "Get your shooting stick, Kitty." He turned to Donal. "Tell Fergus I'll come looking for the pair of you."

"Right, sir."

Kitty stood at his side. He took her free hand. "Heel, Arthur. Come on, Kitty . . . Donal. Let's see what kind of a spread His Lordship's put on today."

19

To Hear Him Crow

So much for his plan to get to the Yacht Club after lunch, Barry thought, as he drove along the main road toward the council housing estate. When Kinky came upstairs, he'd assumed she was calling him for lunch, but it was to say that Elaine Kearney had phoned. Her four-year-old son, Kevin, was hot, having difficulty breathing, and making a rasping noise when he breathed in. Fever and respiratory symptoms in such a young child were not to be taken lightly.

With the Volkswagen parked on one of the narrow streets of the estate, he grabbed his bag, and in a moment was knocking on a mud-coloured front door and noticing that it was badly in need of painting.

The door swung open. A woman stood in the doorway. "Doctor Laverty? Thank God you've come."

"Mrs. Kearney?"

"Aye. Come on in, please." With a red, rough hand she beckoned to him. "And shut the door after ye." She started down a poorly lit hallway and after two paces began to climb a narrow flight of stairs.

Barry followed, trying not to gag at the smell of cabbage water and dirty nappies. He guessed Elaine was in her early twenties, but already the lank black hair peeping out from under her head scarf was greying. Under the scarf, her hair was wound around plastic curlers called spoolies.

He heard a crowing noise coming from above and instantly recognized it as the stridor, the harsh breathing of croup. Some cases of measles might have this symptom too. Kiddies' air passages were small, and any inflammation narrowed them further.

He remembered the main causes of croup: acute laryngitis affecting only the voice box, acute laryngotracheobronchitis affecting the whole respiratory system, a foreign body stuck in the larynx, and diphtheria. Fortunately there was a vaccine for that now, but just before doing Mr. Coffin's trachy, O'Reilly had mentioned seeing cases in his early days.

"In here, please," she said.

Barry followed her into a bedroom. There was barely room for the bed, a wooden chair, and two adults. Patches of mildew stained the cheap wallpaper, but the windows had been recently washed. A small boy lay on the bed under a thin blanket. He looked at Barry from glittering, sunken blue eyes and struggled to draw breath. His nostrils flared, and again Barry heard the crowing, as the little air the boy could pull in struggled past his narrowed larynx. He coughed weakly.

"This here's Doctor Laverty, so it is, Kevin," Mrs. Kearney said. "He's going to make you all better."

Barry smiled at Kevin and then looked at his mother. "Can I get past you there, please, Mrs. Kearney?" He managed to wriggle closer to the head of the bed as she stood crushed against the wall.

Barry sat on the bed, set his bag beside him, and took the boy's wrist. "How are you, Kevin?" he asked.

The child's voice was raspy and hoarse. "I'm all cold and shivery, so I am." He coughed. "My throat's sore." Tears and mucus from his nose trickled down his face.

His skin was hot and clammy, his pulse racing, but his cheeks were red, not cyanosed; the blue of cyanosis would have indicated a severe oxygen lack.

"We'll have to see if we can put that right," Barry said. He turned to Mrs. Kearney. "How long has Kevin been sick, Mammy?"

"He's had the wheezles for about four days. All the kiddies get them sooner or later, and they usually get over it."

So she thought the child had had bronchitis. Certainly most of the kiddies of this estate had regular attacks. The houses were damp, drafty, and poorly heated. They'd been put up at minimal expense by—and with maximum profit to—their builder, Councillor Bertie Bishop.

"I had him in bed and I give him a paper, so I did," Mrs. Kearney said.

"A paper?" Barry could not visualise the boy reading the *Times*.

"Aye. For his wee chest. It's what my mammy did for us when we was little. You take mustard powder, wet it, mix it with honey, and spread it on brown paper, you know. Then you bind it to the chest."

Barry nodded. He'd seen patients treated with a mustard plaster before, but he'd never heard it called a paper. "I see," he said.

Kevin made another crouping noise.

"I don't think," she said, "it done him much good, for the sickness went into his thrapple this morning, so I took off the paper and I sent for you there now, sir."

"You did the right thing. Once there's infection in the voice box, the wee ones croup," Barry said. He turned back to Kevin. "I'm going to examine you, all right?"

The little boy nodded.

"I'll help you sit up." Barry put an arm around the shoulders. He was reasonably sure the boy had acute laryngitis following acute bronchitis, but he wanted to be sure the lad had had his immunizations.

"Has Kevin had his needles?" he asked.

"Och, aye. The district nurse gives them."

Barry had met Colleen Brennan, the nurse who, like the district midwife Miss Hagerty, looked after patients in their own homes. Colleen was a tiger when it came to ensuring children's inoculations were up to date. It was very unlikely that Kevin had diphtheria.

Barry rummaged in his bag and fished out a wooden spatula. He took a pencil torch from his inside pocket. "Open wide," he said to Kevin. Barry shone his torch into the mouth. "Stick out your tongue." Kevin obeyed, and Barry, taking care not to put the spatula so far back the boy would gag, examined the cheeks opposite the boy's molars. He was looking for tiny bluish-white dots known as Koplik's spots. He'd missed a case of measles last July and wasn't going to make that mistake again. Good. No spots.

"Say aah."

The back of Kevin's throat was red and inflamed, but as Barry had anticipated, there was no evidence of the filmy membrane of diphtheria.

"Right," Barry said. He removed the spatula, and Kevin hauled in air with a loud crowing.

When he lifted the boy's pyjama top, there was no rash and no evidence of the muscles between the ribs being drawn inward when Kevin inhaled. The characteristic rasping sounds were obvious when Barry put his stethoscope on the chest. "All done," he said, helping Kevin to lie down and pulling the blanket up.

"Kevin has inflammation of his Adam's apple and bronchial tubes." It was, as O'Reilly would say, hardly a diagnosis to challenge Sir William Osler.

"Is that serious, Doctor?" Mrs. Kearney asked.

"Not at the moment," Barry said, "and it's easy to treat. He'll need antibiotics and nursing in a tent full of steam to loosen up all the mucus."

"Can you fix one up here and give him them pills, like?"

"We could, but I'd rather not. It's unlikely, but he could take a turn for the worse, need oxygen"—or even a tracheostomy, he thought—"and we're not equipped for that here. He'd be better in the Children's Hospital for a few days."

She stared at the little boy, then turned to Barry. "I don't like them hospitals, so I don't. I remember when I'd my tonsils out when I was four—"

"I think they're better now than they were then," Barry said, deliberately interrupting her. He didn't want her scaring Kevin any more than he already must be. "They'll take care of him. They really will."

She tutted. "If you say so, sir." Then she managed a weak smile. "You're the doctor and all, so you are."

Barry cleared his throat and busied himself with his bag, his back turned to Mrs. Kearney so she'd not see his blushes. "Have you a telephone?"

"No, sir. There's one in the sweetie shop on the corner, just up the road."

"Fine," Barry said. He turned back to Kevin. "I'm going to make a phone call, and you're going for a ride to Belfast. You'll be fit as a flea in no time."

Kevin tried to say something, but another bout of crowing cut him off.

"The ambulance men will let themselves in. If there's one available in Belfast it'll come straightaway, so they should be here in about half an hour."

"Thank you, Doctor Laverty," Mrs. Kearney said. "I'm dead grateful, so I am."

"I'll let myself out. You stay with Kevin." Barry made his way down the narrow stairs, through the cramped, foetid hallway, and out into the fresh air again. Across the street a group of children were hanging onto ropes tied to the top of a lamppost. The kids were running around and around it. The game was as old as street-lamps, and the kids called it a Maypole. The twisting of the ropes around the pole shortened them until all the players were drawn inward. Then they reversed direction and ran around the other way. All this was accompanied by high-pitched squeals, shouts, and giggles.

No roundabouts, no slides, no swings here.

None of these children would be going on to university. The boys might find work in the shipyards, the girls in the linen mills as shifters and weavers, but Ulster's shipbuilding and linen weaving were both dying industries.

Further up the street Barry walked past two girls playing hop-scotch, their pitch a series of squares drawn with chalk on the pave-ment. No grass, no trees, no flowers here. The sun barely penetrated the narrow streets.

He wondered if Patricia had played hopscotch as a child in Newry. She'd not be facing an unsure future as a shifter in a linen mill. She was headed for the top, far further than being the wife of a country GP. *But I'm not suited for country life.* He should have seen that from day one, set his own sights higher, but damn it all, he'd thought he really liked it here.

What was it like in Cambridge today? he wondered. Even if it was only January, it might be warm enough for Patricia and her new man to be out in a punt on the River Cam. Barry could picture him poling langorously along past the Backs, as the long lawns rolling down from the colleges to the river were called. Barry could imagine Patricia reclining in the boat, expounding her views on the place of women in the twentieth century. Cambridge, its ancient buildings, and nearby London, where perhaps *he'd* take her for dinner or to a show, were a far cry from Ballybucklebo and this slum.

He stepped onto the road to pass a girl, pigtails flying as she jumped over her skipping rope and chanted:

> One potato, two potato, three potato, four.
> Five potato, six potato, seven potato, more.

July, August, and half of September. That was all the time he'd had with Patricia, and those months had sped by. The empty weeks from the start of her term at Cambridge, with nothing but the occasional phone call and letter, hardly counted.

Barry sighed. They were weeks that had dragged by, just as the four weeks had dragged by since she first said, "It's over," and now she had confirmed it in that last damn letter.

O'Reilly was right. The work did occupy Barry's mind, but once it was done and his mind unfettered, Patricia filled his thoughts.

He reached the sweetshop. Barry pushed through the door. Its upper edge struck a small bell, and the jangling announced his arrival. Once inside he was surrounded by stacks of newspapers, magazines, comics, shelves full of bottles of unwrapped sweeties, racks of cigarettes, cans of tobacco, small tins of snuff. A distinct aroma of liquorice came from an open bottle of aniseed balls sitting on a glass countertop.

From behind the counter, the proprietor, Bernard Cowan, who had a waxed moustache and a hernia controlled with a truss, smiled at Barry. "How's about ye, Doctor Laverty?" His words were indistinct, probably, Barry thought, because the lump in Bernie's cheek was an aniseed ball.

"Have a sweetie?" He pointed at the bottle.

"No, thanks, Mr. Cowan. But could I use your phone?"

"Aye, certainly. Thonder it's at." He pointed to the far end of the counter to a stand receiver with a detachable earpiece on a bracket. "Help yourself."

"Thanks." Barry, feeling like a latter-day Alexander Graham Bell, held the earpiece and started to dial with his other hand.

"Sending wee Kevin Kearney to hospital?"

"How did you know?"

"Och, sure, wasn't his mammy only just in here ringing up to get yourself?"

Barry smiled.

The owner tapped his head with one finger. "Just a matter of using the oul' loaf."

Barry spoke to the doctor on call at the Royal Belfast Hospital for Sick Children, known to all as Sick Kids. The registrar said he'd make the necessary arrangements and send the ambulance. It saved Barry making another call.

"Thanks," Barry said to the shopkeeper, as he hung up.

"Anytime, Doc. You reckon the wee lad'll be all right?"

"I shouldn't discuss patients . . . but yes. Yes, I do."

"Sticking out a mile." He pushed the bottle to Barry. "Go on. Spoil yourself, sir. Have a sweetie."

It would be churlish to refuse. "Thank you." He nodded at the phone. "Can I leave you a shilling to pay for the call?"

"Not at all. Sure it'd only be a couple of pennies. As long as the wee lad's going to be mending." Cowan shrugged.

"Thanks," said Barry, and sucking on a large boiled sweet, he walked back to his car. That was typical of this place—concern for your neighbours. There'd been no question about his using the phone, even though local calls cost money.

Barry frowned. He was making too many phone calls to get help for patients he knew perfectly well how to treat, because he lacked the facilities. He gagged on saliva and the sweet syrup of the aniseed ball. For a moment he thought it was going to lodge in his gullet, but he managed to get it down.

Having to refer so many interesting cases to specialists was becoming hard to swallow, too. Siobhan and her meningitis, Alice with her possible hepatic abscess, now little Kevin. Barry chucked his bag back into the car, hopped in, and headed for home. It was pleasant enough to bask in the customers' thanks, as he had just now, and in Elaine's childlike trust. "You're the doctor." And he enjoyed being a respected part of this tight-knit community. But was it enough? And if it wasn't now, what would it be like when he got to be O'Reilly's age?

20

I Wish He Would Explain His Explanation

The mulligatawny soup they'd started lunch with had been delicious, just the thing to warm folks in from the field. O'Reilly stretched out his legs under the trestle table. His right calf felt stiff. Age, he told himself. Can't be helped. He finished the last remnants of his portion of what had started as a spectacularly poached and glazed whole salmon. The fish had been garnished with dill and served cold. It was probably one the marquis had taken last season from the river Lennon in Donegal and had frozen.

O'Reilly chewed happily, savouring the delicate flavour and surveying the wreckage of the feast. The table was strewn with bowls containing the scraps of beetroot-in-jelly salads, potato salads, aspic jelly, homemade mayonnaise, and sliced lemons.

Butter dishes stood among plates of freshly baked wheaten bread, white loaf, and brown bread.

In keeping with the teetotal nature of the guns' day, they had been offered only tea or white or brown lemonade. But the spectators had done very well, starting with a Bollinger to accompany the melon and ham that had followed the soup, and a white Bordeaux with the fish.

Donal was right. The marquis did put on a right tightener, although it was doubtful if the beaters would be dining quite as handsomely as the guests. Kinky would not be pleased by how much Fingal had eaten, but then he thought with guilty pleasure, Kinky's not here, is she? He grinned, wiped his mouth on a linen napkin, rubbed his tummy, and hauled out his briar.

As O'Reilly stood, Kitty looked up from where she sat opposite, between Myrna and Sean MacNeill.

"Keep an eye on Arthur, please, Kitty. I've to see a man about a horse," he said.

"Of course," she said and puckered at him.

No questions asked. She hadn't needed any explanation other than his mentioning earlier that this business was hush-hush. He felt so . . . so comfortable with her, and he liked that. He liked that very much.

"Don't leave her too long, Fingal," Myrna said. "You never know who might come and carry Kitty off. She's a very good-looking woman."

Sean and Kitty laughed.

O'Reilly guffawed, but he realized if another man did become interested in Kitty O'Hallorhan, he, O'Reilly, would take very unkindly to it. Very unkindly indeed. He lit his pipe and strode across the cobbles of the courtyard in search of Fergus and Donal.

The pair of them waved to him from where they were standing near the stables.

Donal had a half-finished bottle of stout clutched in one hand. " 'Bout ye, Doc," he said.

"Donal . . . Fergus."

"Doctor O'Reilly," Fergus said and lifted his duncher.

"Fergus, we've a bit of a difficulty. Donal here knows about it. Doctor Laverty thought maybe you could help us. And it's hush-hush."

"I'm all ears, Doc." Fergus grinned.

O'Reilly noticed Fergus had hair sprouting in tufts from the insides of his bat ears.

"And," Fergus continued, "I've a mouth like a steel trap."

"Thank you," O'Reilly said. Then he quickly told Fergus the story of how some friends of his had invested in a horse and how the controlling shareholder put up the cash for bets on the animal for everyone and was using the friends' shares in the filly as collateral.

Fergus squinted. "And if the horse doesn't win, the controller takes a bit of the others' shares and gets to own more of the horse. Isn't that right, sir?"

"How did you know, Fergus?" O'Reilly asked.

"There's no flies on Fergus when it comes to the ould gee-gees," Donal remarked.

Fergus grinned. "Sure, thon trick has whiskers on it. When I was an apprentice jockey, I heard tell of a crooked trainer pulling that one at Newmarket, over in England."

"Oh," said O'Reilly. This was a damn good idea of Barry's to talk to Fergus. "But the way I work it out, it's costing the controller—"

"Away off. No harm 'til ye, sir, but 'controller'? You mean Councillor Bishop, don't you? And the notion of him losing money?" Fergus shook his head rapidly. "Me arse."

"How in the name of the wee man do you know it's Bertie, Fergus?" O'Reilly asked.

"Flo's Fancy? Sure everybody knows about that wee filly." His face broke into a grin, and for such a small man his laughter was remarkably deep. Fergus cocked his head, narrowed his eyes, and looked at Donal. "The word's out she's owned by a syndicate of Bertie Bishop's workers. The lads have eighty percent and he's twenty percent, so he has."

O'Reilly said nothing.

"Jesus," Donal said, "the word's out?"

"Och, come on, Donal," Fergus said. "You can't expect the other seven lads to keep a thing like that to themselves."

And, thought O'Reilly, this being Ballybucklebo, what more does the jockey really need to say? O'Reilly was grateful he wasn't going to have to pretend that the individual in trouble was Barry.

"Sure haven't you told Doctor O'Reilly?" Fergus continued.

"Shite," said Donal. He frowned, pursed his lips, then spat.

"Take a daisy, Donal," said Fergus.

How that Ulsterism had come to mean "relax" was beyond O'Reilly.

"Us jockeys and stable lads do know a bit, and from what I hear Doctor O'Reilly saying, Bertie Bishop's trying to rook youse. Whose side do you think we'll be on?'"

O'Reilly was delighted by the prospect of acquiring a team of insider allies. "Will you all help?" he asked.

"Teetotally," Fergus said.

Donal's frown fled.

"Youse was trying to tell me that you think the councillor's *los-ing* money trying to get control of the whole horse. How's he los-ing? I don't understand. Councillor Bishop's so mean he'd wrestle a bear for a ha'penny. I mind one night in the Duck and it was his shout. Says he, 'I've a heifer to buy tomorrow so I've a rubber band around my money tonight,' and divil the bit would he pay. I don't see that man deliberately losing a brass farthing."

O'Reilly glanced at Donal, who nodded. "He appears to be los-ing by betting," said O'Reilly.

"By betting? How?"

O'Reilly continued. "Say he puts up money from his own pocket for ten bets and loses. That's his own stake and the money he bet for the lads gone, but he gets part of their shares of the horse—"

"But if it cost us say, eighty pounds, it still cost *him* a whole hun-dred because he used his own money for us and twenty pounds for himself, his twenty percent," Donal added. "It's daft, so it is."

O'Reilly could see the way Fergus's brow wrinkled. "It *is* daft,"

O'Reilly said. "Bertie Bishop might be a right bastard, but he's no fool. I don't understand. I'd need to think on it. We can't let Bertie away with this just because he thinks he's a highheejin and can fool a bunch of working lads." He turned to Donal. "All the times she's been out, the wee filly's never won, isn't that right?"

"Aye."

"Never wins," Fergus repeated. "I think I can guess why that is. None of us here knows her jockey. He's from County Cork."

"I don't understand," O'Reilly said.

"Owners can tell a crooked jockey to hold a horse back. We'd all know if Bertie tried to get at a local, but—"

"A stranger? I see," O'Reilly said. It was beginning to make some sense.

Fergus stopped and the others followed suit. "It's still crackers, so it is." Fergus snorted down his nostrils just as His Lordship's hunter had done this morning.

"Thanks for trying to help, Fergus, but I think we're bollixed," Donal said sadly.

"Hang about," Fergus said. "I'm getting a feel for what he's up to."

"God, I hope so," said Donal. "Go on then. Spill it."

"Well, I think your man Bishop's getting the jockey to slow the horse *and* fiddling the betting somehow."

"How?" O'Reilly asked.

Fergus shook his head. "Dunno."

"Och, *blether*," Donal muttered, but Fergus was not to be deterred.

"I don't know right now," he said, "but I've a notion how to find out. Me and the rest of the lads'll find out about the Cork jockey— see if he's pulling the wee filly."

O'Reilly had a mental picture of the great detective mobilizing his Baker Street Irregulars.

"And Donal, you know the bookie, Willy McArdle?"

"I do, so I do. I work as a runner for him sometimes."

"Is he a sound man—for a bookie?"

"Sound as a bell."

"Great. Ask him how he thinks Bertie's finagling the betting. If anybody would know, it'd be Willy McArdle, so it would."

"You reckon?" Donal asked.

"Damn right, I do." Fergus turned to O'Reilly. "And then, Doctor O'Reilly, if all of us get the right answers, you and maybe Doctor Laverty could use them to have a go at Mr. Bishop and get Donal and the lads' money back from the councillor?"

O'Reilly laughed. The wheel had come full circle. Barry had suggested Fergus. Now Fergus was suggesting Barry. It would suit O'Reilly's purpose ideally to have the young lad up to his neck in this kind of plotting. Just the thing to lift his mind off a broken heart. "Do you know, Fergus Finnegan," he said, "you're as smart as an egg's full of meat."

"Run away on, Doctor." But Fergus bobbed his head and smiled at the compliment.

"And I know you'll help us, sir," Donal said.

"Oh, indeed," said O'Reilly. "Doctor Laverty's onside. I promise, if you two get me the ammunition, I'll let Bertie Bishop have it. And it'll not be a couple of barrels from a twelve-bore he'll meet. He'll think he's walked into a fifteen-inch broadside from my old *Warspite*." He noticed his pipe had gone out, and he started to look for his matches. "Right, lads," he said. "I'm off now to see to Miss O'Hallorhan and then get on with the afternoon drives."

Kinky had drawn the curtains in the lounge. Barry had gone out into the darkness half an hour ago on an early evening call. O'Reilly sat by the fire cleaning his gun. He had spread a couple of pages of the

County Down Spectator on the carpet. Arthur had been bathed and towelled, fed and watered, and was now in his kennel; Kinky was in her kitchen, where a brace of pheasant hung behind the door; and Kitty was in her room getting changed for dinner. O'Reilly was taking her to the Culloden, a refurbished bishop's palace near Cultra.

O'Reilly wrapped a rag around the knurled head of a long ramrod and shoved it through the left barrel. He lifted the gun and put his eye to the chamber. He smelt the burnt powder inside. The barrel needed a few more run-throughs with the rag. He was repeating the first step as Barry came into the lounge. "Evening, Barry. How'd it go? Interesting case I should know about?"

Barry shook his head as he headed for an armchair, shoving Lady Macbeth out of it before sitting. "An eejit with a toothache he'd had all week, who didn't want to disturb his dentist on a Saturday, but thought a doctor was fair game seeing, and I quote: 'Youse is always on call, so youse are.' I sent him up to the dental emergency room in the Royal."

"Where he'll wait for hours," O'Reilly said. "Rule number one in action?"

"It's what you told me my first day here: Never let the patients get the upper hand."

"You're learning," O'Reilly said and chuckled.

"How was your day, Fingal?"

"Wonderful. And you were right to suggest talking to Fergus. He's full of ideas." O'Reilly looked up the barrel again. It was clean now. He started on the right one.

"Great," Barry said. "I'd like to be able to help Donal."

"Me too," O'Reilly said. He rapidly outlined the state of play with Fergus and Donal, the possibility that the jockey was pulling the horse, the hint Bertie was finagling the betting. "And when we get the facts, I want you to back me up like you did the last time."

"Of course."

"We need to put one over on Bertie, and not only because the little bugger bloody nearly shot Kitty and me today."

"Good Lord. How?"

O'Reilly continued cleaning as he explained to Barry exactly what had happened.

"It's a good thing he didn't hit anyone, Fingal. With you out of action they'd have sent for me, and I know nothing about treating gunshot wounds."

"I do, son. Only too well," O'Reilly said, thinking of his sick bay during the war. "I'm glad I don't have to treat those injuries anymore. I'm happy enough looking after coughs and colds, and the weary, walking wounded."

"Does it never get boring for you?"

O'Reilly put his gun back into its case. "Boring? I suppose it does sometimes. I'd be pretty surprised if that's not the case with every job, but I think there's enough interest—human interest—to keep me on my toes, and once in a while we do get something out of the ordinary."

"I just did."

"Oh?" O'Reilly closed the lid.

"Alice Moloney. I think she may have an amoebic abscess of her liver."

O'Reilly whistled. "What gives you that notion?" He listened carefully as Barry explained his reasons. "Begod," he said, when Barry finished. "You might just be right. I saw one rupture on *Warspite*. Chief petty officer. He'd been on the China station twenty—no, twenty-one—years previously. We'd better get her looked at."

"Who'd you suggest?"

"Sir Donald Cromie. He'll soon sort her out."

"I'll see to it on Monday."

"Good lad. That was some pretty fine reasoning, Barry. I'm proud of you."

Barry smiled.

"Makes my point too, I think. Once in a while something medically very interesting does come along."

O'Reilly wasn't prepared for Barry to stand up, shove his hands in his pockets, and say, "And every single time it does, we have to refer them on to a specialist."

O'Reilly pursed his lips. "That's all part of general practice. Don't forget, you sorted out Cissie Sloan's thyroid and Flo Bishop's myasthenia."

"I know. It's just . . . I don't know. Maybe I'm tired." He looked Fingal straight in the eye. "Maybe I'm missing Patricia. Maybe I'm trying to puzzle out what I'm really looking for in a woman. In life."

"No maybe, son," O'Reilly said, as softly as he could. He stood and put an arm round Barry's shoulders. "No maybe about it."

"Thanks, Fingal."

"I tell you what. I know Kinky's making a special supper for you tonight, but if you like I could ask her not to cook the steak and put the rest in the fridge until tomorrow. It'll keep. You could come to the Culloden with Kitty and me."

Barry shook his head. "It's very kind of you to offer, but I couldn't intrude."

O'Reilly heard the finality in Barry's words. He realised it would be useless to insist. "Fair enough," he said. "And Barry?" He looked up as Kitty came in. "You will find the answers and it will get better with time."

21

Thy Waves and Storms Are Gone Over Me

Spray rattled off the Volkswagen's windscreen and along with the downpour defeated the efforts of the wipers. Barry halted at the kerb and looked at his watch. Four o'clock and already it was almost dark. A gust from the northeasterly gale battering in from the Irish Sea rocked the car on her springs. He could hear the wind howling in the telegraph wires above the Shore Road. The thoroughfare itself was a shallow river, where rain in torrents mingled with seawater bursting over the seawall.

Like the blood vessel that had burst in Sheilah Devine's head.

He'd just been to see the octogenarian—she'd been discharged from hospital the day before, and Fingal had asked Barry to pop in on his rounds today. It was more of a courtesy call and had saddened Barry. He'd felt so helpless. There was nothing he could do for a stroke victim. What practical attention Sheilah needed would come from the district nurse, Colleen Brennan.

Two weeks had passed since Barry had had his heart-to-heart with Fingal. Two weeks of routine practice like this afternoon's call, a trip to Belfast to see *Doctor Zhivago,* and three evenings spent at the Yacht Club. And it had been two weeks since he had received what he now thought of as "the letter." He'd not replied nor had he heard any more from Patricia. Often sleep did not come until the small hours, and since the sunshine on the day of the marquis' shooting party, the weather had been grey, dull, and damp.

Perhaps if it were spring, or if the sun would only blink through for an hour or two, Barry's mood might lift, even though a few minutes earlier he had stood helplessly beside an old woman's wheelchair in the tidy living room of her cottage, trying to comfort her and her husband, Joseph, who waited at the other side of the chair.

Barry had held her right hand in his own. It was limp and clammy, the blue veins tortuous under skin blotched with liver spots. "Can you squeeze my hand, Mrs. Devine?"

He felt no pressure, no movement.

Her head lolled on her shoulder. Her hair, thin grey wisps, had been neatly combed. Barry looked at a face where the left side was deeply wrinkled, the other side smooth and the skin thin as tissue paper. The right corner of her mouth drooped and a thin dribble of saliva ran from it. She tried to speak but only managed a garbled mumbling.

"Excuse me, Doctor," Joseph said, then bent forward and dabbed the drool away.

Barry had finished examining the patient. She was completely paralysed on her right side and had lost the power of speech. That was exactly what the letter from the hospital had said before adding there was nothing more the neurologists could do. Nothing anyone could do, Barry knew, but the responsibility for her now rested with her GPs.

He'd been at a loss for something to say. He'd patted Sheilah's hand and smiled at her. "Doctor O'Reilly or I will come back and see you soon." To do what? he asked himself. Curing the victim of a stroke was impossible. "The district nurse will be in tomorrow."

She'd mumbled and gestured with her left hand as if waving good-bye.

"I'll see you out, Doctor." Joseph led the way, his tartan carpet slippers making a susurration as he shuffled along. He was stooped at the shoulders, the result, Barry assumed, of osteoporosis, a thinning of the vertebrae with age. It was another condition about which he could do absolutely nothing. In the hall, Joseph Devine said, "Thank you for coming. I understand youse doctors can't help herself, but it's a comfort to know you and Doctor O'Reilly care about us, so it is. Between me and the district nurse, and youse, we'll keep Sheilah out of the home, so we will."

The old folks home, more dreaded than a prison sentence by the elderly of Ulster.

"Call us anytime." Barry put on his sodden raincoat.

"It's in the hands of the Lord, Doctor," Joseph said. "Mr. Robinson, our minister, is very kind too."

Barry had never regretted his agnosticism, but he envied the comfort the old couple could take from their church in this time of distress. Being dumped by the woman he loved wasn't as serious as a stroke, but he wished he could take solace like the Devines did. "I'm sorry for your troubles, Mr. Devine," Barry said.

"Take you care in that there gale, sir."

And that was exactly what he was doing, sitting here on the road while the rain came down in torrents and mingled with the spray.

Another sheet of water was blown across the road. The waves had started building south of Aran Island up past Scotland's Mull of Kintyre. They'd been heaped higher by the living gale until, like rank after rank of grey-uniformed storm troopers, they hurled themselves against the seawall's granite blocks. Those bastions repelled the attacks, smashing their assailants into wind-driven spume or sending them reeling back.

Barry'd grown up in Bangor, and the sea had been a lifetime companion. He'd swum and fished in it, kayaked, and sailed. He loved all its faces, not just its summer serenity. There was a primal majesty when the lough was in a destructive mood and trying to smash its way ashore.

Barry sighed. His own frame of mind was more subdued, inward-looking. Since "the letter," he'd been trying to puzzle out where he'd gone wrong. He'd been stupid to ignore the fact that she would always want a life of her own, would want a career. What the hell was there for a civil engineer to build in Ballybucklebo? A new local landmark like the red barn for Willy John McCoubrey's black-and-white cow?

He shook his head. Home, Barry, he told himself. For the moment the spray was less dense and it would be safe to drive again.

He passed under the railway bridge and stopped at the village traffic light. Across the road the top of the Maypole bent like the topmast of a reefed-down square-rigger. He hoped the wood was strong. If the timber snapped and toppled, it would make a mess of the nearby Ballybucklebo Boutique.

Alice Moloney would be working in there today, not that she'd be getting much custom in such a gale. Barry wished he'd been able to do more for her, but Sir Donald Cromie, whose waiting list for appointments was long, had felt that there was no urgency, and he was the expert. The surgeon had been most complimentary about Barry's diagnostic acumen. Alice would be seen on the seventeenth of February, the week after next. In the meantime, she'd already had an X-ray, so the films and report would be ready for Sir Donald when he saw her.

Barry drove ahead after the light flicked from amber to green. It was frustrating having to wait for answers, but Alice'd been most grateful when he'd popped in to explain his suspicions and ask her to go to Belfast for an X-ray. Her thank-yous that Monday and later, when he'd phoned to tell her that her X-ray was normal, had been heartfelt. O'Reilly was right about that too. It was pleasant to bask in the customers' thanks—but was it enough? He was still no closer to finding out what was wrong with Alice. Only a specialist could.

Barry wondered if Jack Mills would see her too. Probably. Sir Donald was his boss. Jack and the specialist would be able to finish what Barry had started.

He parked in front of Number 1, Main Street. He'd phone Jack tonight, see what he was up to tomorrow. It had been a while.

Barry opened the car door and felt it nearly ripped from his hands. He got out, hauled the door shut, and started up the path. As he was about to go inside he saw a woman approaching, shoulder to the wind, dragging a small boy by the hand.

"Come in." He had to yell to make himself heard.

Barry took off his Burberry. He recognised Colin Brown and his Pac-a-Mac–clad mother. "Mrs. Brown . . . Colin," he said. "Take off your coats, then come into the surgery."

Barry sat in the swivel chair. He wondered if Colin's back-to-schoolitis was playing up again. You never knew what divilment the boy could get up to.

Mrs. Brown sat in one wooden chair, Colin in the other. His legs, one with a grazed knee, didn't quite reach the ground.

"Terrible day, Doctor," Mrs. Brown said. "The wires are shaking, so they are."

"It is very windy," Barry said. "I was driving along the Shore Road and had to pull over."

"I'm dead sorry, so I am, not to come when the surgery was open, but I didn't want to take Colin out of school, you know."

"I think you should have, Mammy." Young Colin looked straight at Barry. "It was math this morning. I hate math, so I do." He squinted and pretended to stick a finger down his throat.

Barry tried hard not to laugh. "What can I do for you?"

"What with him cutting himself, and getting the cold, now he's got an itch. I'm dead worried about it, so I am. Show the doctor, son."

Colin slid off his chair and walked over to Barry. "It's me dome," he said, pulling off his school cap and pointing to the centre of his head. "It's terrible itchy, so it is." He put on a serious face. "I think it's the leprosy, so I do. Mrs. Aggie Arbuthnot, our Sunday-school teacher, was telling us all about it at Sunday school last week. I'll not have to go to real school if it is."

Barry didn't know if it was young Colin's solemnity or the mention of Aggie Arbuthnot, the six-toed cousin Cissie Sloan seemed able to introduce into any conversation. He couldn't keep a straight face and had a sudden desire to tease Colin. "If it is, it's you for a leper colony, Colin Brown. And they have schools—and no summer holidays."

"What?" Colin took a pace back. His eyes widened, then he said disdainfully, "Away off and feel your head, Doctor Laverty. They do no such thing."

"*Colin.*" Mrs. Brown turned on her son. "Don't you *dare* call the doctor stupid nor contradict him neither."

"It's all right, Mrs. Brown," Barry said. "No harm done. I don't need to feel *my* head, but I want to have a look at Colin's."

Barry leaned forward and saw a bald patch in the middle of Colin's scalp. At first sight it looked as if he'd been making an attempt to create a miniature tonsure about two inches in diameter. But when Barry looked more closely, it was clear that no monk's deliberately shaven bald spot would have looked like this.

The central part of the lesion was covered in lustreless, broken-off stumps of hair and greyish-white scales. The rim was angry red. Barry was certain Colin had ringworm, a fungal infection. Diagnosis was usually aided by examination in a dark room using a Wood's lamp to make the affected area glow blue. Damaged hairs could be pulled out, soaked in reagents, and examined under a microscope to identify the fungus. Naturally these latter tests would be done by a dermatologist, not a GP.

Barry knew he was right by the look of the sore alone. "Colin's got ringworm," he said.

"Aye. That's what his granny thought. She said she could cure it with a mixture of turpentine and baking soda, and if that didn't work she'd blend together gooseshite and pig lard and rub that on."

"Really?" Barry said. By now he was no longer shocked by the folk remedies the villagers told him about. He had learnt not to deride them.

"I didn't think he'd've been very popular at school stinking of either salve," she said, "so I said I'd get your advice first, sir."

"You did right," Barry said, "but I'm afraid Colin's popularity at school isn't going to matter for a while."

Colin's head jerked up. "Why not?"

Barry smiled at him, then turned to his mother. "Because your mammy's going to have to keep you at home from MacNeill Primary for two weeks."

"Wheeker," Colin said.

"Until he stops being infectious. It can go through a class like wildfire."

Mrs. Brown nodded.

"And he'll need to take pills four times a day for a month."

Colin grimaced.

"It's all right. They don't taste awful," Barry said. He saw Mrs. Brown frowning. "And you'll not need goose droppings. I'll give you an ointment too."

She smiled.

Ah, the power of the ointment, Barry thought. He explained to her how she'd need to boil Colin's school cap because the fungus would be growing inside.

That amused Colin enormously. "I've wee mushrooms in my cap, like?" He peered into it. "I don't see none."

"They're too small to see," Barry said, "but the things that cause your itch have got into the lining, and if you leave it there it will reinfect you when you put your hat on again."

Colin's eyes narrowed. He cocked his head. "So don't boil it, Mammy, and I'll *never* have to go back to school."

After Mrs. Brown and Barry stopped laughing, he explained that Colin's sheets and pillowcase would have to be washed every day. "The fungus that causes ringworm is a persistent little devil and quite contagious," he said. Then he swivelled back to the roll-top desk and wrote the prescription for the fungicide Griseofulvin, 250 milligrams to be taken four times daily, and an iodine-based ointment.

"Excuse me, Doctor Laverty," Mrs. Brown said, "could you give me a line for Colin's teacher?"

"Of course." She'd need a doctor's letter to keep the truant officer from calling to see why Colin was not in class. "Maybe the teacher could give Colin some homework too. I'll ask."

Barry turned his head in time to see the boy withdrawing a recently stuck-out tongue. Better to pretend not to have noticed. "Whose class are you in, Colin?"

"Miss Nolan's. She's a wee corker, so she is." He smiled. "All the big boys is in love with her, like."

Barry smiled. For a moment he had a vivid picture of her conducting the children's choir and of him remarking to himself on her very good legs, green eyes, and hair that shone like burnished copper. Barry sighed and started to write, *Dear Miss Nolan* . . .

He finished the letter, rose, and handed it to Mrs. Brown along with the prescriptions. "Here you are," he said, ushering Colin and her to the door. "And don't forget about the bedclothes and boiling his cap."

"Thanks very much, Doctor," she said. "You've took a great load off my mind, so you have."

"Don't worry about it," he said. That's something else O'Reilly would comment on, he thought. How a GP's job was less about curing major diseases than alleviating patients' worries. He waited for them to put on their coats; then he opened the front door and flinched as the draught made a picture on the wall rattle. "Off you go."

"Thanks a million, Doctor," Mrs. Brown said.

Barry closed the door. As he turned to head upstairs, he noticed the phone. After the usual, seemingly interminable, hospital switchboard delays, he heard a curt "Mills."

Not like Jack to answer the phone without putting on an accent. "Jack? Barry."

"Hi. Can't talk long. I'm due in the operating theatre."

"Are you free tomorrow?"

"Aye. Give me a bell in the morning."

"Sure."

"Great. Gotta go." The line went dead.

Barry replaced the receiver. From that snapped exchange he had no doubt that his friend was fully occupied. Barry unfortunately had time on his hands. He climbed the stairs and decided that as he was free the next day, he'd make the trip to Belfast, Jack or no Jack. He wanted to do some shopping for things he couldn't buy locally.

He shooed Lady Macbeth from an armchair, picked up his book, settled down, and tried to finish reading *The Spy Who Came in From the Cold*. Sensible chap, he thought, as rain lashed against the bow windows and a tied-back curtain flapped where the seal of the window sash was none too tight.

Barry rose to see if he could make the frame sit better. He looked through rain streaming down the pane. Over in the graveyard opposite, the old yews thrashed. What a miserable day. When Barry had gone out into the gale to see poor Sheilah Devine, he'd thought nothing could cheer him. Thank you, Colin Brown. Nobody, but nobody, could stay gloomy for long around young Colin. He'd put that sort of patient encounter on the positive side of the mental ledger he was creating about life as a GP.

He shoved on the window sash and was gratified to feel it settle and the draught diminish. He had to smile, because at the exact moment the window settled more firmly against the sill, the streetlights came on. He knew it wasn't cause and effect, but the coincidence amused him.

22

Have Seen a Glorious Light

O'Reilly stepped over shattered roof slates, the wind flapping his wet trouser legs against his calves. On this, the second night of the gale, the light from the streetlamps was instantly swallowed up by driving raindrops that glowed like swarms of fireflies. Gusts of wind pushed him along Main Street almost as quickly as it hurled discarded fish-and-chip wrappers, cigarette packets, newspapers, and someone's battered bowler hat.

He regretted his decision to leave the warmth of his fire to give Arthur a walk. Despite being on call this evening while Barry was up in Belfast, O'Reilly had headed out into the weather. Kinky knew that his evening walks with Arthur inevitably ended at the Mucky Duck, so if he was needed, she'd know where to find him. This evening he was going to arrive there earlier than usual. It had been too miserable trying to walk into the wind.

"I think," he said to Arthur, "I'll have a hot half-un when we get to the Duck. I'm bloody well foundered."

"Arrghhh," Arthur agreed. The wind ruffled the fur of his back against the grain and made his ears flap.

As they waited to cross the road O'Reilly noticed that the lights were on in the Ballybucklebo Boutique. That was odd. Alice Moloney, who usually closed at noon on Saturday, appeared to be working late. She was probably stocktaking so everything would be in order if she was admitted to hospital next week. He thought it was highly likely she would be. O'Reilly heard a series of bangs as the heavy wrought iron–framed sign for the Black Swan struggled against the gale.

As he crossed the road, the sign succumbed to another blast of wind, and with an eldritch screech it was ripped from its hinges and clattered to the footpath.

"Begod, Arthur, someone could trip over that in this murk," he said. "Better get it out of the way." Soon, with the sign, miraculously still intact, propped against the pub wall, O'Reilly shoved open the Duck's doors and let himself and Arthur in. The warmth was welcoming, but the tobacco fug was like something from the set of a Hammer horror film. If Christopher Lee playing Count Dracula appeared clutching a pint of Guinness, O'Reilly would hardly be surprised.

In the dim light he had difficulty identifying individual customers, but the place was full of men who recognised him and who, after a momentary hush, were not shy in greeting him.

"It's himself. Doctor O'Reilly, so it is."

"Evening, Doc."

"How's about ye, sir?"

"Brave shot last Saturday, so it was, at that pheasant Bertie Bishop made a right Henry's of."

"Is wee Doctor Laverty all right?" That voice sounded concerned.

"Where's *your* lady friend, Doc? Blown you out, has she?"

He didn't know who'd enquired about Barry, but O'Reilly did recognise Archie Auchinleck, the milkman, who'd made the crack about Kitty. O'Reilly wasn't letting those last remarks go. "Doctor Laverty is fine," he said. "He's up in Belfast. He deserves a break from the likes of you, Archie." O'Reilly moved toward the bar, and Archie made room.

"Sorry, sir. I didn't mean to be rude. Just a bit of *craic*, like."

The *craic* ("crack"), for which there is no English word—the leg pulling, the friendly insults that to a stranger might sound hurtful—was all in good humour. The *craic* was what made an Irish pub what it was, a place where a milkman could suggest to a doctor that his girlfriend had dumped him. No offence was taken—as long as the doctor came back with a snappy riposte.

Loudly enough for everyone to hear, he said, "Miss O'Halloran is spending a week with her mother in Tallaght. When she comes back, *I'll* be seeing her again—often—because she enjoys *my* company." If his remarks had let them understand that he and Kitty were walking out, should he care?

"Good for you, Doc. She's a cracker," a voice said.

"Thank you." O'Reilly recognised Gerry Shanks. "She is, Gerry, very lovely, so I'll not be exposing a lady like Kitty O'Hallorhan to a mob of bowsies like you lot. Talk about pearls before swine. She's far too good for you." He let it hang. His own first law, Never let them get the upper hand, was just as applicable to a crowd in a pub as to his patients. "Especially you, Archie Auchinleck, standing there with a face on you not even the tide would take out."

There was a gale of loud laughter, and a voice called, "Nice one, Doc."

O'Reilly put his hand on Archie's shoulder and smiled at him.

Archie shook his head and smiled back. "Nice one, indeed, sir. 'Not even the tide . . .' I'd not heard that one before."

"Pint, Doctor O'Reilly?" Willy asked from behind the bar.

"Smithwick's for Arthur and give Archie a half-pint of—?" His order signalled that the whole exchange had been just a bit of fun.

"Guinness. Thanks, Doc," Archie said.

"And I'll have a hot half. The wind out there's like a stepmother's breath. It would cut you in two. It just blew your sign down, Willy."

Willy switched on an electric kettle. He shrugged and said philosophically, "It's not the first time. It won't be the last."

O'Reilly didn't mind that Willy had started Archie's half-pint before making the hot whiskey. The water needed to boil, and Guinness needs to be poured slowly. Willy held the glass at a forty-five-degree angle beneath the spigot and pulled the pump handle until the upper edge of the stout had reached the top of the tilted glass. The black liquid frothed. Then the publican set the half-pint aside to settle before topping it off. He put sugar and cloves into a mug, squeezed in lemon juice, and added a measure of Jameson's.

"Make it a double," O'Reilly said.

The second tot went in. While they waited for the kettle to boil, Willy went to a beer pump and filled Arthur's bowl.

"How's your soldier son in Cyprus, Archie?"

"I'm quare and relieved, so I am. His regiment's coming home next month." A huge smile split his face. "They're coming to Palace Barracks up the road a wee ways."

"I'm delighted," O'Reilly said. The man had been worried sick about his only son, who was a member of a British peacekeeping force interposed between the Greek and Turkish Cypriots.

He looked over to see how Willy was getting on. He'd finished topping off Archie's Guinness. Once more the glass sat on the bar top settling.

O'Reilly was aware of someone at his elbow. He half turned.

"Could we have a word, sir?" Donal, glass in hand, stood waiting. "Fergus and me has a table, like."

"Grand," said O'Reilly. "Enjoy your drink, Archie, and I am tickled that your boy's coming home."

Willy set the half-pint with its ebony body and thin creamy head by Archie's elbow.

Archie lifted it. "Thanks, Doc. Cheers." He drank. "Not even the tide—"

Archie was still chuckling as O'Reilly paid. "Now, excuse me, I have to go and have a word with Donal." O'Reilly was pleased to have run into Donal, who so far had not reported any progress on the Bertie Bishop front. Perhaps he had news today.

"I'll bring the drinks over for you and Arthur," Willy said.

O'Reilly followed Donal to a table where Fergus Finnegan nursed a pint of Guinness. "Under," O'Reilly told Arthur. O'Reilly's eyes had grown accustomed to the light in the pub, and he saw how Fergus was frowning.

"How's about ye, Doc? Dirty day," Fergus said.

"Evening, Fergus." O'Reilly sat. "It's as black as Old Nick's hatband out there." He unbuttoned his raincoat. "What is it you'd like to tell me?"

"One of the stable lads, Henry Kelly, ran into the Cork jockey fellah at Leopardstown Races."

O'Reilly leant forward, thanked Willy when he delivered the hot whiskey and Arthur's pint. The steam from the glass bore the scent of whiskey and cloves. O'Reilly turned back to Fergus. "And?"

"Our Henry says he's a decent enough wee lad—for a Corkman."

O'Reilly grinned. Regional rivalries were very much alive in Ireland. "*Sláinte.*" He sipped his whiskey.

"Cheers," they said, and they drank.

"Come on, Fergus, what did Henry find out?"

Fergus screwed up his narrow face. "Henry—and the price of ten pints—found out that your man, Eugene Power, rides for Mr. Bishop when he's racing Flo's Fancy. Eugene comes from Newcestown, County Cork; is related to the old Yankee movie star Tyrone Power and the family that makes Powers Irish whiskey. And he can hold his drink a damn sight better than our Henry."

"Ten's a brave wheen of pints, so it is," Donal said. There was a hint of awe in his voice.

O'Reilly ignored Donal. "But . . . ?" he prompted Fergus.

"But as best as Henry can remember, when he asked your man Eugene straight out was he pulling Flo's Fancy, all he got was 'Who'd do a thing like that, bye?'" Fergus screwed up his face. "Them Cork folks and their 'byes' and 'sos' at the ends of their sentences. Dead comical, so it is."

O'Reilly muttered, "Indeed," managed to keep a straight face, and asked, "And that's it?" No wonder Donal hadn't been in touch. "You're no further ahead?"

"Not quite," Fergus said. "When Henry kept at him, he winked; then he said, 'And I'm saying no more. I'm going to hold my breath to cool my porridge, so.'"

"Do you think when he winked he was trying to incinerate something, Fergus?" Donal asked.

"Insinuate, Donal," O'Reilly said. "Maybe, but it's not much to go on." He took a swallow of the Jameson's.

"I'm sorry we can't be more helpful, Doctor," Fergus said, "but poor oul' Henry got himself tight as a newt trying to get your other fellah stocious and talkative. Henry had a terrible strong weakness for a whole day after."

"I'm sure he did," Donal said. "Who'd not have a hangover after ten pints?"

"It's all right, Fergus," O'Reilly said. "Thank you and thank Henry for his noble sacrifice." O'Reilly folded his arms. So the jockey angle had yielded a possible answer, but it was tenuous. Certainly nothing strong enough for him to beard Bertie Bishop with. *Damn.* He swallowed his whiskey, then grinned. If he remembered correctly, Newcestown was no distance from Beal na Bláth. Kinky or her folks living there might know the Power family, and if so, could they help?

So that was one avenue to pursue. Donal might have news too. "Have you had any luck with McArdle, the bookie?"

"Sort of," Donal said.

O'Reilly looked at his almost-empty glass and realized if he called another for himself he'd be duty-bound to buy for the others. Fingal decided to heel-tap and sip the rest of his drink more slowly. "So what did he tell you, Donal?"

Donal shook his head and finished his pint. "I'll explain in a wee minute, sir. Fergus?"

Fergus nodded. "Pint."

"Doctor O'Reilly, would you go another wee half?" Donal grinned. "They'd another round of the shampoo judging this week. Julie's photo's in the last three now."

"Wonderful."

"Aye. She's guaranteed a hundred pounds now no matter what."

"I'm delighted," said O'Reilly. With his own tightfistedness embarrassed by Donal's generosity, he called, "Two pints on me and a half-un. Not hot this time, please, Willy. I'm warmed up now."

Willy pointed under the table.

"No, thanks. Arthur's on a diet."

"Thanks very much, Doctor," Donal said.

"Aye," Fergus agreed. "Dead decent, sir."

"Come on, Donal," O'Reilly said. "What else did McArdle tell you?"

"Bertie Bishop's not betting with McArdle, so he's going to see who *is* taking the councillor's money. And our money. McArdle also told me there's a way Mr. Bishop could be cheating us. It's so bloody simple I should have thought of it myself, so I should."

O'Reilly could sense Donal's irritation for having missed a trick. His whiskey arrived. "The pints'll be a minute," Willy said.

O'Reilly paid for all the drinks and took a swallow. "Go on, Donal."

"If somebody's wagering for a syndicate, what's to stop him telling his partners he'd laid the bets, but actually he didn't give the bookies a penny, like? Then he can look all long-faced when the horse doesn't perform, you know—and pocket the lot, and in our case that's the shares."

"Jesus," said O'Reilly. "The brass neck of the man. Do you think that's what he is doing?" He drank.

"Dunno." Donal shrugged. "McArdle's a right decent bloke so he's going to put out the word among the other bookies. See who Mr. Bishop's using. Find out how he's betting, if he's betting at all, but it'll take a wee while. I just hope he can find out before next Saturday. Flo's Fancy's running at Clonmel." He sighed. "It'd be great if she won, but she'll not."

"Because—" O'Reilly, delighted he'd suddenly found another piece of the puzzle, leapt to his feet. His boot must have kicked Arthur, who sprang up, fetched his head a ferocious thump on the table, and gave vent to a loud strangled yodelling.

O'Reilly bent and patted the dog's head. "Sorry, pup," he said. "Lie down."

The dog obeyed, but the look in his big, brown eyes would have softened Pharaoh's hard heart.

"Willy? When you bring the pints, Arthur can have a half-pint too."

"Right, Doc. I'll just be a wee minute."

Now that order was restored, Fingal sat and felt as if he were Saint Paul on the road to Damascus suddenly seeing the light. "As long as she keeps losing, the odds get longer and longer, and I know—I just bloody well know—the minute he's got rid of all the shareholders, she'll start winning. He'll bet a bundle on her just for himself and win at long odds. If she's as fast as you say, Donal—"

"She is that."

"Then she'll keep on winning and the sale price will go up with only one owner. Bertie 'The Great Panjandrum' Bishop. Not only that, he'll be an owner who only spent two hundred pounds in the first place. He'll make fortunes on the bet and on the sale—by God, and on prize money too."

Willy brought the pints and Arthur's drink.

Above the sound of lapping from under the table, O'Reilly heard Fergus say, "Cheers, Doc. Begob, I believe you're right, sir. You *can* win on the swings and on the roundabouts."

A neat reversal, O'Reilly thought, of the old adage "What you gain on the swings you lose on the roundabouts."

Fergus sipped his new pint and sighed. "And I don't see what we can do to stop him—unless McArdle can come through."

O'Reilly drank again. He'd keep his notion about talking to Kinky to himself. No point giving Donal false expectations. Instead he said, "Perhaps he will but until we hear, Donal—and I know it's no great comfort—you'll just have to hope for the best and prepare for the worst." O'Reilly reckoned that when old biblical Job had needed a bit of comforting and all he got was gloom from a bunch of miserable pessimists, he, Fingal O'Reilly, could have filled that bill too. He wished he had better ideas for Donal.

"Thank you, sir. I suppose you're right." Donal sighed and raised his pint. "I'll give you the nod the second I hear from McArdle, so I will, sir."

"Good. Maybe you'll hear soon." He looked at his watch. Kinky'd be getting ready to serve dinner. O'Reilly finished his drink. "I'm off. Come on, Arthur." He waited for the dog to emerge from under the table. He raised his voice. "Night, all."

"Night, Doctor O'Reilly" came back in chorus.

As he pushed through the doors he saw the lights still on in the boutique across the street. O'Reilly remembered he'd promised to buy a handbag from Miss Moloney for Kitty to give to Kinky. He was sure if he knocked on the door she'd serve him. He crossed the road and peered through the shop window.

Dear God. History was repeating itself. Alice lay on the floor curled up like a scared hedgehog.

23

Dangerous to the Lungs

O'Reilly shoved the door shut, told Arthur to lie down, and knelt beside Alice Moloney. She lay on her side. Her eyes were closed and her breathing came in short gasps. Her hair, usually in a tight bun, now lay splayed out on the floor like a salt-and-pepper fan. "Alice?"

No reply.

"Alice?" He put his fingers beneath the angle of her jaw. Her skin was afire, and her cheeks were feverish blotches on a grey, earthy face. The carotid artery pulse was racing. She tried to sit up, but he laid his hand on her shoulder. "It's all right, Alice."

She rolled onto her back. Her eyelids fluttered, opened, closed. She blinked, then rubbed her eyes with her hands. "Doctor O'Reilly?" Her voice was weak. "What happened?"

"I was hoping you could tell me."

"I . . . must . . . I must have fainted." She was racked with a fit of coughing. Her eyes rolled up and the lids closed.

"Alice?"

Only her rasping breathing and the battering of the storm against the windows replied.

O'Reilly felt for her pulse once more. Fast, thready, and weak. She needed to be in hospital—and soon. He stood. No phone on the counter. How about through that bead curtain? O'Reilly crossed the floor, thrust the beads aside, and ignoring their clattering, found a wall-mounted telephone. He needed no notebook to remind him of the ambulance dispatcher's phone number, so he quickly dialled, spoke to the woman on duty, and was relieved to be told a unit taking a patient home to nearby Cultra would be diverted to Ballybucklebo on its return journey.

When O'Reilly went back to the shop, he found Alice's colour had improved a little, but he saw the sheen of sweat on her ashen brow. He knelt beside her.

Her eyes opened. She coughed—a dry rasping sound—then tried to inhale, but she caught her breath and grimaced. "Aaah . . . ah. It's sore. There," she said and put a hand to her lower right ribs. "When I take a deep breath." She panted, then whimpered. "And my right shoulder hurts."

"It's all right, Alice." O'Reilly brushed her hair from her forehead and squeezed her hand. "The ambulance will be here soon."

Her eyes sought his, and he saw the trust in them. "I've . . . I've to go to hospital?"

"I'm afraid so."

She nodded and closed her eyes.

O'Reilly thought the pain in her chest would be coming from the pleura, the nerve-rich, double membrane that clothed the lungs. The diaphragm, which lies on top of the liver, shares a nerve supply with the shoulders. Something irritating the diaphragm could be experienced as referred shoulder pain.

She coughed again and clutched her right side.

"It's all right," he said. "Don't try to talk. Just concentrate on breathing." He let go of her hand. "I'm going to examine you, but I'll close the curtains first."

He crossed the floor. If Barry was right about Alice having an amoebic abscess, it was almostly certainly the cause of Alice's collapse. The damn things could rupture at any time, and he was certain this one had. Thank Christ he'd been passing.

He drew the curtains shut and locked the door. "There," he said, "privacy—unless you count Arthur as an audience."

She managed a weak smile.

He went back to her, his mind like a detective's reconstructing the probable course of events. The pus in the abscess had lain dormant for more than twenty years, like magma beneath the crust of a sleeping volcano. The diaphragm was a big flat muscle. It lay as a transverse partition between the liver in the abdominal cavity and the lungs in the chest. It and part of the liver were the dam holding the pus, the lava, in.

Just as a volcano may start venting steam and causing small earth tremors as warnings, so had Alice developed anaemia, had an earthy complexion, and lost weight. Barry, more power to his wheel, like a good vulcanologist, had read the signs of potential eruption.

The pus had ripped through the diaphragm and the pleura, and gone into the lung. No wonder she'd passed out.

He knelt, rummaged in his jacket pocket, hauled out his stethoscope, and put the earpieces around his neck. "I'm going to pull up your top things." From the waistband of her skirt he hauled up her jumper, a nylon blouse, and an interlock-cotton liberty bodice.

O'Reilly'd thought that piece of antique feminine underwear had gone out with the horse-drawn tram. "Can you sit up?" he asked, and as she started to move, he helped her with an arm around her shoulders. She was light as an empty egg carton. The skin of her belly was pasty-coloured.

O'Reilly laid the palm of his left hand flat beneath her right shoulder blade and tapped the middle finger with his right index and middle fingers. He heard a resonant sound. He gradually worked down her back, percussing all the while, until he encountered a dull "thump." There was fluid at her lung base, something easily confirmed when he stuck his stethoscope in his ears and asked her to take the deepest breaths she could tolerate. Air made a particular sound when it entered a healthy lung base. In Alice Maloney that sound was absent.

She started coughing, and O'Reilly was treated to an amplification of the harsh racket through the stethoscope. He yanked the earpieces free. Her cheeks were puffed out as if she were holding something in her mouth. O'Reilly fished out a handkerchief. "Alice," he said, giving her the hanky, "spit into that."

Her eyes widened and she shook her head. A woman of her breeding would die before spitting in front of anyone.

"Please, Alice. I need a specimen."

She put the cloth to her lips, turned her head away, and spat. Still looking away, she handed him the hanky.

O'Reilly examined the specimen. It was odourless and a dull grey-brown colour, which the textbooks described as looking like anchovy paste. To his knowledge, the only thing that fit that description was pus from an amoebic abscess.

The thing *had* erupted into her lung. She was a very sick woman, but it was preferable to it having burst into the peritoneal cavity. That would have caused Alice agony and carried the risk of sudden death from whole-body sepsis. Not that lungs contaminated with pus were any picnic either.

He carefully laid her flat and rearranged her clothes to cover her belly. O'Reilly stood, pulled off his raincoat to make a makeshift pillow, then knelt and slipped it under her head. "I think Doctor Laverty was right. You do have a liver abscess, and it's burst through into your right lung."

She looked up, straight into his eyes. Her voice was little more than a whisper. "That's . . . that's very serious . . . isn't it?"

O'Reilly took a deep breath and held her hand. "It can be treated," he said. "There were cases in the old days where letting the pus escape by way of the lungs actually cured the patient."

"I see."

"But it's more likely the surgeon will want to operate on you tonight, then have you take medication. What's important is to get you up to the Royal. The ambulance will be here soon. You'll be admitted to the ward accepting emergencies tonight, and on Monday transferred to the care of your surgeon, Sir Donald Cromie."

She swallowed and nodded.

"It's lucky I was passing," he said.

Alice coughed and then made a grunting noise between her clenched teeth.

O'Reilly heard knocking. He got up to open the door. "Come in, lads. Glad you're here."

Two ambulance men entered carrying a pole-and-canvas stretcher.

"This is Miss Moloney. Go easy with her. A liver abscess has burst into her right lung."

The leader turned to O'Reilly, grimaced, and mouthed, "Oh, shite." He clearly understood the gravity of the situation. He turned to his mate. "Bobby, run you on back and bring a portable oxygen tank. I'll get the stretcher lined up."

O'Reilly heard Alice call his name.

"Yes, Alice?" He knelt so he could hear her.

"Doctor O'Reilly?" She paused for breath. "My sister Ellen in Millisle . . ."

"I'll let her know."

Alice took three gasps, then said, "Her number's under *E* in a little blue book beside the telephone."

"I'll do it the minute I see you safely away."

He heard a snuffle and saw she was crying. "What's the matter?"

"Billie . . ." she coughed, "and Felix."

"Who?"

"My budgie and my pussycat."

O'Reilly felt a lump in his throat. Other than her sister, her pets were her only family and her closest friends. Of course she'd be concerned about them. "Will you trust me to take care of them?" he asked.

She nodded.

Bobby knelt beside Alice. "I need for to put this on you, missus, so I do," he said.

O'Reilly moved back as the ambulance man adjusted a plastic oxygen mask over Alice's face and turned on the flow.

She pulled the mask aside.

"No . . . no. Leave that there mask alone, dear," Bobby said, replacing it.

O'Reilly saw the pleading in her eyes. "I think she wants to tell me something." He lifted the mask and bent his head.

"Instructions for the animals are in the cupboard under the sink with cat food and birdseed."

"Don't worry about them. I'll make the arrangements, if you'll let me have a key." He hoped Sonny and Maggie Houston would help out.

She coughed twice. "In my handbag, on the counter."

"I'll see to it."

She let her head sink back onto his coat. The poor creature was exhausted but had refused to rest until she'd made sure that her loved ones would be taken care of. O'Reilly felt his throat tighten.

"Thank you," she whispered.

He stood aside as the men lifted her onto the stretcher. "Gimme the oxygen bottle. I'll carry it," he said. The metal cylinder was cold. "Stay, Arthur." O'Reilly walked beside the stretcher-bearers, through the gale and into the brightly lit interior of the ambulance.

He waited until they'd made Alice comfortable on the shelf-bed. "Here." He handed Bobby the oxygen and bent to her. "They'll look after you well, Alice," he said.

She nodded.

"What surgical wards are on emergency take-in tonight, Bobby?"

"Eleven and twelve, sir."

"I'll give them a ring, let them know about my patient."

"Thanks, sir."

O'Reilly touched Alice's shoulder. "You're going to be fine," he said, and he was gratified to see a small smile under the mask. "I'm going to get my coat, Arthur, and the key, and then lock up. Don't worry about your sister, or Billie and Felix. I'll see to it."

O'Reilly left the ambulance with Bobby's "Night, Doc" in his ears. Inside the shop he found Alice's key, made a note of Ellen Moloney's phone number, put on his coat, called Arthur to heel, and left. He'd phone Ellen from his home.

Head bowed to the wind, he marched in the direction of Number 1, Main Street. Pity, he thought, Barry hadn't been here to see how astute his diagnosis had been. O'Reilly let himself into the house. He was very late for supper, but he knew Kinky would understand. He'd be dining alone tonight because Barry was up in Belfast—out, he hoped, having fun with his friend Jack Mills.

Again he wished Barry had been the one to find Alice Moloney and make sure she was properly looked after. It would have been quite the object lesson for the lad in how, even though much of their work was routine, country GPs could be lifesavers.

24

A Faithful Friend Is the Medicine of Life

"Still windy, begod," said Jack Mills, peering past the red tassels of a Chinese lantern through the window of the Peacock Restaurant. The air was redolent of spices, and a strange discordant music came from a couple of loudspeakers. "That lass's brolly out there's not going to stick the pace much longer."

Barry looked up from a plate of lychees and saw a woman wearing a cream trench coat walking backward into the wind howling along Queen Street. She was wrestling with a green umbrella, and as he watched, it snapped inside out. He half rose. "I'll go and—"

"Eat up your pudding, Sir Galahad. Looks like her boyfriend's arrived."

As Barry sat, a man helped the woman through the door. They were greeted by the same Chinese waitress, wearing a green cheongsam, who had served Barry and Patricia last summer.

Tonight the server had finished taking Jack's order by asking in her thick Belfast accent the identical question she'd posed back then: "And would youse like chips with that?" Jack had been chuckling as he'd politely refused.

On Saturday afternoon, after he'd finished shopping, Barry had gone to Jack's flat and suggested nipping over to the Club Bar for a couple and then going somewhere other than Smoky Joe's for a bite. He wanted to eat here in central Belfast. They'd taken Jack's Mini.

It had been a good meal, but for Barry there were memories here. He'd made Patricia laugh when he'd told her that in China it was considered polite to burp after eating.

"Enjoying those lychees?" Jack asked. "I find them a bit sweet." He sipped his Tsingtao beer.

"I like them."

"They're good for you; Sir Donald told me," Jack said. "Cure gastritis, inflammation of the glands"—he paused and looked at Barry—"and orchitis. So if you've got inflamed testicles, lad, you're on the way to being fixed already."

Barry laughed so hard he choked on the lychee syrup. It took him several moments before he managed to say, "My goolies are perfectly fine, thank you. You're an eejit, Mills."

"Indeed I'm just a culchie lad from back-of-beyond round Cullybackey, but it's good to see you laugh, Laverty. I was beginning to think you'd forgotten how."

"Not quite." Barry pushed the plate away. "I miss her like all be-jesus, Jack, but maybe it wasn't meant to be."

"Go on." Jack leant forward.

"She was smart, beautiful, bloody good cook, fun, sexy—"

"She certainly was restful on the eye."

Barry looked at Jack and realised he meant no disrespect; indeed coming from him it was a compliment.

"She was that," he agreed. "I think my downfall was that I wanted her to be my mother too. Someone who'd stay home, darn my socks—"

"Enjoy living in the country basking in the reflected glory of the local, highly respected GP?"

"That's right." Her sixteen-day-old letter came to mind. She'd said he'd be a wonderful country GP.

"From what I've seen of your ex, Barry, I think you were being a mite optimistic. That girl's going places." Jack sipped his green tea. "Don't take this hard, Barry."

"Go ahead."

"She has a new fellah?"

Barry glanced down and snapped, "Yes, damn it."

Jack said quietly, "She'll not be coming back here when engineering school's over. We both know that . . ."

Barry, still looking down, nodded.

"But this new man?" Jack shrugged and said dismissively, "I'll not give him six months."

Barry looked up. "Six months?"

Jack inclined his head. "Remember in the summer you told me she said her career was more important than a boyfriend?"

"Aye." He remembered well, and it had hurt then. "I persuaded myself it wasn't true."

"Och, sure, don't we all only ever hear what we want to?"

"I suppose."

"Barry, I know I act the goat a lot, but I can be serious. I've learned a few things about girls in all my . . . *experience*." He lingered on the word and rolled his eyes. "I dated someone like your Patricia. She was one of this new breed that I'm buggered if I understand. They're on the lookout for something. They're like . . . like . . ."

Jack was obviously struggling to find the right words. Barry, remembering Patricia's vehemence when she explained that her fight to get into Cambridge was on behalf of all women, said, "King Arthur's knights searching for the Holy Grail?"

"Exactly. And I think they're willing to make sacrifices to gain whatever it is they're after, but I'll tell you what, Barry."

"What?"

"They're never going to be entirely happy with their careers, no matter how much they achieve—they'll always want more."

Barry knew Jack was trying to make him feel better, but the prospect of Patricia being unhappy and dissatisfied, for whatever reason, made him ache inside. Because suddenly Jack's words seemed right. She'd said she needed a wider horizon. And she did, but at the heels of the hunt, wherever she went, she'd still be looking for something—and probably never finding it.

"You know what they told us in psychiatry class. People like Patricia—strivers, perfectionists—are like that because they're never completely happy with themselves. They always have something to prove."

Barry had been in those same classes, but he had forgotten them until now. He knew his friend had a point. "So what you're saying is, if she can't be content with herself she'll never be happy with another man either? That's what they taught us."

Jack inclined his head. "That's absolutely right," he said, then sat back as if he knew he needed to give Barry time to mull things over.

Barry remembered something else they'd been taught. He looked at his friend. Was Jack able to identify Patricia's pattern because it took one to know one? Was his relentless pursuit of anything in a skirt a sign? Or his need to specialise and probably be a leader in his field? Or his intense desire to play rugby for his country? Were these all reflections of Jack's inner doubts?

Barry stared at the red-flocked wallpaper on the far wall. He put away his uncharitable thoughts about his best friend and tried to digest what Jack had said about Patricia.

It was like the advice one of his teachers used to give to patients considering embarking upon the long, arduous, and almost certainly futile treatment of infertility. "I'll try to help you, whatever you decide, but I'm afraid the truth is that you can take the grief now for a capital sum and refuse treatment, or you can have the therapy. If it doesn't work, and it probably won't, the years you are going to invest with disappointments every month because you're not pregnant will be like grieving on an installment plan—and paying the interest as well when you could be moving on, trying to put the ache behind you."

Jack was trying to get Barry to see that he and Patricia had never had a future and that getting it over with quickly was less painful than a gradual drifting apart. Perhaps in the face of the inevitable it was the easier course. Barry looked at Jack. "So what do you suggest, Sigmund Freud?"

Jack grinned, narrowed his eyes, and said gutturally, "Zere are more fish—"

"In the sea. I know. But I don't much feel like going fishing."

"Ach so, but ven you do start ze anglingk again?"

"Your German accent needs work and you're having hearing difficulty, Jack."

"Himmel, und Donner, und Blitzen." His own voice reappeared. "You're right about my accent but not about my hearing. You *will* go looking again. You're a young healthy man. You're hurting, but you will get better."

"I hope you're right."

"I am. And when you decide to cast again, will you still want a fighting fish or are you going to set your bait for a gentler species?" He held his hands cupped in front of his chest. "One with a nice pair of pectoral fins"—Jack made sinuous movements with his hands—"and an alluring tail? One who'd be perfectly happy swimming in the pond rather than heading out into the deep oceans?"

Barry managed to smile. "You really are an eejit, Mills. You know bloody well I'm not thinking about my future with girls, any girls, right now. I've one to get over. Remember?"

"I do." Jack leant back. "How long have we been friends?"

"Since 1953."

"That gives me the right to say what I'm going to say next."

"You can always tell me what you like."

Jack leant forward and said seriously, "You're a born-again romantic, Barry Laverty. You've never been able to have fun with girls. You always fall head over heels in love with 'em."

"I do not."

"Oh? Really?" Jack said. "Right after we went through puberty, boy, there was the chorister with the cute blonde bangs, and dimples. You never even spoke to her. Just sat and drooled every Sunday when the school sent us to church. Moped all week until you saw her again."

"Saint Mark's at Dundela," Barry said, remembering the crocodile of black-jacketed and pinstripe-trousered pupils winding down from his boarding school to the local church.

"When her folks took her to England, you swore blind you'd never look at another girl." Jack was counting on his fingers. "Then there was the one whose dad ran an ice-cream shop in Bangor. You took her out twice, lost your heart forever, until an older lad whisked her off. You declared that was definitely it."

"Gina," Barry said. "Gina . . ."—he had to try hard to remember—"Luchi." And Jack was right. Way back then, Barry'd thought his heart would never mend.

"Then you started shooting for the moon."

"I what?"

"You were fifteen. We got a new Mamselle."

Barry did remember the young, sloe-eyed, brunette Frenchwoman. The school employed a new one every year so the pupils could practice conversational French. "Come on, Jack. Every boy in that sex-starved boarding school had—"

"Fantasies about her." Jack pointed a finger at Barry. "You fell in love. Wrote her poems. You were still moping when we came back after the summer holidays. But she was gone—they each stayed for only a year."

Barry had to laugh at himself. "Well," he said, "her replacement had a moustache."

Jack grinned. "And legs like a Mullingar heifer's—beef to the ankle." His grin faded. "We all had crushes as kids—but you, Laverty, you never stopped. It was always undying love." He finished his beer. "After we started medical school there was one of the girls in our class, Hilda something-or-other."

"Cleary."

"Right. Then a couple in between we've both forgotten. Hang on." He frowned. "Mandy . . . Mandy Baird, the unit clerk on Ward 22."

"Come on, Jack. I think I took her out twice. I wasn't serious about her."

"The exception, my boy, that proves the rule. After her there was a certain green-eyed nurse in our houseman's year—"

"Who married a surgeon."

"That's when you decided to devote your life one hundred percent to the celibate priesthood of medicine."

Barry grimaced. It was true. "Go on."

"I'm not going to say much about your most recent amour."

Barry felt a lump. "Thanks, Jack. I appreciate that."

"But I *am* going to observe, as your oldest friend, that after all your previous . . ."

Barry knew Jack was hunting for the right word. What he'd said already was quite a mouthful for a man who usually hid his emotions behind foreign accents and a boisterous bonhomie.

". . . your previous *liaisons*, your recovery *was* slow and painful, but eventually it was complete. You may have been left with some scars, but you didn't develop any antibodies."

"Antibodies?"

"Aye. You didn't become immune to women, despite what you might have thought at the time."

"You're right," Barry sighed. "Six months after the nurse I took a hell of a tumble for Patricia."

Jack waved to the waitress and made a scribbling action on the palm of his left hand. "So, me old son, I'm betting that it won't be too long until you'll be telling me you were wrong about—"

"Patricia?" Barry frowned. "That's pushing the friendship thing a bit far, Jack. Patricia *was* the real thing. Still is. I'll never get over her." He sat back in his chair and hunched his shoulders. Jack didn't know what real love was. He was too interested in "a nice pair of pectoral fins and an alluring tail." But he, Barry Laverty, knew about love. He looked over at his friend, who was still grinning at him.

Barry frowned as a thought struck. Am I being just a tad supercilious claiming to be the only one of the pair of us who's ever been in love? Is there just an outside chance that at the moment I'm enjoying feeling sorry for myself? Am I welcoming the extra sympathy from O'Reilly, Kinky, and the folks in the village? Is it possible that based on my past record, Jack is right?

Jack, perhaps regretting coming close to the line, retreated into his usual self. Barry could have sworn John Wayne was sitting opposite when his friend drawled, "In that case, pardner, let's settle up in this here saloon, saddle up, and mosey over to the Royal Victoria Corral."

"Jack, I—" Barry shook his head.

"Listen up, pilgrim, back at my homestead you agreed we'd go. If yuh wanna, you kin sit when we get there and carry a torch fer the lil' lady. Me? I sure figger I'm gonna enjoy the hoedown at the nurses home."

And despite his inner ache, Barry grinned, shook his head, and said, "Eejit, Mills. Buck eejit."

Jack parked the Mini. The gale whistled between the two halves of the Clinical Sciences Building that sat on each side of the road running through the grounds of the Royal Victoria Hospital. They were joined by an umbilical cord in the form of an overhead, enclosed walkway. "Down here's like the wind tunnel at Short Brothers aircraft factory," Jack said.

Barry had to agree. "Bugger," he said, as his tweed cap blew off. He didn't catch it until he was opposite the Royal Maternity Hospital, which stood behind the Royal Victoria.

He picked his cap from the gutter, dusted it off, and waited. Jack was a friend, a man who could make Barry face up to himself. It was beginning to dawn on him that he had expected, and still did expect, to marry one day, and when he did, he was pretty sure he'd want the same kind of marriage as his folks. Dad worked. Mum ran the house. That's the way it had been when they got married back in the thirties. Granted, more women were having careers since the war, but here in Ulster traditional ways died hard.

And that kind of arrangement was a damn sight less complicated than having an ambitious engineer and a doctor under the same roof.

Jack caught up with Barry. "You, Laverty, if you were able to run *and* carry a rugby football, could play on the wing for Ireland." As Barry fell into step with his friend, Jack continued: "You took off there like a liltie. I thought you were going right up the front steps of the Royal Maternity."

"Not tonight," Barry said. "I'm off duty."

"That was a great two months we spent there in '62, learning obstetrics," Jack said, "and chatting up the student midwives. There was a wee one from Magherafelt . . ." He let his voice drift off.

"I left that side of the business up to you, Mills," Barry said, "but I really enjoyed the training."

"Did you think any more about what we talked about last time you were up in town?"

"Me specialising in obstetrics?"

"Aye."

"A bit. Having to refer every interesting case has been getting to me. I sent one to your boss. I think she's got an amoebic liver abscess."

"In Ballybucklebo? Crikey." Jack slipped into *The Goon Show*'s Mr. Banerjee's accent. "They are being things of great rarity in this green land I am tinking. In my country they are ten for a paisa."

"A what?"

"A paisa, Sahib. There are being one hundred to each rupee. It is being a diagnostic coup of the first magnitude for the young man of healing, isn't it?"

"Not really," Barry said, smiling at his friend's perfect mimicry. "I've only been able to suspect what she has. But you and your boss have the tools and the training to make a definite diagnosis and start treatment. I'd find doing that satisfying."

"True." Jack's native speech had returned. "On the other hand, she'll thank us—they all do—but she'll not give us a bottle of whiskey for Christmas. I'll bet you get lots from grateful customers. And I'll bet it lets you feel satisfied in a different way."

As they turned into the lee of the multistorey nurses home, Barry remembered Donal and Julie Donnelly's thank-you bottle and how gratifying it had felt to be the recipient. "I suppose," he said, looking down at his feet as he climbed the steps to Bostock House.

"Hi, Doctors. Nice to see yiz."

Barry looked up to see Joe, ex-prizefighter and now doorman and guardian of the nurses home, holding the glass door ajar. "Hi, Joe."

"Go on, on in," Joe said. "There's a wheen of your oul' mates and a whole clatter of pretty nurses, you know." Joe's grin always looked faintly out of place on his battered face with its broken nose and heavily ridged eyebrows. "But just remember, it's still like when yiz was students. Them wee girls is in *my* charge, so they are. So you two behave yourselves. Savvy?"

"Oh, I will," said Jack. He winked at Barry.

"Me too," Barry said, but he meant it.

25

Dance 'til Stars Come Down from the Rafters

"Behave myself?" Jack said, as he took off his coat and watched a young woman walk past, his head moving from side to side in time with the sway of her hips. "Och, sure, this fox is only going into the henhouse for a bit of warmth."

"Mills, you're incorrigible," Barry said, hanging his coat beside his friend's. Then he followed Jack through the foyer and into the main hall, which for tonight was a ballroom.

Couples thronged the dance floor. Single women sat on chairs along the left wall and partnerless men sat, stood, or lounged along the right. Smoke from cigarettes curled lazily upward and was thrown into bright contrast with the room's dimness by flashes from a mirror-covered ball. It rotated slowly over the centre of the room and sent florin-sized silver discs of light racing each other through the smoke and across the floor.

The Stanley Coppel Band, a jazz combo, played on a raised stage at the far end of the room. Barry recognised the number as "Skokiaan." Their drummer, Barry Lowry, and their trumpeter and leader, Chris Blencoe, had, like Barry and Jack, attended Campbell College.

"Speak of the devil," Jack said. "I see Mandy Baird's here." He nodded toward a jiving young woman with shining black hair that fell in a cascade to her midback, then flew out behind her as she spun. "Wonder if she's here on her own."

"You'll see at the end of this set." Barry watched Harry Sloan go by; he was holding Jane Duggan, the blonde nurse who had scribbled Peggy Duff's phone number on a piece of paper. The same piece of paper on which he'd scrawled the Yacht Club's number for Kinky.

When the music stopped, couples stayed together on the floor or moved toward the foyer. Single people went back to their respective sides of the hall, women to the left, men to the right.

"Mandy is on her own," Jack said. "I'm off."

"Warmth in the henhouse, I suppose? Off you go," Barry said. "I'll sit this one out and study the talent." In fact, he simply intended to sit. He wasn't interested in dancing tonight.

Barry shook his head and watched Jack stride across the floor and nip in front of a gangly lad with buckteeth who looked as if he'd been going to ask Mandy to dance. If the armed forces ever needed a missile that unerringly homed in on pretty girls, they'd use Jack Mills as a template. As Barry moved toward the men's row of chairs, he became aware of a scent he recognised. Je Reviens. He'd been here the last time he'd noticed it. He felt a tap on his shoulder and turned.

"Hello, Barry." The young woman's lips and dark eyes smiled at him. "How are you?"

"Peggy." Barry swallowed. "Peggy Duff. Nice to see you." She wore her black hair as she had before, shoulder-length and curled in under her chin, contrasting smartly with her high-collared, white silk blouse.

She shrugged. "I'm fine. Still single. I didn't expect to see you here tonight."

He remembered that she'd been getting over a two-timing boyfriend.

"So how are things with you, Barry? Has your girlfriend gone back to study at Cambridge and you're off the leash again?"

"She's gone back," he said, realising how flat his voice sounded.

"Oh-oh," she said. "Bad as that?"

He nodded.

"So you're not just having a night out with the lads? Harry's with Jane, I know, and I remember Jack . . ." She inclined her head to where Jack had Mandy on her feet. "I run into him on the wards now and then." She smiled. "Handsome devil."

"He is." And you're a very pretty nurse, Barry thought. I'm surprised he hasn't asked you out.

"He asked me to dinner a few weeks ago," she said.

Barry smiled. "That's my Jack."

"But I made an excuse." She looked directly at Barry. "He's a nice boy, but he's not my type."

"He's my best friend," Barry said. He wondered if his comment had sounded as defensive to Peggy's ears as it had to his own. He got his reply in her awkward laugh.

"Well, you know what I mean. He's a nice man, I'm sure, but he's a bit . . . fast."

Barry nodded. "That's Jack."

"So he's dragged you here to force you to have fun? Jane did that for me. It does help. A bit. She keeps trying to mother me."

What had he said to Jack not an hour ago about wanting to have a girl who might mother him?

"Friends can come in handy," he said. He wondered if Jane had told Peggy about giving Barry her phone number. Probably not. If Peggy'd known and he hadn't phoned, she was smart enough to understand he wasn't interested and would not have approached him tonight.

She reached and took his hand. "She found someone else?"

He nodded.

"I'm sorry, Barry. I truly am. I know how you feel."

As he always did when offered well-meant sympathy, Barry felt close to tears. He was relieved when a voice made tinny by the microphone announced, "Ladies and gentlemen, next a set of blues. 'Saint Louis,' 'Saint James Infirmary,' and 'Beale Street.'" The music started slowly, sadly, a hoarse lament for a lost love.

Barry would have preferred to be on his own, but convention left him no choice. "Would you care to dance?" He'd thought it would be difficult to ask a girl, would somehow be disloyal to Patricia, but since his conversation with Jack in the restaurant the words were not as hard to utter as he'd expected.

At least it was a slow set. He'd be less likely to trample on Peggy's feet. She was warm in his arms. Putting her lips close to his ear, she sang along in a pleasant soprano:

I got the Saint Louis blues, just as blue as I can be . . .

Jack and Mandy moved by. Jack winked at Barry, took his hand from the skirt over her buttock, and formed an "O" with his thumb and index finger.

Barry was unsure if Jack meant he was already set up with Mandy, or that he approved of Barry's choice. It didn't matter. This Peggy was a nice friendly lass, even if she wasn't Patricia. Her voice was pleasing, her breath gentle on his neck, and her slim waist fitted neatly into the crook of his arm. He held her more tightly and brought the warmth of her closer. She rested her head on his shoulder.

There was a comfort to be had, and although she was the one being cradled, he felt like an infant, held and insulated from the gale raging outside and protected from the hurt in his heart. Barry sensed her lips brush his cheek, thistledown on an arid plain. He planted a chaste peck on her forehead and was pleased when she did nothing to indicate she wanted him to go any further.

He might dance with her again later in a slow set, even buy her a drink as the night wore on if she'd not paired up with some other fellah, but that was as far as Barry wanted things to go tonight.

They shuffled around the floor until the last chorus of "Beale Street Blues" soared and died. The nearness of this pretty girl in his arms had been comforting, but it also brought memories of his holding Patricia, and that hurt.

Still together and holding hands, they drifted to the edge of the dance floor.

"Ladies and gentlemen," Chris Blencoe called into the mike, "we're going to take five; then we'll be back with a fast set: 'Tiger Rag,' 'Twelfth Street Rag,' and 'Cross Hands Boogie.'"

"I think," Barry said, not wanting to dance a fast set and also needing time alone, "I think I'll be sitting them out. I can just about manage slow ones without stamping all over my partner's toes." She was still holding his hand, but before he was forced into being more blunt about being on his own for a while, a voice warbled in his ear:

Why don't you go where fashion sits?

Barry had to smile. Then he said to Peggy, "Contrary to what you may think you just heard, this is *not* Fred Astaire, and he's not putting on the blooming Ritz. Peggy Duff, I think you know Jack Mills, and this is Mandy Baird."

Jack and Mandy nodded to Peggy, who nodded back.

"I heard you, Laverty, saying you were going to sit out the next set. Great idea. Come on the four of us, and we'll have a wee wet." He grabbed Barry by the arm and started toward the door.

Barry scowled at Jack, but had to follow. There was no getting out of it. He fell into step as they made their way, along with a small scrum of others heading in the same direction to a bar in a side room off the entrance foyer.

"Grab that one, Barry," Jack said, pointing to a circular table with an oilcloth covering, surrounded by four metal folding chairs. "You're nearest."

Barry fussed about pulling out the girls' chairs and getting them seated.

"Right," said Jack. "Peggy?"

"Vodka and orange, please."

"You'll be having a brandy, Mandy?"

"Please."

Barry saw the look she gave Jack from under lowered eyelids.

"Come on, Laverty. I'll need a hand to carry four drinks."

Barry stood at Jack's shoulder behind three other men who were waiting for their turn to order.

"I was hoping for a bit of peace and quiet," Barry said.

"Not when you're with your uncle Jack," he said. "Pretty girl, Peggy," Jack said. "I asked her to dinner once. No luck." He shrugged and winked. "If you don't ask, you'll never succeed. Hope you've better luck with her than I had."

"Not tonight, Jack."

"Why not? Come on, Barry. She's good-looking. Remember what I said in the Chinese place? Nice pectoral fins under that silk blouse. Bloody fine legs too."

Barry couldn't help himself. He looked over at the table. The young women were both leaning forward in conversation. Peggy sat with her left side turned to Barry. Her blouse had opened slightly at the neck, and he could see the rounded top of her right breast. He glanced down. Like many of the women here she wore a flared skirt over layers of petticoats. She had crossed her legs, and Barry admired the curve of her calves made silky beneath black nylons. He sighed. "Another time, another place perhaps, but not tonight, Jack. I'm not ready. Not yet."

The queue moved on when a short man, wearing a blazer with

the crest of Methodist College on the breast pocket, left the bar carrying two drinks.

"I despair, Barry, but all right if that's how you feel." Jack shook his head. "You can lead a horse to water—"

"And if you're buying, Mills, you *can* make this one drink. I'll have a small Jameson." Barry remembered what Fingal had said about men who were disappointed in love crawling into the bottle. Not Barry Laverty. "A small one."

"You'll have to wait until that bloke ahead gets his. Slow service tonight. Still . . ."—he waved over at Mandy—"I'm in no rush. Mandy'll wait for me." Jack pursed his lips. "I need a favour, Barry."

"Sure."

"Can you get yourself home?"

"To Ballybucklebo?"

"No, you eejit. To my place."

"Why?"

"We've only my car—"

The man ahead moved away from the bar.

As Jack quickly placed his order, Barry understood why Jack had asked. "And you've already told Mandy you'll run her home."

Jack grinned. "She lives out the Antrim Road way at the other end of town."

"I know. I took her out too, remember? Sure I'll get myself home. As long as you give me the key." And, he thought, if I need one, I now have the excuse of not having any transport if Peggy wants me to see her home.

"Good man ma da." Jack paid and picked up his and Mandy's drinks. He waited for Barry to grab the other two. As they moved aside and walked back to the table, Jack winked at Barry. "You'll know who said it, Barry, and he was right: 'Candy is dandy, but liquor is quicker.'" He set the glass on the table in front of Mandy. "Here you are, my dear."

"Ogden Nash," Barry said. He gave Peggy her vodka and orange, and sat beside her.

"Thank you," she said.

Barry was content to sit quietly, sipping his whiskey, occasionally contributing to the conversation, and being amused, as he always was, while his friend went into his act to impress both girls.

Barry enjoyed the company of the two pretty young women, enjoyed the *craic*. Half an hour passed, half an hour after which he suddenly realised he'd not thought about Patricia. Not until Peggy said something about the Belfast Opera Company and Barry remembered having eaten lasagne and being enthralled by the melding of two soprano voices in "Viens, Mallika," the "Flower Duet" from *Lakmé*. That was the night Patricia'd told him she wanted to be an engineer and hadn't time to fall in love. A smarter man than he would have listened and—Barry looked down to where Jack was surreptitiously caressing Mandy's thigh through her scarlet pencil skirt—moved on.

Damn it. There were more fish in the sea. Jack was right, but not for a while, and—he looked over to a young woman who was finishing her vodka and orange—not Peggy Duff. Not tonight anyway.

"Anyone for another?" Barry asked. It was after all his shout. Jack had bought the first round, and girls weren't expected to buy their own drinks. Jack and Mandy said yes. Peggy demurred.

As Barry went up to the bar to order, he decided he'd stay for this drink, take Peggy for a slow spin around the floor. Then he'd make his excuses and get a bus back to Camden Street.

26

Ill News Hath Wings

Barry could hear O'Reilly yelling from the landing. "That you, Barry? Keep your coat on. I need to have a word with you, but I'm going out to make a call. I want you to come with me."

Barry, having driven back from Jack's flat on a pouring Sunday afternoon, had no plans other than to curl up with *Trader to the Stars*, Poul Anderson's latest. Barry had found that science fiction could distract him, but if O'Reilly wanted to talk, it was fine. The novel would keep.

O'Reilly clattered downstairs. "Just on my way to Maggie's. I was going to go earlier, but I've been busy today."

"Anything exciting?"

"Not today. Yesterday there was. We can talk about it in the car."

"Is Maggie sick? Sonny?" Barry would have been surprised if Maggie Houston, née MacCorkle, was ill. She was a tough old biddy and, as Kinky might say, "wouldn't tear in the plucking," but Sonny had a history of chronic heart failure, which was controlled by drugs.

"No. They're both fine. I need to ask them for a favour." O'Reilly headed for the front door. "The Rover's out in front. With all that rain the back garden's like the Slough of Despond." He glanced down at Barry's pants and grinned. "Kinky won't mind if you don't get them covered in glaur."

O'Reilly pulled away from the kerb. "I'm going to ask the Houstons if they can do a bit of pet-sitting."

"Oh." So O'Reilly as usual was keeping the machinery that ran the village oiled—as if looking after the sick wasn't enough. Barry stared through the rain-streaked windscreen and tried to see if the moving blur immediately ahead was a cyclist. He was relieved, and surprised, when Fingal slowed and swerved to give the sodden pedaller room. Perhaps, Barry thought, after his senior colleague's own recent trip into a ditch, a certain old dog had been taught a new trick.

"There's no easy way to tell you this, Barry," O'Reilly said.

"Tell me what? About pet-sitting?"

O'Reilly shook his head. "The pet-sitting's only part of it. You were right about Alice Moloney."

"Alice?" Barry frowned. "I was right? How do you know?"

"Her abscess ruptured into her right lung yesterday evening." O'Reilly's voice was flat. "I wanted you to know as soon as you came home from town. I know you're going to take it hard, but it's not your fault the thing burst."

"My God." Barry sat hard back into his seat, grasped the dashboard. "Did it . . . ?" Please don't say she's dead. "Did it kill her?"

"No," O'Reilly said, "but she's pretty sick. I sent her up to the Royal. They operated straightaway. The surgeon phoned me when he'd finished. It took him three hours to clean out the abscess cavity, cobble up her liver, and close the hole in her diaphragm."

"But she's going to be all right? Isn't she?"

O'Reilly pulled over at the verge beside the front gate to the Houstons' house. He leant over and put a hand on Barry's shoulder. "Too early to say. She's getting a lot of morphine. She has drains in her belly, her chest. She's had a blood transfusion and she's still on a drip. Nasogastric tube in her stomach. Chloroquine as an antiamoebic drug, antibiotics to prevent any superimposed bacterial infection. It'll be a rough few days, but she should pull through."

"But if she doesn't, it's my—"

"Fault? The hell it is." O'Reilly pounded his fist on the steering wheel. "I've already told you that it's not. It wasn't your doing that she was put on a waiting list. I reckon it was close to bloody genius you making the diagnosis in the first place."

"Eventually," Barry said. His voice was flat. "I saw her at the Bishops' party. I thought she looked pretty rotten. I didn't follow up for nearly a month." And I know why, he thought.

"She can't have been feeling too bad all that time, or she'd have come to see us. Wouldn't she?"

"I don't know," Barry said. "She's like a lot of country patients. She'd put up with a lot."

"Barry, stop blaming yourself. Come on. We've to see Maggie and Sonny." He got out and switched on a torch.

Barry followed into the darkness and the rain. The wet paved path reflected the torch's beam. He walked behind O'Reilly to the house. Dear Lord, not another disaster? Poor Alice. And even though he was trying not to be self-pitying, he couldn't help but think, poor Barry too. Was he going to be doomed to a future of medical calamities simply because he didn't, in rural practice, have the tools and training to do his job properly? Was working here really going to be worth the candle?

Barry waited. Even before O'Reilly pushed the bell, Sonny's five dogs began barking.

Above the yapping Sonny's voice could be heard through the closed door. "Into the kitchen. Now. *Now*, dogs." The noise faded, and light from the hall spilled onto the path. Sonny Houston, silver hair shining, stood ramrod stiff and offered his hand to O'Reilly. "Doctor O'Reilly, Doctor Laverty, please come in. Let me take your coats. Sorry about the dogs, but I hadn't the heart to put them out in their caravan on a night like this."

As he followed Fingal, Barry was still fretting about his tardiness in seeing Alice Moloney and his inability to treat her. He looked around as he took off his coat.

The last time he'd been to this house, on the morning of Sonny and Maggie's wedding day, the hall walls had been bare and freshly painted. Now they were decorated with photographs of the ancient city of Petra, carved out of a canyon in the Jordanian desert around 300 B.C. Sonny was an authority on the Nabataean civilization and had spent years on the archaeological site in the late 1940s.

Between a picture rail and the ceiling hung an oar, its blade blue-painted and adorned with gilt. Sonny Houston in his youth had been a Cambridge University rowing blue. Only those so honoured, or who had represented their college, were awarded an oar once it had been suitably decorated with their crew's names. Barry knew from O'Reilly that Sonny Houston, a man who used to live in an old motorcar, held a Ph.D. from Cambridge.

That university bedevilled Barry. Two weeks ago when he'd been walking to a sweetshop to make a phone call, he'd found himself thinking of Patricia with her new man in a punt on the River Cam. The subject of that call—Kevin Kearney—had been discharged home four days ago, well recovered from his croup.

Now Barry was here visiting an old Ulster couple, and there on the wall was yet another reminder of the place that had taken her.

He heard Sonny saying, "Please come into the living room," as he ushered them into a big room on the right side of the hall. "It's the doctors, pet," he said and moved to stand near Maggie's wing-backed armchair beside the fireplace.

Maggie, wrinkled as a prune and toothless as an oyster, grinned, set aside her knitting, and shooed her one-eared cat, General Sir Bernard Law Montgomery, off her lap.

"Doctors dear, come on, on in out of that there dirty night." She leant forward, picked up a poker, and stirred the glowing turf into a blaze. "Come on up to the fire. Get yourselves warm. Would you like a cup of tea in your hand? A slice of cake?"

Barry relished the homely smell of the burning turf, but he had previous experience with Maggie's tea, so stewed you could stand the spoon in it. And her fruitcake was heavy enough to ballast a yacht. He was relieved to hear O'Reilly say, "We don't have time for tea. Sorry, Maggie. We just popped in for a minute to ask you both for a favour."

She cocked her head to one side. "Another kiddie needs a sitter? Like Eileen Lindsay's wee Sammy before Christmas?"

"Not this time," O'Reilly said. "It's a cat and a budgerigar."

Barry immediately recognised whose animals they were. The first time he'd visited Alice Moloney for her anaemia, he'd met the spherical cat and had a run-in with the bird. His words spilled out: "Alice's budgerigar bit me once." Feeling responsible for Alice's present condition gnawed at him now.

O'Reilly ignored Barry's remark and said to Maggie, "Alice . . . Alice Moloney's had to go to hospital—"

"Och, dear," Maggie said. "I'm main sorry 'til hear that, so I am. Is she going to be all right?"

"We hope so, Maggie," O'Reilly said.

Bloody right we do, Barry thought, while noting Maggie's lack of curiosity about what specifically ailed Alice. Here in the country the details of a patient's illness were nobody's business until the sufferer chose to reveal them.

"What can we do to help?" Sonny asked.

"If it wouldn't be too much trouble, could you pop round every day and see to her animals? There are instructions and pet food in a cupboard under the sink."

"A cat and a budgie did you say, Doctor?" Sonny asked.

"Aye," said O'Reilly.

"We'd be delighted, wouldn't we, Maggie?"

"Aye, certainly. Sure don't we look after the General and this ould goat's five dogs?" She reached up and squeezed Sonny's hand. "Your man Noah could have used our help on his ark, so he could've." She chuckled and pointed a bony finger at Sonny. "My ould fellah was a dab hand at the digging in the desert for them bits of pottery. He could've taken care of dunging out the elephants— never mind cleaning a wee budgie bird's cage and a pussycat's litterbox."

Despite her teasing, Barry saw the adoring look that passed between Maggie and Sonny. Both in their sixties and daft about each other. He breathed in deeply, then exhaled. Their road to romance had been riddled with potholes, but love, abetted by O'Reilly, had conquered all. He knew he shouldn't envy them, but he did.

"That would be marvellous," O'Reilly said. "If you pop in at Number 1, Kinky'll have the keys to the dress shop and Alice's flat."

"Never you worry your head, Doctor dear," Maggie said. "We'll see to it."

"We will," said Sonny.

Maggie went on. "Now that's all settled, are you *sure* you'll not have a wee cup, like?"

"Positive," O'Reilly said. "Time we were off."

Sonny accompanied them to the hall, gave each man his coat, and said, "It'll be our pleasure to help."

O'Reilly shook his hand. "Thanks, Sonny. It'll take a load off Alice's mind, I know. Her sister will be visiting her at the hospital.

I'll make sure she tells Alice that the animals are being well looked after."

Barry buttoned his coat. He could sense the satisfaction—no, pleasure—in O'Reilly's voice. He was doing what he must always have been cut out to do. Sorting out yet one more difficulty as he cared for the whole village. Everything he'd told Barry in the last seven months, and the number of problems Barry'd seen and indeed helped O'Reilly to solve, attested to the big man's need to be completely involved with the lives of his patients and apparently deriving complete satisfaction from being so.

"Come on, Barry. Home." O'Reilly headed down the path.

"Night, Sonny," Barry said. He followed into the teeth of the gale.

As O'Reilly drove, he didn't seem to want to talk. He didn't even light his pipe. It suited Barry fine. He sat staring ahead, listening to the rhythmic sweeping of the windscreen wipers, feeling the jolting as the big car bounced along the uneven road.

Barry was still feeling envious of the strength of the feelings between Sonny and Maggie, a love that had persisted for years despite their being apart. He was envious too of the big man driving this huge old car. Would he, Barry, regardless of what career he chose, ever be as content as Doctor Fingal Flahertie O'Reilly? Was Barry Laverty's mounting dissatisfaction with rural practice perhaps a reflection of his own lack of contentment with how he'd bungled his affair with Patricia Spence and were his thoughts about specialisation motivated by a hope that if he did he might win her back?

His reverie was interrupted when O'Reilly parked outside Number 1. "Come on," he said, "let's see what Kinky has for us tonight."

27

Shorten and Lessen the Birth Pangs

O'Reilly let Barry in and swiftly followed. Fingal inhaled. He knew that aroma instantly. Kinky was making beef stew for dinner, and it would be studded with suet dumplings. He started unbuttoning his coat, smiling happily at the thought of her dumplings, but before he had time to take it off, Kinky appeared in the hall.

"I'm sorry," she said, "but your dinner's going to have to wait. I've just had the district midwife on the phone. She wants you to come at once. Hester Patton's in labour and far on, so."

"She's what?" O'Reilly said. "She's what?" He felt his nose tip blanching. "She's bloody well meant to be in hospital." It wasn't annoyance about being kept from his grub that had him tried. The farmer's wife, pregnant for the second time, was expecting twins. Three weeks ago he'd arranged for her to be admitted, in her thirty-second week. That was customary with multiple pregnancies. Admission for bed rest was meant to try to prevent premature labour. And if it did start, at least the patient was in hospital, the best place for delivery to occur. The actual delivery was often tricky, and preemie babies needed specialist nursing. Now Hester was in labour, five weeks early—and at home. Blast. Both Hester and the babies were in danger.

"Miss Hagerty said Hester took her own discharge yesterday.

She was bored and missing her family so she signed the papers and took herself off by the hand, so."

"Silly woman," O'Reilly said, shaking his head, "but it happens. Come on, Barry. We'll need to get a move on. I'll get the midwifery bags."

O'Reilly went into the surgery and reappeared clutching a heavy bag in each hand.

"Give me one of those, Fingal."

"I'll keep your dinner warm," Kinky said and closed the door.

They marched along the front path. The rain had stopped and the winds of the dying gale were pushing the clouds away.

O'Reilly opened the car's boot and waited for Barry to chuck his bag in before putting in the second.

O'Reilly started the engine and took off, muttering, "Out the Bangor-Belfast Road toward Maggie's old cottage, next right after that." He willed the car to go faster.

"I hope," said Barry, "Miss Hagerty's sent for the flying squad."

"She's bound to have. GPs shouldn't be trying to cope with premature twins in the patient's home." The pregnancy was only thirty-five weeks advanced. The babies would be small. The first one could slip out past a cervix that was not fully dilated. Either or both might be coming buttocks first. And after the babies were born, Hester might not expel the placentas or could haemorrhage. The potential for complications was enormous.

The flying squad was a backup for unexpectedly complicated home deliveries. Once Miss Hagerty had phoned, the Royal Maternity Hospital would have dispatched an ambulance with a crew of specialists and midwives, blood if Hester was to need a transfusion, and oxygen-supplied incubators for the wee ones.

"Trouble is," O'Reilly said, "even if they're on the way, they might not get through."

"Why not?"

"You'll see."

O'Reilly concentrated on the road ahead. Already he'd driven along a series of country roads, each more twisty and narrow than the last. They were going up into the Ballybucklebo Hills, past Sonny and Maggie's house.

The land's rolling contours were lit by the silver glow of a waning moon and Venus shining like a diamond solitaire. He craned forward to look up. The Milky Way seemed like a long smudge of chalk on a damp blackboard. Orion hung sideways, low in the eastern sky. From a distant hillcrest, the stark branches of a huge sycamore curled in silhouette.

As the car rounded a bend, O'Reilly saw a man outlined by the headlight beams. He was waving them down. O'Reilly slowed and parked behind Miss Hagerty's Morris Minor and a Massey-Harris tractor.

The car's lights and engine died, but the night was made bright by the tractor's beams.

O'Reilly and Barry were getting out as the man yelled above the roar of the tractor's engine. "Doctors, I'm main glad to see yiz, so I am."

"Doctor Laverty," O'Reilly bellowed, "this is Freddy Patton."
Barry nodded at the man.

"We'll have to go the rest of the way on the tractor," Freddy called. "After all the rain, the dip in the lane's flooded, so it is. I'll be back in a wee minute, Doctor." He drove out onto the road and turned left.

There was a wider place fifty yards away where Freddy Patton could turn the massive vehicle. O'Reilly listened to the notes of gears being changed, and he waited as the red taillights moved away and then the twin headlight beams drew nearer.

"Let's get the bags," O'Reilly said.

"Right."

O'Reilly opened the boot and grabbed the heavier of the two bags; Barry took the other. The air bore diesel exhaust and the scent of burning turf coming from the Pattons' farmhouse. The Massey-Harris grumbled to a halt. O'Reilly bellowed, "Have you room for two, Freddy?"

"Aye," Freddy called, with his hand cupped round his mouth to make a megaphone. "One of yiz can fit in the cab, t'other'll have to hang on behind, so they will."

"Never worry. Into the cab, Barry. Take this bag too." O'Reilly clambered up behind the driver, stood on the tractor's body, held onto Freddy's shoulders, and roared, "Damn the torpedoes. Full steam ahead." From force of habit he mentally cited his source. Rear Admiral David Farragut apparently uttered those words during the American Civil War battle of Mobile Bay.

With the engine rumbling and filling O'Reilly's nose with exhaust fumes, the tractor jolted along a lane so narrow that he had to keep ducking and dodging to avoid being scraped by the branches of the hawthorn hedge. The wind nipped at his cheeks.

The lights of the farmhouse beckoned, then vanished as the tractor headed into a hollow where O'Reilly could see the oily waters of a small lake disappearing through both hedges and stretching for a good ten yards ahead. He'd told Barry the flying squad might have trouble getting through. There was no "might" about it. He, Barry, and Miss Hagerty were going to have to manage.

The tractor's huge, ribbed, rear tyres drove through the flood, and soon the machine was climbing from the hollow. They rumbled into the well-lit barnyard.

"Get yiz down, Doctors. I'll bring the bags, so I will," Freddy said. "And mind yourselves. It's slippy, so it is."

Barry dismounted and headed for the house.

O'Reilly jumped down and his boot skidded. He had to twist violently to keep his balance. "Bugger it," he roared, as something ripped in his back. His left lumbrical, the big muscle that runs alongside the spine, was knotted in spasm. "Holy thundering Mother of Jay—" He sucked in his breath and scrunched his eyes shut as his left hand sought the sore spot. He blew out his breath through pursed lips, arched his back, and felt the knotting ease a little—but not enough. It would be impossible for him to bend over a labouring woman to deliver her babies.

Barry would have to manage.

Despite his pain, O'Reilly smiled. He already knew from earlier experience that Barry was a gifted *accoucheur.* Indeed sometimes he wondered why his assistant hadn't decided to specialise in obstetrics. Tonight, particularly with twins to be dealt with and himself *hors de combat,* he was grateful the young man had not. He'd make a fine partner. No doubt about it.

O'Reilly hirpled across the yard to where Freddy held the door open. He was a very tall, thin man, angular, balding, with sunken cheeks the colour of ripe tomatoes.

"Come on, on in, Doc." Freddy closed the door behind O'Reilly. "Your man Doctor Laverty's gone upstairs to Hester and Miss Hagerty, so he has. He took them big bags with him." He held out a hand. "Gimme your coat."

After the open-air ride along the farm lane, O'Reilly was grateful for the warmth coming from the range at the far side of the kitchen. He winced as he managed to shrug out of his coat.

"Bad back?" Freddy enquired.

"Aye. I wrenched it getting off the tractor."

"Boys-a-boys, but that can smart, you know." He frowned, then cocked his head to one side. "I've some powerful horse liniment. Will I get you a wee taste?"

O'Reilly shook his head. "Hester's in your bedroom?" He knew the house of old.

"Aye."

"I'll find her."

"Go ahead, Doc. I'll take a look at wee Jimmy. He's dead excited, so he is, that he's going to be the twins' big brother. I got him over about half an hour ago, and I have him asleep in his room. Then I'll have a wee cup of tea in my hand, like."

It took O'Reilly longer to climb the stairs than he'd anticipated. Each step sent twinges through his back. Twice he had to rest and rub his back. It felt like the time he'd cracked a couple of ribs playing rugby.

He heard panting, a woman's loud grunting, Barry speaking, then a high-pitched wailing. That must mean twin one had been delivered.

O'Reilly stood quietly in the doorway. His nostrils were filled with the acrid smell of amniotic fluid jostling for attention with the reek of disinfectant.

Barry, wearing a rubber apron and bloody rubber gloves, was handing a tiny baby to Miss Hagerty. The little one's reedy cries came in short bursts. While Miss Hagerty cleaned the newborn, Barry stood at Hester's side, talking to her and examining her belly.

"That's a boy. Miss Hagerty'll show you him in a minute. The other one's coming head first, so it shouldn't be long."

Barry kept a hand on Hester's tummy as he waited for the next contraction.

Miss Hagerty bundled up the newborn and put him into a blanket-lined drawer taken from a dressing table. A second, similarly prepared, jury-rigged cot waited for twin two. "I'll bring him over in just a wee minute, Hester," she said, "but I need to listen to the other one's heart." She lifted a foetal stethoscope from where it sat on the dressing table between a jar of Pond's face cream and a tin of talcum powder. Miss Hagerty put the wide end on Hester's bulging belly, bent over, and laid her ear on the flat circular end. O'Reilly saw her eyes widen. She looked straight at Barry. "Ninety-six," she said quietly.

O'Reilly grimaced. It should have been 144 beats per minute. That baby was in distress from lack of oxygen. He overrode his temptation, ricked back be damned, to intervene. Hadn't he been thinking moments ago that his young colleague was very good at obstetrics?

Barry turned and saw O'Reilly. "Fingal—"

"You carry on."

Barry hesitated, pointed a finger at his own breastbone, and mouthed, "Me?"

O'Reilly smiled and nodded. Come on, Barry, he thought. You're right to be scared, but I know you'll do fine.

Barry shrugged. "Open the forceps pack, please." He began to examine his patient vaginally. "Checking the other twin, Hester."

O'Reilly laid the pack on a small bedside table and moved the table to where it would be handy for Barry. As O'Reilly opened the pack, he silently cursed Hester's stubbornness in leaving the hospital despite medical advice. She was perfectly within her rights to have done so, but now was the time she and her premature babies needed a fully equipped facility. "Ready, Barry," he said.

"The heart rate's down to eighty." Miss Hagerty spoke softly.

Barry swallowed and squared his shoulders. "Doctor O'Reilly . . . Miss Hagerty . . . can you bring Mrs. Patton across the bed, buttocks over the edge, and each one of you support a leg?"

He turned to Hester. "Mrs. Patton, I'm sorry. I'm going to have to give your baby a hand to get born. It's going to be uncomfortable."

As the midwife and O'Reilly positioned the patient, he felt the spasms start in his back. He gritted his teeth, tried to ignore the pain, and willed his young assistant to get a move on.

28

Willing to Pull His Weight

Barry's hand trembled. He'd only ever done three forceps deliveries when he was training, all of those under supervision in a teaching hospital. He wished O'Reilly was in charge.

"The heart rate's sixty," Miss Hagerty said.

Barry gritted his teeth. He was sorry he'd not been able to put in a nerve block to numb the entire birth canal, but by the time he'd scrubbed his hands and put on his gloves, the first baby was nearly born. Nor had he time now. The second twin's heart could stop at any second so there was no time for a block, but he'd risk the minutes it would take to inject some local anaesthetic before he cut a wide episiotomy. "Just a jag, Hester."

She flinched as the needle went in and Barry injected. He waited for the local to take effect.

When he had examined Hester moments earlier, he'd found that the widest part of the baby's head had entered the pelvis, a precondition for a forceps delivery of a premature baby. Not only was the head engaged, it was also properly positioned, with the baby's chin well tucked into its chest and the back of its skull, the occiput, facing the mother's front.

"Heart rate's forty-eight," Miss Hagerty said.

Barry had to ignore the fact that the slowing of the heart was due to oxygen lack, but it was lack—not total deprivation. If the heart stopped and the oxygen supply to the little brain failed, he'd have four minutes before the baby would suffer irreparable brain damage, and not long after that it would die. The temptation was to rush. His mentor in the Royal Maternity had had a great Latin expression for situations like this. *Festina lente.* Make haste slowly.

He took heavy scissors. The imminence of the act he must perform stilled his tremor for the moment. He made the incision. It would give him extra room in which to work.

"We're ready, Barry," O'Reilly said. His voice was steady with no hint of the urgency Barry knew the far more experienced O'Reilly must be feeling. Barry started to sweat, pulled in a very deep breath, closed his eyes, opened them, and saw the trembling in his hand was worse.

He pursed his lips, clenched his fist, and when he opened it to pick up the right forceps blade, the tremor had stopped. He felt the metal cold through his glove. The heavy handle, grooved to allow a firm grip, ended in a lock that would be fitted to the second half of the instrument once it also had been inserted. Past the lock, the blade was curved out to one side to fit around the contours of the baby's skull and shaped in a fore-and-aft direction to accommodate the direction of the birth canal. It looked like an enormous spoon, except that most of the bowl had been removed, leaving only a rim of metal around the circumference. A set of Wrigley's obstetrical forceps was simply a pair of tongs. The blades were for grasping the object to be moved, and the handles for pulling.

"Eighty," said Miss Hagerty.

Better, but still too slow. Barry knew what he must do, but the thought of it made him queasy. Both halves of the forceps must be inserted into the birth canal to fit snugly around the baby's head.

The blades were unfeeling steel, impervious to any hurt. The canal was tearable flesh, and the premature, soft little head could easily be damaged.

Barry glanced at O'Reilly, who supported Hester's right leg. The big man's lips were drawn back in a rictus, as if he was in pain. But there was no time to worry about that. Barry moved to stand between the patient's legs, with his back to O'Reilly.

"I'm going to start, Hester," he said. "You'll feel a fair bit of pressure." Barry slipped his four right fingers into the vaginal opening, feeling the warmth on his knuckles and the firmness of the head beneath his fingertips. As gently as he could, he advanced his fingers between head and canal until the base of his upcocked thumb rested against Hester's pubic bone.

He heard her moaning.

"Sorry," he said, knowing he was going to have to hurt her more. In his left hand, he held the right blade of the instrument vertically at the opening, then positioned the tip between the baby's head and his fingers, which were protecting the mother's soft tissues.

"She's not contracting at the moment?"

"No, and the heart rate's sixty," Miss Hagerty said.

Festina lente. Barry stifled the temptation to rush and perhaps bungle things. Gradually he allowed the weight of the blade to carry the instrument down and forward so that it slid deeply inside and fitted snugly around the head.

Hester groaned and tried to squirm. Barry heard O'Reilly gasp, glanced round, and saw the big man's eyes were screwed tightly shut and the veins in his neck standing out.

"You all right, Fingal?"

"Fine." O'Reilly growled. "And you're . . . doing . . . fine."

Grateful for the encouragement, Barry repeated the manoeuvres with the left blade, and with both inserted it was simple to engage the two halves of the lock by bringing the handles tightly together.

Some of the tension ebbed from Barry. He'd inserted the forceps by feel. If he'd not positioned them correctly, the lock would not have been closable and he would have had to remove the instrument and start all over again.

And time was moving on.

He looked at Miss Hagerty. "I'm ready. Can you get her to push with the next contraction?"

"Aye."

Barry waited until he heard Miss Hagerty saying, "Push, Hester dear. Puuuuush."

Now the contracting uterus and Hester's efforts were acting on the baby, moving it down deeply into the canal. To these efforts, Barry added traction with the forceps. At first he exerted pressure downward. He had to keep the baby's chin tucked in until it had negotiated the curve of the pelvic canal before beginning to ascend. He saw the vaginal opening distended by a dark circle about two inches in diameter. Twin two had dark hair.

"All right, Hester. Take a rest," Miss Hagerty said.

Barry had to steel himself to hold the forceps steady until the next contraction started. The three minutes before Miss Hagerty's exhortation "*Puuuush*" seemed like an eternity.

He pulled the forceps toward himself, and more of the head appeared. As the expulsive forces of the uterine contractions combined with Hester's pushing caused the baby to extend its neck, Barry directed his pull upward. Then he stopped and held the instrument still. He wanted the baby's head to come out slowly. Letting it appear with a rush could rip the mother despite the episiotomy and by sudden decompression damage the little brain.

Slowly, slowly, a wrinkled forehead appeared, then the bridge of the nose, the mouth. Barry used the little finger of his left hand to clear mucus. Cry, he thought, holding his breath. Cry, please cry, and in obedience the baby gulped and gave a tiny reedy wail.

Barry exhaled. Now the head was delivered, he removed the blades of the forceps, rapidly set them on the table, and guided little girl Patton into the world. It was a matter of moments to doubly clamp, then cut, the umbilical cord.

"It's a girl," he said.

Simultaneously he heard Hester's "Thank you, Doctor," sounding as if she was speaking through tears, and O'Reilly telling Miss Hagerty to move the patient back onto the bed.

Barry stepped back to let O'Reilly swing Hester in a quarter circle so she could lower her legs onto the rubber-sheeted bed. For that, Barry was grateful because now that Miss Hagerty's hands were free, he could give the little girl to her.

That would in turn allow him to take care of the delivery of the afterbirths and sew up the episiotomy while O'Reilly and Miss Hagerty saw to the babies.

Barry inhaled deeply. When moments earlier the baby's heart had kept slowing, he had wondered what had happened to his own heart rate. It was probably back to normal now, but certainly it must have exceeded a hundred then. His hands were clammy from sweating inside the gloves, and Barry reckoned that anyone with his lack of experience would have had sweaty palms too. Proper training was what allowed his senior obstetrical colleagues to approach difficult deliveries with the same confidence that Barry would have had when examining a sore throat.

Yet despite the stress, if he asked himself how he felt after the forceps delivery of premature twins, his answer would be "Good. Damn good."

Barry snipped the last stitch. "All done, Hester."

"Thank you, Doctor Laverty."

He straightened and offered up silent thanks that he'd had no difficulty delivering the placentas, nor had there been any haemorrhage. Periodic reports from Miss Hagerty as he'd been suturing had reassured him that both babies were doing well. Don't get a swollen head, Barry Laverty, he told himself, but he could take pride from having successfully delivered twins, the second one with forceps. It was a good feeling, a gratifying feeling, and more satisfying than dealing with the coughs, sniffles, and sprains he saw every day. Barry stood and stripped off his gloves.

For the first time since he had walked into the room he became aware of the details of his surroundings. A two-bar electric fire made it pleasantly warm. He noticed a pot of Dutch hyacinths on the small dressing table, their white blooms reflected in a mirror. But their usually powerful scent was no match for the smells of a delivery room. On each side of the bed were prints of famous Irish racehorses. He was pretty sure the one on the right was Himself, the great Arkle.

He dropped the gloves into a metal basin. "Thanks, Miss Hagerty," he said to the midwife, who was starting to tidy up. "The babies still all right?"

"Both pretty small. I'd guess just over five pounds, so they are the right size for their age. We have the pair of them in the kitchen in their drawers near the range. You mustn't let a wee one get chilled."

Barry knew all about cold syndrome, a potentially lethal condition brought about by not keeping newborns, particularly premature newborns, warm.

"Doctor O'Reilly took a very good look at them both and he says they're grand—but they need right now to be in incubators in forty percent oxygen." She looked hard at Barry. "He's below sorting that out with Royal Maternity."

Barry understood why. Premature babies were greatly at risk of developing RDS—respiratory distress syndrome—or hyaline membrane disease, as it was better known. Two years earlier, the condition had killed the premature son of Jackie Kennedy and her husband, American President Jack Kennedy.

Hester's pregnancy had been only three days more advanced than Jackie Kennedy's, and if RDS wasn't to claim two more victims, the only hope of prevention was to keep the twins in an oxygen-rich atmosphere until the risk period was over.

Should he explain this to the drowsy Hester? He decided not to distress her—not yet. He untied his rubber apron. "I'll nip down and see what Doctor O'Reilly's up to."

"Go on . . . and . . . Doctor Laverty?" Miss Hagerty said.

"Yes?"

"You've a quare soft hand under a duck. I've seen specialists, so I have, not make such a good fist at delivering twins."

Barry felt himself blushing. "Thank you," he said. "Thank you very much." And when he left to get washed, there was a spring in his step. For a moment he wondered, not for the first time since he'd come to Ballybucklebo, about a career in obstetrics.

Jack Mills had suggested it too in the Club Bar back in January. And last night he'd said he thought Barry was going to run up the steps of the Royal Maternity. Barry'd thought Jack had not meant anything by it, but then Barry wondered about men in mediaeval times running to, and taking sanctuary in, the great cathedrals. For all Jack's I'm-just-a-yokel-from-the-wilds-of-Cullybackey, underneath he was as sharp as paint. Had his old friend been more than hinting at Barry considering a career in obstetrics? It was worth thinking about.

Barry hardly noticed the twins sleeping before the kitchen range. His nose was filled with an astringent odour. His senior colleague, stripped to the waist, was bent over, while Freddy Patton rubbed something into O'Reilly's back. Whatever Freddy was using, the smell of it would have gagged a maggot.

"Fingal?" Barry asked.

"I ricked it getting off the tractor," O'Reilly growled.

That would explain why he had seemed to be in pain while he supported Hester's leg. Typical of the man to put the patient first.

"Freddy's rough as a badger's arse, but he—ouch!—swears by this horse liniment." O'Reilly screwed up his face.

"I do so, so I do." Freddy rubbed vigorously. "Your man Mr. Porter, the vet over in Conlig, give it me. I tell you it surely beats what I used to do if a horse injured a shoulder." Freddy kneaded O'Reilly's flank as if he were working with bread dough.

"Jesus Murphy, Freddy," O'Reilly roared. "You're marmalizing me. Go easy."

"I'm sorry, sir, but I cannot, you know. Mr. Porter was very particular, so he was. It's to be rubbed in hard if it's to do the horse a power of good."

O'Reilly stepped away. "It may have escaped your attention, Freddy Patton, but I am *not* a bloody equine. That's enough."

"Don't blame me, sir, then, if you don't get the best of it." Freddy sniffed and rubbed his hands together.

Barry chuckled. This was the second time he'd seen his senior colleague on the receiving end of treatment and advice. The last time was when Kinky had sorted out O'Reilly's bronchitis. And fair play to Freddy. Next to Kinky, he must be one of the very few folks in Ballybucklebo not overawed by Doctor Fingal Flahertie O'Reilly.

"Never mind that." O'Reilly started to put on his shirt. "It's time you got back to the end of the lane, Fred." He tucked in the tails and spoke to Barry. "I got on the phone to the Maternity ambulance dispatchers. They've got on the radio to the squad. They had come, but took one look at the flood and headed back. He's told them to come back and park by our cars. Freddy'll meet them and bring the paediatrician and one incubator on the tractor."

"One?"

"Aye." O'Reilly nodded at the babies. "The twins're small enough for both to fit inside—at least until they get to the ambulance. Then they'll get one each."

"What about Hester?"

O'Reilly shrugged, winced, and thrust a hand into the small of his back. "Horse liniment. I might as well have rubbed it with vegetable marrow jam." He blew out his cheeks. "Hester'll have to stay at home, and between Miss Hagerty and us we'll keep an eye to her. Did you explain to her about RDS?"

Barry shook his head.

"Fair enough. We'll not yet for a while. Usually if it's going to happen it'll be in the first twenty-four hours. We'll not cross our bridges until we come to them. Now," said the shirted O'Reilly, "help me on with my jacket."

Barry eased the big man gently into his tweed coat as O'Reilly told him that Miss Hagerty knew to sort out the delivery bags and that Freddy would help her carry them to her car when she was finished here. "We'll wait for the incubator, and once Freddy's taken it and the babies to the ambulance and come back again for us, we're for home. I'm not looking forward to being bounced on his tractor, and you'll have to drive the Rover."

"Fair enough."

"I want a handful of aspirin, a huge Jameson, and my dinner." He grimaced. "Dear God," he said, "I've more knots in my back than a Chinese silk carpet. This is going to take a day or two to settle down. I'm afraid, Barry, you're going to have to run the shop single-handed." He clapped Barry's shoulder. "And I'm absolutely confident you'll do a great job."

Barry smiled. If he handled all the cases like the last one, he'd justify O'Reilly's confidence. The question was, was running a GP's shop here in Ballybucklebo the way he wanted to spend the rest of his life? A life without Patricia Spence.

29

In a Handbag?

O'Reilly put down the Somerset Maugham classic *Ashenden: Or the British Agent.* It was almost forty years old and Fingal had read it many times. He grimaced and shifted, trying to make himself more comfortable in the armchair. Bloody back. Although it was on the mend, he wasn't up to much yet, but O'Reilly reckoned that the medical matters of Ballybucklebo and the surrounding townlands were in good hands and had been for the last three days. Barry had had full surgeries, enough home visits to keep him occupied in the afternoons, and fortunately for him, not a single night call.

He was out now visiting, of all places, the school. The principal had phoned to say some of the children had head rashes and perhaps it would save the doctors time if one of them came around and saw the kiddies en masse.

O'Reilly heard the phone ring in the hall and Kinky's tread as she went to answer it. If it were a patient calling, poor old Barry might have to go out again as soon as he came home. It wouldn't be pleasant for him, driving on the narrow twisting roads after dark, and already the evening was drawing in. O'Reilly guessed it was about four thirty. He glanced at his watch. It was four twenty-nine.

Kitty would be here soon. He'd missed her. Since they'd dined at the Culloden Hotel on the evening after the pheasant shoot more than two weeks ago, he'd only spoken to her on the telephone twice. When she'd got back from Tallaght last week she'd been busy, and last weekend she'd gone to the painting workshop in Donegal, the one she'd put off to be with him last month.

He'd phoned her on Monday to see when she'd be free, told her about his back, and taken the opportunity to explain why Alice Moloney was in no position to advise about Kinky's handbag. Kitty said she'd find one in Anderson and McAuley's or Robinson and Cleaver's in Belfast.

Poor Alice was recovering. When he'd spoken to Sir Donald this morning, O'Reilly had learnt that her temperature was normal, the tube in her stomach and her intravenous drip had been removed, and she was eating a light diet. Very promising.

He switched on a table lamp that Kinky had moved close to hand and picked up the book again. Interesting chap, Somerset Maugham. He'd been a doctor but gave it up to write. He lived on the French Riviera and would be ninety-one this year. O'Reilly particularly liked his short stories and this tale of Ashenden, the British secret agent. He wished that something would give him the man's powers of deduction. O'Reilly was no closer to solving the riddle of Flo's Fancy.

"Excuse me, sir."

He looked up. He hadn't heard Kinky coming in. "Yes, Kinky?"

"That was my sister down in Cork phoning. You asked me on Saturday night to find out about a jockey, Eugene Power, from Newceston."

"I did, by God. I was thinking of Flo's Fancy only a moment ago."

"Aye, so," she said. "I phoned Fidelma that night. I'm sorry it's taken so long, but she *thought* our brother Tiernan, who's run the family farm since our da passed away, might know something. It seems Mr. Power's a great road bowler like Tiernan."

"And?"

"Tiernan was in Philadelphia visiting our big brother, Art. He'd been expected back this morning, but the flight into Shannon Airport was delayed and it's quite the drive from there to Beal na Bláth."

O'Reilly grunted. "Rather him than me. The roads down in the Republic are even worse than those up here."

"True, sir, but he's home now. Fidelma's had a word with him, so."

O'Reilly quickly sat forward and immediately regretted it. "Arrrgh. Jesus Murphy." His hand flew to his back. He gritted his teeth. "Sorry, Kinky."

"I've heard worse," she said. "And I'm sorry for your back." She moved behind his chair. "Now do you sit forward, sir."

He did and she fussed about rearranging his cushions. "Sit back."

He did. "Thanks, Kinky. That's better."

She came round, stood in front of him, cocked her head to one side, and frowned. "I'd rest more contented if you'd see a proper doctor."

O'Reilly laughed. "You think I'm an improper one?"

"I do not, but it does be well known that a physician who treats himself has nothing but an *amadán* for a patient, so."

O'Reilly would not let many people call him an idiot to his face. He simply said, "Kinky, I appreciate your concern, but it's only a sprain. Time will heal it. More to the point, what did your brother say?"

"Tiernan told Fidelma he knows Eugene. Says he's mostly a sound man, but—"

"But?"

"Two years ago he was cautioned at Newmarket Racecourse in England for perhaps pulling a horse so a slower animal could win at very good odds. The Jockey Club couldn't prove it—they'd have had his licence if they'd been able to—but they were mighty suspicious."

"Pulling a horse, by God?" A jockey who'd do it once would do it a second time. Now there was something he might be able to use. "Thank you, Kinky. Thank you very much."

"I hope it helps you, sir—and lets you help that eejit Donal Donnelly. He should stop acting the lig now he has that wee Julie to look after."

O'Reilly shook his head. Did anything of importance in Ballybucklebo slip past Kinky Kincaid? "I'm sure it will help, Kinky. I'm sure it will." He heard the front doorbell. "I think that might be Kitty," O'Reilly said. He studied Kinky's face. It was expressionless.

"Excuse me, sir," she said. "I'll go and see."

O'Reilly wondered if Kinky's information about the jockey would be enough to confront Bertie Bishop and ask him just what the divil he was up to. Fergus Finnegan's opinion would be welcome, and surely by now Donal must have been told something by Willie McArdle, the bookie. Patience, he told himself. Time will tell. O'Reilly heard women's voices from below and a tread of the staircase creaking.

"Come in, Kitty. Welcome back to Ulster and to this house," he said, as she appeared in the doorway. "You'll forgive me if I don't get up."

"I will. How are you?" He heard the concern in her voice and relished having her worrying about him. "I'm sure you're stiff and sore."

"I am."

"You poor old thing."

His smile belied his next words. "Less of the *old* thing."

She crossed the floor. Lord, but Kitty O'Hallorhan was one of the most graceful women he had ever known.

"Fingal," she said, bending to drop a kiss on his forehead, "you're no spring chicken, but you're wearing well. You're still nearly as handsome as you were when I met you—"

"Nearly?"

"Your nose was straight then."

He remembered the bout when it had been broken.

She bent over and gave his tummy a prod. "And there is a bit more of you than there used to be."

He laughed. "It's just more of me for you to appreciate." He pointed to the other armchair. "Have a pew."

She sat and crossed her legs. "New shoes?" he asked, admiring a pair of brown, stiletto-heeled pumps. "Very smart."

"Mmm," she said. "I thought, seeing I was in Robinson and Cleaver's, I might as well do a bit of shopping for myself as well as—" She lowered her voice as she handed him a paper shopping bag. "Have a look."

O'Reilly pulled out crumpled tissue paper. He could see a maroon suede handbag with a shiny gilt clasp. "Kitty," he said, "for me? You shouldn't have."

She burst out laughing. "Idiot."

Her laughter warmed him, even if it was the second time today he'd had his mental abilities questioned. "You know what Graham Greene said?" he asked.

She was still laughing as she shook her head.

" 'Beware of a man who makes you laugh.' Or something like that."

Her laughter faded, to be replaced by a gentle smile. "And should I beware of you, Fingal Flahertie O'Reilly?"

He smiled at her and said, "Begod, you should, Kitty O'Hallorhan, for if I could get out of this chair I'd give you a great big hug and a kiss."

"I'll save you the trouble," Kitty said, rising, but then she hesitated. "I hear Kinky coming."

"I'll give you the money for the bag later," he whispered.

"Ahem," said Kinky. "I do not wish to intrude, so, but I thought you might appreciate a cup of tea and some toasted, buttered barmbrack."

"Marvellous," O'Reilly said. "Can you put the tray on the sideboard?"

"I can."

When Kinky turned to put it down, O'Reilly stuffed the tissue paper back and handed the shopping bag to Kitty. As he did so, he inclined his head to Kinky.

Kitty nodded at him. "Mrs. Kincaid?"

Kinky turned.

"It still bothers me that I upset you about not washing the pancake dishes. This is just a wee something to say I'm sorry." Kitty handed her the bag.

Kinky blushed. "I'm sorry too, Miss Kitty. It does be a long journey from County Cork. I was tired that day. I should have held my tongue and not taken the hump, so."

"Open it, Kinky," O'Reilly said. "Let's see what it is."

She pulled out the handbag. Her eyes widened. "Och, Kitty, *achara*. It's beautiful."

O'Reilly smiled. Kinky had called her Kitty not Miss, and for good measure had chucked in *achara*, Irish for "my dear."

"I'm glad you like it."

"Like it? And my old one just about ready for the knacker's yard." She took a deep breath, stood close to Kitty, and pecked her cheek. "I do love it, Miss Kitty. Thank you . . . thank you very much."

"I'm glad," Kitty said.

"And you can come and cook in my kitchen anytime you like, so."

"There you are, Kitty," O'Reilly said. "You've been given the keys to the kingdom. That's very gracious of you, Kinky."

She set her present on the sideboard beside the whiskey decanter. "And Miss Kitty," she asked, "what do you take in your tea?"

"Just a drop of milk, please," Kitty said, sitting again. She accepted a cup of tea and a plate of barmbrack. "Thank you."

"And here is yours, sir."

O'Reilly thanked Kinky. She picked up her new bag and its wrappings. "I'll be going along," she said. "There'll be braised shank of lamb for dinner with champ and roast parsnips. It's time I was seeing to them."

She headed for the door, then turned and said to Kitty, "I'd take it as a favour, Miss Kitty, if when you come down you'd bring the tea tray." Kinky's chins wobbled as she laughed and then said, "As I recollect, your mother doesn't work here."

O'Reilly was still laughing as Kinky left. He took a bite of the spicy speckled loaf, savoured it, and thought how delighted he was that any rift there might have been between Kitty and Kinky seemed to have been healed. He smiled at Kitty, and she puckered into a pretend kiss. He sent one back.

Braised lamb shank for dinner, Barry coping with the patients, Kitty here, and Kinky in her kitchen. Apart from his aching back, as far as O'Reilly was concerned, God was in his heaven and all *was* right with the world.

30

Yet Meet We Shall

All was not right in Barry's world. The number of cases of probable ringworm at the school worried him. "You've six boys for me to see?" he asked Mrs. Redmond, the principal of MacNeill Primary School, who sat behind a desk in her office.

"I'm afraid so, Doctor Laverty." She was a late middle-aged woman. She wore no makeup, her lips were thin, her eyes pale, her nose narrow. She looked falcon fierce and was known as a strict disciplinarian, and yet Barry also knew of her reputation for kindness. She was highly regarded locally.

"They're all in a single class," she said, "so I told their teacher to wait with them in their room until you got here." She rose and headed for the door. "Come this way, please."

Barry walked with the principal down a high-windowed, linoleum-floored hall. Neon strips in the ceiling provided extra light. The walls were hung with photos of girls' hockey teams and boys' soccer elevens.

A cleaner, her hair tied up in a triangular scarf, worked an electrical floor polisher, a "bumper" in local parlance. When she stooped, an ankle-length calico apron brushed the tops of a pair of shiny black brogues. The smell of floor polish was overpowering.

She switched off the machine and bobbed in a shallow curtsey. "Mrs. Redmond . . . Doctor."

"Carry on, Jessie," Mrs. Redmond said.

"Thank you, ma'am." The electrical motor made a harsh buzzing.

Not for the first time Barry thought how feudal things were in Ballybucklebo.

"In here," Mrs. Redmond said, opening a door with a frosted-glass upper panel.

Barry found himself at the back of a classroom.

"Miss Nolan," Mrs. Redmond said.

The teacher was in front of a large blackboard, sitting behind her desk on a raised platform at the head of the room. Of course. Colin Brown was in Sue Nolan's class. The outbreak had probably started with him and infected others among her pupils.

"Doctor Laverty's here."

"I'm glad he is," Sue Nolan said. "The natives are getting restless." She pointed to where six boys, all seven or eight years old, were rising from their desk seats and turning to look at the back of the room in deference to a visit from the principal. "They think they're being kept in," she said.

Kept in. It brought back memories for Barry of his time at Connor House in Bangor, the school he'd attended before he went to Campbell College. He'd not like to think of the number of times he'd been in detention there.

"You may be seated, boys," Mrs. Redmond said. "And Hubert Flynn? *Stop* picking your nose."

As desk seats rattled, Barry quickened his pace. He could understand how the boys must feel when all their classmates were outside playing, and they were in here under the eye of the principal.

Bright pictures done with poster paints, pastels, and potato cuts, all the handiwork of children, adorned the side walls. There was a distinct, well-remembered smell of chalk dust and ink in the air. Ranks and files of single-unit desk-and-chair combinations stood on a planked floor. They were as regularly spaced as a well-drilled army platoon.

Barry and Mrs. Redmond arrived at the head of the room. Sue Nolan came out from behind her desk and smiled at him. He had forgotten what a startling green her eyes were and how she wore her long copper hair done in a single plait. It shone and brightened the subdued tones of her black blouse.

Barry said quietly, "Good afternoon, Miss Nolan," then waited because he was the guest. Mrs. Redmond was in charge.

"This is Doctor Laverty, children," she said. "Say hello nicely."

Six treble voices piped, "Hello, Doctor Laverty."

"Hello," he said and raised his right hand in greeting.

"He's going to examine your heads."

Hubert Flynn, the nose-picker, a towheaded boy wearing a navy-blue blazer with the school crest on the breast pocket, held up his hand. The knot of his blue-and-chocolate striped school tie was askew in the V-neck of his grey uniform sweater.

"Yes, Hubert."

He lowered his hand. "Please, Mrs. Redmond, can the doctor start with Art O'Callaghan?"

Barry saw a smaller boy in short, grey flannel pants and wearing thick-lensed, wire-framed granny glasses turn and stare at Hubert.

"Why?"

"Because . . ." Hubert sniggered, "because Art's been needing his head examined for months, so he has."

Barry found it difficult not to join in with the children's laughter. He glanced at Sue Nolan. She too was having trouble keeping a straight face.

Mrs. Redmond was not. Her voice was icy. "You will apologise to Art for that remark, Hubert Flynn. Art O'Callaghan is *not* stupid."

Hubert lowered his head. "I'm dead sorry, Art, so I am," he said meekly.

"Good," she said, "but there's no need for 'so I am.'"

"I'm sorry, Mrs. Redmond, so I—"

Mrs. Redmond fixed Hubert with a gaze that Barry thought would have done justice to Balor, a mythical one-eyed figure from Ireland's past, whose stare could kill.

"Sorry." Hubert Flynn seemed to shrink.

"Accepted—this time, but if there's any more nonsense out of you, Hubert, or anyone else"—her gaze swept over the six little boys, lingering on each individual for a measurable moment—"I'll ask Miss Nolan to give you all a hundred lines before you go home."

Writing out neatly, "I must always behave in class," one hundred times must seem like fifty years at hard labour to an eight-year-old, thought Barry, with a stab of empathy for the little boys before him. He hadn't much liked school himself, and he marveled that he'd made it through his medical training with good marks. Perhaps it had something to do with how interested you were in the subjects.

"Now, Doctor Laverty, how would you like to proceed?" Mrs. Redmond asked.

"I'll examine one to start with, please."

"Hubert, come here. The rest of you sit," she ordered.

Barry took a quick look. The sore was exactly like Colin's red-rimmed bald spot. He turned to Mrs. Redmond. "Ringworm," he said.

She nodded and said to young Flynn, "Go and sit down."

Hubert obeyed.

Why, Barry wondered, did Hubert's recent, seemingly mortal enemy Art O'Callaghan now give Hubert a great grin as Hubert passed by?

"Is it reasonable to assume the other five probably have the same thing?" Mrs. Redmond wanted to know.

"It is." He turned to the children. "Stay at your desks," he said, then looked back to Mrs. Redmond. "I'll do a bit of production-line medicine." He remembered O'Reilly lining up a batch of patients and giving them injections one after the other. "Nip round and look at them all."

It hadn't taken long to peer at each pupil's head and make the diagnoses. All of the boys would require treatment. With the disease spreading so rapidly in the school, he, alone or with O'Reilly, must find the source and try to prevent more cases. "Ringworm," he said. "I'll need to write prescriptions and letters to their parents—and will you need a sick line for each of them, Mrs. Redmond?" Barry said.

"A certificate will not be necessary."

"Then apart from the paperwork, I'm finished." He spoke to Mrs. Redmond, loudly enough so everyone could hear. "I'll have them out of here in no time."

She didn't object when there was a small cheer.

"Thank you, Doctor Laverty," she said, then glanced at her watch. "I'm most grateful. Now if you'll forgive me, I have to run. Curriculum meeting in Belfast. If you need anything else, I'm sure Miss Nolan can help you and pass on any instructions to me." With that, Mrs. Redmond strode toward the door.

From the corner of his eye Barry saw the recently chastised Hubert Flynn frown and cross his eyes at her departing back. He heard Sue Nolan's soft but firm "Hubert."

Barry bent, rummaged in his bag, and found his prescription pad. He was vaguely aware of Sue Nolan moving closer.

"Here," she said and handed him a writing tablet. "You'll need this if you're going to write letters."

He looked up and found himself staring into those green eyes. Barry couldn't help notice her subtle, musky perfume. He accepted the pad, but fumbled and nearly dropped it. "Thank . . . thank you." He inhaled. That musk was delightful. "I'll just be a tick. May I borrow your desk?"

"Of course. And Doctor Laverty, if you give me the first letter I'll start making copies for the other parents."

"Terrific." Barry followed her to the back of the desk to two hard wooden chairs. He automatically pulled hers out and waited for her to sit.

"Thank you, kind sir," she murmured. And not missing an instructional moment, she continued more loudly, "A gentleman should always help a lady into her seat."

"That lets you off, Hubert Flynn," Art said. "It's only for gentlemen, so it is."

She ignored the remark, but said, "Settle down, boys. The sooner Doctor Laverty and I are finished, the sooner you'll be out of here."

Barry sat beside her.

"Boys in Ulster," she said quietly, "seem to learn the fine art of mutual slagging very young."

Barry thought of all the times he and Jack had traded what to an outsider would sound like mortal insults, but were in fact only banter. "Must be something in the water," he said and was gratified by her throaty chuckle. "Now to work."

He had to interrupt Sue Nolan to ask the names of the other four boys, but in what seemed like no time, he'd finished the sixth prescription and was waiting for her to complete the last letter. Barry looked into the classroom, past where the little boys sat chatting quietly to each other. Each sloping, hinge-lidded desk had a two-inch-wide trough at the top edge for pens, rulers, and pencils, and at the right corner a circular hole holding a ceramic inkwell. He recalled sitting at desks like these, dipping his steel-nibbed, wooden-shafted pen into the well and leaving spidery, blot-marred words on the page.

"Finished," Sue said, sitting up from her task. "Sorry I've no envelopes, but they can stick the letters in their schoolbags."

"You're a wee glipe, Art." Hubert Flynn's voice was clearly audible. "And yer mammy wears army boots, so she does." There was an edge to his voice.

Barry looked up and grinned. That was fighting talk. How would she handle it?

Her voice was soft. "Hubert," she said. "Hubert Flynn." She shook her head, and her copper mane tossed back and forth. "Dear, oh dear. Is that any way to talk to anyone? I don't mind a bit of teasing, but that was very rude, and Art's supposed to be your friend." She waited—and waited—her unblinking gaze never leaving the boy's face.

Barry saw Hubert lower his eyes.

"You've made me very disappointed," she said and waited some more.

Barry watched as the little boy looked up at his teacher. His face was starting to crumble; his lips turned down. She rose and went to him, and to Barry's amazement she bent and hugged the lad.

Now the tears did start. "I'm awful sorry, Miss Nolan. I'll never do it again, so I won't. Honest to God."

"Promise?"

"Promise."

She gave him a hanky. "Good. Now blow your nose, tell Art again you're sorry, shake hands, and sit there quietly, and we'll say no more about it."

"Yes, miss."

Barry was impressed by how Sue handed things.

"Here, Doctor Laverty," she said, handing him his own letter and five copies.

"Terrific." He compared his scrawled words to her immaculate copperplate. "Thank you. Now I need to tell them a few things."

She spoke to the boys. "Doctor Laverty has something to say."

Every face turned to him.

"Boys, when your name is called, I want you to come up here one at a time. I'll give you a prescription and a letter to take straight home for your mammy. She'll make sure you'll be better in no time." He noticed another boy whispering to Hubert. The other four were intently watching the conversation. Hubert held up his hand.

"Yes, Hubert?" Barry asked. The boy seemed to be quite recovered from his tears.

"Please, sir, we'd like to know, like . . . Colin Brown got off school, so he did?"

Barry smiled. "He did. And so will you." He turned to Sue Nolan. "I'm afraid they'll all have to stay at home for a couple of weeks." From the corner of his eye he saw Hubert give Art a surreptitious thumbs-up, as if things were going according to plan.

"It can't be helped," Sue said. "I just hope this'll be the end to the outbreak."

"Me too," Barry said. "Now let's get them and us out of here." He glanced at the first letter and called, "Art O'Callaghan."

Art came up and Barry gave him his papers. Funny, Barry thought, as he called another name. It's like Prize Day with me handing out the trophies, and by the looks on their faces you'd think each one *had* won a prize.

As soon as the last boy had been given his prescription and instructions, Sue said, "Class is dismissed."

The boys made a dash for the door, but young Flynn got left behind. He hesitated to bend down and pull up his left sock, which had slipped down around his ankle. "And don't forget to tell your mammy to boil your cap," Barry called to him. The instructions were in the letter, but it didn't hurt to send a verbal reminder too.

"I know, Doctor. Colin Brown's mammy had to."

"Fair enough. Go on with you."

Hubert tore off, yelling, "Take your hurry in your hand. Wait for me."

31

Considerably Worried and Scratched

"I don't want to hold you up, Sue, but could you stay a few more minutes?" Barry said.

"Of course."

"Just a few questions."

"Ask away."

"Before I do, I must say I was impressed by the way you handled young Hubert. In my day if I'd tried it on like that, I'd have got a swift clip round the ears."

"Honey," she said, "catches more flies than vinegar." Her eyes, green as fine jade, held a most delightful smile.

"Thanks for doing the notes. I'm impressed by your penmanship," he said.

"I'm learning to do Japanese ideographs too," she said. "Calligraphy's a hobby. Completely old-fashioned, useless in today's world, but pleasant to look at."

Barry almost found himself remarking, "So are you pleasant to look at, Miss Sue Nolan," but instead he said, "I need your help to try to stop the ringworm outbreak from spreading."

"Certainly."

"Ask the cleaning staff to use Dettol to wash down the desks in here and the basins in the gents toilets. Have all the old towels in there changed, and the used ones washed. You've seen what ring-worm looks like; I don't think there'll be any more, but if any new cases do crop up, shoot them over to us at Number 1 or send for us again."

"Fair enough."

He looked at her blouse. "I'd suggest you give your hands a good wash before you leave here, and boil that blouse tonight. You hugged Hubert. I'd hate to see you with a bald spot." The words slipped out. "You do have lovely hair. Quite stunning. It would be a shame to spoil it." What on earth possessed him to say that?

"Thank you," she said, "for the advice. I'd not fancy my hair looking as if the moths had got at it." She shook her mane. "It took a while to grow."

Barry knew he was blushing. He wanted to get the conversation back on a professional footing. He cleared his throat and said, "With a bit of luck I think that should do it, now we've sent all the affected cases home, but to be on the safe side you'll have to try to keep the children from sharing clothing, combs, hairbrushes, tow-els. Lots of handwashing."

"I'll see to all that too," she said levelly. "I really hope the out-break is finished now. I'd not be happy with an empty classroom. I love teaching here."

"Have you always taught here?"

She shook her head. "I did my practice teaching in Belfast, but the minute I was ready for a full-time job I got out of the city as fast as I could."

"Ballybucklebo's pretty small."

"Not to me. I'm a small-town girl. Broughshane, where I grew up, isn't San Francisco, you know."

Broughshane was about seven miles from Cullybackey, where Jack Mills's family had a dairy farm, and close to the larger Bally-mena. Barry knew of the small town in the Glens of Antrim but had never actually been there. He smiled and said, "Ballybuck-lebo's no hiving metropolis either, and a ringworm outbreak's hardly as serious as the 1906 California earthquake, but I still need to get to the bottom of it. That's where you can help."

"How?"

"Every one of the infected kids is yours—"

"Doctor Laverty, what do you take me for?" she said, with mock indignation. "I'm a single woman." She raised her right eyebrow and chuckled in the same deep tones he remembered from the first time he'd met her.

It pleased him to have made her laugh. "That's not *exactly* what I meant."

"I know," she said with a smile. She lightly touched his sleeve. "I was just taking a hand out of you. And yes, it did start with one of my pupils: Ballybucklebo's answer to Dennis the Menace, Colin Brown." She chuckled again. "Mind you, Hubert Flynn runs him a close second."

"I noticed . . . Kids." He shook his head. "My guess is that Colin got infected first, and somehow it was passed on. Boys are always wrestling and grabbing each other by the hair. They probably share combs." Barry shook his head. "I don't know yet where Colin got it. Cats and dogs carry one kind of fungus, cattle another, and mice harbour a different strain. Youngsters are usually infected by their pets or farm beasts; then it's passed from one child to another by close contact. It'll be hard to find the original source in a rural community. There're animals everywhere."

"You mentioned mice."

"The mouse fungus is called *Trichophyton mentagrophytes*."

"Colin has a white mouse."

Barry whistled. "That's probably where the whole thing started. Did he tell you about his pet?"

She chuckled. "He did better than tell me. He showed me. He

brought it to school in his pocket four weeks ago. Held it up by its tail, poor wee thing. I had ten little girls all standing on their seats shrieking like banshees. He nearly scared the pants off them."

"Sounds like something Colin would do," Barry said. "He is an imp. I'll need to look into it, but I'm sure the mouse will be the primary source. Maybe Colin let the boys pet the creature. It doesn't sound as if the girls wanted to. Maybe that's why only boys are affected." He frowned. "It's certainly plausible. I'll follow up on that. You have been most helpful, Sue. Thank you. Sorry I've held you up."

She looked at her watch. "Damn. I've missed my train to Holywood. No matter. It was fun being a medical detective for a few minutes, and there'll be another train."

"There are more fish in the sea" was how Jack Mills had expressed matters in a different context. "It's my fault you missed the train, and Holywood's no distance. I'll give you a lift if you like."

"Really? That's sweet. I'm in no real rush"—she glanced at her watch—"but I've had enough of this classroom for one day and I don't fancy hanging about at the station, so I'll get a move on, try not to hold *you* up." She made a grab for a stack of exercise books on the desk and knocked them onto the floor. She surprised Barry by laughing. "My dad, he was a terrible tease. When I was little, he used to call me T.A.O."

"T.A.O.?"

"Mmm. The Awkward One. He said if there was only one tree in a field I'd find a way to bump into it. I was always dropping plates, knocking my head on things." She pointed at the books. "Still am."

Barry started to bend to help pick them up.

"Don't you dare," she said with a smile.

Barry stopped. "Why not?"

"Because if you do, guaranteed I'd bend at the same time and we'd clonk heads. I'll get them," she said and knelt. Her skirt rode up her thighs, and Barry had to force himself to avert his gaze from the reinforced tops of her nylons.

She stood and tucked the books under her left arm. The action lifted a pair of neatly formed breasts under her black blouse. "Come on," she said. "My coat's in the staff room."

"Remember," he said, "to wash your hands."

Barry left the gents toilet. He too had needed to wash his hands. He waited outside the staff-room door for Sue to reappear. So, he thought, she's clumsy—or believes she is, anyway. Perhaps having a dad who, not unusually for the times, had mocked her about it had made her try to be more considerate of other people's feelings. Look how gently she'd handled a mischievious little boy. And how tactful she'd been in setting him at ease after blurting out that remark about her hair. She'd been quick off the mark with a riposte when he'd inadvertently suggested the children were hers. Barry smiled. The lass had a sense of humour.

The door to the staff room opened. "Sorry to keep you," she said. She wore a powder-blue raincoat and carried her books. "No rest for the wicked," she said. "I've last night's homework to mark."

"Poor you." Barry had an urge to offer to carry her books, but thought better of it. "The sooner I get you home, the better. My car's out on the street."

Together they walked along the corridor. Jessie and her floor polisher had vanished. "What else do you do after school?" he asked.

"I've a gormless springer spaniel, Max. Dad gave him to me when I came up here. Thought I might need a bit of company. He needs lots of attention—and his walk every day. Keeps me fit."

Barry smiled. "Dogs are good company. I had an Irish terrier when I was a kid. I wasn't very original, though. I called him Paddy." He shifted his bag to his other hand. "I'll bet you do other things too."

"I like music," she said. "You remember the Christmas pageant, when I conducted the kiddies' choir?"

"I do." How could he forget that pageant and the Colin Brown episode?

"I particularly like choral music," she said, "so I'm in the Philharmonic Choir in Belfast. We practice every week."

"I remember my dad taking me to hear them do the *Messiah*. To tell you the truth it wasn't my cup of tea," Barry said, "but I did like the 'Hallelujah Chorus.'"

"What my father calls 'a good sanctified shout.' The Philharmonic's been performing it every Christmas since 1886. I like that about Ulster," she said. "There's a great sense of history here . . . Some of my school friends emigrated." She shook her head and said, "I'll not."

"Nor me," Barry said, as he held open the school's front door and let Sue pass. Together they walked down a short flight of steps onto the playground.

The gravel crunched under their feet, and the noise of distant traffic mingled with the high-pitched, happy cries of children playing tag over by the green-painted iron railings.

A shriek rang more loudly than the kids' laughter. Barry spun to look for its source. The tag players were huddled around one of their number on the gravel. He dashed over and pushed his way through the knot of children. Art O'Callaghan sat howling and clutching his right knee. His wire-framed granny glasses lay on the gravel beside him.

"Let's have a look, Art," Barry said, kneeling by the boy.

"It hurts, so it does," Art sobbed.

"I'm only going to look," Barry said. He put a hand on the boy's shoulder and could feel the child heaving.

"Here, Art," Hubert said, "here's your specs." He handed them to the seated Art, who clipped the frames in place, one bendy, curved wire earpiece at a time. Hubert's words tumbled over each other. "We was playing tag, and he was it, so he was, Doctor Laverty, and he was chasing me, like, and he took an awful purler, so he did." He paused for breath.

Barry was aware of Sue kneeling on Art's other side, dabbing his tears with her hanky. She must have a limitless supply, he thought. The little boy had leant his head against her breast for comfort. Barry made a mental note to insist once more that she wash the blouse as soon as she got home.

He smiled at Art and bent further to look at the knee. Poor wee lad. He had a graze covering his right kneecap. The skin had been abraded, and the whole area was raw and oozing blood. Here and there, stones stuck up like chocolate chips in strawberry ice cream. The wound was going to have to be washed, and the pieces of gravel removed, before Barry could dust it with Cicatrin antibiotic powder, dress it with a Vaseline-impregnated nonstick gauze, and put on a bandage. At least that would reduce the risk of infection and make it a little less sore. They'd have to go back to Number 1 unless . . . "Where do you live, Art?" Barry asked.

"Up on the estate. Seventeen Comber Gardens. Next door to Mr. and Mrs. O'Hagan." Art sniffed and drew the sleeve of his blazer from elbow to wrist under his nose.

"Here," Sue said, handing the boy her hanky. "Use this."

Kieran O'Hagan. Enlarged prostate, Barry thought. One on an increasing list of villagers he was getting to know. Comber Gardens wasn't far. He knew he had all the supplies in his bag needed to deal with the abrasion. "Miss Nolan," Barry said. Titles were always used in front of children. "I'm afraid we'll have to make a small detour before Holywood."

"That's perfectly all right."

Barry slipped his arms under Art's legs and shoulders and stood. "Home with you, Art O'Callaghan. I'll need to put a bandage on that for you. Can you bring my bag, Hubert?"

Art started to sniffle. "It's too far to walk, so it is. My knee's awful sore."

"I know," Barry said. "That's why I'll take you in my motorcar."

"And you can sit on my lap, Art. All right?" Sue said.

Hubert picked up Barry's bag and waited.

"Come on then," Barry said. But before he started to walk, he said to the children, "You other four I gave the letters to. Straight home. I told you that when I gave you your prescriptions. I don't want you infecting anyone else."

"You hurry up and get better, Art," Hubert Flynn said. "And I *am* sorry, so I am, that I said you needed your head examined."

Barry walked to his car. "It's not locked," he said to Sue. "Hop in and I'll give you Art."

When Sue was settled, Barry stooped and put the boy in her lap.

"Thank you, Hubert." Barry took his bag from the boy. "Now straight off home."

As he started the engine, he said, "I'll not take long to fix you up, Art. Sorry about the detour, Miss Nolan."

"I don't mind a bit," she said. "I can start marking the homework while I wait."

"Terrific," Barry said. "Then I'll get you home." He was looking forward to driving the schoolmistress from Broughshane back to her flat in Holywood.

32

Things Fall Apart

O'Reilly heard the front door closing. "That must be Barry," he said to Kitty. "Just in time for dinner." The prospect of tonight's meal—braised shank of lamb with champ and roast parsnips—pleased O'Reilly. And sticky toffee pudding to follow. It sounded delicious. Kinky'd got the new recipe—it was English—from a friend at the Women's Union just before Christmas and had waited until tonight to try it out.

"How's Barry been managing?" Kitty asked.

O'Reilly shifted in his chair. His sprained back was definitely on the mend. It would be a lot easier getting downstairs to the dining room than it had been earlier in the week. "Barry's a good diagnostician," he said, "and he has a fine pair of hands." After the way Barry had conducted the recent delivery of Hester Patton's twins, O'Reilly had no trouble paying his assistant the highest of surgical compliments.

"Thank you, Fingal," Barry said from the doorway. "I appreciate your saying that." He came in. "Hello, Kitty. Good to see you. How's your mum?"

"She's fine, for a woman of eighty," Kitty said. "She's sharp as a tack and I still enjoy her company—in small doses. But it's good to be back up north."

O'Reilly saw the smile she gave him. "It is good to have you back, Kitty," he said. "We missed you, girl, didn't we, Barry?"

"Indeed we did," said Barry, with only the slightest emphasis on the "we."

O'Reilly noted that, as well as Barry's smile. There was no sarcasm in it, and O'Reilly was convinced that Barry would understand that it was difficult for an Irishman of O'Reilly's generation to tell Kitty, "I missed you," in front of someone else. He cleared his throat, then said, "The sun is very definitely over the yardarm. Barry, will you do the honours?"

Barry went to the sideboard. "Gin and tonic, Kitty?"

"Please."

O'Reilly knew he'd be getting a Jameson but wondered if Barry would settle for a sherry. "So, Barry," he said, "while you're pouring, tell us what you found at the school."

"Six cases of ringworm. All boys. All sent home for two weeks. And a grazed knee. Now cleaned and dressed." Barry came over, carrying two glasses. "Here you are, Kitty." Barry gave her the G & T. "Fingal." Another glass of whiskey waited for Barry on the sideboard. Barry wasn't a drinker, but when he did take a drop these days it was usually whiskey. O'Reilly saw in that a small sign of young Laverty's gradual maturation.

"*Sláinte,*" O'Reilly said and drank.

"*Sláinte mHaith,*" Barry and Kitty both replied.

"Six?" O'Reilly said. "That's one hell of a lot."

"And all in Colin Brown's class," said Barry. "I think I know the original source. Colin Brown has a pet white mouse."

"Has he, begod?" O'Reilly said. "How do you know?"

"His teacher, Sue Nolan, told me."

O'Reilly thought he heard something light in Barry's voice, and his use of the Christian name rather than the more formal "Miss Nolan" was interesting too.

Barry laughed. "She told me he'd once brought it to school and scared the living daylights out of the little girls."

"Charming," said Kitty, but she too was smiling. "When I was a girl, my version of your Colin put a slug down the back of my dress."

"And did you scream, Kitty?" O'Reilly asked.

"I did not." Her grin widened. "*He* did."

"Why?" Barry asked.

"Because I belted him one and made his nose bleed."

O'Reilly choked on his whiskey, felt it burning the back of his throat. He could just imagine Kitty as a child. He looked at her appraisingly. As a boxer himself, he'd be prepared to bet she had a wicked right hook. "Good for you, Kitty," he said, "and seeing as you mentioned slugs, I'd agree Colin Brown can be the living exemplar of, to quote Mother Goose, 'Slugs, and snails, and puppy-dogs' tails, that's what little boys are made of.' Colin was the first case, but I don't think it gets us closer to understanding how the epidemic is spreading." He sipped. "Any ideas, Barry?"

"Not really. I am pretty sure he caught ringworm from his mouse. But the animal's not being taken anywhere else as far as we know, and now Colin's full of griseofulvin I don't think the wee rodent's going to pass on any more fungus to Colin. I'll maybe pop round and have a word with Colin's mother." He sipped. "There was one thing today . . ."

"Oh?"

"Colin's being kept home from school, but one of the boys in his class knew what I'd advised Colin's mum to do with his cap. I suppose he'd been over to see Colin. We didn't put the boy in isolation."

"No need to really," said O'Reilly, "if you told Colin's mum all the steps to take. She's a smart woman. He shouldn't be too contagious unless there is real contact with the fungus. It's only a precaution keeping him at home."

"I certainly told her about his cap."

"To burn it, I hope?"

"Burn it?"

"That's what we were taught to do. And the bedclothes."

"Fingal, Colin's folks aren't the Rothschilds, and we do have griseofulvin now. I told her to boil his cap and wash his sheets and pillowcases every day."

O'Reilly thought for a moment. Barry's argument was perfectly logical—but Fingal recalled an outbreak he'd had to handle nine years ago. "That's sound common sense, Barry," he said, but still he was thinking of a case where a boy who could have been Colin's twin brother in the mischief stakes had been the first to be diagnosed. O'Reilly decided to say nothing about it now. He'd wait until they'd had a word with Colin. "Maybe next week, when my back's recovered, we might pop in on the Browns. See how Colin's getting on," he said.

"I was going to go over after dinner," Barry said.

O'Reilly shook his head. "I don't think there's any rush, and I want to come with you."

"Fair enough," Barry said.

O'Reilly sensed movement. He turned and saw that Kinky had come in. "Yes, Kinky?"

"I'm here to tell you the lamb's coming on a treat," she said. "It'll be ready in ten minutes."

O'Reilly felt his mouth start to water.

"I'd like you all down in eight minutes," Kinky said, "and seeing you're here, Miss Kitty, I've a nice bottle of claret breathing on the sideboard."

"Thank you, Mrs. Kincaid," Kitty said.

She was still minding her p's and q's, O'Reilly thought. Taking no risk that offence could be taken because she was too familiar.

He was delighted when Kinky looked straight at Kitty and said, "The wine does be a very lovely colour. Deeper red than my new handbag, so, and that will be very much envied by my lady friends, Cissie Sloan and Flo Bishop."

"Och," said O'Reilly, "you'll be the fashion plate of Ballybucklebo, Kinky Kincaid."

"Go on with you, Doctor O'Reilly. I'll be no such thing." She was blushing. "But I am most grateful for the present."

"You deserved it, Kinky," Kitty said. "You really did."

"Thank you," said Kinky, "thank you very much, Miss Kitty." She turned to O'Reilly. "And my lamb shanks do deserve to be eaten at their best, so."

"Come on then," said O'Reilly, managing to lever himself out of the chair without too much discomfort. "And the sticky toffee pudding will get its just desserts too."

"That, Fingal Flahertie O'Reilly," said Kitty, "is the worst pun I've heard in a month of Sundays." She took his arm and O'Reilly was grateful for her help and warmed by her touch.

"That was wonderful," said O'Reilly, from his place at the head of the table. Barry sat to his left, Kitty to his right. He pushed aside his dinner plate and swallowed a mouthful of claret. "That's not a bad drop either. What do you think, Barry?"

"It's lovely; mind you, I'm not what one senior gynaecologist in Belfast calls a connooser. I think he means connoisseur."

"It is very good," Kitty said. She turned to O'Reilly. "You surprise me, Fingal. I know you're not much of a wine drinker."

"True," he said, "but I know you like it." It was pleasant when she reached over and squeezed his hand.

He caught a whiff of caramel sauce a moment before Kinky appeared with the sticky toffee pudding. "Wonderful," he said, and grabbed his spoon and fork in his fists.

Kinky cleared the plates and served the dessert. As she set his before O'Reilly, she said, "I did have a word on the telephone with my sister Fidelma this afternoon, so. She says Tiernan says your man Eugene, the jockey, will be riding for Mr. Bishop two weeks from Saturday at Downpatrick. I thought you'd like to know, sir."

"Thank you, Kinky," he said. "That is indeed helpful." Although how, he wasn't quite sure. Not yet. "I think," he said, "that's a day I'll ask you to hold the fort here, Kinky. Barry and I will be going to Downpatrick."

"It would be no bother, sir," she said, then left with a tray of dirty plates.

"You'll come too, Kitty?"

"I'm not sure if I'll be free," she said.

"I'm sure you'll be able to arrange it," he said, and without waiting for an answer O'Reilly got stuck in. The sponge cake melted in his mouth, and the hot caramel sauce was sweetly delicious.

"I'm curious," Kitty said. "It's not by any chance to do with the same horse you had to talk to a man about at the marquis' pheasant shoot, is it?"

"None other than," O'Reilly said. He knew Donal didn't want to appear foolish in front of the citizens of Ballybucklebo, but Barry already knew, and Kitty was . . . Kitty was practically family. "Bertie's running a swindle with a racehorse," he said. "He's bamboozling Donal and a bunch of his friends. You'll keep what I'm going to tell you to yourself, Kitty?"

"Of course."

O'Reilly took another huge bite of pudding then quickly outlined how by betting with the syndicate's shares—and losing, Bertie Bishop was on the verge of owning the animal outright, and quite likely to be in a position soon to make a lot of money from the filly. By O'Reilly's calculation, knowing how many times the horse had run and lost, Donal and his friends now owned no more than the last ten pounds each of their original investment of a hundred pounds apiece.

"The race at Downpatrick is critical," he said. "And I'm stuck for an answer. Kinky's family knows the jockey. He's a Corkman. He may be pulling the horse to stop it winning, but we've no way of proving it."

"You're not going to let Bishop beat you, Fingal?" Kitty asked.

"Bloody right we're not, are we, Barry?"

Barry shrugged. "I'd love to help . . . I'll certainly come with you to Downpatrick."

"Good lad." Clearly Barry couldn't resist being involved. O'Reilly smiled. "Donal's our great white hope. He's got a local bookie, Willy McArdle, asking around. We think Bertie's not betting at all. If we can confirm that, Barry, you and I will be having a word in the councillor's delicate, shell-like ear. We might even head him off before the races—but I'd not mind a day out anyway."

The phone rang in the hall.

"Fair enough," Barry said. "Any idea when we might hear from Donal?"

O'Reilly shook his head. "Soon, I hope." He finished his dessert.

Kinky came in. "I'm sorry, Doctor Laverty," she said, "but it's a patient for you."

"Excuse me." Barry rose and followed her into the hall.

"Poor old Barry," Kitty said. "You've had him hard at it since you did for your back."

"I know." He leant over and kissed her forehead. "I'm sorry, Kitty, but as soon as I'm better I will have to make up my share of being on call."

"I understand."

"I was hoping that now you're back from the south I'd be able to see more of you. A lot more." He looked into her eyes. "The day Bertie nearly shot you I told him I was very fond of you. I am. Very." He took her hand in both of his.

"I know you are, Fingal," she said levelly, "but it's been seven months."

"And you've been very patient."

"I did say I'd wait, but—"

O'Reilly felt a chill. He'd not seen this coming. The toffee pudding's aftertaste was sour. "But?" he asked. Tell her you do love her, you eejit, he told himself, but the words wouldn't come.

"I had a good chance to think in Tallaght."

"And?"

"Fingal, I'm not one for ultimatums. I was daft about you when we were students. I am again now. I don't think I ever stopped."

O'Reilly's heart sang. Tell her. Go on. "Kitty, I—" Still he couldn't bring himself to spit it out. The silence hung—and hung.

"Can't quite say it out loud. I know." She stood and patted his shoulder. "I think what we both need is a break. Time to think hard about where we're going." Her voice was matter-of-fact.

O'Reilly took a deep breath, looked up into her eyes, and said, "If that's what you want." Tell her you fool. You're going to lose her. She just said she's daft about you, but it's quite possible to be daft about someone and still know that it won't work. Perhaps she wants out and is trying to break it off gently? Or does she want more? Does she expect me to propose or—? O'Reilly stood. He enveloped her in a huge hug, kissed her hard, and felt her respond. Then he stood back. Her eyes sparkled. He was breathless. "Kitty, I . . ." Damn it, he wanted her now, and he'd sensed her need. Perhaps if—to hell with convention—if he made love to her, but with Kinky in the house . . . He stepped back. "Do we really have to take this break?" he asked. He waited for his breathing to slow.

She managed a small smile. "I don't have much choice," she said. "I'm being taken to London on Monday for ten days."

"Taken?" He stiffened. "Who by?"

"Mr. Roulston."

"Roulston? He's the new neurosurgeon?" In Ireland, surgeons took as their title "Mister" rather than "Doctor."

"John Roulston. That's right," she said.

O'Reilly had heard of the man's appointment in November of last year. Roulston had come from a London teaching hospital. "I believe he's very good."

"He is. He's introducing several new procedures and wants me to go with him on a course so I'll be prepared to supervise the post-operative nursing."

"I'm sure you will be," O'Reilly said. He rose and put his napkin on the table. "I hear tell he's about my age. Divorced." An edge had crept into his voice that he couldn't hold back.

"Yes. Yes, he is." She looked straight at him. "Fingal, I'm going on a professional course, not a dirty long weekend."

"I wasn't suggesting that." But it could turn out that way. Two professionals. Professional respect. Mutual attraction. A couple of after-class drinks. She was already thinking of him as John. A hotel room. It didn't bear thinking about. He shivered. "I understand," he said, although in truth he didn't want to. He only knew that inside he was chilled. He moved closer and hugged her. She didn't rebuff him. He held her at arm's length. "You go on your course. I'll get on with the practice here. Just promise me one thing."

"What?"

He swallowed. "That I can take you for dinner—today's the tenth—on Friday the twenty-sixth. That's a bit more than two weeks from now and a couple of days after you get back."

"Yes, you can, Fingal," she said. "I'll look forward to it." And she kissed him.

33

Dreamless, Uninvaded Sleep

"Pass the bloody milk," O'Reilly said.

Barry did as he'd been asked or, he thought, more like ordered. It must be the enforced idleness that'd been making Fingal so grumpy for the last couple of days.

O'Reilly munched a slice of toast and marmalade. "I'll take the surgery this morning," he said. "My back's well enough for me to park my arse in a chair and listen to the customers' complaints." He sounded gruff. "And I'll take call this weekend. I want you to have tomorrow and Sunday off. You've worked hard all bloody week."

"Are you sure, Fingal?" Barry asked. "I thought that as Kitty has just come back from visiting her mother in the south, you'd want—"

"Of course I'm bloody well sure."

"If you say so." Perhaps a taste of his own medicine—being kept busy—might cheer Fingal up. "It'll do you a power of good to get back into harness." And make him more pleasant to live with.

O'Reilly grunted.

Barry shrugged. As he buttered a slice of toast, he heard the phone ringing in the hall. He looked expectantly at the door. It opened and Kinky came in.

"I'm sorry, Doctor Laverty," she said. "The waiting room's

packed, but that was Joseph Devine. He says he can't get Sheilah to wake up."

"You'll have to go round straightaway, Barry," O'Reilly said, "but she's probably gone, poor old thing."

"Right." Barry rose.

"Don't worry about the waiting room being full, Kinky. I'm doing the surgery," O'Reilly said and then stiffly stood.

She tutted. "Doctor O'Reilly dear, you should be resting."

"That, Mrs. Kincaid, is for *me* to decide."

Barry heard the finality in O'Reilly's voice. The tip of the big man's nose was pallid, a sure sign he was angry. Barry looked at Kinky and raised his eyes to the heavens. He headed for the door.

He heard Kinky say calmly, "Indeed it is, sir," and by the clinking of crockery Barry knew she was clearing the table—and setting the plates on the tray with that bit of extra force.

O'Reilly was calling to him. "You'll likely need a death certificate. They're in the top left-hand drawer of my desk. And hurry up in there. I want to get started."

"Thanks." Barry crossed the hall into the surgery. He rummaged around in the drawer among referral forms, sick lines, prescription pads, and a paperback copy of *The Old Man and the Sea* until he found what he was looking for. It was his statutory responsibility, if a patient had been under his care, to certify the date, place, and cause of death. The undertaker could not proceed with his duties until the form had been lodged with the Registrar of Births, Deaths, and Marriages and the necessary paperwork issued. Signing a death certificate was not one of Barry's favourite jobs, although when he'd been a houseman they'd all been happy to sign one of the two doctors' forms required before a cremation could go ahead. That paid a good two guineas, known to the less reverent as ash cash.

As he headed for the front door, he heard roaring coming from the direction of the waiting room. "Will you move it, Ian Kilpatrick? I haven't got all bleeding day."

Clearly Fingal was in the kind of mood he usually reserved for obstructive admissions clerks, slovenly nursing-home receptionists, Doctor Ronald Hercules Fitzpatrick—and Councillor Bertie Bishop. Barry was glad to be going out.

He parked outside the Devines' low brick wall. It surrounded a neatly clipped lawn bordered by narrow, empty flower beds. Come summer, those borders would, he knew, be a riot of nasturtiums, pretty much the only flowers that could grow in such salty soil.

Across the wind-ruffled lough he watched cloud shadows swooping over the dappled faces of the Antrim Hills. The Knockagh obelisk on their crest was spotlighted by a single sunbeam. Gulls screamed overhead as Barry walked along a short path to the pebble-dashed bungalow.

Joseph Devine answered the front door. He was wearing an old woollen dressing gown, striped pyjamas, and his slippers. "Come in, Doctor Laverty."

"Thank you, Mr. Devine." Barry noticed the man was unshaven, his eyes were bloodshot, and his stoop seemed more pronounced.

"Sheilah was all right, if you could call it that, when we went to bed, but she won't wake up. She's in there," Joseph said, indicating a room to the left. "I'll wait in the hall."

Barry went into a small bedroom. There was a distinct odour that he had learnt from the more experienced nurses was always in a room immediately after a death.

Old embossed wallpaper had been painted over with a light-blue wash. A photograph of an antiquated twin-engined biplane bomber and its crew hung opposite where Mrs. Sheilah Devine lay on her back on the nearest side of a double bed with a maroon eiderdown pulled up to her chin.

The wrinkles were gone from the left side of her face. Her eyes were wide, staring at the ceiling. Her mouth hung open. He noticed that there was no movement of the bedclothes over her chest.

"Mrs. Devine?" Barry said, not expecting any answer. "Mrs. Devine?"

He sat on the edge of the bed and felt for her carotid pulse. There was none and her skin was clammy. He bent his head and put his ear close to her mouth. He did not hear nor feel her breathing. Barry straightened, took a pencil torch from an inside pocket, and shone the beam into each eye in turn. Neither dilated pupil reacted. The ebony-coloured discs, each with an encircling narrow white *arcus senilis*, stared fixedly into eternity. Barry used his right thumb and index finger to pull the upper lids down. He knew he should take out his stethoscope and listen for a heartbeat, but somehow he felt it would be sacrilegious to disturb her last sleep. He stood, head bowed, and unbidden the words from his childhood formed on his lips: "Our Father, which art in Heaven . . ."

Barry didn't pull up the sheet to cover Sheilah Devine's face. Instead he smoothed the place where he had been sitting and went back into the hall. "I'm sorry, Mr. Devine," he said. "She won't have suffered."

"It's all right, Doctor Laverty," the old man said, and Barry heard the trembling in his voice. "It's all right. Sheilah's at her rest now." His tears unheeded ran trickling through the grey stubble on his cheeks.

Barry put a hand on the man's shoulder and felt the bony prominences beneath his palm. "Would you like to go and sit with her for a while, Joseph?" he asked quietly.

"Thank you, Doctor. I would."

As he shuffled into the bedroom, Barry went through to the lounge. Sheilah's wheelchair sat empty. The blanket on the seat was neatly folded. The last time he'd been here he'd not noticed the upright piano against the far wall. He read the title of the sheet

music on the rack, "In the Sweet Bye and Bye," and he wondered
who had played the instrument and if they'd sung together. The
Lord only knew when that song had been all the rage. Probably
near the turn of the century when they'd been very young.

Barry walked to the mantelpiece, pulled the book of certificates
from his pocket, used the mahogany shelf as a desk, and started
filling in one buff form. By rights, Mr. Devine or a member of the
family should take it to the registrar over in Newtownards. But
Barry didn't know if the Devines had any relatives living in the village, and Joseph was frail and in no condition to go.

As Barry walked back along the hall, he could hear soft singing.
The bedroom door was ajar, and not wishing to intrude, Barry lingered in the hall and peeped in.

Joseph Devine sat on the bed holding his wife's hand. He sang
in a gentle tenor:

> . . . in the sweet bye and bye,
> We shall meet on that beautiful shore.

Then he bent and kissed his wife's forehead. "We will, pet," he
whispered. "We will."

Barry waited until Joseph stood up before slipping into the room,
coughing and asking, "Can I do anything for you, Mr. Devine?"

"No, thank you, Doctor Laverty. You've been most kind." He
took a hanky from his dressing-gown pocket, dried his eyes, and
blew his nose.

"I'll fill in the certificate so there'll be no need for a postmortem,"
Barry said. It seemed so . . . so coldly clinical to be talking about it
at that moment, but Barry knew how country folks hated the idea of
a loved one being cut open. "I just need to know Sheilah's date of
birth and marriage."

Joseph gave the information, and Barry completed the form.

"I'm on my way to Newtownards anyway this morning"—it was not entirely true, but it was only eight miles away—"so I'll pop in and give the papers to the registrar."

"I'd be greatly obliged."

"Joseph, I hesitate to ask, but will Mr. Coffin be looking after the . . . arrangements?"

He nodded.

"He's quite recovered from his accident at Councillor Bishop's on Boxing Day," Barry said. "His place is on the way back. Would you like me to drop in, give him the paperwork, and have him get in touch?"

"Would you?"

"Of course." Barry turned to leave, but then asked, "Can I do anything else for you?"

Mr. Devine shook his head. "We've got very good neighbours," he said softly.

Barry felt humbled by the remark. He was no stranger to how this community pulled together in the face of any disturbance. As soon as the word was out, Mr. Devine would not be able to eat all the food that would be prepared for him. Nor, unless he asked for privacy, would he be left on his own for long.

"It's time I got myself shaved and dressed," he said. "Then I'll have to make phone calls. We have a grown daughter in Vancouver—"

"I don't think she'll be up yet," Barry said. "There's an eight-hour time difference."

"I should have remembered. Sometimes these days . . . some-times I get forgetful."

And I can't cure that either, Barry thought.

"We've a son in Enniskillen. I'll have to phone him. And I suppose I'd better let my friends in the Masons and my old comrades at the British Legion know."

Many Ulstermen belonged to the Masons, a fraternal order,

Barry remembered, which had counted Rudyard Kipling among its adherents. The British Legion, with branches all over the United Kingdom, was a wonderful organisation for ex-servicemen. Joseph Devine must have served in the forces during the First World War. In the Royal Flying Corps, if that photo of the Vickers Vimy bomber was anything to go by.

"Perhaps," Barry said, "you might like to put an announcement in the *County Down Spectator?*"

"I will. And in the *Belfast Telegraph*. When Mr. Coffin's been and we know the date of the funeral." He sniffed. "I'll have to have a word with Mr. Robinson too. Sheilah will want him to give the service. She'll like that."

Barry noted how Joseph was referring to his wife in the future tense. Poor man. Barry felt helpless to offer any comfort. "If you're sure there's nothing more I can do, I'd best be running along," he said.

"Please go, Doctor. I'll be all right. It's just going to take a bit of getting used to, that's all."

When Barry reached his car, he turned back to see Mr. Devine standing, watching from the doorway. His eyes glistened, and a sunbeam was reflected from the fresh tears on his cheeks.

It wasn't far to Newtownards. Barry drove carefully along the narrow twisting roads. The car climbed hills, went down into shallow valleys, then climbed higher. In the morning sun, wisps of vapour, diaphanous as bees' wings, drifted up from the dark earth of ploughed furrows. In a field, a single white Charolais bull plodded ponderously ahead, his dewlap swinging in time to his stride.

The little Ulster fields on each side of the road were bounded by drystone walls, rusty barbed-wire fences, or hedges of hawthorn in early bud. Green pastures held flocks of ewes heavy with lambs, cows in calf. Spring would be here soon.

But not for poor Sheilah Devine. Barry took a deep breath.

According to its destination board, an approaching green Ulsterbus was bound for Portaferry at the tip of the Ards Peninsula. Barry stopped to give it right of way at the Six Road Ends. It didn't seem like almost nine months since he'd stopped Donal Donnelly near here and asked directions to Ballybucklebo so he could have an interview with a Doctor O'Reilly. Barry'd not been sure of his career destination then, but he had been ready to give country general practice a try.

In those short months he'd certainly had a fair sampling of the medical side of general practice, but he hadn't been prepared for the village. Gradually he'd come to learn it wasn't simply a collection of houses, shops, a pub, and a couple of churches. It was an entity, and as an animal was the whole of its parts, so too was the village a many faceted, living organism.

To liken O'Reilly to its heart would be carrying the analogy too far, but Ballybucklebo, Barry knew, was a composite of the people. The marquis, the Browns, the Donnellys, the Auchinlecks, Father O'Toole, Cissie Sloan and her cousin Aggie Arbuthnot with six toes, Mister Robinson, the Presbyterian minister, Mrs. Redmond, the school principal, Sonny and Maggie—aye, and Bertie and Flo Bishop. It was a place where the bereaved Joseph Devine could say with confidence, "We've got very good neighbours." That had brought a lump to his throat then. It did now.

Barry moved slowly ahead, Ulster country roads not being conducive to fast driving, no matter what Fingal might think. They meandered gently toward their destinations, much like life in Ballybucklebo.

A life he was now part of. He was accepted here as—what had Jack said?—"the local, highly respected GP." Barry wasn't so sure about the "highly," but certainly there was respect. It was a place he could already think of as home. He'd miss it if he left.

He crested a last hill, pulled over, and parked. Ahead and below lay Strangford Lough. Barry wanted to take a good look at one of his favourite views.

The nearby town of Newtownards lay at the lough's head, watched over by the multiturreted Scrabo Tower perched on an escarpment immediately to the west. Light aircraft, by the distance made tiny as dragonflies, were practicing takeoffs and landings on a small aerodrome.

The tide was out, and broad mudflats glistened as beaten silver in a candle's glow. Further out, the blue waters were studded with islands and low seaweed-covered reefs called pladdies. On the distant horizon, the Mourne Mountains loomed magenta against a blue sky.

Strangford Lough took its name from the Viking invaders of the tenth century. *Strangfjorthr,* the turbulent fjord. The native Celts had called it Lough Cuan, the peaceful lough.

Sheilah Devine had found her peace this morning, and the grieving Joseph must surely find his soon, as inevitably as the hawthorn buds Barry had seen earlier must burst, the ewes lamb, and cows drop their calves.

It was a privilege to know the Devines, be trusted by Joseph, and to have been able to save him the inconvenience of delivering this certificate.

Barry started his descent. He'd be glad to get this job done and head home to Ballybucklebo, a small haven in the Ulster he loved.

34

Earnest Advice from My Seniors

O'Reilly gazed at a slice of uneaten black pudding on Barry's plate. Kinky, he thought, might be working on slimming him, O'Reilly, down, but if the size of this Saturday's Ulster fry she'd set in front of Barry was anything to go by, she had different plans entirely for the young man. O'Reilly reckoned when it came to her self-imposed mission of making sure Barry was well fed, Kinky took a line like those who force-fed geese to produce paté de foie gras.

He lowered his *Irish Times*. "You going to eat that?"

Barry shook his head.

O'Reilly grinned and speared it with his fork just as Kinky came in to put a fresh pot of tea on the table.

"*Doctor O'Reilly.*" Her chins quivered. Her eyes flashed. "Put that down, sir. This minute."

O'Reilly flinched. She was as protective as a mother hen of her chicks. He set the fork-impaled pudding on his plate. "Sorry, Kinky," he said. And he thought that while he was at it, he might as well apologise for snarling at her yesterday and for growling at Barry. This business with Kitty wanting breathing space and going off to London was troubling, very troubling. "Ahem."

They both stared at him.

"Thank you both for putting up with a cantankerous old man

yesterday. I'm sorry that I was so bloody growly," he said, noting the look of total surprise on Barry's face. That fooled you, boy, O'Reilly thought. I know you can't believe I'm willing to apologise for anything.

"Doctor O'Reilly, sir," Kinky said, "you are *not* an old man, and it is in all of us to get as cross as a wet hen once in a while. I know that a pain that goes on and on can make a body grumpy, so. I've heard you say it often enough about patients. You've had a bad back all week that's not well mended yet."

"My back's pretty much better," O'Reilly said, "and it's still no excuse for taking it out on other people."

Kinky smiled. "It does take a true gentleman to say sorry, so."

O'Reilly saw Barry nodding his agreement.

"And a lady to remark on it," O'Reilly said. "And a hungry man to eat this." He grabbed the fork, popped the black pudding in his mouth, chewed mightily, and swallowed.

"You are enough to make a body despair, Doctor O'Reilly, so," Kinky said, but she was still smiling. "It's soup for you at lunchtime."

Good old Kinky, he thought. She doesn't argue often, but when she does, she likes to try to get the last word. This time he wasn't going to let her. "As long as it's one of yours—and not out of a can," he said slyly.

"Doctor O'Reilly." Her look would have frozen a small pond. "As if I'd let such a thing in my kitchen, and well you know it." Her face softened. " 'Tis a terrible tease you can be, sir."

As Kinky turned to Barry, O'Reilly picked up his morning paper. "And will yourself be in at lunchtime?" she asked Barry.

"No, Kinky. I'm going down to the Yacht Club in Bangor. I'll get a bite there."

O'Reilly finished the story he was reading and set his newspaper aside. Kinky had left. Barry was spreading marmalade on a slice of toast.

O'Reilly said, "The Yanks are sending bombers over North Vietnam, General Franco's started a blockade of Gibraltar to try to force Britain to give it back to Spain, the bill banning tobacco advertising on television has been given royal assent, so it's law now, and—*mirabile dictu,* wonderous things are spoken—Ringo Starr married a hairdresser on Thursday. I'll sleep better tonight for the knowing of it." He chuckled. "Her maiden name was Maureen Cox. I wonder if her married one will be Starr or Starkey?"

"Fingal," Barry said, "why on earth did you bother to remember the real name of the Beatles' drummer?"

"I've always had a pretty nonselective memory," said O'Reilly. "But I like their music, and do you remember what I said to you last July about the new stuff?"

Barry frowned. "Haven't a clue."

"I said the other long-haired mob would do well too."

"The Rolling Stones with Mick Jagger? Jack Mills calls him Mick the Lips." Barry smiled and his smile pleased O'Reilly.

"Apt," he said. "And their second L.P., *The Rolling Stones No. 2,* came out mid-January, and it's been top of the album charts ever since. It'll be there for a while."

Barry shook his head. "Fingal, sometimes you really are a suppository of trivia."

"That's the kind of malapropism I'd expect from Donal Donnelly. I think you mean repository." He added as an afterthought, "Malapropism. Thought to have originated in the play *The Rivals,* first staged in 1775—"

"At Covent Garden and written by Richard Brinsley Sheridan, an Irishman," Barry said and with a flourish took a bite of toast.

Good. Barry hadn't played their duelling quotations game since Boxing Day.

"But I do mean suppository, not repository. With your wide experience of general practice, intimate knowledge of modern rock-and-roll groups, ability to quote practically the entire canon of English literature, fluent French, and apparently complete familiarity with the King James version of the Holy Bible, to say nothing of the Book of Common Prayer, the blarney pours out of you. There is only one word for what causes it. I chose it with extreme care. *Sup*-pository."

O'Reilly burst out laughing. "Nice one, Barry. Oh, nice one."

Barry made a small bow to accept the compliment.

"I take it that if you're willing to poke fun at me your own mood has taken a turn for the better?"

"I'd a good night's sleep last night, I'm pleased your back's better, and to tell you the truth I'm glad you're looking after the shop today. I could use the break. I'll be seeing some friends."

"And I've been bored silly all week." That wasn't all that was bothering Fingal. He hesitated, trying to decide whether or not to confide in Barry.

"I know what you mean," Barry said. "Sitting round is no great shakes. The work does occupy your mind. Keeps it off other things."

"True," O'Reilly said, guessing that Barry was ready to open up some more. "Losing Patricia hurt you sorely, Barry. I hope being busy has helped." Come on, talk to me, he thought. Catharsis is good for the soul. Damn it all, after nearly nine months they were more than professional colleagues. And he, O'Reilly, had been thinking about Kitty going to London with a divorced brain surgeon who was something of a medical star. O'Reilly might talk to Barry about that.

Barry stared at the tablecloth. "It has but it still hurts," he said quietly. "A lot."

"And damn it, as strange as it may seem, I still miss Deidre after more than twenty years," O'Reilly said. "It's in the little things. She loved birds. Even now, every time I see a blue tit or hear a chaffinch . . ."

Barry looked O'Reilly in the eye. "Patricia was an amateur ornithologist—like her dad."

"I understand." O'Reilly saw how the young man was staring into the middle distance. "Is it paining you as badly as it did at first?"

Barry shook his head. "At first I was numb; then it started to hurt like hell. Now? Not quite as much."

"Good. I know it's early for you yet, but there will be another lass. Honestly."

"Perhaps," Barry said. "I went to a dance with Jack last weekend. I saw a girl I'd met before. Very pretty, very accessible, but I simply didn't feel a thing. Nothing. I don't think I'll be seeing her again."

O'Reilly wondered if Barry had trusted anybody else with that confession. "Ships that pass?" he said.

"Yes."

"Sometimes vessels do meet again." He knew his voice had a hint of sadness.

Barry sat back. "Go on, Fingal," he said quietly.

That's exactly what good doctors should do, sense when patients wanted to talk and let the sufferers know they'd be listened to, but O'Reilly didn't think Barry had his doctor's hat on. He was simply being a friend. "You know about Kitty and me?"

"That you were together once? Yes."

"Once I got married I never expected to see her again. I probably wouldn't have if you'd not run into her at the Royal last summer and told me she was asking about me."

"I'm glad I did. If you don't mind me saying, the pair of you seem to be . . ." He frowned.

O'Reilly understood that Barry wasn't sure how far he might go.

"Having a lot of fun together," Barry said.

Tactfully put. "We are," O'Reilly said. "I'm very fond of Kitty O'Hallorhan."

"It shows, Fingal," Barry said. "I'm surprised you've let me have this weekend off. I'd have thought that given she's been away, you'd have wanted—"

"To be with her?"

"Yes."

"I did." But she didn't. Go on, tell Barry. "I think Kitty's assessing her future. I'll not be seeing her for a couple of weeks. She's going to be in London."

"Why?"

"She's doing a refresher course."

"Hardly a reason to be worried. You'll see her when she comes back."

"I know. We have a dinner date, but . . . but I'm concerned that it could be our last."

Barry put his left thumb under his chin and stroked his upper lip with his index finger. "I'm hardly an expert, Fingal, but I can tell you what Jack Mills—"

"Ulster's answer to Casanova *and* Don Juan?"

"He *is* experienced. Probably more than the pair of us put together. I can tell you what he told me last summer when Patricia decided her career was more important than falling in love."

"Go on."

"He told me to let the hare sit. Either she'd come back, or if she didn't, I'd get the message." His eyes clouded. "She did come back . . . for a while."

"And is there anything you could have done to keep her?"

"I suppose I could've tried proposing, but I wasn't ready."

Am I ready to propose? O'Reilly asked himself. Was that what Kitty was hinting?

"I don't think she'd have accepted anyway. She has her sights set on more important things. She wrote to me a few weeks ago, told me she'd made a mistake. Wasn't suited for country life. Needed a wider horizon."

O'Reilly watched as Barry inhaled, held the breath, then let it escape slowly. Is Barry blaming himself? Fingal wondered. Those suffering a loss usually did. It had taken him years to accept that he could have done nothing to prevent his wife's death. When he'd suggested Deidre leave Belfast in 1940, she'd flatly refused. He'd told her the city's shipyards were building a lot of escort vessels and that it might make the city a target for Göring's *Luftwaffe*. But she'd laughed it off. If he'd insisted, tried harder . . .

Barry fiddled with a spoon. "I suppose I could have gone to Cambridge to be near her," Barry said. "There's a damn fine obstetrics and gynaecology unit at Addenbrooke's Hospital."

And is that a hint you're not altogether satisfied with general practice? O'Reilly wondered, but he said, "Och, Jasus, have you got a dose of the most pernicious disease in the world, if-only-I'd-itis?"

"I like obstetrics, Fingal."

"So did I, Barry, but life interfered."

"I know. You told me, but you also said you were very happy as a GP."

"I still am," O'Reilly said. He hesitated before asking, "It's been nearly nine months since you joined me, Barry. Are you happy?" He waited.

"Honestly?"

"Christ, Barry, if you've to ask that—"

"I'm sorry, Fingal, but you've just been telling me you're worried about Kitty. You don't need to be worrying about me too."

"And why not? Isn't it my job? Worrying about Donal and Bertie Bishop, Julie's photo contest, about the ringworm outbreak, Alice Moloney's progress—she's improving by the way—about the

Patton twins?" He leant over and put a hand on Barry's shoulder. "It's all part and parcel of what being a country GP is all about, and for me it makes up for not making the great diagnostic break-through or curing someone with an heroic operation."

"I understand. And you needn't worry about the twins. I spoke to their paediatrician yesterday. They're both off forty percent oxygen and thriving."

"That's a relief. It's one less concern." He leant closer to Barry. "And I like how you didn't want to worry me, but it's been clear as the nose on your face for the last few weeks. You're having second thoughts. And you *are* a damn fine midwife."

"Well—"

"It's all right. I think I know a way out for you."

"What do you mean?"

"I'll explain it all to you next week. Are you willing to wait 'til then?"

"Of course, but—"

O'Reilly put out a hand as if to stop Barry's curiosity. "Next week. And you will go on working here until July?"

"Of course. That's what I agreed to when I started last summer. I'd not renege on you, Fingal."

"Good man. I shouldn't have asked. I've always known I could trust your promises."

"Thank you for that." Barry smiled.

"Aye . . . well." O'Reilly wanted to move on. "I need to make a phone call, and the fellah I have to talk to won't be around at the weekend."

Barry rose, then walked to the window and back. "I haven't the foggiest notion what all this is about, but thank you, Fingal. Thank you very much."

"Och, run away on off and chase yourself. No need for thanks." And in truth there wasn't. O'Reilly'd miss Barry very much if he moved on, but a volunteer was worth ten pressed men. Young Laverty would be no use as a partner if he wasn't happy at his work.

O'Reilly picked up his paper. "You told Kinky you were going down to the Yacht Club. Away you go. Have fun this weekend, and it's my turn in the surgery on Monday."

35

To Have a Friend Is to Be One

Barry drove along Bangor's familiar Seacliffe Road, heading for the Yacht Club, still wondering what O'Reilly had in mind that might help him reach a decision about his future. The old sweater he wore had the familiarity of an old friend. The trousers were ones Kinky had not been able to save, despite her best ministrations; the shirt's collar was worn, soft against his neck. It felt good to be dressed in his oldest clothes. He was hoping to help out a crew with their spring refit, a job that usually entailed getting dirty. He was ready.

He passed the two-storey terraces on the inland side of the lough-shore road from Bangor to Ballyholme. Built in the 1850s to serve as boardinghouses in the summer, they had catered to the down-from-Belfast-for-a-week or over-from-Glasgow-to-be-beside-the-seaside holiday makers.

The big attraction had been the sea, which lay to Barry's left behind a stone wall. Belfast Lough was gunmetal grey, churning and bursting in sheets of spray on jagged, barnacle-encrusted rocks. Although the sky was dour and flat as the armour-plating of a battleship, it wasn't raining.

Halfway round the road, a single, L-shaped, two-storey building sat on a promontory that jutted into the lough. Barry knew it had been built in 1780 and later converted into flats. The building was a newcomer by Irish standards, where the megalithic passage tomb at Newgrange predated both the Great Pyramid at Giza and Stonehenge in England.

A fellah called Patrick Taylor, another sailor, had been in the year behind Barry at Queen's. His folks lived in the flat closest to the sea. Taylor'd be a houseman now—assuming he'd passed his finals last June.

Barry turned right onto Ward Avenue past Kingsland Park and wondered what interesting buildings his classmates who'd emigrated might see. Nothing as old as things here, that was for sure. But although moving on might be in Barry's plans, emigration, as he had tried to tell Sue Nolan, definitely was not.

He pulled into the car park of Royal Ulster Yacht Club.

Inside, the old building's wood-panelled walls were adorned with pictures and memorabilia of five yachts, all named *Shamrock*. On those vessels, between 1901 and 1930, Sir Thomas Lipton, the multimillionaire tea merchant, had mounted five unsuccessful challenges for the America's Cup. Royal Ulster had been his club because the aristocratic members of the Royal Yacht Squadron at Cowes on the Isle of Wight had blackballed his application for membership. Despite having been knighted, Sir Thomas was "in trade" and *not* the kind of person to be welcomed by the English gentry. But the Ulster folks were more interested in his abilities as a sailor and had been more than happy to have him.

Barry walked on and immediately met a man coming out of the club.

"Barry Laverty? My God." He stuck out his hand. "Barry? How in the hell are you?" He wore a tattered Aran sweater that one day might have been white, paint-splattered jeans, and canvas gym shoes known locally as guttees. He was about Barry's age but taller, and his sandy hair was receding so fast that Barry thought he could almost see the margin between shiny scalp and hair moving toward the back of John Neill's head.

"Hello, John. How the hell are *you*? It has been a while."

"Must be five or six years. And don't ask how I am." John pursed his lips and shook his head. "I should have taken your advice even more years ago when we sailed your dinghy. I can see you on the helm saying, 'Go to Queen's, John. Your school marks are great. Get a degree.' Would I listen?" He shrugged. "Selling life insurance is about as exciting as putting antifouling paint on my hull."

Barry smiled. "I'll bet you have a few quid saved up though. You've been earning good money since we left school. All the years I was a penniless student."

"And I've still no wife or rugrats to support, so I can afford a Glen-class keelboat."

"Good for you."

"What about you, Barry?"

"Me?" He shook his head. "Debonair bachelor. Footloose and fancy-free." And not happy about it either, but he'd not tell that to John.

"You've not had much time to sail though, have you? Duty calls and all that?"

"True."

"That's why we've not seen much of you lately."

Barry nodded. "But you will. I'm working as a GP in Ballybucklebo—and my boss gives me every other weekend off."

"That's not too bad." John ran a hand over his head, looked hard at Barry, and asked, "Didn't you sell your dinghy?"

"*Tarka*? She went to a fellah from Carrickfergus. I needed the money to buy a car."

"So you've no boat?"

Barry shook his head.

"I don't suppose you'd be looking for a racing-crew spot?'"

"On your Glen?'"

"Aye. Three of us can handle her, but a fourth man would be handy on spinnaker runs or in anything over twenty knots."

Cruising boats would sensibly reef down in winds like that. He knew the heavy Glen could be a beast to handle under those conditions, and only racing sailors would even think of hoisting the spinnaker, a great balloon of a sail, in high winds, but that was what made racing so exhilarating.

Barry thought for a moment. He'd agreed to stay with O'Reilly until July. He missed his sailing. John Neill was a good head. "I might," he said, "but the skipper would have to be pretty understanding."

"Why? Have you forgotten how to sail?'"

Barry laughed. "Not at all. Maybe I'm a bit rusty, but I can still tell a sheet from a halyard. The trouble is, I can't always be free when I want. Do you still race on Thursday nights?'"

"Aye."

"Doctor O'Reilly's pretty decent about time off. I can ask for every Thursday, but there are things he might want to do once in a while. I couldn't always guarantee to be here midweek for club races, and it'll be only every other Saturday for regattas."

"That won't be a problem as long as you let me know. I can always find a youngster hanging about the clubhouse, hoping for a ride, but it's good to have a semipermanent crew. You and I've raced together. You're a good tactician, good helmsman. I can often use a break in a race."

Barry hesitated. He wanted to keep his uncertainties to himself, but he had to be fair to John. Losing a crew member, even a part-time one, spoiled the harmony of the teamwork that developed over time. "I might not be available after July," he said.

"Why not?'"

"I'm still making up my mind. I might want to specialise, and trainee specialists work bloody awful hours."

John clapped Barry on the shoulder. "You will make up your mind one way or the other. You never wavered for one minute about wanting to be a doctor. And sure July's months away. We could still have three good months racing."

"In that case—"

"Welcome aboard." John stuck out his hand and Barry shook it. "Now, crew . . ." John hunched his shoulder, screwed up one eye, and in a faithful imitation of Robert Donat's Long John Silver, growled, "Aaaar, Jim lad, us'ns 'ave a job to do. Waas you ever at sea, Jim lad?"

Barry laughed. "I left myself open for that, didn't I?" And fair play. If he expected to enjoy the pleasures of sailing on somebody else's boat, he'd have to do his share of the chores. Hadn't he been hoping to be asked to help out today? "What's the job?"

"Antifouling. And Barbara and Ted Orr, the rest of my crew, can't get down today. Kid's birthday party."

"So old Ted did finally marry Barbara?" Barry asked, once more realising how out of touch medicine had made him.

John lowered his voice. "Had to, two and a half years ago. Michael's two today."

"Oops," Barry said, doing the necessary subtraction. "Bit premature was he?"

John laughed. "You *could* say that, but the pair of them seems to be happy as pigs in shite."

"Lucky them," Barry said quietly. *Barry, I made a mistake.* She would never have settled for domesticity. He saw that now. The letter had made it plain. If he'd been less besotted, he would have seen that.

"And lucky me," John said. "I've got help with the painting after all."

"I've a pair of wellies in the car. I'll get them."

"Better still, if your car's handy, *Glendun's* up on the hard standing at the Ballyholme Shipyard, so run us down and you can run us back up here about one. I'll buy lunch."

"Super." Barry led the way. Kinky, as she so often was, had been right. He was enjoying the company of his nonmedical friends. It sure as hell was better than sitting feeling sorry for himself when he was off duty.

He'd always liked being around boats, even if he was only there slapping special paint on the underside. It was applied annually to inhibit the growth of sea plants during the summer, when the boat would be on a permanent mooring in Ballyholme Bay. And at least until July, he'd be going out on the club launch to *Glendun* to race in a crew of old friends.

Next door to Caproni's ice cream shop and ballroom on Seacliffe Road, the shipyard's workshops and their extensive forecourt were connected to the waters of Ballyholme Bay by two iron rails. The slipway crossed the road and ran down a gently sloping concrete slab beside a dinghy park. Here boats were hauled ashore or launched.

In the forecourt, John's boat, deep-wooden-hulled and beamy, squatted on the legs of a cradle beside several other vessels. Barry, who was working on her keel, stood up, paintbrush in one hand, the other hand massaging the small of his back. Across the road, skippers and their crews were sandpapering or painting the bottoms of upturned little craft. The rasping of rough paper and the scratching of paint scrapers could be heard over the noise of the occasional passing car. The annual refurbishing ritual was a reminder that spring was not so very far away.

Past the park, on the far side of Ballyholme Bay, whins grew dark green and chrome yellow on Ballymacormick Point. There were quiet places among the gorse there, hidden paths where a young man could kiss his girl in private. *I wish everything good for your career and you.* Could he think it so soon after Patricia had gone? Could he think of kissing a girl in the quiet places on the point?

Barry pursed his lips and turned back to the boat. *Glendun* was one of a number of identical yachts, all of which had been built near Strickland's Glen. The early ones had been named for the Glens of Antrim. *Glendun,* he knew, meant "the glen of the river Dun." John had told Barry that her leading rival was *Glenariff,* "the glen of arable land."

He dipped his brush into a can of red antifouling, squatted, and went back to painting the cast-iron keel. The fumes stung his nostrils. He could see John's guttees and the legs of his paint-spattered jeans on the other side of the keel.

"It's quarter to one," John yelled. "Ten more minutes, then lunch. My back's bollixed."

Barry's own back was stiff. "Right." He slapped on more red paint.

From behind him a woman's voice said, "It's hardly the Sistine Chapel, Michelangelo."

He recognised the tones, and turned. "Sue . . . Sue Nolan. What are you doing here?" He started to stand. "Hang on." Was it the effort of standing up that had made his pulse a little fast?

"I noticed your car five minutes ago, then I saw you stand up, so I came over to say hello and to thank you again for looking after Art and taking me home."

"Taking you home on Wednesday was my pleasure." It had been. She had been easy to talk to on the run up to Holywood. He'd almost accepted her invitation in for a cuppa, but at the time

O'Reilly was pretty much *hors de combat* and Barry had pleaded the call of duty. "What brings you down here today?" he asked.

"I was over in the dinghy park doing the same as you," she said, "only on a smaller boat." Her one-piece brown dungaree was liberally splattered with white enamel. Vagrant copper wisps of hair, piled under a man's floppy cap, escaped at the nape of her neck and over her forehead. They fluttered in the breeze like ribbon telltales from the shrouds of a yacht. She used her left hand to brush away a thin lock hanging over her right eye. "You remember in the car the other day I told you I was learning sailing theory?"

Barry nodded.

"Do you know Dennis Harper?"

"Dennis? I've known him for years. He has a GP14. Nice little dinghy."

"He went to Queen's with my older brother, Michael. They're both lawyers, and I've known Dennis for years too. He's been coming to Broughshane with Michael since I had pigtails. Been like a big brother."

She'd have suited pigtails, Barry thought.

She pointed across to the dinghy park. "He's over there. He's an instructor on the sailing course. That's why I'm here today. He needed his bottom scraped. I offered to give a hand."

Barry chuckled. "Did he indeed? Scraped? And did it hurt him much?"

"Barry." She grinned at him. "Eejit. I meant Dennis's dinghy needed—"

"I know. Just like I'm giving my skipper a help with the antifouling." He enjoyed the easy familiarity of a young woman who at their third or fourth brief meeting would let him tease her and would not be one bit reticent about calling him an eejit.

"I must say," she said, "you look more relaxed than you did when I saw you last. You look like you belong here."

He had to laugh. "Well, it beats looking at little heads being attacked by a fungal infection, and patching up skinned knees." He scratched his cheek. "I've sailed for years. Now I sail when I can get time."

"When did you learn? Did you take a course?"

Barry shook his head. "When I was twelve I lived beside the shore. I was fishing for crabs in the Long Hole—"

"The harbour at the start of Seacliffe Road?"

"That's right . . . and this little dark man came up to me. He was olive-skinned, had a hooked nose like Mr. Punch, and he was hunchbacked. He spoke to me in a thick foreign accent and asked me if I knew how to sail."

"You're not making this up, are you? His name wasn't Quasimodo by any chance?"

Barry chuckled. "No, it was Joe, Joe Bellini. His folks had come over from Italy after the war. Opened an ice cream shop here. Joe'd had TB of his spine as a child."

"That's sad," she said. He heard the compassion in her voice.

"When Joe left school at sixteen he couldn't work because of his handicap. His dad bought him a clinker-built dinghy so he'd have something to do. He'd been sailing that boat single-handed for ten years. He kept her in the Long Hole."

"With the fishing boats."

"Right. Anyway, when I told him I didn't know how to sail, he asked me if I'd like to learn."

"You said yes?"

"I told him I'd have to ask my dad. He agreed, and I spent five summers sailing with Joe." Barry could feel a lump starting. "Those were the happiest summers I've ever spent."

"Why?" Her question was gentle.

"I don't think Joe had any friends his own age, but he had his boat. He loved her; he loved the sea, the birds. He'd put her on course, hold the tiller, and roar out a sea chantey or a come-all-ye." Barry, who couldn't carry a tune in a bucket, warbled:

Come all ye dry-land sailors and listen to my song.
It's only a hundred verses so I'll not detain yiz long.

Sue bent over laughing. "Barry, that's terrible."

"I know," he said, "but it's one of the songs I learned from Joe." His smile faded. "It wasn't the only thing he taught me. He could see beauty in the most ordinary things. He once showed me a simple jellyfish and asked me to admire its exquisite filigree architecture. I've never forgotten that phrase."

"Filigree architecture," Sue said. "I like it."

"I've a lot of memories of that little, bent man. He taught me to sail all right, and he taught me to love it as much as he did. For him, sailing was freedom and it came to mean that for me too." Barry was surprised to feel Sue's touch on his arm. He looked into her eyes and felt he could trust this young woman. "I loved Joe like a brother, and it's to my shame I've not seen him in years. Medical school, moving to Ballybucklebo—"

"Barry, that kind of thing happens. We grow up, grow apart. I'll never forget the groom who taught me to ride when I was little, but I moved away, went to Stranmillis Teachers Training College, got my job in Ballybucklebo . . ."

"Do you still ride?" he asked, happy to change the subject.

"My uncle has horses. When I'm home, if I get the chance I'll exercise them for him."

"I've never ridden."

"And I've never sailed—not yet."

"And I've never had a more useless painter, standing there

blethering away while the antifouling dries." A grinning John Neill appeared from around the other side, rubbing his paint-splashed hands on a piece of turpentine-soaked rag.

"John," Barry said, "meet Sue Nolan from Broughshane. She teaches up in Ballybucklebo. Sue, John Neill."

The two nodded at each other. Ulster men and women rarely exchanged handshakes, and anyway John's hands were still smeared with paint and turpentine.

"Aren't you one of the students in Dennis Harper's 'Learn to Sail' class?" John asked.

"I am."

"Thought I'd seen you about the place." He looked around. "With Dennis today?"

Even though she'd said Dennis was like a big brother, Barry was surprised that the question "With Dennis today?" could make him feel envious.

"He's over in the dinghy park," she said. "We were just going to walk up to the club."

"I'll give him a yell," John said. "Barry has his car and we're going back up to Royal Ulster for lunch. Barry, you won't mind giving Sue and Dennis a lift, will you?"

"Not at all. Why don't you two join us for lunch?" It slipped out, but he knew he wanted to spend more time with Sue Nolan today.

"Love to, and I'm sure Dennis would too," she said.

"Right," said John. "I'm going to go find the worthy Harper and invite him to join us." He started walking down to the road.

Sue looked up at *Glendun* again. "What kind of boat is this, Barry?" she asked. "If I'm going to be a sailor, I need to know things like that."

"Doesn't it feel funny? You, a teacher, learning in a class?" he asked.

"Heavens, no," she said. "Life would be very dull if you didn't learn new things."

"Fair enough, and to answer your question, this boat's one of a local class called Glens."

She smiled. "Like the ones near Broughshane?"

"Exactly. This one's *Glendun*."

She looked admiringly at the curve of the hull. "She's a very graceful shape," she said.

And so are you, Sue Nolan, boilersuit notwithstanding. He remembered the glimpse of her thigh, the uptilt of her breasts under a black blouse when she'd picked up spilled exercise books the day he'd come to see the ringworm cases. He coughed. "I hear the places they're named for are very beautiful too."

She cocked her head to one side. "I told you that before Christmas. The invitation to visit still stands."

"You coming, Barry?" John yelled from the road. "We need you to drive."

"I'll take you up on that one day, Sue. I'd like to learn about that part of Ulster," Barry said. He put his paintbrush in a jar of turpentine and wiped his hands clean. "Come on," he said. "Lunch."

And as they walked together across the shipyard to join the others, Barry, for the first time in two months, felt a spark, a tiny glimmer of a kind of contentment he would have sworn he was never going to feel again.

36

Each to His Choice

"I'm delighted with your progress, Hughey," O'Reilly said, "and Doctor Laverty will be too." O'Reilly left the swivel chair and helped Hugh Gamble, his final patient, to his feet. Monday morning surgery was over.

"The knee's a whole lot better, but I'll not be running the hundred yards for a wee while yet," Hughey said. "Thon Deep Heat's great, and the physiotherapist at Bangor Hospital . . ." He winked slowly at O'Reilly. "She's a wee cracker, so she is."

O'Reilly smiled. "I hope she's helping your knee as well."

"She's doing a powerful job but, Doc . . . if I was forty years younger and I'd never met my Dora . . ." Hughey leant his head slowly to one side, grinned, and clicked his tongue between his cheek and teeth.

O'Reilly opened the door to the hall. "You're a terrible man, Hughey Gamble. You love to take a hand out of folks. I know bloody well you never looked at another woman in your life."

"Och sure, Doc, a cat can *look* at a king, as long as he doesn't mistake the monarch for a mouse."

"True," said O'Reilly, and he chuckled. "Let yourself out, and come back and see us in a month."

As Hughey left, O'Reilly picked up the telephone and dialled the number for the Royal Maternity Hospital. Barry was out making home visits, and O'Reilly had a promise to keep. It was clear to him that Barry believed he had only two choices: leave Number 1 and train as a specialist, or stay, perhaps reluctantly, and become a partner in July. But there was a third option.

"Professor Dunseath's secretary, please." He waited. "Jane? Fingal O'Reilly. How's your tennis elbow?" He listened to her lengthy description. He'd known Jane for years. Early in his career, O'Reilly had learnt that it paid to be on good terms with specialists, and the way to have easy access to these busy people was to get to know their secretaries. "Aye, I know," he said sympathetically. "Hydrocortisone injections can sting like bedamned. Did they help? . . . Great. You'll be taking on Billie Jean King next." He heard Jane laughing. "Now, any chance I could get a word with his eminence, your boss? Great. I'll hold on."

Paddy Dunseath, M.D., F.R.C.S., F.R.C.O.G., professor of obstetrics and gynaecology at the Queen's University of Belfast, was responsible for all the training positions in his discipline in Ulster. "Hello, Paddy . . . Fingal . . . I need a favour."

O'Reilly heard the County Roscommon man's brogue accentuated by the phone. "What can I do for ye, Fingal?"

"I've an assistant, Barry Laverty."

"Fair-haired chap? He was here in '62. He'd a flair for obstetrics, as I remember."

"He still has. Will you have any junior positions open in the summer?"

"Does he want to specialise?"

"He doesn't know, but *I* think he needs to test the waters. If he likes it, he'll make a damn fine obstetrician."

"Hold on. I need to look in a file. Just a sec."

O'Reilly heard papers being shuffled.

"I've nothing in Belfast, but I'm going to have a vacancy for a trainee at the Waveney Hospital in Ballymena in July."

"Terrific."

"You say he's not really sure about wanting to specialise?"

"That's right. He needs to find out what suits him best. He's a good lad, young Laverty. If he doesn't want to stay with you, Paddy, I'll have him back with pleasure."

"I'm a wee bit hesitant, Fingal. I prefer youngsters who have their hearts set on our speciality."

"But you said you'll have a vacancy in July. Does that mean no one's applied yet?"

"It does."

O'Reilly waited. He knew Paddy of old, knew he was a man who made up his mind easily, but didn't like to be pushed.

"All right, Fingal. I know the boy's good. I'll give him a six-month job and make him sit his Diploma of the Royal College at the end of it. That way, if he does come back to you he'll be better qualified, not only with more experience, but with a piece of paper to prove it."

Jasus. You don't need a brain. You need a diploma, O'Reilly thought. L. Frank Baum had been right. "And if he doesn't want to come back here?" he asked the professor.

"As long as he gives me two months' indication before his term is up, if he wants to stay on. And if he proves as good as you say, I'll keep him for the full specialist training, and he'll have the first six months under his belt."

"Terrific. And I promise you, Paddy, he is good."

"I'll take your word for it."

"How soon do you need to know if he wants the position?"

"He's got two weeks to make up his mind."

"Fair enough. You'll hear by then. Thanks, Paddy."

"No need to thank me, but if you could get me a couple of tickets for the next Ireland-England rugby international in Dublin—?"

"Done." As an ex-international player, O'Reilly could get tickets for himself. "I'll post them to you." Considering the favour the prof had just done, O'Reilly would give him his place with pleasure.

"Thank you, and I'll wait to hear from Laverty . . . What, Jane?" O'Reilly could make out the secretary's voice in the background. "Sorry, Fingal," Paddy said. "I've got to go." The phone went dead.

O'Reilly replaced the receiver as the front door opened and Barry came in. "More work for me this afternoon?" he asked.

O'Reilly shook his head. "How did your morning go?" He headed for the dining room.

Barry followed. "I took care of the phone calls you asked me to make. The Patton twins'll be home tomorrow, and Alice Moloney's being discharged on Wednesday."

O'Reilly took his seat. "Enemy nil, country GPs two—three if you count each twin individually. We do make a difference, you know."

Barry sat and smiled. "True enough," he said. "But I wish I could make some headway with the ringworm."

"Oh?"

"Miss Redmond chose to call me rather than send the patients over. Four more cases today."

"Four? How many's that altogether?"

"Eleven, counting Colin." Barry sat beside O'Reilly. "I'm blowed if I know what the source is. I thought it might be Colin Brown's white mouse, but with Colin safe at home effectively in quarantine, and the mouse with him, how are the others getting infected?"

"I think I know," said O'Reilly. "You said something that jogged my memory last week. I had an outbreak here in 1956. I probably should have acted on this one sooner, but we'll go and see Colin after lunch."

"What did I say last week?" Barry leaned forward. "And what happened in 1956?"

"1956?" If O'Reilly was right in his guess about the ringworm, he wanted to surprise Barry. "1956? Arthur Miller married Marilyn Monroe, the Hungarians rebelled against the Russians, Britain and France invaded Suez—"

"And Bertolt Brecht fell off the perch. I'm getting to know you, Fingal Flahertie O'Reilly. You want to surprise me at Colin's with your wisdom and experience. I can wait."

"Good lad. I do want to get out to the Browns. I hope we'll not have to wait too long for our lunch."

"You will not, so," Kinky said, bringing in a tray. "I've done toad in the hole today, with brussels sprouts and onion gravy."

"Wonderful," O'Reilly said. He could smell the gravy. He looked at his plate. Six sprouts, a small lake of gravy, and a Cookstown sausage—Kinky would use no other kind—nestled in a wrapping of Yorkshire pudding. "Oh, lovely." He glanced at Barry's plate. Damn it, the boy had two sausages. O'Reilly glanced up at Kinky and had to look away. She clearly would brook no argument. "Just bloody lovely," he muttered.

"It does only be luncheon, sir, not a Celtic feast with a whole roast ox. Maybe you'll like your dinner better. I've Guinness beef, carrots, mushrooms, and champ, with apple crumble to follow."

"I like the sound of that," said O'Reilly.

"And you might like the news I have from Cork," she said.

O'Reilly's fork stopped half an inch short of a sprout. "Go on."

"He was a terrible man for the craythur, our Tiernan, when he was a youngster. Last night he had a few with Eugene Power, the jockey man. They've been friends through the road bowling. Tiernan reckons Eugene is one of the best jockeys riding these days; he made a slip a few years back, but ordinarily he rides to win. Now he's in trouble."

"Trouble?" O'Reilly said.

"Eugene told Tiernan he does not know what to do. He's terrified he'll lose his licence. He's just got the word he's to pull a horse at Downpatrick on the twenty-seventh; he doesn't want to, but he's being forced."

"Is he, by God? Is he? And no prizes for guessing who by." O'Reilly ignored his lunch. "Barry, we'll need to see Donal. If he's got word about how Bertie's betting and now this—"

"Excuse me, sir," Kinky said, "but I saw Julie at the grocer's this morning. She's coming in tomorrow for an antenatal visit. I took the liberty of mentioning that it might be a good idea if Donal came with her. I did not say why, so."

"Kinky, you're a genius," O'Reilly said. He made a quick calculation. Julie'd been eight weeks when she was married in early December. This would be her twenty-week visit.

"Have you been seeing her, Barry?"

"I have and she's doing fine."

"Any word on the photo contest?"

"She'll hear next week."

"I do hope the little lamb wins," Kinky said. "She's a darlin' girl, so." Kinky tutted. "And with all that blether, Doctor O'Reilly, you've let my toad go cold in its hole." She whipped away his plate. "I'll bring you another," she said.

"Any old chance of two?"

Kinky sniffed—and left.

"Oh, well," said O'Reilly, "it was worth a try." He sat back. "Good old Kinky. Trust her to ferret things out." He drummed his fingers on the tabletop. "Now, Barry, you'll be in the surgery tomorrow. Take Julie and Donal first so I can be with you before I start the home visits."

"Right."

"Then," O'Reilly said, "if Donal has good news for us and we combine that with what we've just heard—"

"We might just make a call on His Exaltedness, Councillor Bishop, in the afternoon?" Barry suggested.

"Indeed we might." O'Reilly watched Barry dig into his second sausage. "So Julie's pregnancy is going smoothly?"

"Very smoothly," Barry said. "I've seen her at twelve and sixteen weeks. She's been a bit anxious after what happened last time."

"Twenty weeks? She should be out of the woods now," O'Reilly said, "but you never know with pregnancy." He looked at Barry. "And while we're on the subject of obstetrics, since our chat on Saturday I've had a word with the bloke I said I'd speak to."

Barry frowned, put both wrists on the table, and leaned forward. "Please go on."

"I know you are having second thoughts about general practice—" O'Reilly held up his hand. "Let me finish. You're hurting about Patricia, this place is full of memories . . ." O'Reilly saw Barry nodding slowly. "You're frustrated with the run-of-the-mill work and having to make referrals of so many interesting cases."

"I really enjoy feeling that I fit in here, am part of the community. I've always loved the country . . ." Barry stared at the tablecloth for long seconds before looking at O'Reilly. "But frustrated?" he asked quietly. He nodded.

"You're bloody good with pregnant patients. I think you should go and work in an obstetric unit for a while."

"But—"

"I'll hold your job here for six months."

"How? The practice has grown since I came, even with Doctor Fitzpatrick up in the Kinnegar. You'll need help."

"Do you know about Barry Bramwell?"

"Wasn't he a trainee obstetrician?"

"He was, but he started a thing called the Contactor's Bureau. It's not like the old days when I started. Single-handed GPs can get temporary locums from it, or someone to cover if they want a day or night off. For a fee, of course. I'm going to use them in a couple of weeks for the Downpatrick Races. You want to come, don't you?"

"Wouldn't miss it."

"Ordinarily Kinky would hold the fort, but she likes a day at the horses. It'll be a little break for her."

"That's decent of you, Fingal."

"The hell it is. That woman's worth her weight in gold ten times over."

"How much will a locum cost?"

"I'm not sure. Why?"

"I'd like to pay half. I'm getting a day off too."

Typical Barry. O'Reilly shook his head. "My treat."

"Thank you, Fingal, for paying for the day, but I don't see why you should be out of pocket for me if you have to get a locum for six months."

O'Reilly laughed. "That's decent of you, Barry, but I said I'd hold your job. I didn't say I'd go on paying you and locums as well."

Barry took a deep breath.

"Barry, it'll give you a bit more time for getting over your girl, and it'll let you see what obstetrics and gynaecology is all about. I know I liked the obstetrics very much, but gynae? I'm not so sure. Gynae surgery is certainly challenging, and infertility and endocrinology will stretch your mind, but outpatients?" O'Reilly grimaced.

"I've done gynae outpatients, Fingal. Clinics full of patients for cervical smears, with vaginal itches, painful periods, asking for contraceptive advice. It could become pretty dull. None of it's trivial to the patients, I know, but you don't have the satisfaction of getting to know those patients as people. It's conveyor-belt medicine because you're always pushed for time. I'm sure it could get pretty routine, but I'd hope the sorting-out of the more difficult cases would make up for it. Every job has its dull bits."

"That's why I think you going in at the deep end for six months will give you every chance to see if you really like the whole package, warts and all," O'Reilly said.

"Allegedly Oliver Cromwell's instructions to Sir Peter Lely, who was to paint a portrait."

"True, but we're not talking about your picture. We're talking about your career, and I'm asking you to think about giving obs and gynae a try."

"Fingal, I don't know what to say."

"Then don't say anything. There's a job starting in July."

"July?"

"That's right, for six months. So if you want to come back, you could get experience, write the diploma, and be better qualified for here. If you want to stay on and specialise, you'll have six months already done of the four-year training you'll need."

"I really don't know what to say."

O'Reilly saw how the boy's eyes glistened. "Prof. Dunseath says he'll hold the job for two weeks to give you time to decide. Only two weeks, so think hard about it."

"Fingal," Barry rose. "Fingal, that's the most generous, most considerate—"

"Bollocks. It's entirely selfish. I can't lose. If you decide not to accept and to stay here, great. We'll be partners in July. If you decide to go, I'll either get a better-qualified partner back in time for next New Year's or you'll be doing what you want with your life."

"But you'll be short an assistant."

"Holy thundering Mother of Jasus, I *know* you, Laverty. If you're going to stay on specializing, you'll tell me early. I'll have no trouble finding an assistant among the locums. He won't be Barry Laverty, but I'll manage. Might even get a young woman doctor these days. You, take your time. Think about it. Be sure it's what you want to do."

"And the job's in the Royal Maternity?"

O'Reilly laughed. "The Royal and the Jubilee in Belfast aren't the only training centres. This job's in the Waveney Hospital."

"In Ballymena?"

O'Reilly nodded and wondered why Barry had a small smile when he said, "That's only a few miles from Broughshane."

"And I'm sorry this has taken a few minutes longer than it should, sir," Kinky said, bringing in O'Reilly's plate. "Her Ladyship's in disgrace. I didn't think such a shmall little white cat could eat up so much Yorkshire pudding batter. I'd to make a fresh batch."

"It's all right, Kinky," O'Reilly said. "Better late than never. Thank you." He sliced into the sausage. "Now, Barry Laverty," he said, "you've two weeks to make up your mind about the prof's offer."

"Thank you, Fingal."

"And there's something else I've not forgotten, Barry." He chewed a mouthful of toad in the hole. "Delicious. When I get the rest of this into me, we're going to pay Colin Brown a visit and I'll tell you what happened in 1956."

37

The Schemes o' Mice an' Men

"We'll walk," said O'Reilly, and with a resonant bang he closed the door to Number 1. "You remember where the Browns live?"

"Down Station Road. Thatched cottage next door to the tobacconist's." Barry was looking forward to this. If Fingal wanted to preserve an air of mystery about the ringworm affair, so be it. Barry was happy to play along.

The gales and downpours of earlier in the month had given Ballybucklebo's face a good scrubbing. The road was litter-free and the air salty clean, but Barry had no doubt that after a few more weekly cattle markets the place would again be wearing its familiar attar of cow manure.

"Afternoon, Doctors," Freddy Patton yelled from across the road. "It'll be great to get the wee ones home tomorrow. Brave day today, so it is."

Barry waved back.

"Afternoon, Freddy." O'Reilly's quarterdeck roar soared over the traffic noise. Barry reckoned it probably let mariners far out in Belfast Lough know they were within two miles of the County Down shore.

Freddy was right. It was a lovely afternoon for the middle of February. Patches of blue played hide-and-go-seek between masses of cumulonimbus. The onshore breeze barely stirred the rehung sign of the Black Swan. Ahead of Barry, a hen pigeon fled along the gutter. She was trying to avoid the amorous intentions of a cock that strutted jerkily after her, his enamel-blue and green head iridescent in a beam of sunshine.

As they waited at the traffic light, Barry watched two women go into the Ballybucklebo Boutique. Sally must be justifying Alice Moloney's faith in her ability to run things. He'd seen Sally in follow-up last week. For the moment she was pimple-free, possibly as a result of the chocolate-free diet he'd suggested last month.

From across Station Road a voice called, "Yoo-hoo, Doctors."

Barry saw Sonny and Maggie Houston hurrying across from the direction of the dress shop. Maggie wore an ankle-length, dark-blue overcoat, Wellington boots, and her old straw boater. A wilted red rose drooped from the hatband. When the couple arrived hand in hand, Barry was pleased to see that Sonny's cheeks were not blue, nor was he short of breath. His heart failure was still under control. "Good day," he said and touched the brim of his Paddy hat. Maggie grinned. She was wearing her dentures today.

"How are you both?" O'Reilly asked.

"Fit as fleas," Maggie said, "and never mind us, how's about Miss Moloney? I reckon she should be well mended by now."

"She is, Maggie," Barry said. "She'll be coming home next Wednesday."

"Do you think," Maggie asked, "she will need us still for to look after her pets?"

"Why not pop round on Wednesday afternoon, see to them, and ask her?" O'Reilly said. "My guess is she'll be a bit peely-wally yet and will be glad of the help—and the company."

"We will," said Sonny. "I shall miss Felix when we finish. He is a *very* well mannered animal."

If Barry was interpreting correctly the look Sonny gave Maggie, the implication was that Maggie's battle-scarred cat, General Sir Bernard Law Montgomery, was not.

The criticism clearly ran off her like water off a duck's back. "Felix may be nice," she said, "but that bird, Billy, the bloody biting *bastún* of a budgerigar, should get a dose of fowl pest." She held up a finger and showed Barry an Elastoplast dressing.

I warned you, Barry thought. Moving to safer ground, he said, "I like your rose, Maggie."

She smiled up at Sonny, who smiled back at her. "He's a sentimental oul' goat, my Sonny."

Barry heard the fiercely protective "my" and once again envied them.

"He brings me a red rose every Monday."

"I hate to tell you, Maggie," O'Reilly said, "but that rose's a bit—"

"Elderly?"

He nodded.

"Of *course* it is. It's last week's." She put a hand to her hat brim. "Waste not, want not, and sure the only thing in flower so far this month is speedwell. Our snowdrops are up, but won't be blooming until next week. When they are, that's a dead-sure sign spring's on the way, so it is."

"And if you'll excuse us, Sonny, Maggie, we'd best be on our way too. We've a patient to visit, and the light's going to change again," O'Reilly said. "Good to see you both."

Sonny lifted his hat. "Good afternoon." He turned away, and still holding hands, they walked along Main Street.

"There are, it seems," O'Reilly said, as if to himself, "advantages to the married state—at least for some folks."

And advantages to the closeness of the community in a place like this, Barry thought. Ballybucklebo was much smaller than Ballymena. If he went there as a trainee specialist, he'd not be wrapped up in the day-to-day life of the place the way he was here.

He had to lengthen his stride to catch up with O'Reilly, who was already knocking on the door of the Browns' cottage.

"Now, Barry," O'Reilly said, "if I'm right and this is a rehash of my previous experience in 1956, I'm going to need your support."

"Certainly."

Colin answered the door. He was clutching a half-eaten slice of bread that was liberally smeared with strawberry jam. A lump of red stuff clung to the corner of his mouth. "Hello, Doctor O'Reilly," he said indistinctly, through a mouthful. He tried to hide the slice behind his back. "My mammy's out at the shops doing her messages, so she is."

Barry had never understood why in Ulster errands were called "messages."

"She said I could make myself this here piece," the boy said, using the Ulsterism for bread and whatever it was spread with.

Barry very much doubted the truth of Colin's statement but decided to let it be.

"It's you we came to see, Colin," O'Reilly said. "May we come in?"

"Aye, certainly." Colin took another huge mouthful.

Barry followed along a narrow hall, where a bicycle was propped against one wall. They went into a small kitchen. Clothes were spread to dry on two collapsible clotheshorses. There was a faint aroma of detergent. Dishes were drying in a rack on a shelf beside the sink.

"Will youse sit down, please?" Colin asked, indicating plain wooden chairs at a pine kitchen table.

Mischievous Colin might be, Barry thought, but he'd been taught manners.

"My mammy would make youse a cup of tea, so she would, but I don't know how to, like. I'm not allowed to boil water, you know."

"That's a good thing," O'Reilly said, parking himself.

"Finish up your piece," Barry said, "and wash your face." Colin grinned, gobbled down the last morsel, and washed his mouth at the kitchen sink.

"We'd not want Colin's mammy to see him smeared with jam, would we, Doctor O'Reilly?" Barry hated to see kids getting into trouble, and pinching a slice of bread and jam was hardly a felony.

O'Reilly said, "Doctor Laverty's right, son, not when we've come here to see about your head. How is it anyway?"

"A bit itchy yet," Colin said, "and that ointment stings."

"Can't be helped," O'Reilly said. "We've got to get you better and back to school."

Colin sighed.

"Doctor Laverty, will you have a look, please?"

Barry bent and peered at Colin's scalp. "The patch is much smaller. It's on the mend."

"Good," said O'Reilly.

"Colin, have you a pet mouse?" Barry asked.

Colin sighed again. "I had. I had him two years. I called him Morris. He was a great wee thing, so he was. He could climb wee stepladders and all."

"Had?" Barry asked.

"Aye," said Colin. "He was very old. About a week ago I went to give him his brekky . . ." Colin shrugged, swallowed, then smiled. "We give him a super funeral in the flower bed, so we did. My daddy's a carpenter, you know. He made Morris a wee coffin and everything."

"Did you not feel sad?" Barry asked, torn between sympathy for the child and a feeling of relief that the probable source of the outbreak was no more.

"Och, I did for a day or two, but my daddy and mammy's for getting me a tortoise."

The resilience of childhood in the face of loss, Barry thought. Would that it had persisted for me—and for Joseph Devine.

"Something to look forward to," said O'Reilly.

"Aye," said Colin. "I'm going to call him Adolf Kilroy, like the one in *The Perishers.*"

Barry could picture the tortoise in the *Daily Mirror* comic strip. He had a Hitler moustache, and dark German script appeared in his speech balloons. "Did you ever see it, Dr. O'Reilly? That tortoise was shaped like a World War Two German helmet."

O'Reilly nodded. "It's very funny," he said. "An old English sheepdog called Boot; his master, a little boy called Wellington; your tortoise with a carapace like a German helmet . . ." He chuckled, then said, "Colin, talking of headgear, did your mammy do like Doctor Laverty asked?"

"And boil my cap? Aye." Colin, who had been smiling at the conversation about the comic strip, lost his grin.

"Could I see it?"

Colin's eyes narrowed. "What for?" he asked. "My mammy boiled it, so she did."

"I'd just like to see it," O'Reilly said.

"Doctor Laverty said the mushroom thingys was too wee to see."

"They are," said O'Reilly.

"Then why do you want to look at my cap?"

Barry was surprised by the resistance.

"Colin," O'Reilly said, and Barry heard the steel in his voice.

"Och, all right." Colin left.

"Now," said O'Reilly. "Just follow my lead."

"Here y'are." Colin handed O'Reilly the school cap. "But she did boil it. Honest to God."

O'Reilly turned it inside out and peered at the lining. His frown was so deep his eyebrows met. "Hmm," he grunted.

Barry's bafflement grew, and it grew further when O'Reilly whipped out a magnifying glass. Lord, Barry thought, he just needs a deerstalker and meerschaum pipe, and—Barry smiled—I suppose that would cast me as Doctor Watson.

"Aha," O'Reilly said. "Ah-ha." Barry stole a glance at Colin. The boy's eyes were wide, his mouth hung open.

"Doctor Laverty." O'Reilly handed the cap and glass to Barry. "Take a look at *that.*"

Barry accepted the cap and peered through the lens. All he could see was an enlarged section of cap lining.

"So," said O'Reilly sternly to Colin, "your mammy boiled your cap?"

"She did."

"But Colin, it's crawling with ringworm. Isn't that right, Doctor Laverty?"

Barry gave the cap back to Fingal. "Oh, indeed," Barry lied. You'd need special preparation and a microscope to see the fungus. What the hell was Fingal up to?

"She boiled it." Colin's voice cracked. He was near to tears.

O'Reilly leant forward so his face was close to Colin's. "Did you know that doctors have to keep secrets, Colin?"

"What about?" Barry heard Colin's note of enquiry.

"Anything a patient tells them."

"That's right," Barry said.

"You mean, like, if I told you something, you'd not have to tell my mammy, nor Mrs. Redmond?"

"Not a word," said O'Reilly. "Not . . . a . . . dicky bird."

Barry watched Colin frown, purse his lips, breathe out through his nose.

"How much a rub, Colin?" O'Reilly asked softly. "How much?"

How much a what? Barry wondered.

"You'll not tell nobody?" Colin sounded urgent. "Promise?"

O'Reilly crossed his heart. Barry nodded.

"Sixpence," Colin whispered.

"Sixpence?" O'Reilly said and looked at Barry. "Inflation's a terrible thing. In 1956 it was tuppence. How many boys?"

"Ten."

"That's five shillings. About five weeks' pocket money?"

Colin nodded.

Barry was still at a loss.

"Honest to God, you'll not tell?" Colin begged.

"We'll not," said O'Reilly, "provided you tell us the names of all the boys you sold to."

"And they'll not get into trouble?"

Barry had to admire the little lad's sense of honour.

"Not at all," said O'Reilly. "We just want your cap—and theirs."

"All right. It was Hubert—"

"Before you tell us any more," O'Reilly interrupted, "have I got this right? Your mammy boiled your cap. When it was dry, you wore it again on purpose?"

And reinfected it, Barry thought. Griseofulvin and the ointment would not have killed the fungus in one day.

Colin nodded.

"Then you saw some of the boys and told them you could get them out of school for two weeks—for sixpence each?"

Barry remembered Hubert Flynn asking if they'd have to stay at home, and giving Art a thumbs-up as if there'd been some plan. Now he understood.

"And they came over and you rubbed them with this?" He held up the cap.

Colin nodded. "And I told them that only *my* cap worked. So there'd be no competition, like. None of the ten of them selling rubs, maybe even cheaper. When their mammies boiled their caps, they'd not know to do what I done with mine."

Barry couldn't completely stifle his grin. This little devil should sign on as an apprentice to Donal Donnelly—or perhaps Colin could give Donal a few pointers.

"Doctor Laverty, how many patients have you seen?"

"Ten, plus Colin," Barry said.

"In that case," said O'Reilly, "we'll not need their names. If Colin only made ten sales and they can't pass the disease along, the outbreak's contained. Can you phone Mrs. Redmond and let her know we think it's all done?"

"Of course." Typical Fingal. Solving a problem and letting Barry get the thanks.

"Least said, soonest mended about the other lads, don't you think?" O'Reilly asked and cocked his head. "Professional confidentiality?"

Understanding the wisdom of what O'Reilly was saying, Barry was relieved that he'd not be under any obligation to tell the principal the names of the culprits. Having seen her in action, he was sure retribution would have been fair but swift. He might tell Sue Nolan in confidence if he saw her again. Not the names, but how the mini-epidemic had been spread. She'd certainly get a laugh. He spoke to Colin. "Doctor O'Reilly promised you nobody would get into trouble, so we'll be saying nothing about you or the other boys. Just telling Mrs. Redmond there'll be no more trouble with ringworm."

A very humble-sounding Colin said, "Thank you, sir."

"I thought, Doctor Laverty, that we were going to have to collect up all their caps too—and burn them. But I'm pretty sure you've treated everybody, and none of the others, thanks to Colin, will be in the fungus retail trade."

"I wish I'd suggested burning yours when I saw you first, Colin," Barry said.

Colin looked at his feet and scuffed one toe on the rug.

O'Reilly said, "You didn't have the advantage of having been down this road before in 1956 when the perpetrator of an identical scheme did very nicely. He is, by the way, known to you, Doctor Laverty."

Barry was not surprised that Fingal had been able to mine his seemingly inexhaustible lode of experience to understand what was going on now. He was curious about the 1956 fungus seller. "Who was it, Doctor O'Reilly?"

O'Reilly nodded at Colin, shook his head, and said, "I'll tell you later."

Barry heard the front door opening. Mrs. Brown, carrying a laden wicker shopping-basket, came into the kitchen. She stopped dead. "Is everything all right?" She moved to Colin.

"Indeed it is," said O'Reilly. "Colin's been a hero. He's helped us solve the riddle of the ringworm outbreak."

Barry saw a look of adoration cross Colin's face as he stared at O'Reilly.

"Has he? That's great. I was talking there now to Hubert Flynn's mammy. She'll be dead pleased, so she will."

"Good," said O'Reilly, fixing Colin with his gaze. "And Colin's promised me that from now on he'll always do his homework before he goes out to play. Every last bit," O'Reilly said.

Colin's worshipful look turned to a scowl. Barry realised that although it might appear O'Reilly had let the boy off lightly, there'd been a sting in the tail. Colin's mother would hold him to the promise the doctor had invented, and the boy might just learn the lesson that crime did not pay.

Even though the patient was a small boy, O'Reilly was in complete compliance with his own first law of general practice: Never let the customers get the upper hand.

"Now," said O'Reilly, pulling out a ten-shilling note. "We'll have to take his cap for more tests."

What tests? Barry wondered.

"Fortunately," O'Reilly said, handing Mrs. Brown the money, "there's a public health fund that reimburses parents, so buy him a nice new cap."

"Thank you, Doctor," she said. "That one was getting a bit wee for him, anyway."

"Come on, Doctor Laverty," O'Reilly said. "We'll see ourselves out."

Once on the street, and before Barry could ask who the fungus salesman had been in 1956, O'Reilly, holding the cap by the peak between his finger and thumb, said, "When we get home this is going on the fire. We'll have our own little bonfire of the vanities."

"Our what?"

"Bonfire of the vanities. It's an old Italian custom of burning objects like mirrors and cosmetics that might lead one's feet from the path of righteousness and into sin. The most famous one was in Florence on February seventh, 1497."

Barry muttered, "Suppository."

"I heard that," said O'Reilly. "I'll let it pass."

"There's another thing," Barry said. "I didn't know about a public health fund to reimburse parents."

"Because there isn't one," O'Reilly said, "but you're the one who said she's not a Rothschild."

Barry shook his head. He knew it would be a waste of time trying to compliment O'Reilly on his generosity. The big man would merely growl, and there was another matter to be resolved. "Fingal," Barry said, "you said you'd tell me who was involved in 1956."

"'56?" O'Reilly said, and his grin was huge. "Even back then his hair was bright carroty and his buckteeth—"

Barry stopped in his tracks. "Donal? Donal Donnelly? Go away. I don't believe it." But he did.

"Who else?" said O'Reilly, who had stopped to wait for Barry.

"I just hope young Colin doesn't grow up with an interest in race-horses and greyhounds. I'm not sure Ballybucklebo's big enough for both of them."

Barry, who was laughing so much he had to bend over and put his hands on his knees, couldn't speak. But he thought and if that did happen, you, Doctor Fingal Flahertie O'Reilly, would still have the measure of them both.

38

You Have Sown Much, and Bring in Little

Barry answered a chorus of "Good morning, Doctor Laverty" with "Good morning, everybody." The surgery's waiting room was half full, not too busy for a Tuesday morning. Those god-awful roses on the wallpaper still made him cringe.

Elaine Kearney's young Kevin was down on his hands and knees on the carpet, pushing a red Dinky Toys car along and making broooom-broooom noises. Was it really a month since the boy had been admitted to Purdysburn Fever Hospital with croup? The boy looked up and piped, "Hello, Doctor Laverty. I'm all better, so I am." He certainly sounded as if he was completely recovered. It was satisfying, Barry thought, to know he'd helped the lad, even if only by making the diagnosis and arranging hospital admission.

"I'll have you and your mammy in in a minute," Barry said and smiled at Elaine. Then instead of announcing, "Who's first?" as the patients would be expecting, he said, "Doctor O'Reilly needs a favour from the Donnellys today and wants to see them at once before he starts his home visits. Sorry about that."

"Come on," Barry said, as the couple rose from their seats. Then he stood aside to let them precede him. He was as impatient as Fingal was to hear what Donal had to say.

There were a few mutterings and one voice said distinctly, "It's not right, so it's not."

"I'll be back soon, and I'll take you all in order." If he didn't quickly revert to the age-old practice of seeing patients in the sequence in which they had arrived, he knew the ensuing ructions would make the upheaval that spoiled Lieutenant William Bligh's afternoon on HMS *Bounty* look like a storm in a teacup.

He followed the Donnellys into the surgery. Fingal, half-moon spectacles on his bent nose, was in the swivel chair. "Morning to you both," he said. "Have a pew, Donal."

"Over here, please, Julie," Barry said, indicating the examining couch. Her raincoat front was open and she was starting to show. Her stomach under a navy-blue skirt was visibly swollen.

She handed him a small glass bottle. "My sample."

"Doctor O'Reilly," Barry asked, "could you do the dipstick tests? Speed things up a bit?"

"Sure. Just be a minute, Donal; then we'll get down to business."

And that, Barry thought, was proper. Looking after patients must take precedence over sorting out other matters. Barry gave O'Reilly the bottle, followed Julie to the couch, and waited for her to climb up, lie down, and expose her lower belly. As he wound the sphygmomanometer cuff round her arm, he told her, "Your blood tests are back. They're all normal."

"That's great," she said, "and I'm taking the tablets like you told me, sir."

Iron and folic acid supplements. He popped the stethoscope in his ears, blew up the cuff, and listened as he let it deflate. "Blood pressure's normal," he said.

She smiled.

Barry carried on with the routine of making sure her ankles weren't swollen, confirming that the top of her uterus was palpable at the level of her belly button—exactly where it should be at twenty weeks.

"Aye," she said, "and I felt the wee one kicking me last night, so I did. I was dead excited. I made Donal feel it too."

"The kicks of him?" Donal said. "He'll be playing centre forward for Linfield in no time."

"And if it's a girl, Donal?" Julie asked.

By the look on Donal's face it was clear he hadn't considered that eventuality.

"Don't worry," Barry said. "What's important right now is that by twenty weeks, and that's where Julie's at, she should be noticing movements, what we call quickening. I should be able to hear the baby's heartbeat." A moment bent over with the Pinard stethoscope confirmed that he could. "It's going like a steam engine," he said, as he straightened up.

"Urine's okay," O'Reilly called from beside the sink.

"So everything's fine," Barry said. "Just have to weigh you."

Donal's, "Sticking out a mile," was reflected by Julie's wide smile.

"You can fix your clothes and get down, Julie," Barry said and waited.

She was, he thought, a perfect example of what was so attractive to him about obstetrics. Nearly all of the time it meant dealing with happy events. The patients were young and usually healthy. Pregnancy was not a disease, and in the hospital the midwives, working under medical supervision, took care of all of the normal deliveries, freeing up the specialists to deal with more technically taxing cases.

His job as an obstetrician would be to know how to act when a complication did occur antenatally or during delivery or postpartum, and even more importantly to do everything possible to try to stop anything going wrong by detecting potential difficulties.

He was doing that preventative supervision today for Julie, who was now sitting up. Barry gave her his arm to lean on as she hopped down. "Come on over to the scales when you're ready," he said and then waited for her to finish rearranging her clothing.

It was at these routine antenatal visits that so much could be detected in the early stages and managed effectively—but by specialists, not GPs. GPs certainly weren't trained in, nor did they have the equipment to deal with, complicated deliveries. He remembered with satisfaction Hester Patton's twins, babies who really should not have been under his care at all and who would not have been but for Hester's decision to leave hospital.

Barry helped Julie onto the scales and was pleased to note she'd gained only four pounds since her last visit, well within the recommended limit of five pounds per month. "So," he said, "everything's going exactly as planned."

"Thank you, Doctor," Julie said and beamed. "Will I come back in a month?"

"Please. Unless you're worried about anything in the meantime."

"I don't think *I'll* be concerned, Doctor Laverty," Julie said. "Donal's the one who's sore worried, and it's not about our wee one neither."

Donal glanced at Julie.

She nodded to him and said to O'Reilly, "I know about Flo's Fancy." Julie sat on the other wooden chair and took Donal's hand. "He told me on Saturday." She looked directly at O'Reilly and shook her head. "Thick as a couple of short planks sometimes this husband of mine, but he's a heart of corn, so he has." She turned to Donal. "I know you did it for me and the child, didn't you, honey?"

Barry smiled. Donal could be stupid, no question, and Barry wasn't fully convinced that Donal's motives were ever entirely unselfish when it came to wagering on horses or dogs, but if Julie chose to believe it were so, Barry'd not interfere.

Julie looked Donal straight in the eye. "And you're very sorry, aren't you?"

Donal hung his head. "Yes, love. I am, so I am."

"You'll not do nothing as daft as that again, will you, Donal Donnelly? Not without talking to me first?"

"I promise," Donal said.

"And anyway," Julie said, "thanks to Mr. Bishop's cousin, even if Donal loses his whole hundred pounds in the horse, we'll still be one hundred and fifty pounds better off. I heard on Saturday I'm in the last two for the hair model's job, so I'm guaranteed two hundred and fifty pounds if I only come second."

"That's wonderful," O'Reilly said. "Bloody marvellous."

And very generous of her, Barry thought, to forgive Donal so readily.

"They'll announce the winner next Friday," Donal said. "Julie'll knock their socks off, so she will. That money'll get us a start in a wee house."

It would be a tremendous boost for them, Barry thought. Patricia had been right encouraging Julie to go ahead, just before she'd said to Kitty, "It's over." Eight weeks ago. He inhaled. Oh, well, one day, maybe one day, God knows when, I'll be house-hunting too. He looked at Julie. She did look radiant. "The very best of luck," he said.

"Och," she said, and Barry saw her squeeze Donal's hand. "I had that when this eejit married me." Her eyes shone.

Barry looked at Donal's carroty thatch, the buckteeth exposed by his wide grin. Love might not be blind, Barry thought, but in Julie's case it probably needed pretty strong spectacles.

"Does that mean, Donal," O'Reilly asked, "that as the Donnelly finances are going to be restored, there is less urgency in the matter of Bertie Bishop?"

"It does not indeed, sir. There's my mates to consider and all.

And this next race is make-or-break. Each one of us has only ten pounds left in the wee filly. If Mr. Bishop bets that and she loses—"

"You lads are out a hundred pounds each and he owns the whole bloody horse," said O'Reilly, and Barry saw those hellish lights burning deep in O'Reilly's eyes. "We can't be having that, can we, Barry?" O'Reilly rubbed his hands together. "So what can you tell me, Donal?"

"Your man Willy MacArdle kept his word, you know. It's took him a while, but he has asked all about. Not a one, not a single one of the local bookies has seen hide nor hair of Mr. Bishop nor his money. Willy was dead pacific about that, so he was."

"Specific," O'Reilly muttered. Then he added, "So Bishop's been lying. He's simply not betting. He's a gobshite of the first magnitude." He glanced at Julie. "Sorry, Julie."

"It's all right." She smiled and shook her head. "You should hear Donal and his friends after a few jars."

"Bishop does that to me," O'Reilly said. "And he is what I called him."

"I know," Donal said. "So can you get our shares in the wee horse back, sir?" Barry saw hope in his eyes.

"I can surely try, Donal," O'Reilly said. He turned to Barry. "*We* can surely try, can't we, Doctor Laverty?"

Donal grinned and said, "I'll bet when you and Doctor Laverty here have a go at him, sir, after what I told youse Willy told me, like . . . well, I'll bet Mr. Bishop'll cave in the way a sandcastle does when the sea comes in."

Barry was flattered to be included in Donal's obviously sincere belief that O'Reilly and he were miracle workers. He could certainly picture Fingal as an irresistible tide.

"He might, but when it comes to money," O'Reilly said, "Bertie Bishop and the Rock of Gibraltar have a lot in common. Both are big, both are thick, and both are very hard to budge."

"Even for you and Doctor Laverty?" Julie asked.

" 'Fraid so, Julie," O'Reilly said, "but by God, we're going to try, aren't we, Dr. Laverty?"

"Indeed we are," Barry said, and he felt a lot more optimistic than O'Reilly seemed to be. Of course, O'Reilly'd had years of experience in dealing with the councillor. Barry was glad to be involved once more in the affairs of the village.

"Good," O'Reilly said. His grin was vast. "This evening, barring acts of God, nuclear war, or a patient who really needs us, Doctor Laverty and I will have a word with Bertie Bishop."

"Thank you, sir."

"And I want your help, Donal."

What was O'Reilly planning now? Barry asked himself.

"Aye, surely, Doctor."

"Does Bertie still go into the Duck after work on a Tuesday to have a jar with that fellah from Belfast?"

"Ernie MacLoughlin? Him who supplies Mr. Bishop with bricks and cement? Five thirty," Donal said. "Like clockwork."

"Good," said O'Reilly. "So, Donal, I want you to be in the Duck too today, along with as many of the lads from your syndicate as you can round up. But I don't want you to come anywhere near the councillor, Doctor Laverty, and me until I call you over."

"Fair enough, sir."

Barry thought Donal sounded more cheerful.

"Right," said O'Reilly. "Off you two trot; Doctor Laverty will finish the surgery this morning, and I'll do the home visits."

"Time for work," O'Reilly said, as the couple left, "but if we get finished early we'll take Arthur for a run and then . . ." He grinned. "I'm really looking forward to my pint tonight."

39

On the Kingdom of the Shore

O'Reilly stood at the edge of Belfast Lough and hurled a stick out to sea. "Fetch."

Arthur shot off, tearing through the shallows, then swimming strongly until he grabbed the wood, turned, and, snorting mightily, returned, ran to O'Reilly, sat, and presented his retrieve.

"Good dog." O'Reilly took the stick, and the sodden animal stood and ambled to where Barry waited further back up the beach.

"No, Arthur," O'Reilly bellowed, but it was too late. He heard Barry yell, "Gerroff," saw him lean sideways like a matador evading a bull's charge as the big Labrador shook himself. The spray glittered in the rays of the setting sun, and Barry's pants visibly darkened.

"Come here, Lummox," O'Reilly called. "Sorry about that, Barry."

"I'll let you explain about my pants to Kinky," Barry said. "Bloody dog." But there was affection in his voice as he patted Arthur's flank.

"And bloody Bertie," O'Reilly said. "Let's head up to the Duck. His Exaltedness should be settled in with his supplier friend by now." Fingal strode across the beach. "Time for the councillor and me to have a little tête-à-tête."

Barry fell in step.

Arthur, who had not been called to heel, ranged ahead across the rippled sand and chased a group of dunlin into flight. The little brown waders flew in tight formation, jinking and weaving as one, so the flock looked like a puff of wind-driven smoke.

"Fingal?" Barry asked. "You know and I know that Bertie's diddling the lads out of their shares. Do you think telling him you're positive he's not betting at all will be enough to stop him?"

O'Reilly shook his head. "I doubt it. It's a puzzle to me how he's managed to go on betting and losing for as long as he has, and only betting to win. I know he's got the right to, because Donal and his friends all signed a contract. I think he's gambling on their being too ashamed to tell anybody, because they don't want to look like a bunch of buck eejits, but . . . the brass neck of the man. It's as plain as the nose on your face that he wants to own the whole horse. The bloody arrogance of him." O'Reilly kicked a float that must have broken loose from a fishing net. The cork soared over a dune's crest like a well-struck rugby ball over the crossbar.

"What I don't understand, Fingal—and I don't know a quarter as much about racehorses as you do—is why he would want to own the animal. If I were looking for a horse, I'd certainly not buy one that never wins."

Barry was right. "Nor me," said O'Reilly, "but I've a half-notion about what he's up to."

"What?"

"I know she's not winning now, but what if she does once he owns her outright? Donal tells me she's a flyer." And after Kinky's news from Cork about Flo's Fancy's jockey pulling the horse, having her start to win once Bishop gave the order was entirely feasible. "He's determined to get that filly," O'Reilly said. "And by God, I'm going to stop him, Barry."

"How, Fingal?"

O'Reilly grunted, then said, "First of all, I want some answers, and I'm damn sure the syndicate will want some too. Donal should have the lads at the Duck by now. They'll all be too scared to ask him as individuals. He's their boss. But if they go at him together, he can't fire half his workers, and . . ." O'Reilly scratched his head. "I might even get him to say publicly he'll answer questions without any risk of retribution."

They crested the first dune, the sand rasping underfoot as the breeze whispered through the marram grass.

"Do you know about jujitsu, Barry?" O'Reilly asked. He had to skirt a part of the path where the sand had crumbled.

Barry frowned. "Japanese kind of fighting? I thought it was a bit passé now that anyone who's read James Bond knows about karate."

"Karate's probably more lethal, but jujitsu has its points. It's more subtle than boxing. The object isn't to belt your opponent harder than he belts you." He tugged at one cauliflower ear. "You turn your opponent's strength back on him. And that's what I want to do to Bertie."

"How?"

O'Reilly stopped. "First, I'll accuse him of not betting locally—and we know that for a fact, thanks to Donal and his friend McArdle. If I keep at him, suggest he's *never* bet and has lied about it, I should be able to get him to lose his temper so that he won't be thinking straight."

"And then?"

"I'm sure Bertie's one step ahead," O'Reilly said. "I'll almost guarantee he'll say he's betting offtrack."

Barry frowned. "Betting offtrack. What's that?"

Sometimes, O'Reilly thought, it was hard to believe Barry was Irish. He must be the only one in the country over the age of sixteen who knew virtually nothing about horses or horse racing. O'Reilly said, "It's been legal here since 1961. You don't have to go to the races to wager anymore. You can bet by phone or at a betting shop, known rather quaintly as a turf accountant's. Ladbrokes has been around since 1886. They're the biggest bookies in the U.K., and they've set up premises all over the place. If Bishop swears blind he's betting with Ladbrokes . . ." He let his words hang.

Barry frowned. "It doesn't sound very promising. Not if you're right about those English bookies. He'll call your bluff straightaway."

"Right, but that's where the jujitsu comes in. I'm going to set myself up so Bertie *thinks* he's beaten me, and in front of an audience. His delight in that will make him vulnerable to what comes next, and my name's not Fingal Flahertie O'Reilly if I can't manoeuvre him into putting himself in an inescapable position in front of those witnesses."

"You'd not mind looking like an idiot, Fingal?"

O'Reilly laughed. "It's in a good cause, and don't forget the old proverb 'He who laughs last, laughs best—and longest.' A Japanese fighter will often let his adversary push him down, but by dragging his opponent with him and exerting just the right pressure, he'll use the force of the enemy's shove to hurl him head over heels."

Barry laughed. "You've something up your sleeve, haven't you? Something to do with the Cork jockey going to pull the horse?"

"Right on target," O'Reilly said, "but I'm keeping that for later. All I want today is to get Bertie to make some promises—in front of witnesses." They'd reached Shore Road. "Come in, Arthur. Heel," O'Reilly called.

The big dog obeyed.

They crossed the road for the short walk to the Duck. "How in the name of the wee man are you going to get the last laugh, Fingal?"

"If what I'm planning works, then my being embarrassed today will be only the first step to getting back the lads' shares in what might suddenly become a valuable animal. And better still, if I'm able to close the trap, I'm going to hit Bertie Bishop where it really hurts."

"Where?" Barry asked.

"Right slap-bang in the middle of his wallet," O'Reilly said and laughed. "Now come on, we're nearly there and my tongue's hanging out for a pint."

O'Reilly pushed open the doors to the Duck. "Evening, everybody." To Mary Dunleavy, who was behind the bar, he said, "Two pints and Arthur's usual, please."

O'Reilly, accompanied by Barry, moved to the bar and waited for his eyes to become accustomed to the dim light. He saw Donal with a group of men at the far end of the room. They must be the other shareholders. He knew them all. The most recognisable, Billy Brennan, the district nurse's elder brother, a man of six foot two, towered over Donal and the rest. Billy sported an old-fashioned crewcut and wore patched blue dungarees. His gallbladder had a habit of flaring up, but the surgeon at the Royal didn't think he needed to have it out.

"Doctor O'Reilly."

O'Reilly watched as Councillor Bertie Bishop hoisted his bulk from a chair, where he had been sitting at a table. The lit cigar he clutched in his chubby left hand would have cost a bob or two. Opposite him sat a middle-aged man wearing a three-piece brown suit. The newcomer had a bald spot that reminded Fingal of illustrations of Friar Tuck, and a face like a russet potato with bulging red cheeks and a bulbous nose. He'd be Ernie MacLoughlin, the builders' supplier Donal had mentioned that morning.

"Doctor O'Reilly. Doctor Laverty. Good evening."

"Bertie," O'Reilly said and inclined his head.

"Councillor Bishop," Barry said, and was ignored. Bishop directed his entire attention to Fingal. "Doctor O'Reilly?"

"Yes, Councillor?"

"I hope by now you will have accepted my apology for that . . ."
—he coughed—"most unfortunate incident at His Lordship's."

O'Reilly clapped the councillor's shoulder. "Water under the
bridge." O'Reilly winked at Barry. "Sure accidents can happen to
anybody. That old saying's appropriate, don't you think? It could
have happened to a bishop—Bertie."

The councillor's laughter, a high-pitched, braying noise,
echoed from the Duck's ancient roof beams. "Boys-a-dear," he finally managed, "you're so sharp you'll cut yourself, Doctor."

"Probably," said O'Reilly agreeably. "So what can I do for you?"

"I thought, seeing you're for letting bygones be bygones, like,
you'd mebbe let me buy you and Doctor Laverty a wee wet?"

"Delighted," O'Reilly said. "And don't forget Arthur." He
turned to the bar. "Are you finished pouring yet, Mary?"

"Nearly, sir."

"Grand," said O'Reilly. "Bring them over to the councillor's
table. Mr. Bishop's shout." O'Reilly positively beamed. He'd anticipated having to make an excuse to strike up a conversation
with the councillor. Now here was Bertie treating them like long-
lost friends.

O'Reilly led Barry and Arthur to the table where the balding
man in the brown suit sat.

"Mr. MacLoughlin, I believe?" O'Reilly said. "Don't get up.
I'm only the local GP, not royalty, and this is Doctor Laverty."
O'Reilly lowered himself into a chair and put Arthur under the
table.

"How's about ye, doctor? And it's Ernie, so it is." He stuck out
a hand, which O'Reilly shook.

"Ernie." Barry sat.

Mary Dunleavy set a pint in front of O'Reilly. "Councillor
Bishop's bringing yours, Doctor Laverty," she explained. "My

hands was full." She set Arthur's bowl of Smithwick's on the floor and petted the big dog.

"Here you are, young man." Bertie handed Barry a pint of Guinness. "And here's ten shillings, Mary." He pinched her bottom. "Keep the change."

Mary straightened up. She was blushing furiously as she accepted the note and stalked away. O'Reilly was tempted to come to her defence but didn't want to rock the boat. Not yet. The councillor plumped down between Barry and O'Reilly.

"Cheers, Bertie," said O'Reilly, rather than his usual "*sláinte.*" Bishop, worshipful master of the local Orange Lodge, was unlikely to take kindly to the use of the Irish language.

Barry and the rest toasted, "Cheers."

O'Reilly sank the top third of his Guinness in one swallow and savoured the taste. He grinned. "Thanks, Bertie. Thanks very much. Flann O'Brien, a fine Irish writer, was right: 'A pint of plain *is* your only man.' "

"My pleasure." Bertie Bishop smiled, then took a draw on his cigar.

"How's Mrs. Bishop?" O'Reilly wondered when he'd be given the opportunity to mention the horse.

Bertie lowered his voice. "Tell you the truth, Doctor, I was all pleased a while back when Doctor Laverty here fixed her up."

O'Reilly saw Barry smile, and rightly so. The boy had made a really tricky diagnosis.

"But no harm to you, Doctor Laverty—"

O'Reilly smiled at the Ulster precursor to a criticism.

"—there's times when she's running round like a bee on a hot brick I could prefer the old, slow Flo."

"Maybe . . ." O'Reilly said, inwardly thanking Bertie for opening the door to the next remark, "maybe your wee horse could use some of Doctor Laverty's medicine too." O'Reilly sank the rest of the pint, turned, and waved to Mary, who clearly understood and started to pull another one. O'Reilly winked and grinned.

Bishop's brows furrowed. The hand holding his cigar dropped to his side. "What are you talking about, O'Reilly?"

"You know very well, Bertie. Flo's Fancy."

Bishop's frown deepened. "My wee filly? What about her?"

O'Reilly noticed the proprietory "my." "I do think," he said calmly, "we need to have a word with you about her, Bertie. I honestly do."

40

To These Crocodile's Tears They Will Add Sobs

Barry watched as Bertie set his whiskey on the tabletop so forcibly that some of the contents of the glass splashed over the rim. He looked O'Reilly right in the eye. "I don't see why my filly's any business of yours, O'Reilly, so I don't."

Barry noticed the "Doctor" had vanished.

"But, Bertie, as I understand it she's not *yours*. Eight other men have shares in her."

"It's no secret. All of them's grown-ups. Nobody twisted their arms to buy in."

"I hear she's not been doing very well," said O'Reilly.

Bishop held both hands in front of him, palms up, smoke from his cigar drifting past his fingers. "I know. It's bloody awful, so it is." He leant forward. "I thought I'd bought a real flyer, you know. I was going to sell her for a fortune, so I was. Make me *and* the lads a great big bundle of the oul' spondulix on the sale and the betting. I'm right sorry for them, so I am." He forced a huge sigh. "It's desperate. I can afford to lose a bit, but they're all working lads. It's hitting them right sore." He put his cigar in his mouth.

"It is, Bertie," O'Reilly said calmly, "because you're acquiring their shares, and I know you're cheating to get them."

Bishop frowned, ripping out his panatela. "Did I hear you right? I'm cheating? *Me?*"

"You heard," O'Reilly said calmly.

"You're calling me a cheat, O'Reilly? Are you? Are you?" Bishop's wattles quivered and his voice rose.

"You are. The men think they've lost because you told them you wagered on their behalf. I don't think you've actually placed a single bet. And instead of their money, you take part of their shares. I'd call that cheating—and lying. You're swindling them, Bertie. Do you steal sweeties from chisellers too?"

O'Reilly accepted his second pint, and Mary scuttled away as Bishop roared, "What do you mean by that? What do you mean by that?" His face was rapidly turning puce; his voice was rising. "Are youse accusing me? To my face?"

Ernie MacLoughlin leant forward, tugged at Bishop's sleeve, and said in a hushed voice, "Bertie, keep your voice down, for God's sake. Everybody's looking."

If O'Reilly's plan had been to get Bishop's temper up, it was succeeding, Barry thought. He looked down the room. Every eye in Donal's group was on this table.

"I don't give a bugger who's looking," Bertie Bishop roared. "That man there, that man there—" He stabbed his cigar at O'Reilly. "He called me a liar—to my face. You're my witness, Ernie. And you too, Laverty."

Barry pursed his lips. Was Bishop thinking of taking legal action for slander? He'd not put it past the man. Barry hoped Fingal knew what he was doing.

"Do you want more witnesses, Bertie?" O'Reilly asked.

Bishop struggled to his feet, planted both fists on the table, and leant forward on his braced arms. "Witnesses? Bloody right, I do." Little drops of spittle flew. "I don't have to stand here and take this—"

"But you do, Bertie," O'Reilly said.

"Don't be so feckin' sure. I demand an apology, so I do."

"What for? We've done our homework," O'Reilly said. He looked Bertie straight in the eye. "You're not betting at all. Not one of the local bookies has ever seen you. I know that. You're telling lies about it."

"Is that a fact?" A flicker of a smile crossed Bishop's florid face. "Is that a fact?" He lowered his voice. "When I prove you're wrong, O'Reilly, you *will* apologise. Won't you?"

O'Reilly shrugged. "Naturally. A gentleman would—although I'd not expect you to know that, Bertie."

Barry watched the councillor's face turn a deeper shade. Not surprisingly, after that last remark. Ireland had a long tradition of dueling, and for a split second Barry had a grotesque vision of O'Reilly and the councillor at dawn, at ten paces—with pistols.

Bishop stood upright and folded his arms on the shelf of his belly. "You've gone too far, O'Reilly," he roared. "Far too feckin' far."

"For God's sake, Bertie, lower your voice," Ernie pleaded.

"I will not. I can prove I've been betting, so I can. I'm no liar. And I'm going to do it in front of everyone here, so I am."

"I'll enjoy that," O'Reilly said. "If you can."

And, Barry thought, I know and Fingal knows that Bertie has a trump card if he claims he's using Ladbrokes.

"Donal Donnelly," Bertie yelled. "Bring your friends down here. I want you all to see Doctor Know-all proved wrong."

Barry heard the scraping of chair legs as Donal and the rest of the horse-owning syndicate stood and started moving down the bar.

"Now you're for it, O'Reilly." Bishop's eyes narrowed. "I've got you by the short and curlies, so I have."

"I doubt it," O'Reilly said calmly.

Donal and seven other men formed a half circle around the table. Other patrons, who were standing or sitting further back, craned forward to catch what was happening. Barry smiled at Donal and got a wink back. There was an undercurrent of conversation.

In the dunes, O'Reilly had said he needed witnesses for his plan to work. His tactic of taunting Bertie Bishop was paying off, and it was Bertie himself, not Fingal, who had called for the little crowd to be assembled.

O'Reilly raised one hand. "Gentlemen," he said, "Councillor Bishop and I are having a disagreement about your horse—"

"Flo's bloody Fancy," a deep voice said. "About as much use as tits on a boar."

"That's neither here nor there," O'Reilly said. "I think Mr. Bishop here's diddling his shareholders."

"I'd not be surprised," a voice said.

"Who said that?" Bishop yelled. "Who the hell said that?"

The silence that followed, Barry thought, was eminently sensible.

"I tell youse all, right now, I'm not cheating nobody, so I'm not."

"And if you're not," O'Reilly said, "I will apologise for my remarks."

There was a communal in-drawing of breath. Doctor O'Reilly apologise?

"Before we settle the matter, there is a favour I'd like to ask of Mr. Bishop," O'Reilly said.

"You'll be dead out of luck, O'Reilly," Bishop snarled. "You'll get no favours from me."

"It's not for me. I know these men are shareholders, and I'm sure they'd like to ask you some questions." O'Reilly produced a tiny smile. "It's possible some of the answers might strengthen your case. I'm all for being fair."

Bishop's eyes narrowed; his brows moved down. "Aye?" he asked.

O'Reilly nodded. "Might clear the air of any suspicions folks might have too."

"Prove I am an honest man, like?"

O'Reilly said nothing.

"Fair enough," Bertie said, seemingly a little calmer. "Fire away."

"I know all these men work for you," O'Reilly said. "Have we your word you'll not go after any of them for anything they might say now?"

Bishop hesitated before answering, "You do." His gaze swept the crowd. "You can ask what the hell you like. I've nothing to hide, so I've not." He shoved the half-smoked panatela back between his lips.

The men continued to stand, glancing at the floor and each other. Billy Brennan was whispering into the ear of the man next to him. Clearly no one wanted to pose the first question, so Barry asked, "Councillor Bishop, we've heard you only ever bet to win, never to win or place. Why?"

Bishop removed the cigar. "Are you a betting man, Laverty?"

Barry shook his head.

"If you were, you'd understand. You've to double your stake for the place part. Ten pounds to win, twenty pounds to win *or* place, and you only get a quarter of the odds for a place. Ten to one for a win drops to two and a half to one for a place." Bishop's tones were those of a schoolteacher addressing a not very bright pupil. Bishop turned to the little crowd. "If I had done that at twenty pounds a race, all youse men's money, aye, and a pisspot full of mine too, would have gone twice as fast."

Barry heard a muttering, but whether of agreement or disagreement he couldn't be sure.

"Excuse me, Mr. Bishop sir." Billy Brennan, cap held in both hands, stared at the floor. "No harm to ye, but . . ."—Brennan looked down on Bishop—"I can understand that, so I can, but she *has* been placing. We might have got at least a few bob return if you *had* backed her both ways. Or maybe stopped betting on her altogether?"

Another voice said, " 'At's right, so it is."

Barry saw it was Richard Orr who had spoken, a keen sea angler who'd once come to the surgery with a mackerel hook stuck in his thumb.

Orr's remark was followed by a growing swell of grumbling.

Bertie Bishop held up his hands for silence. "You're right, Orr. Dead-on, so you are. I'll not deny it. Mebbe I should have stopped betting, but I just thought she kept coming so bloody close, she was *bound* to win next time. And look, each time she didn't win, we got better odds in the next race. I was so sure she was going to come first, I kept the stake down to ten pounds to give us more chances. Not a one of youse would have complained if I'd put ten pounds on for you at ten to one and you'd walked away with one hundred smackers clear, would you?"

"Fair play," a voice commented. Barry recognised Tom Curran's hoarse voice. The man had a ferocious smoker's cough but staunchly refused to quit. Heads nodded in assent. "Might've done the selfsame thing myself, so I might." The speaker was a stranger to Barry. He watched Bishop. It was as if the man scented success and was determined to drive the message home.

"And if we had won, wouldn't it have bought your shares back for you *and* put a few bob in your pockets too?"

"You'd have given our shares back to us? Right enough, sir? That would have been quare nor decent," Donal said.

Judging by the nods and the looks on their faces, the other men agreed.

"It would have been the right thing to do." Bishop smiled. His voice was back at its normal pitch. He puffed on his cigar again.

Barry glanced at O'Reilly, who was hiding a grin behind his

hand. With the other he gave Barry a surreptitious thumbs-up, then said loudly enough for all to hear, "All very plausible, Bertie—if you ever placed a bet, which I know you never did. Not a brass farthing."

Barry looked at the little crowd. Nothing but frowns. A couple of men had taken a pace toward the plump councillor. "What?" a voice asked. "Never bet?" Every eye was on Bishop.

"That's right," O'Reilly said. All gazes had switched back to him. "I have a witness. A certain bookie has asked around all the others in his trade. Not one of them has seen a stiver from Councillor Bishop."

Barry recognised that O'Reilly was protecting Donal by not naming him as the witness. Bishop's agreement not to exact retribution might only stretch so far.

"You can keep your witness, O'Reilly. Of course I don't use the locals." Bishop started to grin. He removed the cigar.

The crowd stared at him.

Here it comes, Barry thought.

"You're so bloody clever, Doctor. Did you never hear tell of off-track betting?"

"Offtrack—?" O'Reilly's expression, Barry thought, would have done service on the face of someone who had been blindsided by a truck, or on an actor onstage at Belfast's Ulster Hall. This was exactly what O'Reilly had predicted Bishop would claim.

"Ladbrokes, *Doctor* O'Reilly. Lad-feckin'-brokes."

"Ladbrokes?" O'Reilly said.

Barry was proud of the way O'Reilly recovered his poise. "Prove it," he said. "Show us a betting slip. You can't, Councillor, can you?"

Several other voices muttered, "Show us. Go on."

"I can't," he said.

"So we've got you, Bertie," O'Reilly said and grinned.

"Is 'at a fact?" Bishop turned to the crowd. "Any of youse men bet offtrack?"

"I do, Mr. Bishop," Tom Curran wheezed.

"In the shop in Belfast?"

"No. On the phone, sir."

"Do you get a slip?"

"Not at all. I have an account with a password and all, and it's secret, so it is."

Bishop held his arms wide at shoulder height, hands palms up. "And that, gentlemen, is why I can't produce a slip. I bet on the phone. I'm far too busy to go all the way to Belfast to the turf accountant's."

"Honest to God?" Donal Donnelly asked.

"Honest to God, Donal." Bishop hadn't hesitated for as much as a split second in his reply.

I'm sure he's lying, Barry thought, but by Ulster convention anyone who said "honest to God" must be believed.

"I think, *Doctor* . . . I think, in front of all these people, an apology perhaps?" Bishop's voice oozed as greasily as oil slips onto the water from a boat's leaking fuel tank. His grin was ear to ear.

Barry looked at O'Reilly, who had turned to the audience. "Gentlemen," he said, "this isn't easy for me to admit I was wrong, but fair play. If the councillor's been using an offtrack bookie, I was wrong to accuse him. Totally wrong."

"My God," an awed voice said. "Himself's going to say he's sorry, so he is."

Barry wouldn't have believed his ears if O'Reilly hadn't explained in advance what he was going to do.

"Och, sure, only the pope's infallible," a voice said.

"Go on, O'Reilly," Bishop urged. "More."

"I *was* wrong, Bertie," O'Reilly said. "I misjudged you. I called you a cheat and a liar. It was indefensible."

"Holy Mother of Jesus." A voice rose above a loud communal inhalation.

"For which I unreservedly apologise. Unreservedly." Fingal managed to look contrite.

Bishop laughed. "All youse men know your Bible. Second Samuel, book one, verse nineteen. 'How are the mighty fallen.'"

Silence reigned.

"I'm sorry, Bertie," O'Reilly said. "I really am."

Barry expected Bishop to clasp his hands above his head like a victorious prizefighter. He looks, Barry thought, like the cat that got the cream. Far too much cream.

"'Scuse me, Mr. Bishop," Billy Brennan said. "I think Doctor O'Reilly got it wrong, so he did, but he's said he's sorry." He looked from side to side at the other men. "We'd just like to tell him, you know, we think it was right decent of him to look out for us, even if we never asked him to."

There was a murmuring of assent. Barry noticed that Donal was staring at O'Reilly and nodding enthusiastically.

"And we're dead pleased we got them questions out of the way, like. Thank you for that, sir."

Bishop nodded condescendingly.

"There's just one more wee thing, sir," Billy Brennan continued.

"And that is?" Bishop's tone was magnanimous.

He was behaving exactly as O'Reilly had predicted. Wallowing in his victory and happily playing Lord Bountiful with his audience.

"Downpatrick's make-or-break for us, sir. I don't suppose you'd think about an each-way bet there?"

"I'm sorry, Billy," Bishop said. "I've already used Ladbrokes. Got our bets down early to get the best odds. I got twenty to one on the nose."

O'Reilly winked at Barry.

"Them's pretty long odds," Donal said.

"Your ten pounds'll get you two hundred," Bishop said.

"If she wins," O'Reilly said. "Mr. Bishop?" he said. "Just now you told Donal Donnelly that with a win like that you'd keep what was owed from previous bets and give each man back his shares."

" 'At's right."

"Will you still?"

"Look, O'Reilly," Bishop said, "I'm a man of my word. You know that now, don't ye? Don't ye?" He looked around the little crowd. "You're all witnesses to something else now. That's exactly what I'll do. You all heard that promise, didn't ye?"

"Aye. We did," Donal said. "Mr. Bishop, sir, I think what you're doing is dead decent, so I do. I think a lot of us lads'll remember that, come the next council elections."

Bertie smiled.

"But there is one wee thing more."

"Oh?" Bishop frowned.

"You've just told us it's too late for Downpatrick now, but my Julie says if I put any more money on the gee-gees, one brass farthing more, she'll kill me, so she will."

A wave of laughter swept the pub, but when it subsided, Donal ploughed on. "Could we maybe agree, if we do get our shares back, like, not to use them to bet with anymore after Downpatrick?"

"I think," said O'Reilly, "I think your stock would go very high if you agree, Bertie."

"Aye," said Bishop thoughtfully. "Aye, it would."

"Please, sir?" Donal asked, to a loud groundswell of agreement.

"Fair enough. No more betting with your shares after this race," Bishop said. "You've my word on that too."

The sound was muted but it was a cheer.

Bertie Bishop, arms still outstretched, basked in the applause and played the room like the seasoned politician he was, head bobbing, eyes seeking eyes. Then to Barry's amazement Bishop spat on the palm of his hand and offered it to Donal, who spat on his own. That handshake was as binding as a High Court order.

Barry saw the gleam in O'Reilly's dark eyes, the single thumb once more cocked up. O'Reilly rose. "Come on, Barry," he said. "Drink up. Time for home." He turned to the councillor and said, "Bertie, we started off with you apologising to me and finished with me apologising to you. I think we're quits."

Bishop's "All right" was sulky.

Barry noticed neither man offered to shake hands.

"We'll be off," O'Reilly said. "Bye, Ernie."

"Bye yourself, Doctor. Nice to have met yiz both," the man in the brown suit said.

"Just got to settle up for my last pint and say good-bye to the lads," O'Reilly said. "Take Arthur and wait for me outside."

It wasn't long before he appeared. "Home," he said.

"You won, Fingal," Barry said. "You got most of what you wanted."

O'Reilly strode briskly. "Most? What did I forget?"

"You said you wanted to hit Bishop in his wallet too."

O'Reilly grinned. "Bertie was magnanimous in there because, one, he was delighted to have called my bluff and to believe he'd won, so he let his guard down, answered questions, and made those concessions. Two, all his promises were piecrust—made to be broken. They only kick in *if* the horse wins at Downpatrick. He's already arranged for her to lose; we know that from Kinky."

"Of course." Barry frowned. "So why didn't you tell him you knew he was fixing the races and demand he give the men their money back? They'd have been no worse off and you'd have saved face."

"I want Bertie to think he's about to own the animal from appetite to arsehole, because once he does he's not risking anything more. He'll be rid of his syndicate unless we can stop him, and as soon as he is, she'll win. You watch. She'll start winning. He'll bet on her at long odds and win, collect big prize money for coming first, and eventually sell her for a huge profit."

Barry shook his head. "Money is the root of all evil," he said.

"No," said O'Reilly, "'The love of money is the root of all evil'—First Timothy 6:10—and it's my ambition to see Bishop's love blighted. Now if we can get the wee filly to win fair and square . . . and I've a notion that a word with the marquis and Eugene Power might work wonders."

Barry laughed.

"And," said O'Reilly, "if, as I'm convinced, all Bertie's talk about betting at Ladbrokes is only blether, that he's done no such thing, guess who's going to have to pay his shareholders when she wins?"

"Bertie himself, because he just swore in front of witnesses that he *had* wagered. He *is* in that 'inescapable position.'"

"Up to his neck," said O'Reilly. "He's sworn he's bet eighty pounds, the eight men's stake, so when the horse wins, they'll believe that Ladbrokes will pay Bertie eighty times twenty on their behalf and that's sixteen hundred pounds."

"But you're sure he's been nowhere near the bookies?"

"Not within a beagle's gowl. But he'll still have to pay up, out of his own pocket, and it's a brave wheen of money. We have to subtract the seven hundred and twenty pounds of gambled-away shares he's promised to reinstate, but it still leaves—"

"Eight hundred and eighty pounds to be paid out." Barry whistled. "That's more than twice my annual pay."

"And it'll be going up in July—if you stay," O'Reilly said.

Barry was unsure how to answer.

"Right now, however," said O'Reilly, opening the gate and letting Arthur into the back garden, "let's see what Kinky has for our dinner." He glanced down at Barry's damp trousers and laughed. "And what she has to say about your pants."

It was pleasantly warm in the kitchen. Kinky was slicing a loaf of what, judging by the yeasty aroma, was freshly baked wheaten bread. She looked up. "Not again, Doctor Laverty." She shook her head. "I despair, so."

"Sorry."

"No matter." She turned to O'Reilly and said, "While you two were out, sir, Miss Kitty did phone from London. She'll be in her hotel until 7:30. I've her number on the pad by the phone."

"Will she, begod?" said O'Reilly. He charged for the hall with a grin on his face that Barry thought would have lit up the Bally-bucklebo Hills at midnight.

41

Let Me Be Dress'd Fine

On the following Wednesday, Barry set out to walk to the Ballybucklebo Boutique. It had been eighteen days since the rupture of
Alice Moloney's liver abscess, and she had been discharged home
that morning from the Royal. He was bearing a thermos of Kinky's
hot beef tea. She'd sworn it would give Alice strength.

"Sure in County Cork, Doctor Laverty," she'd said as he was
leaving, "couldn't my ma's beef tea revive people half-frozen in a
blizzard, and it's the same recipe in the thermos, so."

She did not explain further, but did add with a spark in her dark
eyes, "And try not to pour any on your clean pants." Halfway to his
destination, Barry was still marvelling at what a good-natured woman
Kinky Kincaid was.

By what was now the last week in February there was less bite to
the wind, although as O'Reilly had remarked earlier, they weren't
going to get rich today by opening a heat-stroke clinic. The skies
were a deeper shade of blue. In another six weeks they would be full
of swooping swallows returned from wintering in North Africa.

Well before the birds came back, Barry was going to have to
make up his mind about staying with Fingal, who today was up at
Aldergrove Airport meeting Kitty's flight, or going to Ballymena
for a taste of specialist work. He had until next Monday to decide.

He'd studied *Hamlet* at school when he was fifteen. At the time he'd been unsympathetic to the Melancholy Dane and his "To be or not to be," seeing the man as nothing more than a haverer. Now Barry felt more empathy with the prince's dilemma and his to-and-fro emotions.

"Hello, Doctor Laverty." Julie Donnelly was coming out of the butcher's shop, stuffing a brown paper–wrapped parcel into her shopping bag. "This here's some nice brisket I've bought for Donal's supper, so I have."

"Hello, Julie. How are you?" She had a discrete bump under her fawn coat. It was a good thing Bertie Bishop's cousin the photographer was only interested in her hair. The final choice of the winning photographs would be made in two days, on Friday. "Getting nervous about the contest?" he asked.

She shook her head. "Sure, like I told youse doctors, I can't lose even if I'm only second. I'm more anxious for Donal and his mates on Saturday. He's cheered up a bit because he knows if the wee horse wins he'll get his shares back—but he doesn't think she will win."

"I wish I could promise you she'll do it."

"Och, sure," she said. "If wishes were horses, beggars would ride. We'll be all right, no matter."

Barry, impressed by her imperturbability, smiled. "We'll know in a couple of days."

"We will. And will Donal see you at Downpatrick, Doctor?"

"Indeed. Both me and Doctor O'Reilly. Are you not coming?"

She shook her head. "Donal doesn't want me getting excited." She patted her tummy. "He says I've to get lots of rest."

"Not a bad idea."

"Anyway," she said, "he'll be busy working as Mr. McArdle's runner, but Donal's particularly anxious to tell Doctor O'Reilly how thankful everybody was last Tuesday at the Duck for everything the doctor tried to do. He's given them back a chance." She hitched the basket up her arm. "I've to be running on now. I need to get some vegetables too." Her smile was angelic when she said, "And I'm getting him some meringues for a wee treat for afters. He just loves meringues, so he does. Bless him."

Barry felt the love in those words. Julie, who was going to be stuck for life in Ballybucklebo, seemed perfectly happy with her lot. She didn't need broader horizons like a certain civil-engineering student. Of the two women, he wondered who would be the more content ten years from now.

He walked on, thinking about how last week a still-grinning O'Reilly, following a thirty-minute telephone conversation with Kitty O'Hallorhan, had explained his further plans over dinner. As Flo's Fancy would not be running until the seventh race on Saturday, there'd be lots of time in Downpatrick before that to have those words with the marquis and Eugene Power. O'Reilly was convinced that if the filly was given her head in a fair race, she could win and very decidedly upset Bertie Bishop's applecart.

O'Reilly did not want there to be the slightest hint that he and Barry were hatching such a plan, so for a while longer Donal and his friends were to be kept in the dark.

Barry had barely shut the door of the Ballybucklebo Boutique when Cissie Sloan, who was standing at the counter, turned and said, "Doctor Laverty dear, is it yourself? Am I glad to see yourself, so I am, sir. I'm having terrible trouble—"

"I'll be in the surgery tomorrow, Cissie," Barry said, hoping to avoid hearing about it here.

"Nooo," she said, "not doctoring trouble, like. Sure didn't you fix me up last summer?"

Barry nodded. He had.

"Them wee thingys you gave me is racing round in me like motorbikes at Dundrod."

She'd certainly taken very literally his explanation of hormones circulating in the bloodstream. In motorcycling circles, the Dundrod Circuit Ulster Grand Prix was as famous for the breakneck speeds of its competitors as were the Isle of Man Tourist Trophy races. Barry had to laugh. Although he had tried to duck becoming embroiled in one of Cissie's endless conversations, he couldn't help himself. "So what can I do for you, Cissie?"

She turned to the counter. "See them two dresses there?" She held up a handful of a blue one and a handful of a red one. "My cousin Aggie Arbuthnot. You know, Doctor, the one—

"I do." Barry quickly headed her off.

"She was meant to be here for to help me choose a new dress for the Downpatrick Races on Saturday, so she was. I can't think where she's got to. Maybe . . . nah. She does that on Mondays. I know that. She's more likely to—" She tutted and frowned. "On the other hand—"

Barry coughed. Loudly. "Cissie," he said, "what can I help you with?"

"Can you wait 'til I try each one on, like? Have a gander at them?"

Sally, who was normally shy, interposed, "I think Doctor Laverty's a bit too busy to look at you modelling the dresses, Mrs. Sloan."

Barry could have hugged the girl.

"Right enough," Cissie said to Sally. "I suppose he is. Och, well." She turned to Barry. "Just mebbe then, Doctor, which . . . which colour do you like the best? Honest to God now?"

Barry had a quick image of Rubens's painting *The Judgement of Paris*. The poor divil had to choose between three goddesses and determine the most beautiful. No matter who Paris picked, he'd have made mortal enemies of the other two. Barry frowned, cocked his head, and said, "They're both very pretty colours." He sensed the door opening and turned.

"Jasus Murphy, Cissie." A short, skinny woman in her early

thirties stood in the doorway, arms akimbo. Her red hair was wrapped in a head scarf that was knotted at the front above her forehead. "Didn't I tell you on Monday I'd meet you outside the post office today because it's close to where we both live? And me standing there for the last fifteen minutes, both legs the same length, and a lazy wind just got up out there. It wouldn't bother to go round you. It would go right through you, so it would."

"I think," Barry said, "I'll leave you ladies to decide on the dresses." He started to climb the stairs to Alice's flat. He couldn't help overhear Aggie going on. "It's not just that I got foundered out there, Cissie Sloan. My very close veins was acting up something chronic, so they were."

Cissie's apologies were profuse. They should be. Aggie's varicose veins did need attention. Barry'd made arrangements for her to be seen at the Royal.

He stopped on the landing and as he knocked on the door to Alice Moloney's flat, he heard Cissie ask, "And do you have them veins in your toes too?"

42

Come to Our Own Home and Rest

"Hello, Doctor Laverty. Do come in." Sonny Houston ushered Barry into the little hall of Alice Moloney's flat. He was wearing a smart tweed jacket and had a yellow paisley cravat knotted at the throat of a crisp white shirt. "Miss Moloney's tucked up in bed. Maggie's making her a nice cup of tea."

Barry flinched. After a cup of Maggie's stewed tea, Alice might feel an intense yearning for a return to hospital food.

"Who's a good boy then?" Billie Budgie screeched.

"Houl' your wheest, you wee bugger," Maggie growled in a stage whisper. She stood in the tiny kitchen pouring boiling water into a teapot.

Barry noticed snowdrops in the silk band of her felt trilby. "How are you, Maggie?" he asked.

Her toothless grin split her leathery face. "All the better for seeing yourself, Doctor dear. You're just in time for tea—once it's stewed a bit more."

"Maybe later, Maggie. I really have to see Miss Moloney." He put the thermos on the counter. "Mrs. Kincaid's beef tea," he said.

Maggie looked at it, then at her teapot, and sniffed. "Miss Moloney'll be glad to see you, sir. I think she's been through the wars, but she's on the mend now, so she is. I have her propped up on her pillows."

As Barry crossed the living room he noticed that the embroidered sampler of the Lord's Prayer now hung straight and the table had been dusted. Maggie hadn't only been looking after Alice's pets. He knocked on the door frame.

"Come in." The voice was quavery.

"Alice," he said, "it's good to see you home."

Alice Moloney sat, her back supported by pillows. She wore a pink bed jacket over her powder-blue nightie. Her salt-and-pepper hair had been neatly brushed and hung to her shoulders. Her complexion was losing its earthy look, but her cheeks were sunken. Beside her was her teddy bear. The spherical, tortoiseshell cat lay curled up beside Alice, purring loudly despite being sound asleep.

"Thank you for coming, Doctor Laverty," she said. "You needn't have. Miss Brennan, the district nurse, has already been. I've no temperature and my pulse is normal. She's looked at all my wounds and says they're healing well."

"That's very good," Barry said. She'd have three wounds, one for the chest drain, one for the drain that the surgeon had inserted into the abdominal cavity, and of course, the main surgical incision. Any or all could have become infected, but that was unlikely now. The normality of pulse and temperature also made it unlikely she harboured any infection inside. "How are you feeling?" he asked.

"Tired," she said. "Weak, but I've no pain, and thank goodness, I'll be able to sleep properly now I'm back in my own bed."

"Are you going to be able to manage on your own?" he asked.

"Oh, yes, thank you. Mr. and Mrs. Houston are being most kind." She screwed up her face. "I think she's making me another cup of tea." Barry heard the concern; then Alice said, "My sister Ellen was most attentive when I was in the Royal and she's coming today to stay, and Miss Brennan says she'll call every day." She sighed and stretched out a wasted hand to stroke the cat. "Everybody's been so solicitous."

"I'll pop in whenever I can," Barry said, "and call us at once if you feel at all unwell."

"I will," she said. "You and Doctor O'Reilly have been wonderful."

Barry was about to dismiss her thanks with a remark about it being their job. In truth, he still felt guilty that because he'd been so wrapped up feeling sorry for himself, he'd forgotten all about Alice Moloney since he'd seen her at the Bishops' Boxing Day party. And she, in her turn, had not sought out medical attention at Number 1.

She forestalled him. "I didn't see much of the great man in the Royal."

"Sir Donald Cromie?"

"Yes. He made ward rounds three times a week, but he left most of the work to his juniors."

Barry smiled. "It was ever thus, Alice. Consultants are very busy." But O'Reilly splits the work fifty-fifty, Barry thought.

"I do understand, and his young man, a Doctor Mills, was quite charming."

"I've known Jack Mills since we were schoolboys."

"He told me. He also said that you and Doctor O'Reilly saved my life. I believe him."

Barry felt the blush start. He knew he was turning beetroot red. Was he, as well as learning about country general practice, also picking up some of his senior colleague's other traits, like an inability to accept praise without feeling uncomfortable?

"I am very grateful to you both," she said. "Because of you I'll be able to live out my days here in Ballybucklebo knowing I've neighbours like the Houstons, and doctors like you and Doctor O'Reilly."

"Thank you, Alice," Barry said. "Thank you very much. Sonny and Maggie are wonderful," he said. But he wondered if her hope to have him as her doctor in the future was misplaced.

"Away on out of that, Doctor dear. Sure isn't it only what any Christian would do?" Maggie dumped a tray on Alice's bedside table. "I've tea for the both of you and pieces of my plum cake."

Barry saw the pleading look in Alice's eyes. "Maggie," he said, "you have a heart of corn, but I'm going to have to disappoint you."

"Oh," said Maggie, frowning.

"Alice has been *very* sick, so she's on what we doctors call a restricted diet. She's not allowed sweet things like your wonderful plum cake."

"Not allowed? Doctor's orders, like?" It seemed to mollify her.

"And there's a thing in tea called tannin."

"Tannin, is it? I heard tell it's what they use to cure cowhides."

"It is," Barry said. There's enough in one cup of your tea to make rawhide tough as armour plating, he thought. "And tannin's very bad for people who've just had operations." He saw the look of gratitude in Alice's eyes. "What is good for invalids is beef tea."

"And didn't you bring a thermos of it, sir?" Maggie asked.

"I did."

"I'll get Miss Moloney a cup," Maggie said. Her eyes narrowed and she fixed Barry with a steely glare. "Yourself's not on a restricted diet, sir?"

Barry swallowed. "No, I'm not, but I am in a rush." By the look on her face, he was sure she was thinking, "liar." "So no tea, but if you'll wrap two of those slices of your plum cake while you're getting Alice's beef tea, I'll take them with me. It's the best plum cake in Ballybucklebo." Forgive me, Kinky, he thought, as he watched Maggie pick up the tray and leave, but I'd not hurt Maggie Houston for the world.

Alice smiled and said weakly, "I think that's the second time you've saved my life, Doctor Laverty—"

Their laughter was interrupted by the entrance of a middle-aged woman. She bore a distinct resemblance to Alice Moloney but, Barry guessed, was two or three years younger. Her features were sharp and her skin bore a slight yellow tinge.

"Alice, my dear," the newcomer said, "how are you?" She rapidly crossed the floor and planted a kiss on Alice Moloney's forehead. "I brought you these," she said and put a bunch of cut flowers on the bedside table.

"Doctor Laverty," Alice said, "I'd like you to meet my little sister, Ellen Moloney, from Millisle."

"How do you do, Miss Moloney?" Barry said. Ellen had retained her surname and so, Barry deduced, was not married. And if she was anything like Alice, she would be punctilious about correct manners. He'd not use her Christian name until granted permission.

"How do you do, Doctor?" she said. Her voice was Anglicised like her sister's, reflecting their having grown up among the English colonists in India. Her yellow tinge almost certainly was the result of steady use of the antimalarial quinacrine. "I am very pleased to meet you."

Barry inclined his head.

"I believe," she said, "we owe a very great deal to you, Doctor O'Reilly, and the specialists at the Royal. A very great deal indeed." She turned to her sister. "I've been worried sick about you, Alice. When I came to visit you in that hospital you looked so lost among all those tubes and wires, and that nurse'd not tell me anything about you."

Barry knew only too well how the best relatives could hope for were stock phrases: "She's resting," "She's comfortable," "Her condition is guarded." He'd never understood why visitors seemed to be regarded as too feebleminded to be given proper explanations.

Ellen sat on the bedside and took her sister's thin hand and began to stroke it with her own. Her gaze was fixed on Alice Moloney's eyes. "I don't know what I'd have done if anything had happened to you, darling. I honestly don't." She bent and kissed Alice's forehead. "You're all I've got," she said. "I've been so *dreadfully* worried about you."

Barry, who did not wish to intrude, stood silently.

"It's all right, Ellen." Alice Moloney's voice had lost its quavering tone.

Barry understood. Since the death of their parents, Alice must have taken on the role of protector to her younger sister, and old habits die hard. Weak as she was, she was making the effort. "I'm on the mend. I'll get a bit better every day, and I'll have you here, dear, to look after me, won't I?"

"Indeed you will." Ellen Moloney managed a little smile. "It will make a change from you looking after me when we were girls."

She turned to Barry. "And Alice is going to get better, isn't she, Doctor?"

He read the hope in her eyes. "She is, Miss Moloney. I promise."

"Thank you, Doctor Laverty, I'm so very grate—" Her voice cracked and he saw a single tear trickle down her cheek. She swallowed, took a deep breath, and squared her shoulders. "I'm sorry," she said, "but it's such a relief to know. I couldn't bear—"

"It really is all right." Alice reached forward and hugged her sister. "It's all right."

Barry Laverty, lump in throat, slipped quietly from the room and left the Moloney sisters together in their love, one for the other.

He'd composed himself by the time he went into the living room, where Sonny was admiring the picture of Mahatma Gandhi.

"Interesting chap," Sonny said. "I met Gandhiji when he was in

London in 1931 for talks. I had to admire such a skinny little fellow putting up with the English climate, and him in only his dhoti. You know, he told me something I've always remembered: The best way to find yourself is to lose yourself in the service of others."

Barry nodded. "I think he must have passed that thought on to Doctor O'Reilly. He believes much the same."

"We know that, Doctor Laverty." Sonny looked Barry in the eye. "And we can see it in you too, young man."

Wanting to change the subject, Barry quickly asked, "And how did you meet Gandhi, Sonny?"

"Through a Cambridge friend of mine who'd gone into the diplomatic service and was in the party from the Foreign Office squiring the Mahatma around."

"I see." The mention of Cambridge irritated Barry, but did not cause the same violent ache as it would have done six weeks ago. "That's Alice's father in the picture," he said.

Maggie appeared from the kitchen carrying the laden tray. "I'll be taking along her beef tea," she said.

"Give Alice and her sister a few minutes," Barry said. "I think they need some privacy."

"I will, so I will." Maggie set the tray on a table. "I've Mrs. Kincaid's thermos and your plum cake here." She gave them to Barry. Maggie grinned. "I put in an extra slice for Himself."

"Thanks, Maggie." Barry accepted the package. "I'm sure Doctor O'Reilly will be delighted." He headed for the staircase, then turned. "And thank you both for helping out here."

"Run away on with yourself, Doctor dear," she said. "I've told you, it's nothing."

"It was a pleasure," Sonny said, "and remember what Gandhi said—so thank you for asking us. She's going to let us take care of her pets for a while longer."

"And we'll keep a wee eye to her too," Maggie said.

"That's great," he said, "and Maggie, remember about the restricted diet and the tannin."

"I will, Doctor, so I will, but you enjoy my cake now."

Assuring her he would, Barry headed downstairs to where Sally was hanging a blue dress back on a rack.

"Cissie took the red one?" Barry asked.

"Aye," said Sally, picking at her pimple. Her voice filled with wonder and dropped in volume. "Doctor Laverty?" she asked. "Did you know Mrs. Arbuthnot has *six* toes on each foot?"

"I did, Sally," he said.

"Boys-a-dear, that's ferocious, so it is."

Barry pulled the door shut behind him and headed for home.

As he passed the Presbyterian Church, he could see in the graveyard under the ancient yews the freshly turned earth in the place where Sheilah Devine had been buried last week. She was among family and friends she had known for more than eighty years.

She could be buried in worse places than Ballybucklebo, Barry thought. Much worse.

43

More Beautiful Than Thy First Love

O'Reilly paced across the upstairs lounge, opened the curtains, then stared through the window and peered along the dimly lit Main Street. The road was empty. He pulled out his pipe, looked at it, shoved it in his pocket, strode back, and sat heavily in the armchair. In what seemed like an hour since he had last consulted it, the minute hand of his watch had advanced by three minutes and it was still only five minutes to seven.

Would Kitty never get here?

She'd said she thought they should take a break. Perhaps she'd been right. Since she'd left this house sixteen days ago to go on that refresher course he'd tried to put her out of his mind, but it hadn't been easy. He kept being reminded by little things. The bottle of gin had been bought for Kitty. It sat forlorn and unused beside the Jameson on the sideboard. On a coffee table, her right glove awaited the return of its fellow. She'd dropped it in the hall and he'd not noticed it until after she'd left.

Fingal Flahertie O'Reilly wanted Caitlin O'Hallorhan here, and he wanted her now. If nothing else, the break had given him time to think and to arrive at a conclusion.

It had been a surprise when she'd phoned last week. She'd sounded in good form when he'd spoken to her in her hotel. The time they'd spent chatting about inconsequential matters had sped by. He'd have talked longer, but she'd said, "I've got to go, Fingal. I've tickets to see Ian McKellen playing Godfrey in *A Scent of Flowers.*"

"I've read he's very good . . . won some award," O'Reilly said. "Enjoy yourself." He hesitated, then asked, "Will I give you a call some other night?"

"I'm not sure what my plans are," she said. "You could always try."

"Fair enough. If I don't, don't worry. Would you like me to pick you up on Wednesday at Aldergrove?"

"That would be great." She gave him her flight number and arrival time.

"Enjoy the play," he said. "Night-night." He'd not asked if she was going by herself.

Over the following days, he'd decided not to phone. Taking a break was a two-way thing. He hoped she was missing him as much as he was missing her. He'd rather not know if she was out, and if she was, he tried to tell himself, why shouldn't she have fun in the big city? And he'd wondered about John Roulston.

O'Reilly hauled out his briar, struck a match, and got the pipe drawing well.

Roulston had seemed to be a decent enough chap. He'd been helping Kitty with her suitcase on Wednesday when Fingal arrived to pick her up at Belfast's Aldergrove Airport. Damn it, he'd been looking forward to having the very first moments with her to himself. He'd been harbouring a dream that, like a scene from a romantic B movie, she'd drop her case, run to his arms, and say breathlessly, "God, Fingal, I've missed you."

She'd not do that with a senior surgeon in tow.

Roulston was a dapper man. Five-foot-ten, slim, good head of neatly trimmed dark hair, small scar under his right eye. He'd been wearing a camel-hair coat with black-velvet collar patches, had knife creases in his charcoal-grey slacks, and wore highly polished black shoes.

O'Reilly glanced at the cuffs of the clean white shirt he'd put on for tonight. His gold cuff links shone. A neatly tied, half Windsor knot secured his Trinity College graduates' tie. Like a nineteen-year-old putting on Old Spice after his second shave of the day, he wanted to look his very best. Kinky had sponged off his sports jacket and ironed his tweed pants. He'd never liked shoes and was more comfortable in his old, ankle-high, brown-leather boots, the likes of which any farmer might have worn. He knew he needed a haircut.

You're no oil painting, Fingal Flahertie O'Reilly, he told himself, then grinned. He would have come a very poor second in a sartorial elegance competition with John Roulston, and he hoped he'd not be vying with the man for anything more important.

At the airport, it would have been churlish not to have offered him a lift into Belfast. His conversation in the car had been light, informed and witty. He'd certainly provoked several chuckles from Kitty and a sympathetic "Och, the poor wee man. He always looked so lost," when Roulston had mentioned the recent death of Stan Laurel.

When they'd arrived at Broadway Towers, Roulston had asked, "May I use your phone to call a taxi, Kitty?"

"I'll run you home," O'Reilly had offered. Was he being polite, or did he not want John Roulston to go inside the apartment with Kitty?

"Not at all. My place on Dorchester Park is away up at the top of the Malone Road, miles from Ballybucklebo—"

In more ways than one, O'Reilly thought. The Upper Malone Road was the domain of *la crème de la crème* of Ulster society. Ballybucklebo was not.

"But thanks for the offer."

"Come on then, John," Kitty said. "I want to get unpacked." She certainly seemed comfortable in the man's company, but then Kitty was like that with just about everybody. "Coming in, Fingal?"

"I'll not, thanks." He had no idea if there was anything between them, but if there was he'd be damned if he was going to set himself up to appear as if he were jealously overprotective. "I'll see you on Friday for dinner. Seven at Number 1, and bring your toothbrush." O'Reilly glanced at Roulston, but his face was expressionless. "Donal's horse is running on Saturday at Downpatrick, Kitty. You'll not want to miss that." He hoped to God she'd not.

"Friday at seven" was all she'd said.

Seven was only a few minutes away. He let go a blast of smoke and paced to the window again. Through a dark clear Friday night, headlights were coming from the direction of Belfast. Maybe that was her? They sped on past the house.

O'Reilly stood staring out into the darkness, past the steeple, over the rooftops to the blackness of Belfast Lough. At its head and to his left Belfast shone like a beacon, and ahead of him the myriad lights of Greenisland and Carrickfergus speckled the far shore and lower slopes of the Antrim Hills.

They'd all have been out for the blackout during the war, he thought. Ulster would have been as stygian at night as the Mediterranean he had stared at so often from the bridge of the old *Warspite*.

That gloom had been torn to shreds by the guns of the great superdreadnought in March 1941 at the battle of Cape Matapan, eye-searing cordite flames belching from the muzzles of her eight fifteen-inch rifles. A month later, the thunder of exploding bombs had echoed from the Cave Hill. Flashes of the high explosives and the flames of Belfast's burning buildings had daubed the hillsides yellow and scarlet, and painted the undersides of the clouds in horrid reflections of the inferno beneath.

God damn the *Luftwaffe*. God grant you peace, Deidre, my love, for I must surely do so, my darling girl. I must surely let you go.

O'Reilly blew out his cheeks, rubbed his eyes with the back of his hand, and was wandering back to his chair when the front doorbell rang. In his rush down the stairs, he almost trod on Lady Macbeth, who was clambering up from below. She leapt onto the banister and he heard her spitting at his retreating back.

Kinky beat him to the door. "Come in, Miss Kitty. Himself will—"

"Be right here," O'Reilly said breathlessly. "Thank you, Kinky." He grinned at Kitty. "And don't bother taking off your coat," he said. "We'll be leaving for the Culloden straightaway."

"In which case, sir," Kinky said, "I'll go back to my kitchen and finish preparing the veal in aspic and Scotch eggs for our picnic for the races tomorrow." She smiled at Kitty. "Doctor O'Reilly has invited me to come, so."

"Wonderful," Kitty said. "I'm looking forward to going too."

She had brought her toothbrush. O'Reilly was delighted.

"I do hear tell," said Kinky, "that Cissie Sloan has a nice new dress for the occasion." She lightly touched Kitty's arm. "I'm sure it's lovely, so, but I think my new handbag will take the light from her eyes." She headed off along the hall.

Vanity, O'Reilly thought, thy name *is* woman. "Come on, Kitty," he said, relishing the faintest whiff of her perfume. "We've reservations for seven thirty and I'm quite looking forward to my dinner."

She laughed. "Was there ever a time you weren't?"

"Ah," he said, "but this is special. Tonight I want to hear if your break did you good."

They chatted on the short drive down about the weather, how much she'd enjoyed the play, the Victoria and Albert Museum, her trips to the Tate and National Galleries. He'd enjoyed listening to her talk enthusiastically about Stubbs's horses, the Turner sunsets, and one of the English painter's most famous works, *The Fighting Temeraire*. He wondered if she'd spent any time admiring Rodin's *The Kiss*.

O'Reilly led Kitty into the Culloden's entrance hall, helped her off with her coat, and gave their coats to the cloakroom attendant.

"That," he said, admiring her cerise, knee-length, short-sleeved dress, sheer stockings, and new patent-leather stilettos, "is some outfit. And you've had your hair done. You look absolutely stunning."

She made a mock curtsey. "Thank you, Fingal. I hoped you'd approve."

"I do. I think," he said, "we'll go through to the bar. It used to be a chapel when this place was a bishop's palace."

"Was it?"

"The widow of the man who built it gave it to the Church of Ireland in the 1880s. Three or four bishops used it as their palace before the church sold it to a gynaecologist in the 1920s. It became a hotel in 1962." O'Reilly took her elbow and steered her across the hall. A small plaque read: Jeremy Taylor Bar.

A fire blazed cheerfully in a huge fireplace. The tables were far enough apart for the other patrons to be unable to overhear each other's conversations. He noticed two small groups and acknowledged bowed greetings from members of both, who clearly recognised him.

Kitty sat in a wingbacked armchair and crossed her legs.

Fingal sat opposite. He admired the curve of her calf. "G and T?"

She shook her head. "Are we having wine with our meal?"

"Of course."

"Then why not start it now?"

"Fair enough." He sat back in his chair and pursed his lips.

O'Reilly hoped his next remark might catch her a little off guard so her reply would be completely spontaneous. He'd been patient in the car, but he wanted to know what had happened in London. He said, "He seems like a decent sort, your Mr. Roulston."

"John?" she said and laughed. "He certainly is." She smiled at him and waited.

O'Reilly laughed. Damn you, Kitty, you've turned the tables perfectly. "Kitty," O'Reilly said, "I've missed you—dreadfully. You went away and left me with a lot to mull over."

She leant forward and put her hands on the polished mahogany tabletop. "I wanted you to think, Fingal. I really did."

"I wondered how you and Roulston were getting on." He started to reach out to cover her hand with his own, but a waiter in a dinner suit and black tie came to the table.

"Doctor O'Reilly. Nice to see you again, sir. Your table will be ready whenever you are." He handed Kitty a leather-bound menu, and O'Reilly a menu and a wine list. "Would sir and madam like a drink while they decide?"

"Yes, thank you, Bernard," said O'Reilly. He glanced rapidly at the menu. "And we've decided already."

Kitty frowned and raised one eyebrow.

He knew she was too much of a lady to argue in front of a waiter.

"You have a good Bâtard-Montrachet?"

"Yes, sir. A '56 if memory serves."

"Good. We'll have a glass here. For our meal, the lady will start with escargots and follow with a filet steak, medium rare."

"And for sir?"

"Scampi and lobster thermidor."

"Certainly. I may have to go to the cold room for the wine, sir. We don't have a lot of orders for the Montrachet."

"Take your time," O'Reilly said.

The waiter left.

Kitty said quietly, "Fingal, that's far too extravagant. Montrachet is horribly expensive."

"And the last time we tried to have a bottle we had to rush off and deliver a baby. Remember?"

She nodded.

He leant forward, put a hand on hers, and looked straight into her grey eyes flecked with amber. "I reckon some things if you've tasted them once are worth a second try."

She smiled. "And that's why you've ordered our meal the way you have? The same menu as the one we didn't finish that night too?"

"No." O'Reilly sat back. "Not exactly. It's because—"

Kitty started to smile. "Before you go any further, Fingal. I want you to know John Roulston is a decent man. He took me to that play and to the Tate."

O'Reilly said gruffly, "No reason why he shouldn't. None at all."

"He did *not* take me to his bed."

O'Reilly knew he was blushing. "I . . . that is . . . well—"

"But you were worried he might have." She turned her hand under his, held and squeezed it. "Fingal, you're jealous and that means you care. Please understand I didn't deliberately set up that refresher course. I did enjoy John's company, and I saw no reason to lie to you about it, but I didn't do any of it to make you jealous."

"Thank you," O'Reilly said, "and thank you for setting my mind at rest. I apologise, but I was worried."

"You'd no need." She uncrossed and recrossed her legs. "Now tell me why you ordered what you have, although"—she looked at his eyes—"I have a pretty fair idea."

"Because it was the first dinner out in Dublin a medical student bought for a student nurse the night she qualified."

"I thought so," she said. "That is sweet." She puckered and blew him a kiss.

O'Reilly rose and walked to her side of the table. He looked down on her shining silver-tipped black hair, her eyes wide and looking up into his. "Stand up," he said.

She stood.

To hell with the other patrons. O'Reilly put his arms around her and pulled her to him. He put his mouth beside her ear and whispered, "When I bought you snails back then, I was in love with you, Kitty O'Hallorhan." He held her at arm's length. "You've been very patient—"

She shook her head.

"Kitty," he said, "I think I've known it since last August. It's just been—"

"Hard for you to spit it out. I think," she said, "you are such a brave man in so many ways you have to have an Achilles heel. In your case, it's your heart. You are terrified of being hurt again."

He hung his head.

"So," she said, "I'll make it easy for you. Fingal O'Reilly, I still—"

He put his great paw gently over her mouth. "No, Kitty," he said. "There's no need. I don't need prompting. I love you and I always will." He let his lips touch her forehead. In such a public place, he had been demonstrative enough.

"Thank you, Fingal," she said, letting her lips brush his cheek. "Thank you very much." She sat gracefully once more and inclined her head to where the waiter was approaching, carrying an ice bucket and two glasses.

She didn't need to say any more, and O'Reilly, now the dam had burst, could no more restrain his feelings out of respect for social convention than a child holding its halter could stop a stallion determined to gallop away. His voice didn't quite reach its quarterdeck volume, but it was loud enough for the other patrons to turn and stare. "Bernard," he roared, "take that away and bring a magnum of chilled Möet Chandon and a tray of champagne flutes."

"Fingal. *Ssssh,*" Kitty said laughing. "Everybody's looking."

They were indeed, so it was too late for *ssssh.* "Miss O'Hallorhan here and I," O'Reilly said, addressing the other diners, "have something *very* special to celebrate, so anyone who'd like a glass of bubbles with us, come on over."

To O'Reilly's surprise there was a round of applause as men and women started rising and making their way over to his table. One voice said, "Bravo, Doctor."

O'Reilly lowered his voice and bent to Kitty. "I'm so bloody happy," he said, "I could burst. I need to celebrate—and I need to tell you, and go on telling you, I love you, Kitty O'Hallorhan. I really, really do."

44

Le Déjeuner sur l'Herbe
(or The Car Boot Lid)

Barry was trotting downstairs to join the race party, but stopped outside the upstairs lounge. "I see you've made a friend, Jennifer."

Doctor Jennifer Alexander, ex-classmate and the trainee cardiologist who had been sent by the Contactor's Bureau, was sitting in an armchair, petting Lady Macbeth. The petite white cat was curled up in the young woman's lap.

"She's a pretty wee thing, Barry," Jennifer said.

"Her name's Lady Macbeth," Barry said, "because she reckons she owns this place."

"Typical cat."

"And if you want any more animal company there's a bloody great Labrador in the back garden called Arthur—"

"*Barry. The races are today. Get a move on,*" O'Reilly bellowed from the hall.

". . . Arthur Guinness." Barry laughed. "His bark's worse than his bite," he said quietly, "and I mean O'Reilly's, not Arthur's," then he yelled, "Coming." He hesitated. "Thanks for coming down, Jennifer. It'll be good for us to get away for a day."

"My pleasure," she said, "and I can use the money."

"*Baaaarry.*"

"I'm off," he said, and he ran down the last flight to join Fingal, Kitty, and Kinky for the drive to Downpatrick.

O'Reilly drove over the Ballybucklebo Hills to Comber, then along the west side of Strangford Lough through Balloo and on to Killyleagh. Green islands, brown pladdies, and low sea wrack–covered reefs studded the calm waters. In the distance, the granite-grey Mourne Mountains tumbled to the shores of the Irish Sea.

Fingal was full of the joys of spring, and in his kamikaze motoring approach of old, he hurled the Rover along the narrow winding road. Fortunately they did not encounter a single cyclist.

As Kinky and Kitty chatted in the back, O'Reilly sang snatches of "Camptown Races," pounding a fist on the steering wheel to accompany each "doo-dah, doo-dah."

His good humour was infectious, and Barry found himself joining in the chorus—that is, when he wasn't clutching at the dashboard while the car took corners or sped up and over the drumlins and became momentarily airborne. He wondered if it was only the prospect of Bertie Bishop's downfall that had O'Reilly so excited.

They crossed the gently flowing River Quoile, where weeping willows lining the banks bowed to a pair of swans gliding sedately past. O'Reilly drove through the ancient cathedral city of Downpatrick—in Irish, *Dún Pádraig,* Patrick's fort—the saint's burial place. He was in good company. Saints Comgal and Bridget were also interred there.

A little more than a mile past the southwestern outskirts, O'Reilly parked in a field beside the racecourse. A drystone wall separated the far end of the temporary parking lot from a pasture, where a herd of black-and-white dappled Friesians stood in a row, heavy heads hanging over the wall. They were, Barry thought, a mute spectators' gallery that, in dim incomprehension, regarded with soft brown eyes the antics of the creatures next door.

Cars were ranked in rows, and many racegoers, like O'Reilly's party, were having picnics. The lunch Kinky had prepared was eaten as they stood around the open car boot. It was superb: cold chicken, ham sandwiches, veal in aspic, Scotch eggs, potato salad, green salad. The two large thermoses of her beef barley soup, brought along in case the day turned cold, lay unopened in the picnic basket. The weather was perfect. Blue skies, puffball clouds, a light southerly wind.

Barry had not been surprised when Fingal produced a bottle of Entre-deux-mers from a portable icebox, but why did the chest also contain two bottles of champagne?

"Doctor O'Reilly sir," Kinky said. "I do think, and I'm sure Miss Kitty will agree, that after veal in aspic *one* Scotch egg is quite sufficient, so."

"Kinky's right, Fingal," Kitty said, grasping his wrist. "Put it back."

O'Reilly grumbled, set the savoury in the basket, and said, "Lord, preserve me from this 'monstrous regiment of women.'"

"John Knox," Barry said, quite happy to play along. He was going to say, "in 1558," but the fond look that passed between O'Reilly and Kitty pulled him up short. Barry wondered exactly what had transpired between them last night.

"Good afternoon, gentlemen," said O'Reilly heartily.

Mr. Coffin, the Ballybucklebo undertaker, tipped his bowler hat, and Shooey Gamble lifted his duncher. The old gentleman was getting along well with the help of a blackthorn walking stick.

"How are you two?" O'Reilly asked.

"Very well, thank you, Doctor," Mr. Coffin replied and touched a finger to a small scar beneath his Adam's apple. "Thanks to you two."

"And I'm getting better use of the knee, Doctor Laverty," Shooey said. "Thon heating pad's a godsend on a cold night, so it is." He winked at O'Reilly, then said, "We're off to the races. We want to see how Mr. Bishop's wee horse does. I think everybody in the whole townland wants to."

As they left, O'Reilly turned to Barry and explained, "Mr. Coffin's late father was Shooey's best friend. Mr. Coffin keeps a filial eye on the old boy. Takes him to the odd soccer game, the races. They keep each other company, and speaking of keeping company—"

"Doctor dear," said Maggie Houston, "I knew we'd see you here. I was just saying to Sonny—"

"Good afternoon, ladies . . . gentlemen," said Sonny Houston, tipping his hat to Kitty and Kinky.

"—we're sure to see the doctors here this afternoon," Maggie continued. Maggie's hatband held two roses, one more wilted than the other. She smiled and everyone could see that in honour of the occasion she was wearing her teeth.

"You're looking very lovely today, Miss O'Hallorhan," Sonny said. "Quite . . ."—he struggled for the word—"radiant."

"Thank you, kind sir." Kitty favoured Sonny with a wide smile.

Barry noticed how she looked at Fingal—and how Fingal looked back.

"And is that a new handbag, Mrs. Kincaid?" Sonny enquired.

Maggie leant over and peered at it. "Thon's a humdinger, so it is, Kinky. New, like?"

Kinky smiled. "It is. I'm glad you like it. It did be a gift from Miss Kitty, so."

"Did you get it locally, Miss O'Hallorhan?" Maggie wanted to know.

"In Belfast," Kitty said. "Miss Moloney was unwell."

"Was," said Maggie. "Was. We were in with her and her sister yesterday. Miss Alice Moloney's up and doing quite nicely now, and she said to be sure if we saw you doctors today to tell you how grateful she is."

O'Reilly inclined his head.

Barry smiled. "Pleased to hear it, Maggie."

Maggie became conspiratorial. "Miss Moloney give me a pound for a flutter, you know, and her so proper, who'd have thought she liked a bet?" She lowered her voice. "Doctor O'Reilly sir. What's nap today?"

"Nap?" Barry asked.

"It's short for Napoleon, reputedly because he always bet on sure things in battles," O'Reilly said. "In track lingo it means what do the experts suggest as the very best bet for any given day." He lowered his voice to match Maggie's and said, "I reckon Flo's Fancy in the seventh."

"Thank you, sir. We'll remember that, won't we, dear?"

"Of course we will," said Sonny. "Flo's Fancy. That's the councillor's animal." He inclined his head to Kitty and Kinky. "And now, if you'll excuse us, we must be running along."

"We'll be close behind," O'Reilly said. "It's half past one and the first race starts at 2:15."

Barry watched him eyeing the uneaten Scotch egg. Kitty, unbeknown to Fingal, was also watching him, clearly ready to head him off at the pass if he made a move. Kinky was taking no chances. After stealing one quick glance at O'Reilly, she grabbed the egg and rewrapped it in greaseproof paper. "If everybody's had enough?" she said, and without waiting for a reply started packing up the picnic hamper.

O'Reilly looked disappointed, but clearly it would take more than being denied the pleasure of one of Kinky's Scotch eggs to dampen his spirits today. When she was finished, he shoved the hamper into the boot and closed the lid with a crash. "Right," he boomed. "It's off to the races with us."

Barry found himself last in the queue of O'Reilly, Kitty, and Kinky at one of the turnstiles of Downpatrick Racecourse. There was a bank of ticket wickets and long lines of people stretched from each.

"How's about ye, Doc?" Gerry Shanks asked from where he stood in the next line with a man Barry recognised as Charlie Gorman. "My Mairead has Angus and Siobhan over with Gertie Gorman today, so I come on down here with my pal Charlie for a bit of *craic.*"

O'Reilly had delivered Gertie's breech baby last year, and the Shanks's daughter's meningitis was still fresh in Barry's mind. "Your Siobhan's well, Gerry?" he asked.

"Fit as a flea."

"I'm glad to hear it." It was pleasant knowing how your patients were doing.

"Still supporting Linfield, Charlie?" Barry asked.

"No team like the Blues," Charlie Gorman said.

"Pay you no attention 'til him, Doctor," Gerry said. "Your head's cut, Charlie. They couldn't beat their way out of a wet paper bag. Glentoran's the team to watch, so it is." Gerry shook his head. "More important, Doctor, how do you reckon Councillor Bishop's wee horse is going to do today?"

"I think," said Barry, "from what I've been hearing, everybody from Ballybucklebo is asking the same question."

He was next at his wicket. He held out a pound note, but the ticket seller shook his head. "Thon big fellah, him with the bent nose and bullock's lugs, he's paid, so he has."

Champagne on ice, O'Reilly paying for their entrance? The big fellah was in crackling form today.

"Come on, Barry," O'Reilly yelled. "Begod, but it's like Paddy's market here. Quite the turnout."

There was hardly elbow room in the concourse between the turnstiles, various buildings, enclosures, and the outer track railings. Men in hacking jackets and cavalry twill pants, most sporting cravats and camel-hair peaked caps—these were the horsey fraternity—mingled with plainly dressed farmers, artisans, and women in their Sunday best. There was constant movement in and out of several buildings to his right. If the number of folks clutching drinks was anything to go by, one at least, must be a bar. The stands stood to his left, and a large marquee was further off past them.

"Hello, Barry."

He turned to see Sue Nolan.

"Hello, Sue." An emerald head scarf complemented her burnished copper hair. "What brings you here?"

"My uncle from Broughshane has a filly in the seventh. Glen Lady."

"I'll be watching for her. Are you on your own?" He found he was hoping she was.

"No—"

It was a pity, Barry thought.

"I'm with my uncle." She pointed to the big tent. "I'm meant to be joining him over there."

Barry smiled. "I'll mebbe run into you through the afternoon." He wanted to keep her talking. "No more ringworm at school?"

She shook her head. "Not one. And Colin's back in class. You'd not believe what he did on Tuesday—"

From ahead he heard O'Reilly yelling, "Barry. Get a move on."

"Sorry, Sue," he said. "That was His Master's Voice, and I don't mean the record company."

"Doctor O'Reilly?"

"Himself. Gotta go, but I really want to hear about Colin."

"If I don't see you today, why not—"

"*Barry.*"

"—give me a call? I'm in the book," Sue said.

"I will." He caught up with his party in front of the stand. O'Reilly was saying, "Kinky, I know you want to find Flo Bishop and Cissie Sloan. I'd try the top bar off to the right."

"Thank you, sir."

"And Kinky, if you decide to stay with your friends, that's quite all right. Meet us back at the Rover after the races."

Kinky looked happily at her handbag and said, "I'll be doing that, sir. I hope you all enjoy the meet, and if you are seeing Mr. Power, I'd take it kindly if you'd not mention what Tiernan told me the wee jockey said."

"Naturally," O'Reilly said. "Off you trot, and come on, you two. The marquis'll be in the private marquee." O'Reilly headed off, holding Kitty's hand. Barry was walking at his shoulder.

"Quite the meet," Barry said.

"Quite the track," O'Reilly replied. "It's the oldest in Ireland. The first race was held here in 1685. The course is a mile and two furlongs long and is set up for both National Hunt races, with six fences on the outer-rail side, and for flat racing along the inner rails. The—"

Barry lost the end of the sentence when a large man forced his way past. Barry dodged more people, then caught up with O'Reilly, who stood outside a canvas marquee talking to a man wearing a brown grocer's coat and sporting a red armband.

"I do understand," O'Reilly said. "VIPs only."

It dawned on Barry that this was not Ballybucklebo and that in the rest of Ireland, except perhaps in rugby circles, O'Reilly's local godlike status did not apply.

"I'm looking for the Marquis of Ballybucklebo," O'Reilly continued.

"I can't help it . . . I'm sorry, sir. VIPs only. Them's the rules, so they are."

Barry felt someone jostle past his shoulder and then try to pass

Fingal. "Out of my way, O'Reilly." Barry had no trouble recognising the portly figure of Bertie Bishop.

"I suppose you're an owner and that makes you a VIP," O'Reilly said quietly.

" 'At's right."

"Good for you, Bertie." O'Reilly looked around. "Where's Flo?"

"Back at the grandstand colloguing with your Mrs. Kincaid and Cissie Sloan. I heard Flo invite them to come with us for the racing. I've space in the private stand."

The unspoken "And you don't, O'Reilly" was clear to Barry.

"Och," said O'Reilly, "anywhere I see your wee horse win, it'll be exciting." He glanced at the doorkeeper, who stood with his arms folded, florid face impassive. "I wonder, Bertie," O'Reilly said, "if you'd do something for me?"

"What?" His eyes narrowed.

"If the marquis is inside, would you tell him I'm here and would like a word?"

Bishop pulled in a deep breath. He grinned. "I could, so I could." Barry knew that Bishop was forcing O'Reilly to plead. Barry saw the muscles at the corners of the big man's jaw tighten before he said calmly, "I'd be most grateful, Bertie."

"All right."

"Thank you and good luck in the seventh. We're all cheering for Flo's Fancy."

Bishop ignored O'Reilly and strutted inside. Barry watched him greeting this one and that, then noticed a young woman with copper hair under an emerald scarf. Damn it, he *would* phone her.

Distracted by Sue Nolan, Barry lost sight of Bertie Bishop. But John McNeill, Marquis of Ballybucklebo, shock of greying hair nodding, had turned, detached himself from a group, and was heading to where Barry, Kitty, and O'Reilly stood.

"Miss O'Hallorhan? Fingal? Young Laverty?" The marquis' words were as clipped as his moustache. "Why on earth did you have to send Bertie Bishop to ask me to come out?"

O'Reilly pointed to the doorman. "Your man there thinks he's Leonidas guarding the pass at Thermopylae."

"Wouldn't let you in? Never mind." The marquis bowed to Kitty. "Miss O'Hallorhan, I'd be delighted if you and your gentlemen friends would join me soon in the private stand. I'll tell the steward there to expect you."

"Thank you, my lord," she said.

"I've already told you. It's John."

"Kitty," she said, and Barry saw the marquis smile before he turned to O'Reilly. "Now, Fingal, what can I do for you?"

O'Reilly pointed to a space over by the fence. "Can we go over there, John?"

"For a bit of privacy? Certainly."

"Is Fergus riding for you today?" Fingal asked, as they crossed the ground to the fence.

"In the fourth and the seventh."

O'Reilly looked thoughtful. "The fourth? That's the Ulster Grand National, over the fences."

"It is," the marquis said. "My Battlecruiser's running."

Barry smiled, remembering the huge steeplechaser's performance at the Ballybucklebo point-to-point in August.

"Good luck to him," O'Reilly said, "but it's the seventh we need to talk to you about, John. Another horse in that last race."

The marquis looked thoughtful. "Bishop's animal?"

"We've reason to believe he's ordered the jockey to nobble her."

"What? Pull the horse?" The man's brow creased.

"I'm afraid so."

"Good God. Can you prove it? We'll have them up before the Jockey Club—"

" 'Fraid we can't do that. We've only got hearsay evidence. It was told to Kinky's brother in strict confidence too. She's asked me not to get her brother involved. I'm sure you understand, John."

"Of course."

"I really don't care about the jockey anyway. It's Bertie I'm after," O'Reilly said.

"Pulling a horse? Why would Bishop do a thing like that?" Barry heard the puzzlement in the marquis' voice.

"It's to do with robbing shareholders of their ownership of the animal," O'Reilly said.

"Has it, by Jove?"

Barry expected the marquis' frown to deepen, but instead he smiled. "And knowing you, Fingal O'Reilly, you've a plot to stop him."

"With your help, John."

"What can I do?"

O'Reilly laughed. "First, don't bet on your own horse to win. If we can bring this off, the best she'll do is come second and I'd hate to see you lose any money."

"Because you're making sure Flo's Fancy will win." The marquis' smile was gone. "You'll not be trying to persuade Fergus to slow down. My Myrna's Magic is the favourite, you know."

O'Reilly laughed. "Divil the bit, John. What I'm trying to do is make sure the wee filly gets a fair run at it, that's all. From what Donal Donnelly has told me, she's a really fast horse and she'll eat your mare alive."

"As long as it's in a fair race, I'll have no complaints."

O'Reilly pursed his lips, cocked his head to one side, and said, "For the sake of the men Bertie's trying to diddle, I almost *would* try to fix things with Fergus to make sure. But when she wins by her own efforts it's going to cost Bertie a lot, and I want him to take that tumble with no chance of appeal. It's simply got to be a fair race."

"It's what I'd have expected of you, Fingal." His Lordship's chuckle was deep and throaty. "Cost Bertie Bishop a lot of money? I don't even want to know the details. Anyone who'd pull a horse, never mind shoot at a walking pheasant, must be punished, and if we can't prove his wrongdoing and go through the Jockey Club—"

"We must invoke divine intervention," O'Reilly said innocently, "and just give the Big Fellah"—he jerked his head upward—"a little shove. I will explain exactly what Bishop's been up to over a wee half, John, but for now I want to know what I can promise Bishop's jockey, Eugene Power, you'll do for him after he wins. Bishop is bound to fire him for disobeying orders and queer his pitch with other owners."

"Vindictive little man, Bishop. He would, wouldn't he?"

"He would."

The marquis frowned. "And you'll vouch for this Power fellow, Fingal?"

"I will. I have it on impeccable authority that ordinarily he's a fine rider, but he's being threatened—"

"By Bishop, no doubt?"

"Who else?"

The marquis nodded. "Fine. Tell Power to come and see me tomorrow at the Big House. I'll make some telephone calls. If he brings that filly home first today, he'll never want for a mount, I promise."

"Thank you, John," O'Reilly said. "And there is one other thing."

"Go ahead."

"The word about Bishop is going to go around among the trainers, stable lads, and jockeys, and it may be difficult for him to get another jockey. Nobody likes to ride for a crooked owner."

"It'll serve him right."

Barry had to agree.

O'Reilly shook his head. "I mentioned shareholders. If they get their shares back, they stand to make a decent profit if Flo's Fancy wins a few more races after today. And from what I hear, she should if she's ridden properly."

"I see . . . I quite see." The marquis frowned, pinched his nose, and then said, "Fergus . . . Fergus Finnegan. He could use a few wins. No reason I can't ask him to ride for Bishop for a while. Fergus won't like that, but he can tell his pals he's doing it on my orders. My guess is that once Bertie does sell Flo's Fancy, he'll get out of racing altogether."

O'Reilly sighed. "Och, Jasus, and what a loss that would be."

The marquis chuckled. "I'll speak to Fergus tomorrow before I see your chap . . . Power, you said? He could ride for me."

"Bless you, John," O'Reilly said. "We're well on our way to the downfall of Bertie, and if you'll excuse us, I have to nip over to the weigh room and get a word with the Corkman Eugene Power to make sure it happens."

45

Are Said to Understand One and Other

"He really is a sweetheart, your marquis," Kitty said, as she linked her arm with O'Reilly's, and the pair of them accompanied by Barry started to walk away from the marquee. She cocked one eyebrow. "Single, I believe?"

O'Reilly chuckled and Barry heard something in the big man's voice when he replied, "And out of bounds, Miss Caitlin O'Hallorhan." It was a tone and a sentiment Barry could only describe as possessive. Fair play to you both, he thought.

The three of them passed the grandstand and headed to the betting ring. They forced their way through the mob to where the on-track bookies had their booths. The enclosure was sited between the stand, the track behind it, and the parade ring off to the right.

"Kitty," O'Reilly said, "will you do me a favour?"

"If I can."

"You know Barry and I have to see a man about a horse."

"I do."

Barry was eager to see how Fingal was going to handle the Cork jockey.

"Will you go and find Willy McArdle and put that on Luke's Point Lass on the nose in the first?" O'Reilly handed her a five-pound note. "For us both. We'll split the winnings."

"Fair enough," she said, taking the money. "Luke's Point Lass on the nose."

And by the sound of things, Barry thought, O'Reilly was backing the favourite. Above the noise of the crowd, the stuttering of a distant petrol generator, and the occasional whinny, Barry could hear the bookies calling the odds, "Luke's Point Lass, two to one on. Evangeline, six to five. Mossbridge Racer, two to one. Longford Lad, twenty to one. Ballina Brave, a hundred to one. Five to one, the field. Five to one, the field."

He looked over to where the on-track bookies were plying their trade. Each had his own platform, with wooden arms rising vertically from the sides of a tall, Dickensian, stand-at desk. Blackboards with the horses' names and prices in chalk were attached to one of the poles. The struts supported a sign bearing in garish colours and flourishing script the name of the bookmaker: Honest Sammy Dolan, Best Odds; William McArdle and Sons, Turf Accountants.

Men stood behind their desks taking money and issuing betting slips as each bettor reached the head of the queue and handed over a wager.

"There's Willy's stand, Kitty," O'Reilly said. "Tell him Doctor O'Reilly says thanks for the help he gave Donal, and after you put on the bets, very quietly tell Willy I say to lay off early on Flo's Fancy. Then head on back to the private stand and meet John. We'll see you there."

"Don't be long," she said, then turned and walked away.

"Sorry, Fingal, but I think I've lost the thread. Were you asking Kitty to tell Willy to shorten the odds early or to lay off, stop taking bets completely?" Barry asked.

"Not at all. Every small bookie protects himself by taking a proportion of all money wagered on any horse he thinks might win or place and then betting on that animal with a bigger bookie. It's called laying-off. That's one of the jobs of a bookie's runner."

"Going and phoning in bets?"

"Right. It's all go, Barry. Odds change all the time as each bookie calculates how the punters are betting and studies the intelligence relayed by his tic-tac man. Look—" He pointed to where some distance away a man wearing white gloves was whirling his hands around like a semaphore. "That lad's sending signals to Donal. See him there beside Willy?"

"Hard to miss Donal's thatch." Barry saw Donal say something to his boss, who immediately wiped Longford Lad's odds of twenty to one off the blackboard and replaced them with ten to one. "I suppose the tic-tac man's sent some info."

"You suppose right," O'Reilly said. "So Willy's shortened the odds. That's why I want him to take my advice and lay off on Flo's Fancy early. He can make a bundle if she wins, and he's covered if a lot of other people bet with him on that filly today, even if she has been losing at other meets."

"Why would they bet on her? A losing horse?"

"Sentiment. Our people, out of pride, will back a local horse at long odds even if its form isn't very good. When they do, you'll see the odds shorten here, and there'll be more laid off against her with bigger bookies, so the odds will shorten off-track too. I just want Willy to be able to get the best he can on Bertie's horse, probably with Ladbrokes. We owe him that much. We'd not be halfway home in the beat-Bertie-Bishop stakes without Willy's help."

O'Reilly drew up short at the side of the weigh room and pointed over at the entrance to the betting ring. "There goes Donal, heading for the phone. Kitty'll have repeated my message. He'll be making that lay-off call for McArdle."

A loudspeaker boomed tinnily, "My lord, ladies, and gentlemen, welcome to Downpatrick Races. It is now fifteen minutes to the start of the first. The horses are moving to the track."

Barry watched the handsome animals being led from the parade ring to line up for the start. Their jockeys, small men all, riding boots firmly in stirrups, knees bent almost on level with the horse's back, sat solidly in their light English saddles, reins held loosely. Each wore the brightly coloured silks of the horse's owner.

O'Reilly's timing of their arrival at the adjacent weigh room was perfect. Fergus Finnegan came out wearing the marquis' colours of green and scarlet squares and carrying his saddle.

"Fergus," O'Reilly boomed.

"Doctors." Fergus grinned. "Good to see youse. What's the word?"

"Can you introduce us to Eugene Power?"

"Aye, certainly. I'll get him."

"Before you go, Fergus, I want you to understand . . . it's only fair to tell you, if Doctor Laverty and I can make what we're planning work, you may not have a winner in the seventh."

"Myrna's Magic get beat?" Fergus narrowed his eyes. "Doctor O'Reilly sir, I know you're up to something, and as long as it's on the level, what the eye doesn't see, the heart doesn't grieve over."

"You've my word it's all honest." O'Reilly offered his hand, which was duly taken and solemnly shaken by Fergus. "And Fergus, we'd not be able to do this if you hadn't given us the tip about Bishop's jockey. Thank you for that."

Fergus winked. "Donal's a right good head, so are his mates, and it's not right what Bishop's doing. I was pleased to help, so I was. I'll be happy to give the wee animal a fair chance, like"—he became serious—"but I'll not pull *my* horse. Bishop's'll have to win fair and square."

"I'd have expected no less of you," O'Reilly said. "Off you go. Bring back Power."

"I'll get the Corkman for you, and then I'm off. Flo's Fancy'll still get a bloody good race from me—and we'll see who's got the best horse, so we will." Fergus headed back into the weigh room.

The tinny speakers bellowed, "My lord, ladies, and gentlemen, the first race, the McCoubrey Stakes for a purse of two hundred pounds, will be twice round the track, two and a half miles over the jumps."

Barry stopped paying attention to the voice when Fergus reappeared followed by another jockey. He was short, narrow-faced with deep-set black eyes, a lopsided smile, and locks of auburn hair straggling from under his peaked, black velvet–covered hard hat. He wore the Bishop syndicate's colours, silks of a light red that clashed horribly with a series of superimposed pink circles. He carried his saddle under one arm.

"Eugene Power," said Fergus, "this here's Doctor O'Reilly and this here's Doctor Laverty."

"Pleased to meet you, so."

Barry heard the gentle Cork inflection, so like Kinky's.

"I'm off," Fergus said. "I want to have a wee word with my mount Battlecruiser before the fourth. Tell him about the fences, like."

Barry did not miss his quick wink to O'Reilly, who inclined his head to Fergus.

"See you in the seventh, Eugene," Fergus said.

Power turned to O'Reilly. "Fergus says you've a question for me, bye."

"I have," Fingal said. "Are you happy riding for Councillor Bishop?"

"It's a job." His voice was flat.

O'Reilly said, "It must be frustrating to have such a great wee horse and never have a win."

The little man took a step back and had to grab at his saddle when he nearly dropped it. His mouth opened and shut.

Barry studied Power's face. The man must be wondering, exactly what did Fingal know?

Power looked at the ground. "She's been unlucky, that's all." He looked back up at O'Reilly. "It does be hard on her other owners. I'm terrible sorry for them, so." He looked as if he really meant it.

So, Barry thought, this man has a conscience.

"Would you like Flo's Fancy to win today?"

Power shook his head. "I'd like that well enough. Wouldn't any jockey want to ride a winner? I just dunno. On her form I can't see her making it at all, at all." He sighed and looked O'Reilly straight in the eye. "But she's a lovely wee craythur. It would be grand, so, if she was able to win."

"I've heard something," said O'Reilly. "His Lordship would like to see you tomorrow, Eugene."

The Corkman's eyes widened. "The Marquis of Ballybucklebo? Wants to see me? Me? What for?"

"He told me not ten minutes ago he's looking for someone else as well as Fergus to ride for him—"

Before O'Reilly could continue, the speaker brayed, "They're under starter's orders."

"The marquis needs another rider?" Power cocked his head.

"That's right, isn't it, Doctor Laverty?"

"Indeed it is."

"He mentioned you by name, Eugene. There'll be a job for you, all right."

"Me?"

"Indeed. He reckoned if Flo's Fancy won today you should go round and see him tomorrow."

"And the marquis'd have a job? For me?"

"I promise you," O'Reilly said. "And I think you might need one. I'm not convinced Councillor Bishop would be overjoyed by a win—if you get my drift."

Power's hand on the saddle was shaking. "I am not convinced myself, in soul I'm not. Doctor O'Reilly?" The Corkman held O'Reilly's gaze, then lowered his voice. "You doctors have to keep secrets?"

"We do," O'Reilly said.

Eugene's face crumpled. Barry thought he looked close to tears. "You'll not tell anybody?"

"That's right."

"I once did a silly thing in England—once, bye." His voice dropped to a whisper, and Barry had to strain to hear. "I pulled a horse."

"We all make mistakes," O'Reilly said, "and confession is good for the soul."

"Aye, so, and I swore to myself I'd never do it again. But Mr. Bishop found out; he said he'd tell the Jockey Club if—"

"Eugene," O'Reilly said gently, "say no more. He can't tell the Jockey Club now because I know he's been blackmailing you. The club would marmalise him if we told them. What I want to hear is that now you know for certain you'll have a job with the marquis, will you give Flo's Fancy her head today?"

"I'd love for to see her win," he said wistfully. "Just the once." He looked from O'Reilly to Barry and back to O'Reilly again. "And that's true about the marquis and a job? Because if she wins, Mr. Bishop will fire me as sure as eggs are eggs."

"You've my word," Fingal said. "I'd not worry about the councillor."

The Cork jockey grinned broadly. "Thank you, sir. Thank you and, by God, bye, Myrna's Magic is a grand fast horse, but so's Flo's Fancy. I'll just need keep up with the leaders, then let her out in the last furlong and give her a taste of the crop."

"I'm sure you know your business," O'Reilly said, and he clapped the little man on the shoulder.

There was a wickedness to the Corkman's laugh before he said, "You're going to see a race the likes of which hasn't been seen since before or after Arkle beat Mill House for the Cheltenham Gold Cup last Saint Paddy's Day."

46

They're under Starter's Orders

"Bertie Bishop," O'Reilly called. He had left his seat in the VIP section and was on his way out of the stands behind Kitty and Barry.

Councillor Bishop spun in his seat.

"I'm off," O'Reilly said, "to have a flutter on your Flo's Fancy in the seventh. It's the last race of the day, but I reckon it's been worth waiting for."

Bishop beamed. "Do like I done, Doctor," he said. "Don't waste your money betting to place. Go for a win. I got twenty to one for me and the lads, so I did. You know 'at."

"I will and I do," said O'Reilly, thinking, *at least that's what you told everybody.* "Myself and the half of Ballybucklebo will be betting on her. It'll be like a Roman triumph when she pulls it off."

"Ah, now," said Bertie, "there's many a slip between—"

"Cup and lip. If there wasn't, horse racing'd be no fun."

"*Fingaaal*" pealed out over the general hubbub. *Good Lord,* thought O'Reilly. *That was Barry yelling at him.* "If you don't come on we'll not have time to go to the parade ring and then place our bets." *Touché. It had been himself roaring at Barry to get a move on all morning.*

O'Reilly hurried along the row and down the steps to the concourse. "Right," he said, when he joined Barry and Kitty, "let's go." He shouldered his way past sandwich-munching punters, workingmen holding pints of stout and arguing over the *Racing Form*, women with what he guessed would be glasses of port and brandy, and kids chewing toffee apples and candy floss.

He sang a snatch of "The Galway Races":

And gingerbread and spices to accommodate the ladies,
and a big *crúibin* for thruppence to be pickin' while you're
able.

Kinky would enjoy a *crúibin*, a pickled pig's trotter eaten cold with vinegar. So would Eugene Power. *Crúibins* were much appreciated in County Cork.

A woman was standing by a baby in a pram, the infant clad in tiny racing silks and a miniature hard hat. A small knot of her friends bent over the pram making clucking noises and admiring the wean. Jasus, he thought, but wasn't a day at the races just what the doctor ordered? Sure there was the excitement of watching the horses, the exhilaration of a winning bet. But it wasn't just the money that made you feel good; it was the easygoing *craic* with friends and neighbours that really made the day. Along with *céilis,* and parties, a night at the Duck, a day shooting pheasants, aye, and even a funeral and the meal after, racing was one of the rituals that bound Ulster folks together in tight communities that O'Reilly wouldn't swap for the keys to the kingdom of heaven. Long may it continue, he thought. And, begod if I'd a glass in my hand I'd drink to that.

He was lucky to find space in the scrum at the rail of the parade ring. "In here, Kitty," he said, making room for her to stand in front of him, his arms on each side of her, his hands on the rail. A tiny whiff of her musky perfume tickled his nostrils. There was just room for Barry to tuck in sideways by O'Reilly's shoulder.

The stablehands were leading the seven thoroughbreds around

the ring so the punters could admire and size up each animal. O'Reilly inhaled the familiar smells of leather, horse sweat, and horse apples. They masked Kitty's perfume.

Now at five o'clock the day was chillier, and the horses' breath came in puffs of vapour that hung like phantasms in the still air. One filly tossed her head and whinnied loudly. The groom had to strain on her head rope to control the animal.

"What do you make of Flo's Fancy, Kitty?" he asked, as the chestnut horse was led past, daintily stepping, ears twitching, head nodding as she chewed on her bit.

Kitty narrowed her eyes and studied the filly. "That's a well set-up little horse," she said, as the animal approached. "Nice gait. About fourteen hands. Deep breast, so her wind should be sound. Heavy quarters. Good gaskins."

O'Reilly inclined his head. "Impressive," he said. "Gaskins. Muscles like the human calf. Did you do veterinary medicine as well as nursing?" He chuckled.

"No, I just like horses. My da was very keen too. He taught me." She looked more closely. "I like that look in her eyes. Fierce . . . fighting," she said. "Like you, Fingal, when someone challenges you or you get your dander up."

He squeezed her gently with his encircling arms and whispered, "And I will get my dander up if you go back on last night's promise."

She chuckled. "Not one chance, eejit. Not one."

Fingal took a deeply contented breath. He heard Barry ask, "Fingal, I'm no judge of horseflesh, but I've looked at Flo's Fancy and Myrna's Magic. I like that blaze on Magic's forehead. And she seems bigger than Flo's Fancy. Do you think she could beat Bishop's horse?"

"Anything can happen in a horse race, Barry. They both look like good animals. So's that one." He consulted his racing programme. "Glen Lady. Good Lord, if I'm not mistaken, isn't that our schoolteacher leading the horse?"

"Sue Nolan. Her uncle's the owner. Sue often exercises her."

O'Reilly noted how quickly Barry had responded, how he'd waved to her and how she'd smiled and waved back. Her black stirrup pants were neatly tucked into knee-high leather boots. The horse's graceful strides were complemented by the ease of Sue's walk, her hips swaying in harmony with her charge's tail. O'Reilly glanced sideways to see that Barry's head was moving from side to side in rhythm with the horse's steps and Sue Nolan's backside, a well-shaped one at that. O'Reilly cleared his throat. "Betting time," he said, backing away from the rail. And still protecting Kitty with his outstretched arms, he cleared a way to the concourse and headed for the bookies. "Jesus," said O'Reilly, "would you look at the scrum in that ring?"

Queues stretched from every bookie's stand, and judging by the number of people he recognized, everyone in Ballybucklebo and the townland was here. "Right," he said, "I'll get in a queue and I'll bet for us, Kitty. What do you fancy, Barry?"

"Can I bet on two horses?"

"Of course." O'Reilly shook his head. Barry Laverty must be the only man in this horse-mad country who was an innocent abroad on a racetrack. "You really don't follow the horses, do you?"

Barry shook his head. "I went to a boarding school from thirteen to seventeen, and nobody there cared. It was all rugby and cricket. Then medical school. A couple of lads in my class bet regularly, but I'd never enough money."

"So I'm leading your feet from the paths of righteousness?" O'Reilly clapped Barry's shoulder. "Just tell me what you want. You can give me the money later."

"Five pounds on Flo's Fancy to win—"

"Good lad."

"And five," Barry said, with a wry smile, "on Glen Lady to place."

"Done," said O'Reilly, who had a pretty shrewd idea of what

had provoked that bet—and the smile. "Now, Barry, you escort Kitty back to the stand. I'll catch up once I've finished." He turned, pushed into the ring, and joined the line in front of Willy McArdle. The odds on Flo's Fancy had shortened to five to one. All the bookies must be taking lots of wagers on her.

It took a while, but Fingal was finally at the head of the queue, facing the florid face of Willy McArdle. The man's oiled black hair glistened under a bowler hat.

"Jesus Murphy, are youse back again, Doctor? It's me for the poorhouse, so it is, what with your wins on Luke's Point Lass in the first, Battlecruiser in the fourth—"

"Sure didn't I lose on him at the Balybucklebo point-to-point?"

"But you didn't bet with me, sir, on that one."

"True," O'Reilly said. He was always amazed by how bookies could remember.

McArdle grinned. "Sure amn't I only taking a hand out of you, Doctor? You done me a right good turn when you told the lady to give me the nod, so you did." He bent forward and, speaking just loudly enough to be heard over the noise of the crowd, confided, "I'm well covered at Ladbrokes even if the whole of Ballybucklebo bets on Flo's Fancy in this race. I owe you one."

"No, you don't," said O'Reilly, thinking that Donal and his syndicate certainly owed Willy McArdle one. "You will do though, when I come for my winnings." He placed the bets, waited for Willy to pop the notes in his leather satchel, and took the slips. "Where's Donal?" O'Reilly asked.

"He's gone to get me a glass of lemonade—I'll not take a jar while I'm at me work."

"Sensible," said O'Reilly. "Could I ask you—"

"Would youse get a move on?" a voice said from behind. "I want to get my bet down before the feckin' race is over."

"Take your hurry in your hand, Ronan O'Rourke, and watch

your language. I'll take your money even if the race has started, all right? The doctor wants to ask me something."

O'Reilly ignored O'Rourke's muttering. "Would you ask Donal to go to my Rover in the car park after the race?"

"I will, and I'll send over your winnings with him—if, of course, there are any." McArdle winked. "Least I can do, Doc."

"Thanks." O'Reilly stepped aside as the bookie said, "Now, Ronan, what'll it be?"

When O'Reilly heard the loudspeaker announce, "My lord, ladies, and gentlemen, the seventh and final race will start in five minutes. Five minutes," he broke into a heavy trot. He was short of breath by the time he'd wiggled past Barry and settled between Kitty and the marquis. "Made it," he gasped, as the speaker announced, "They're under starter's orders."

Fingal strained forward. His view of the track was unimpeded, and he could easily pick out Eugene Power by his colours and Fergus Finnegan by his. The jockeys and their mounts were milling around behind the tape, vying for best position in the starting line.

The start itself was positioned some distance past the finishing post, which stood directly in front of the stand. In the four or five minutes it would take the horses to complete two circuits on the turf and pass the post for a second time, they would have galloped exactly two miles, one furlong, and 172 yards. O'Reilly glanced down at Bertie Bishop sitting directly beneath him in the tier below. In just five minutes, if all went according to plan, a certain chubby councillor was going to be knocked off his high horse—by his own little horse. O'Reilly rubbed his hands together and grinned mightily.

He craned forward. Eugene Power had managed to position Flo's Fancy beside the rail, with Myrna's Magic alongside. Glen Lady was in the middle of the other four horses behind the tape. The crowd had grown silent in anticipation of the start, and Glen

Lady's whinnying echoed across the track as she reared, pranced sideways, and disrupted the line. It would be a few more minutes before order was restored.

In the hush, O'Reilly clearly overheard Bertie saying to Flo, "I've just checked up and the odds is way, way down on Flo's Fancy, so they are. Wasn't I quare nor smart putting on our bets early at twenty to one?"

"Yes, dear," Flo said, "and everybody's seen how you done your very best for the lads. It'll be grand if she wins, so it will."

O'Reilly had to smile. Flo had no idea exactly how grand.

"Once more they're under starter's orders," the speaker announced.

The official was on his raised platform outside the boundary fence and level with the tape. He held a flag aloft. The man snapped the flag down, the tape was dropped, and the speaker roared, "They're off."

47

But One Receiveth the Prize

This, thought O'Reilly, is it, by God. A tight bunch of seven horses jostled for position until halfway down the back straight, when Flo's Fancy moved ahead with Myrna's Magic hard beside her. A length separated Glen Lady from the two leaders, and she had two lengths on the remaining four.

From the loudspeakers the voice kept up a running commentary. "And as they go into the first bend, it's Flo's Fancy . . . Flo's Fancy, by half a length over Myrna's Magic. Glen Lady's closing the gap . . ."

The crowd was fairly quiet. Too early in the race for anyone to get excited—yet. O'Reilly glanced past Kitty to see Barry staring into the distance to where two separate groups of seemingly toy horses rounded the curve and started on their first pass along the home straight. They grew until Fingal had no difficulty seeing the blur of the leaders' hooves pounding on the turf and throwing up divots. He could hear them coming, a low drumming, growing in intensity, until as they thundered past him almost halfway home, he could hear them snorting, see the sweat that lathered their shoulders and the mud clinging to the jockeys' silks.

Around the bend and into the back straight for the second time.

"And as they go away it's still Flo's Fancy, but Myrna's Magic has closed the gap to just over a head and has half a length over Glen Lady, Glen Lady . . ."

"Keep it up, Flo's Fancy," O'Reilly roared. He knew full well Eugene Power couldn't possibly hear him, but the act of yelling was a kind of safety valve releasing the excitement that was starting to build.

He glanced down to see Bertie Bishop craning forward. His copy of the *Racing Form* was twisted into a tight spiral between two tightly clenched hands.

"And halfway down the back straight, it's Flo's Fancy, Myrna's Magic, but Glen Lady is coming on the outside. Glen Lady is coming . . ."

O'Reilly twisted forward and raised himself on his toes to see better.

"And they're into the final turn. And it's Glen Lady, Glen Lady, Flo's Fancy . . ."

It's *what*? O'Reilly leapt to his feet, roaring, "Get a bloody move on, Flo." He was aware that Flo Bishop was staring up at him. "Not you, dear. The flaming filly."

He glared down the track to where four widely separated horses were still in the distant bend, but three were pounding down the undulating, uphill, home straight. The jockeys were hunched over their horses' necks, moving fluidly with their mounts' strides, riding crops rising and falling, the horses' nostrils flaring, jetting steam, their great heads rocking up and down, and sweat flying like sea spume.

It was impossible to tell who was in the lead.

Kitty and Barry were now standing. Kitty grabbed O'Reilly's arm. "Come on, Flo's Fancy," she yelled.

Barry leant so far forward he almost fell into the lower tier on top of Cissie Sloan. "Come on—" The lad was frowning, clearly torn between his two horses.

O'Reilly looked down to the track. He heard the hooves, the spectators' roars of encouragement drowning out the loudspeaker, his own voice screaming, "Come on, Flo's Fancy. *Come ooooon.*" As three horses passed the post seemingly as one, the camera flashed.

"Holy mother of God," O'Reilly yelled, letting his quarterdeck roar soften slightly. "Who in the hell won?" He glanced down at Bertie. The man's face was puce. He'd torn the *Racing Form* in two.

"It's a photo finish," the speaker intoned, "and in fourth place Drumshanbo Darling . . ."

Down on the track the jockeys had reined in their mounts and were letting them canter to a stop before turning them and walking them back. O'Reilly saw a man standing at the track rail, tearing up his betting slip. No joy for him today. The deafening roar that had greeted the finish had been replaced by a subdued muttering as the crowd waited for the announcement of the results. Many punters were staring expectantly at the pole-mounted loudspeakers, waiting, O'Reilly thought irreverently, for the word from on high.

There was a rattling all around as people in the stand sat in their folding-down seats. O'Reilly remained standing, as did Kitty, still holding onto his arm. Bertie Bishop shifted from foot to foot and let the torn papers fall.

"Begod," O'Reilly called to Barry, "it's going to be how the Iron Duke described Waterloo."

"The nearest run thing you ever saw," Barry said. "I'm sure Donal and his mates are on eggs."

"So," said O'Reilly, inclining his head forward and down, "is someone else."

Bertie Bishop was still shifting from foot to foot like a man trying for purchase in quicksand.

"My lord, ladies, and gentlemen," the voice said, "thanks to the magic of the strip camera we have a winner . . ."

The announcer paused for effect, and Fingal, who could cheerfully have strangled the man for doing so, muttered, "Get on with it."

"By a nose . . ."

"Get bloody well on with it."

"In a tightly run race . . ."

"For the love of Jasus and all the apostles, will you come on?"

". . . is Flo's Fancy."

"Right." O'Reilly punched one fist into the air above his head. Kitty swung and, taking him by surprise, kissed him. Barry was clapping his hands. Kinky, dear old Kinky, had both hands clasped above her head like a victorious prizefighter. The seated marquis yelled, "Thanks for the tip, Fingal." It was hard to hear him above the general pandemonium that forced the announcer to pause before continuing: "And it's a dead heat for second place between Glen Lady and Myrna's Magic."

"You'll be a rich man, Barry," O'Reilly said. "A winner and a place. Fair play to you."

Barry grinned and held up one thumb.

O'Reilly looked down. Bertie Bishop's face was a deeper puce. He stood ramrod stiff, arms clamped shut across his chest, jaw stuck out. His scowl held pure vitriol, and his voice rasped above the general noise. "I demand a bloody recount. That result's not feckin' right, so it's not."

O'Reilly squatted and leant forward so his mouth was level with Bertie Bishop's ear. "Bertie, it's not an election and you can't recount a photo finish. I'd have thought you'd've been very happy with a win."

"Happy? I'm out of pocket by near a thousand pounds, and I've to give the lads' shares back to them, and—"

"I'm sure the lads'll be happy to have their shares returned," O'Reilly said, then lowered his voice. "But I'd keep my voice down, Bertie, if I were you."

"What the hell for, O'Reilly?" Bertie roared.

"Because," Fingal said very quietly, "at the moment your stock is up. You've been very decent to eight local men."

Bertie didn't lower his voice. "I don't give a thundering—"

"Stop shouting, dear," Flo yelled, in a voice that O'Reilly reckoned could have cut tin.

"Yes, dear." Bishop's decibel level did diminish, and it seemed to O'Reilly that the councillor had shrunk in stature. A good moment to rub the message home.

"It's not *you* personally out of pocket nearly a thousand pounds. It's Ladbrokes, isn't it? You told everybody at the Duck you'd bet there."

"Aye, well . . ." Bertie's voice tailed off.

"If you didn't, Bertie, perhaps my apology wasn't merited. Perhaps you never bet at all, ever?"

Bishop spat. "I did, in soul I did, so I did. Every bloody time. So there, O'Reilly."

Fingal stared into Bishop's eyes. The pupils were black pinpoints, and hadn't Fingal recently read a paper in a medical journal that correlated contraction of the pupils with telling a lie? That was all Fingal needed to confirm his suspicions. "So," he said beaming, "in that case—and who am I to doubt you, Bertie?—my apology stands." Fingal wondered if his own pupils had just contracted.

"I should bloody well think so."

"Och," said O'Reilly, "my saying sorry is worth eight workingmen getting their shares—and their winnings. It's what you promised in front of all those people, Bertie."

Bertie shook his head so forcibly his wattles shivered, and he made strangly, growly noises in his throat.

"Cheer up," said O'Reilly. "You'll still own twenty percent of a great wee horse, you'll get your cut of the prize money today, and in future if she keeps winning and you sell her for a big profit, you'll get your share of that too."

"I suppose so."

"You will," said O'Reilly beaming, "and your reputation for decency is solid now."

" 'At's right." Bertie managed a weak smile.

O'Reilly moved his head closer and lowered his voice to barely a whisper so only Bertie could hear. "And your share of the prizes and the eventual sale might *just* make up the thousand pounds that I know and you know is as likely to be coming from Ladbrokes as whiskey from a hedgehog."

Bishop hung his head.

"Don't worry, Bertie. All of that's between you and me and the wall."

Bertie mumbled, "Thank you, Doctor O'Reilly," then turned his back and grabbed his wife by the arm. "Come on, Flo. Say good-bye to your friends. We've to go down to the parade ring and accept our prize on behalf of our syndicate"—his little eyes narrowed—"and have a word with that eejit of a Cork jockey."

48

He That Bringeth Glad Tidings

O'Reilly held Kitty's hand, led Barry and Kinky out through the gates of the racecourse, and waited to cross the road to the car park. Lord Jasus, what a day. What a day.

Barry, judging by the lightness in his step and the smile on his face, must think so too. "Thanks for bringing me, Fingal," he said, as they moved ahead surrounded by the now thinning crowd as people made their way to cars or to the nearest bus stops. It took a while to cross the road because so many bicycles were being wheeled along by folks who'd mount up as soon as they could.

"Fingal," Kitty said, "there'll be lots of cyclists on the way home. You'll be careful?"

"Of course, dear." O'Reilly ignored Barry's raised eyebrow and said to him, "Aren't you glad we came?"

"I am."

"I'd not have let you miss it, Barry. It might not be Royal Ascot—"

"Maybe not, but I've had as much fun here as I'd have had at Ascot, probably a lot more. And I'm ahead thirty quid."

"Between us, Kitty and I are up sixty pounds."

"You're a good judge of horseflesh, Fingal," Kitty said and smiled at him.

"I do have an eye for the fillies." He winked at her and they laughed.

"I hope," Barry said, turning to Kinky, "you enjoyed your day, too."

"It was altogether grand, so. Altogether." She showed her handbag. "And Flo and Cissie, even in her new red dress, were most impressed, so thank you, Miss Kitty."

"We need to thank *you*, Kinky Kincaid," said O'Reilly. "It wouldn't have been such a lovely day without you and your brother Tiernan." He lowered his voice. "No hint of him got to Eugene Power."

"Tiernan will be grateful, so. Cork road bowling is a shmall little, closed world, and he'd not want to be thought badly of by his friends. Thank you, sir. I saw you watching the race, then talking to that Councillor Bishop," she said with a grin. "I could tell he was fit to be tied. He'd a face on him like a bulldog that had licked piss off a nettle."

O'Reilly had heard Kinky use the expression before, but clearly Kitty and Barry had not. It would have been worth paying admission just to see the astounded looks on their faces. He saw Donal waving and slowed until Donal caught up and silently fell into stride beside him.

"So are you a happy man, Donal Donnelly?" asked O'Reilly.

"By jizz, Doctor O'Reilly, sir, there's not a happier man in the whole Six Counties, except maybe my seven mates."

"There might be one more," O'Reilly said, glancing at Kitty, "but go on."

"Before I do, sir, Willy said for to give you this here." Donal handed over an envelope. It was satisfactorily fat. "Thank you." O'Reilly slipped it into an inside pocket. He'd give Barry his winnings back at Number 1. "Now, Donal, you were saying you and your mates are the happiest men in Ulster."

"We are that. We got our shares back and a wheen of spondulix in our pockets—the bet winnings and our share of the prize money, you know. Who'd not be happy?"

"And what about Julie, Donal?" Kitty asked. "Did she win yesterday?"

"I didn't get a chance to tell youse, with all this blether about celebrating Flo's Fancy and all. Julie come second."

"I'm disappointed, Donal," Kitty said. "Really and truly. We were all so sure she'd win."

"That's very kind, Miss O'Hallorhan, you know, but no harm 'til ye, Julie and me's quare nor satisfied." He looked down, then back up at her. "To tell you the truth I'd rather not have thousands of people gawping at her photo.

"And with that two hundred and fifty pounds and the oul' do-re-mi from today, the pair of us can buy a wee house and my wages can pay a mortgage dead easy, so they can. Might even pay it off completely when the syndicate sells the wee filly."

"I'm delighted," O'Reilly said, "and I hope you and your mates will be down at the Duck tonight to celebrate. We'll leave that nice young cardiologist to run the shop, Barry, and we'll drop in later."

"You'll be very welcome, sirs, and you too, Miss O'Hallorhan," Donal said. "The lads and Willy Dunleavy won't mind having a lady there, even it is a public bar. Tonight's special, so it is."

"Thank you, Donal," Kitty said, "and will Julie be coming too?"

"I'll ask her if she wants to, but she's been off the drink ever since she started expecting." Donal grinned. "I want to get home to her, make sure she's comfy, like. I'm not on the oul' pushbike today. I've borrowed a motorbike."

"Go on then," O'Reilly said, "and try not to ride into the ditch."

Donal laughed. "No harm to ye, sir, but after what yourself done to the Rover? That's rich, so it is."

"True on you, Donal," O'Reilly said. "True on you."

"I'll be off," said Donal, but he hesitated to leave. "See youse two doctors?" Donal spread his arms wide. "See youse? Me and the lads don't know how to thank youse enough. You're the soundest two men in all the Wee North, so yiz are. Because of youse we was dead jammy today."

"That's what it was," O'Reilly said. "Pure luck." He ignored Barry's disbelieving look. "Go home, Donal, give our love to Julie, and we'll see you later."

As Donal headed off, Fingal opened the boot and started to pull out the picnic hamper.

"Doctor O'Reilly sir," Kinky said. "If you eat that Scotch egg now you'll spoil your appetite for your dinner, and I've four of the loveliest lobsters waiting to be poached."

"Four?" asked O'Reilly. He could feel the saliva start. "Why four?"

"I'd imagine locum doctors eat too," Kinky said, "and more than one meal a day like Arthur. I left her tomato soup, Melton Mobray pie, and a nice salad for her lunch, so."

"Well done," O'Reilly said. "And lobsters for dinner. Begod." He shoved the hamper aside and pulled out the cooler. "If I'd known that, I'd have kept this"—he produced a bottle of champagne—"until then, but I brought it so we could celebrate the wee filly's win right away." He tried hard not to look at Kitty, who had already been told what he was going to do. If he saw her, he might give the game away before their glasses were charged. "There are champagne flutes in the hamper, Barry."

As Barry set the four glasses on the boot lid, O'Reilly popped the cork of the first bottle. He looked around to see that the field, which moments ago had been full of moving cars, was now practically empty. There were only a couple of Land Rovers nearby, each with a horse box attached. A man was accompanying a young woman, who led a horse toward the nearest Rover.

"Now," he said, "to business." He poured the bubbly liquid and handed a glass to everyone. He had to say, "No excuses, Kinky Kincaid," when she tried to demur.

He raised his glass high. "To Flo's Fancy. May she go on winning and be sold for a bundle."

"Flo's Fancy," Barry and Kitty repeated.

Kinky sneezed and tutted, then said, "Those bubbles do get up a body's nose, so." Her eyes widened. "But it's got a lovely taste."

"Good for you, Kinky," O'Reilly said. He took a very deep swallow. God, he thought, I'd imagined this was going to be easy. His hand holding the flute was trembling. Go on you lily-livered gurrier, he told himself. He moved beside Kitty and slipped his arm around her waist. He exhaled and forced his shoulders back. "I've another toast," he said, "and I want you two to drink deeply to it."

O'Reilly could see the questions in the eyes of Barry Laverty and Kinky Kincaid.

He took one deep breath, then announced, "Last night after a delightful dinner I asked Miss Kitty O'Hallorhan . . . I asked her"—the words tumbled out—"if she would do me the honour of becoming Mrs. Fingal Flahertie O'Reilly." His grin was vast. "I'm pleased to tell you she has accepted. We wanted you two to be the very first to know, and drink to our health." O'Reilly bent and kissed Kitty firmly and with all the love in him. "I'll be buying her the ring on Monday."

Other than Kitty's quiet "Thank you, Fingal," there was a stunned silence. O'Reilly looked up. Barry stood there with both legs the same length and his mouth open. It took him several more moments to regain his composure. Then, grinning as he spoke, he said, "I'm so bloody delighted for you both. It's wonderful news." He lifted his glass. "Come on, Kinky. To Fingal and Kitty. Long life and every happiness." He and Kinky drank. She was crying as she did so. Great tears coursed through her smile.

As if to indicate their approval, the herd of Friesians in the adjoining field began frantically lowing.

This is a moment, O'Reilly thought, warmth running through him, this is a moment I'll put into my lifetime book of memories.

When the beasts had settled down, Kinky said, "Doctor O'Reilly, sir . . . Miss Kitty . . . I'm so very happy for you both." She rummaged in her new bag for a hanky.

"Thank you, Kinky," Kitty said. "Thank you very much." She reached out and touched Kinky's arm.

"And Kinky," O'Reilly said, "it's going to make you extra busy. Kitty has a very demanding full-time job. You'll still be running Number 1. You'll be cooking and washing and tidying up after three people now, not two." O'Reilly continued: "So I'll be putting up your wages by four pounds a month."

Kinky dabbed her eyes. "Doctor dear" was all she could manage.

"I think you're worth every penny," Kitty said and was rewarded with a damp smile.

O'Reilly still held Kitty, who put an arm round the big housekeeper's shoulder. He looked at Barry and hoped he didn't feel left out. "Begod," said O'Reilly, "if you'd just come and stand by Kitty, Barry, we could have a class photo taken of the whole Number 1, Main Street, team." It was a team O'Reilly hoped would be facing a long future together.

Barry shook his head and looked at his shoes, then back up to O'Reilly. "Fingal," he said, "this is your moment, yours and Kitty's. I don't want to intrude but . . ." He hesitated, then said firmly, "I think you both might want a bit of room at Number 1." He paused. "I've been havering over this ever since you told me about the job in Ballymena."

O'Reilly frowned and cocked his head. "If you're going to say what I think you are, Barry, the job in Ballybucklebo'll still be yours next January, if you want it." But, he thought, you're making the right choice, boy, and I wish you every success in finding your true path.

"Thank you. I do know that, and I'm very grateful, so on Monday, first thing, I'm going to phone Professor Dunseath and tell him I'd like to take up his offer."

"Good lad," O'Reilly said loudly. He offered Barry his hand. "Well done, Barry. I know deciding's not been easy, and I know you'll enjoy the experience." He sipped more champagne. "And you tell Paddy Dunseath from me, that he'll not get any more rugby tickets unless he gives you July third and fourth off."

"Why? I'll only just have started my new job."

"Because"—he tightened his arm's embrace around Kitty and looked into her eyes—"the third is the day we're getting married, I want you as my best man, and if you do the job right you'll need the next day off to get over it."

"Me?" Barry moved his glass closer to his chest. "Fingal . . . Kitty . . . I'd be honoured. Nothing would give me greater pleasure. I am truly delighted for you both."

O'Reilly heard a tiny catch in Barry's voice. Despite his own recent loss, Barry was a big enough man to rejoice in a friend's happiness. Fair play to you, boy, O'Reilly thought.

Barry continued: "I'd love to be the first—it is the best man's job to propose the toast to the bride and groom—the first to officially call you Doctor and Mrs. O'Reilly."

"Hear that, Kitty? Mrs. O'Reilly. It has a very nice ring to it."

"It has," said Barry wistfully, "and maybe one day I'll get you to do the honours for me, Fingal."

O'Reilly laughed. "Anytime, lad. Anytime." He finished his champagne, and as he turned to put his glass in the hamper, a movement caught his eye. O'Reilly looked up and recognised the young woman with the copper-coloured hair and the bright head scarf, who was closing the door of a horse trailer.

"Huh," said O'Reilly with a grin, "the school summer holidays are July and August, aren't they?"

"That's right," Barry said, following the direction of O'Reilly's gaze and smiling. "And before you ask, Fingal, it's only four miles from Ballymena to Broughshane. I've looked at the map."

Your Questions Answered

The Past Is a Foreign Country: They Do Things Differently There

I promised you in the author's note on page 10 that I would answer my readers' questions. What is Ulster, and how is it related to Northern Ireland and the Irish republic? How were the doctors paid? How did the way of life in rural Ireland and the practice of medicine forty years ago differ from the way things are today? Where *exactly* is Ballybucklebo, and who was Doctor O'Reilly? And could I explain some of the vagaries of English as it is spoken in Ulster?

The answers follow.

The island of Ireland is divided into four provinces: Ulster, Munster, Leinster, and Connacht, subdivided into a total of thirty-two counties. The old province of Ulster was made up of nine counties. For centuries, all of Ireland was governed by the United Kingdom. When the island was partitioned in 1922, three of Ulster's nine counties—Monaghan, Cavan, and Donegal—became part of the new Irish Free State, which later became the independent Republic of Ireland. But they still remained in the province of Ulster. Six of the Ulster counties—Antrim, Armagh, Derry, Down, Fermanagh, and Tyrone—remained part of the United Kingdom of Great Britain and Northern Ireland. Those six pieces of real estate, collectively called Northern Ireland (frequently pronounced

"Nor'n Ir'n"), are often loosely and incorrectly referred to as Ulster—or affectionately as the Six Counties or the Wee North. The terms are used interchangeably in these pages as they are in real life.

I do hope that's clear because it's time to move on to the question of how GPs made their living. Until 1948, payment was fee-for-service. Doctor O'Reilly and many of his kind operated on the Robin Hood principle of taking from the rich and giving to the poor. The wealthy and their families often paid more than the service was worth, but the child of a poor farm labourer would have been treated for free. Often payment was in kind: a couple of chickens, a brace of lobsters, a load of peat.

Northern Ireland was and is an integral part of the United Kingdom. In 1948, the British Labour government introduced the National Health Service (NHS). All citizens paid a weekly national insurance premium, "the stamp," to which a contribution was also made by their employer. These funds provided the entire population with unemployment and sickness benefits, and covered the costs of illness. Each citizen was issued a card and a National Insurance number, like a Social Security number. Citizens were free to pick a GP of their choice, with whom they lodged their card.

A flat annual capitation fee was paid to the doctor for every card held by the practice. About 2,500 were required for a GP to make a comfortable living (hence, in *An Irish Country Christmas*, Barry's concern when a new doctor moves into the district and starts to poach patients). In return, the doctor was obliged to provide medical services at any time, day or night, 365 days a year. This free health care, as it was perceived, led to abuses, and Doctor O'Reilly was not the only Ulster GP who had as his first rule of practice, "Never let the customers get the upper hand." However, in my own experience rural patients tended to be most considerate of their doctor's time.

O'Reilly, as the principal doctor in the practice, would have been paid by the Ministry of Health, and from those monies he would have given Barry Laverty his salary, as together they provided care to the people of Ballybucklebo.

And that leads to the next question: Where is Ballybucklebo, and who was O'Reilly?

Irish names are musical, and every one of them means something. Eight miles from where I live is the village of Drumshanbo, "the ridge (*drum*) of the old (*shan*) cow (*bo*)." Ballybucklebo is literally "the townland of the boy's cow." I made up the name, and it and the surrounding countryside are fictitious, but that has not prevented my friends from Northern Ireland insisting they know exactly where it is. For the very last time, Ballybucklebo is *not* Helen's Bay nor Holywood, although both are in County Down. The same applies to the characters. Although I am medically qualified, I am *not* Barry Laverty. A friend who had read *An Irish Country Village* suggested to me on the very morning I was penning this that Doctor Fingal Flahertie O'Reilly is my late father, Doctor James Taylor, God rest him. Sorry, Fingal and Jimmy are not one and the same.

So now you know that the centre of this book's universe comes from my imagination; even so, I have done everything in my power to recreate the rest of rural Ireland—its geography, its way of life, and the practice of medicine—exactly as it was in 1964–1965.

The chasm that yawns between then and now is vast. Then was a simpler place, a simpler time. Towns and villages were smaller. Roads were twisty and narrow. There were fewer cars. For many people transport was a donkey, shank's pony, the bicycle, and a rural bus service. This last halted not only at official bus stops. Drivers were likely to pull over for you between stops.

City folk might lock their houses. Countrypeople never bothered. The shops had a half day on Thursday in my hometown of Bangor, "the place of pointed hills." The day of this closure varied from town to town, but if you were stuck for milk or a packet of cigarettes you could try knocking on the door. Most proprietors lived on the premises and might well open up for a friend in need. They closed early on Saturday and, except for sweetie shops and newsagents/tobacconists that sold the Sunday papers, were closed all day Sunday, as were the pubs. Attendance at mass or church service was practically compulsory.

Learning was held in great respect. In any rural community the doctor, teacher, priest, and minister outranked the village constable, undertaker, and chemist (pharmacist). All were lower down than the gentry and the aristocracy. The Marquis of Dufferin and Ava had his seat at Clandeboye, not four miles from where I grew up. As a boy I acted as a beater at many of his pheasant shoots, an Irish country custom also practiced by the Marquis of Ballybucklebo.

Everybody knew everybody, their business, and their genealogies. Some folks had never travelled more than a few miles from the home in which they had been born and raised. They brought their new wife there, reared their family, mourned their parents, and could pass away confident that the neighbours would visit for the laying up and removal, and for the meal after the service and interment. Funerals were functions of great importance, as much for their bringing together of the community and the socializing with neighbours as for the paying of last respects.

Amusement was much more do-it-yourself than it is now. No iPods, BlackBerries, Internet, Xboxes. Television was a state-run, one-channel universe until 1955, when a commercial channel was added. Not until 1964 did a second commercial-free station, BBC2, start broadcasting. These stations did not operate twenty-four hours a day and were in black and white until 1967.

For villagers, trips to the cinema in a neighbouring larger town were frequent, except on Sundays. Although the cinemas in Belfast might give a major film a run of several weeks, smaller picture houses still offered two different programs: a B movie, travelogue, cartoon, the Pathé News, and the "big picture" every week, and a matinee on Saturday afternoons. Only a few years prior to the period of the *Irish Country* books, rural cinemas still ran children's matinees on Saturday mornings, with admission of threepence or a two-pound (907-gram) empty jam jar.

And of course there was the public house, with its opening time of 10 A.M., and closing time of 10 P.M., with an extra ten minutes' legal drinking-up time—a bit longer for locals once the doors were shut. These locals frequently included the long arm of the law himself, a reasonable guarantee that prosecution for staying open too long was most unlikely.

The pub was the social hub of village life. In it, deals were done, gossip repeated, local news discussed, and there was, and still is, the *craic* ("crack"), that indefinable, fuelled-by-a-few-jars, Irish mixture of conversation, humour, and good-natured banter, where insults are freely traded but with no malice. As opposed to the rest of Ireland, where many pubs still advertise *Craic agus Ceol* (fun and music), in the Six Counties live music in pubs was illegal. A rebel or loyalist song in the wrong place could lead to a booze-fuelled donnybrook. An ounce of prevention, it was believed, was better than a pound of cure.

It was different, of course, at private social gatherings, weddings, birthdays, and parties. Everybody was expected to perform their party piece, be it a song, a story, a tune, a well-told joke, or a recitation. I have the words by heart to "The Boy Stood on the Burning Deck," "The Charge of the Light Brigade," and "The Green Eye of the Yellow God"—and I didn't learn them in school.

If rural life was simpler, so was medicine. Doctor Cyril Morrison was the first to use a cumbersome early ultrasound machine in Belfast in the mid-1970s. The prototype CAT scanner was not developed until 1971. Diagnosis relied heavily on clinical acumen,

X-rays, ECGs (called EKGs in the U.S. and Canada), rudimentary blood and urine tests, examination of other body fluids, biopsies, and bacteriological culture and microscopic examination.

We saw diseases that are now happily things of the past. Smallpox was all but gone forever. Tuberculosis was on the way out, thanks to an effective vaccine. Better understanding of nutrition and the provision of free milk in the schools were wiping out rickets. Mandatory testing and treatment with penicillin when indicated had nearly eradicated congenital syphilis. Nevertheless the odd cases of all these conditions still showed up. Poliomyelitis was vanishing, thanks to the Salk vaccine introduced in 1953, but doctors in 1964–1965 were still dealing with the aftermath of the 1951 pandemic. I myself failed to escape that one and was lucky to survive with no residual damage. I suspect my three months in the fever hospital may have influenced my decision to study medicine.

We didn't see some of the more recent ills to afflict the human race. The first methicillin-resistant *Staphylococcus aureus* (MRSA) was detected in 1961, but it seemed to have little importance at a time when new and effective antibiotics were coming into use on a regular basis. AIDS was not reported until 1981. Radiation sickness was mentioned in our training. We were in the post-Hiroshima nuclear age, and the Cold War was very much in evidence. We did not have to deal with the aftermath of Chernobyl.

When it came to treatment, the first kidney transplant in the British Isles was performed between identical twins in 1960, and it was not until 1964 that immunosuppressive drugs were introduced and cadaveric transplants became a reality. Doctor Henry Jay Heimlich introduced his lifesaving manoeuvre in 1974.

Cardiac resuscitation was in its infancy. In 1965, Doctor—later Professor—Frank Pantridge, working at Belfast's Royal Victoria Hospital, equipped an ambulance with a seventy-kilogram defibrillator so care could be rushed to the victims of heart attacks. He reported that on the cardiac flying squad's trial run, the mortality rate was two hundred percent. The victim did not survive, and in the rush to reach the patient a pedestrian was knocked down and perished. By 1968, Doctor Pantridge had reduced the device's weight to three kilograms, making it truly portable. I was fortunate to have been his houseman (intern) from October 1964 to January 1965.

The birth of Louise Brown in 1978 following in vitro fertilization was but a dream for Doctor Patrick Steptoe and Professor Robert Edwards, both of whom I had the privilege of working with in 1969 and later in 1987–1989.

The clinical practices described in the *Irish Country* series were in daily use during my own training from 1958 to 1964. My memories are buttressed by a stroke of remarkably good luck: I kept every textbook I have ever owned. Details of some drug treatments have been taken from such now antiquated tomes as *The Essentials of Materia Medica, Pharmacology, and Therapeutics* (1961), and *A Short Practice of Surgery* (1959).

And as the medicine practiced in the sixties differed from that of today, so does the language spoken daily in Northern Ireland depart from standard English. For those unfamiliar with the Ulster variety as it is spoken by my characters, it will be briefly described here. To define more obscure words and expressions, I have appended a glossary (page 439).

The Ulster dialect is rich and colourful, but can be confusing. I am not referring to the so-called Ulster Scots, defined as "the variety of the Scots language traditionally found in Northern Ireland and parts of Donegal," and according to one survey spoken by two percent of the population of Northern Ireland. In this book you will find simply the English used by most of the people of Ulster.

All dialects have their verbal punctuation. In Northern Ireland, "like" is popular. "You know" is not so much sprinkled through sentences as ladled in, usually under circumstances when the listener cannot possibly have the information. And although repetition drives the spell-checker crazy, "Come on, on, on in" is perfectly correct in the Wee North. Emphasis is given by tacking "so I will," "so she did," or one of its many variants onto the end of a sentence.

There is one construct I have rarely used. Reporting direct speech often takes the form of "She says to me, she says, 'Great day,' says she." But I didn't think such usage should be inflicted on the reader because it would slow down the story.

Like all patois, Nor'n Irish is not one bit shy about adopting useful phrases from others. For instance, you'll find examples of Cockney rhyming slang in the book. The Londoners use only the first word of the rhyme—"He made a right cobbler's of it." In full, it is "cobbler's awls" and that rhymes with—balls. 'Nuff said.

The agreement of verbs with their subjects and the strict observance of correct tenses and voices do not trouble many of us from the Six Counties. "I *seen* him at the races," or "She *come* round here yesterday," or "They *was* rightly pleased, so they *was*," are perfectly acceptable.

Often the opposite will be meant. "Will yiz *borrow* me a cup of sugar?" means "Will you lend . . . ?"

If you meet these oddities in the text, they are neither typos nor evidence of my inability to use correct English. I do have some familiarity with its grammar and syntax. I should have, you know, for I done a brave wheen of years, like, getting learned it, so I did.

So I hope that's all the questions answered, but if you have more you can find me at www.patricktaylor.ca, and now if you've a mind to try some Irish cooking, some more of Mrs. Kincaid's recipes follow.

Hello again. *Céad míle fáilte* to my old friends and another hundred thousand welcomes to folks visiting Ballybucklebo for the first time. I'll tell you, I don't mind being here in my nice warm kitchen. It's blowing outside to beat Banagher, and if the rain doesn't stop soon I'll be expecting a visit from a man looking for gopher wood and collecting up animals two by two, so.

Thank the Lord it did be a good day for the Downpatrick Races yesterday. My handbag was much admired. She is a lamb, that Miss Kitty, for giving it to me. The ten pounds I won sits inside the bag. I think I'll ask Himself for a half day next week so I can nip up to Belfast and buy myself a nice new pair of low-heeled brogues, and I can window-shop for a new outfit. The third of July will be here soon enough.

And well you might lie beside the range, Arthur Guinness. Your boss is right decent to you, bringing you in out of the rain, even if you do have a waterproof doghouse. Och, but sure isn't the big man considerate of just about everybody—except that Councillor Bishop? What my friend Flo sees in the man I do not know, but to each his own. It's none of my business.

What *is* my business is running Number 1, Main Street. And that includes doing the cooking.

When that fellah Taylor who spins the yarns about this place first wrote *An Irish Country Doctor*, I did think Doctor O'Reilly had taken leave of his senses, so. Says he to me, "Kinky, so many things Irish are getting lost I want you to write down some of your recipes so folks can try them and see if they like them."

I thought it was a load of malarkey, but I did as I was asked.

The letters asking for more recipes started after that book and have been coming thick and fast since. So now this book is nearly finished, it's me for the kitchen table again, pen in fist, making fair copies of some of the dishes I prepare.

When you do try them, I hope you enjoy them.

Irish Recipes

BRAISED LAMB SHANKS

4 lamb shanks
10 cloves of garlic, unpeeled
3 tablespoons olive oil
2 carrots, chopped
2 celery sticks, chopped
1 onion, chopped
150 ml / ¼ pint / ⅔ cup red wine
150 ml / ¼ pint / ⅔ cup lamb stock or water
sprig of thyme and rosemary
2 bay leaves
salt and pepper to taste

Lamb shanks can be from the shoulder or the hind leg. The shoulder takes longer to cook, so to achieve an even result cook the same types together.

If possible use a heavy-bottomed casserole with a tight-fitting lid.

Brown the seasoned shanks in the olive oil. Remove the lamb, add the vegetables, and sauté for a few minutes. Pour in the red wine, bring to the boil, and simmer for a minute or two. Add the stock and herbs, and place the shanks on top. Bring to the boil, cover, and cook in the oven for 1½ to 2½ hours depending on size and cut. You can also cook on the hob if your pan is very heavy-bottomed, but you will need to check the liquid level from time to time to make sure that it does not boil dry; add extra stock or water if the level looks too low. When the lamb has finished cooking, remove the shanks to a serving dish. Discard the vegetables, and reduce the remaining liquid in the casserole by bringing to the boil for a minute or two. There should only be just enough sauce to coat the lamb.

RED CURRANT JELLY

900 g / 2 lb / 4 cups red currants
900 g / 2 lb / 4 cups sugar, warmed

Place the washed fruit in a preserving pan or stock pot, and bring slowly to the boil. Stir and press the red currants to break down the fruit and release the juice. As soon as the fruit is cooked (about 10 minutes), add the warmed sugar and stir until it is dissolved. Then bring the mixture to a rapid boil, and boil for about 10 minutes. Now you can use either a jelly bag or a sieve lined with gauze placed over a bowl. Pour the jelly mixture into it, and let it drip through. If you don't mind not having a completely clear jelly, you can press to extract as much juice as possible. Pour the juice into warmed jars and cover. This makes two one-pound jars, but the process is exactly the same for a larger quantity.

Toad in the Hole

2 eggs
110 g / 4 oz / ½ cup self-raising flour
a pinch of baking powder
a few thyme leaves
salt and freshly ground pepper
dash of milk
100 g / 4 oz cocktail sausages, cooked

Preheat the oven to 220°C / 425°F / gas mark 7. Beat the eggs into a bowl. Continue to whisk, and add the flour and baking powder gradually, together with enough milk to make a thickish batter the consistency of cream. Add the thyme leaves, salt, and pepper, and pour the batter into a greased casserole dish. Place the sausages on top. Bake in the oven for 10 to 12 minutes until the batter is well risen and golden brown. Serves two.

Sticky Toffee Pudding and Butterscotch Sauce

225 g / 8 oz / 1 cup dates, chopped
300 ml / ½ pint / 1⅓ cups hot tea
oil for greasing
110 g / 4 oz / ½ cup unsalted butter
175 g / 6 oz / ¾ cup sugar
225 g / 8 oz / 1 cup self-raising flour
3 eggs
1 teaspoon bicarbonate of soda
1 teaspoon vanilla essence
1 teaspoon coffee powder

Butterscotch Sauce

110 g / 4 oz / ½ cup butter

225 g / 8 oz / 1 cup brown sugar

225 ml / 8 oz / 1cup cream

225 ml / 8 oz / 1 cup Irish whiskey (I like to use Jameson's, for
    that's what Himself drinks so, but any good Irish one will do)

1 tablespoon vanilla essence

Soak the dates in the tea. Cream together the butter and sugar, and beat in the eggs one at a time. Then fold in the flour. Add the vanilla, coffee powder, and soda to the date and tea mixture, and stir it into the creamed mixture. Pour into six to eight greased individual moulds, and bake in a preheated oven at 180°C / 350°F/ gas mark 4 for about 30 minutes, until the small cakes are firm and starting to come away from the sides. Remove from the oven and cool on a rack.

For the sauce, melt the butter in a pan over a medium heat, and when it is bubbling add the sugar. Then stir until the sugar has dissolved and the mixture is bubbling again. Pour in the cream and then the whiskey, and reduce the heat. Boil for another minute or two, remove from the heat, and allow it to cool slightly before you add the vanilla.

To serve, you place the puddings on plates, and pour the sauce over the top followed by a generous dollop of cream. If you have any leftovers they can be reheated easily in a microwave oven.

So there it is now. I'm going to make myself a nice cup of beef tea. It's my own ma's recipe and just the thing for a day like today. I'll take it up to my own room, put my feet up, and have a good watch at *Sunday Night at the London Palladium* on the telly. I do enjoy a good variety show—nearly as much as I used to enjoy Punch and Judy when I was a youngster.

May all your cooking turn out right.

Oíche mHaith agus beannacht De ort. Good-night and God bless.

MRS. MAUREEN "KINKY" KINCAID
Housekeeper to
Doctor Fingal Flahertie O'Reilly,
M.B., B.Ch., B.A.O.
1, Main Street
Ballybucklebo
County Down
Northern Ireland

GLOSSARY

As promised in the Author's Note this glossary will, I hope, add to your enjoyment and understanding of some of the dialogue.

acting the goat: Behaving foolishly.

afters: Dessert. The logical last course follow-up of a meal that began with starters.

agricultural: Country bumpkin.

amadán: Irish. Pronounced "omadawn." Male idiot.

and all, and everything: Frequently tacked to the end of a sentence for emphasis.

An Gorta Mór: Irish. Pronounced "an gortah more." The Great Hunger. The potato famine of 1845–1849.

anyroad: Anyway.

apples and pears: Cockney rhyming slang for stairs.

argy-bargy: Voluble disagreement.

arse: Backside (impolite).

asked about, asked around: Made enquiries.

at himself/herself, not: Unwell.

aunt Fanny Jane, my: Nonsense.

away off and chase yourself: Go away; I don't believe you.

away off and feel your head: Don't be stupid.

away on, away on out of that: I don't believe you.

back of beyond: The sticks.

bamboozle: Deliberately confuse.

banagher, to beat: Greatly exceed any reasonable expectations.

bangers: Sausages.

banjaxed: Exhausted or broken.

banshee: Irish. *Beán* (woman), *sidhe* (fairy). Female spirit whose moaning foretells a death.

bap: Head.

bap, to lose the: To be temporarily out of control.

barmbrack: Speckled bread (see Mrs. Kincaid's recipes in *An Irish Country Doctor*, page 340).

bashtoon: Irish. *Bastún*. Lout, but often used to signify bastard.

batman: Army officer's servant.

beagle's gowl: Very long way; the distance over which the cry—the gowl, not growl—of a beagle can be heard.

beasts: Cattle.

bee on a hot brick: Running round in circles.

bee's knees: The very best.

bee's knees, he thinks he's the: He's conceited.

bejizzis: By Jesus.

Belvoir: Suburb of Belfast. Pronounced "Beaver."

better than a pantomime: Some activity that is engrossing, usually humorously, often by people making inadvertent fools of themselves.

biddy: Hen.

bigger fish to fry: More important matters to attend to.

bind: Cure diarrhea or cause constipation.

biscuit: Cookie.

bit my head off: Expressed anger by shouting or being very curt.

blether: Talking nonsense.

bletherskite: Nonstop talker.

blew me out: Ended a love affair.

blimey (occasionally, Gor blimey): Expression of surprise. Originally a Cockney corruption of "God blind me."

bloater: Salted and smoked herring.

blowed, I'm or I'll be: Expressing the opposite. "I'll be blowed if I can swim"—that is, "I can't swim."

blow you out: Tell a lover to go away for good.

blue: See *capped*. A university award for athletic excellence akin to a U.S. university letter.

boater: Flat-topped, medium-brimmed straw hat.

bob: One shilling.

bob, a few; a bob or two: A sum of money.

bodhrán: Irish. Pronounced "bowrawn." A circular handheld drum.

boke: Vomit.

boke your ring up: Vomit very forcibly (literally, so forcibly that the anal sphincter [ring] is brought up).

bollixed: Ruined.

bollocks: Testicles (impolite). May be used as an expression of vehement disagreement or to describe a person of whom you disapprove. For example, "He's a right bollocks."

bonnet (of a car): Hood.

boot (of a car): Trunk.

bore, twenty-, twelve-, ten-, eight-: Gauge of a shotgun. Calculated by noting the number of balls fitting exactly into the muzzle that could be cast from one pound of lead.

both legs the same length: Standing about uselessly.

both ways: A bet placed that will pay the odds if a horse wins and one quarter of the odds if the horse places.

boul': Pronounced "bowl." Bold.

bound and determined: Determined.

bowsey: Dublin slang. Drunkard.

boys-a-boys, boys-a-dear: Expressions of amazement.

brass neck: Impertinence, chutzpah.

brave: Very large.

bravely: Well.

breeze blocks: Cinderblocks.

brekky: Breakfast.

Brian Boru: *Ard Rí.* High King of all Ireland who beat the Vikings at the Battle of Clontarf in 1014 and was killed there.

brisket: Cut of beef from the thigh of a foreleg.

brolly: Umbrella.

brung: Brought.

buck eejit: Imbecile.

bullock: Steer (castrated bull calf).

bunk, done a: Ran away.

bun in the oven: Pregnant (impolite).

Burberry: A popular make of raincoat.

bye: Boy. Often used in County Cork to end a sentence.

cailín: Irish. Pronounced "colleen." Girl.

call the cows home: Be ready to tackle anything.

capped: A cap was awarded to athletes selected for important teams. Equivalent to a letter at an American university.

carrageen moss: An edible seaweed.

caubeen: Traditional, peakless Irish bonnet.

casualty: Emergency room.

céilí: Irish. Pronounced "kaylee." Party with music and dancing.

champ: A dish of potatoes, buttermilk, butter, and chives.

champ, thick as: Stupid.

chemist: Pharmacist.

chips: French fried potatoes.

chippy: Carpenter.

chiseller: Dublin slang, a small child.

chuntering on: Talking nonstop.

civil to: Pleasant to.

clabber: Glutinous mess of mud, or mud and cow clap.

claret: Blended red wine from Bordeaux. The single-grape varietals like merlot were not introduced to Ireland until the 1980s.

clatter: Quantity.

clatter, a brave: Large quantity.

clonk: Bang together.

colloguing: Chatting about trivia.

conkers: Horse chestnuts. Used to play a children's game.

comeuppance: Just rewards.

coortin': Paying court to. See also *walk out with*.

corker: Something or somebody of great excellence.

cow's lick: Tuft of hair that sticks up, or hair slicked over to one side.

cracker: Excellent. See also *wheeker*.

crackers: Crazy.

craic: Pronounced "crack." Practically untranslatable, it can mean great conversation and fun ("The *craic* was ninety") or "What happened to you since I saw you last?" ("What's the *craic?*"). Often seen on signs outside pubs in Eire: *Craic agus Ceol*, or Fun and Music.

craking on: Talking incessantly.

craythur: Creature. Equivalent of North American "critter."

craythur, a drop of the: Whiskey.

crick in the neck or back: Painful strain.

crúibins: Irish. Pronounced "croobeens." Boiled pigs' trotters (hooves), served cold and eaten with vinegar.

culchie: One who does not live in Dublin. A hick or rube. See *Jack*.

cuppa: Cup of, usually tea.

cure, wee: Hair of the dog.

cut: Really drunk.

cut to the onion: Emotionally wounded very deeply.

dab hand: Skilled at.

damper: Device for restricting the flow of air to a coal or turf fire to slow the rate of burning.

dander: Literally, horse dandruff. Used to signify either a short leisurely walk ("I took a wee dander over to Jimmy's") or anger ("He really got my dander up").

dead: Very.

dead on: A strong affirmative or excited acceptance of good news or a measure of complete accuracy. Equivalent to "I totally agree," "That's marvelous," or "Absolutely correct."

dead wheeker: Wonderful or marvellous.

deerstalker: A tweed hat with fore and aft peaks and earflaps that can be tied under the chin. Sherlock Holmes is often portrayed wearing one.

dibs: First claim upon.

dicky: Cockney rhyming slang. Dicky bird: word.

diddling: Cheating.

didny; didnae: Did not.

dinner suit: Tuxedo.

divil: Devil.

divil the bit: None. For example, "She's divil the bit sense." (She's stupid.)

divilment: Devilment. Mischief.

doddle: A short distance or an easy task.

dogs are barking: Feet are sore. Cockney rhyming slang. Dogs meat: feet.

do-ray-mi: Money. Equivalent of North American "dough."

dosh: Money.

dote: Something adorable.

dote on: Worship.

doting: Losing your marbles.

do with the price of corn: Irrelevant.

double-breasted gun: Double-barreled shotgun.

dozer: Fool.

dozer, no: No fool.

drip: Intravenous.

drop of the pure: Drink of whiskey or *poitín*.

double: Spirits are poured in Ulster as singles (one ounce), the standard measure if simply "a whiskey" or "a gin" is ordered. A double is two ounces.

doubt: Doubt used alone, "I doubt we'll get there," means "I don't think we'll get there." Used with a following "not," as in "I doubt we'll not get there," also means "I don't think we'll get there."

drouth: Pronounced "drewth." Thirst. "I've a terrible drouth."

drouth, he's a raging: He's an alcoholic.

drúishin: Irish. Pronounced "drisheen." Dish made of cows' blood, pigs' blood, and oatmeal. A Cork City delicacy.

drumlin: From the Irish *Droimin* (little ridge). Small rounded hills caused by the last ice age. There are so many in County Down that the place has been described as looking like a basket of green eggs.

D.Sc.: Doctor of science. Postgraduate degree equivalent to a Ph.D.

dudeen: Short-stemmed clay pipe.

dulse: Seaweed that when dried is eaten like chewing gum.

dummy tit: Baby's pacifier.

duncher: Cloth cap, usually tweed.

dunder: Forcible thump.

dungarees: One-piece coveralls.

dunging out: Cleaning a stall, barn, or byre by removing the old straw and dung.

Dun Laoghaire: Port near Dublin. Pronounced "dun leery." Literally, Leary's Fort.

ECG: Electrocardiogram. In the U.S. and Canada, EKG.

eejit: Idiot.

egg-bound hen: A hen with an egg that cannot be laid stuck in the oviduct. Applied to a person, it suggests extreme distress.

eggs, on: Extremely worried.

elected: Have won or have been chosen, usually to receive good things.

ex-serviceman: Veteran.

fag: Cigarette.

fair play to you: To be fair or well done.

fall off the perch: Die.

feck: Steal. See also *fecking*.

fecking: Dublin corruption of "fucking."

fenian: Catholic (pejorative).

fiddle, on the: Rigging, embezzling, achieving an end by dubious means.

finagle: Achieve by cunning or dubious means.

fist of, make a good: Do a fine job.

fit to be tied: Very angry.

flat: Apartment.

flex: Plug-in cable of an electrical appliance or light cord.

flies, none on: Smart. Streetwise.

florin: Silver two-shilling piece about the size of a silver half-dollar. Worth about 40 cents today.

flue, up the: Literally, up the chimney. Can be used to signify being in difficulty or being pregnant, usually unplanned.

flutter: Bet on a horse race.

fly (out) half: Player who in rugby football receives the ball from the forwards, usually from the scrum-half (quarterback), and sets the backs in attacking motion.

flying: Drunk.

for having none of it: Not allowing.

for it: About to be in deep trouble.

form, racing: Known performance of a racehorse.

fornenst: Beside.

forward: Impertinent.

foundered: Chilled to the marrow.

frigging: Euphemism for "fucking."

full: Drunk.

full of beans: Energetic.

full of it: Either stupid or excessively flattering.

furlong: Archaic measure. One-eighth of a mile, or 220 yards.

gaiters: Leg protectors that run from the knee to the ankle and are held to the shin by straps and buckles.

gander: Look.

garage: A shed for housing a car, or a service station, often with the services of a mechanic.

garsún: Irish. Pronounced "gossoon." Boy.

gas: Originally, Dublin slang. Fun.

gas, great: Great fun.

gas man: Bit of a wit. See *gas* for origin.

gawp at: Ogle.

gee-gee: Childish expression for horse. Often used by adult horse fanciers to mean racehorse.

get (away) on with you: Don't be stupid.

get on one's wick: Get on one's nerves.

get your head examined: How can you be so stupid?

give over: Stop it.

git: From "begotten." Bastard.

glaur: Glutinous, muddy mess.

glipe, great: Stupid (or very stupid person).

gnat: Tiny flying insect of the suborder *Nematocera*.

gobshite: Dublin slang. Literally, dried nasal mucus. Used pejoratively about a person.

God's (honest) truth: Emphatically absolutely true.

good head: Decent person.

good man ma da: Good man my father. Expression of approval.

goolies: Testicles.

gormless: Witless.

grand man for the pan: One who really enjoys fried food.

great: An Ulster accolade; can be used to signify pleased assent to a plan.

Great Hunger: In the nineteenth century the potato crop in Ireland often failed. The disastrous failure from 1845 to 1849 is known as the Great Hunger (*An Gorta Mór*). Also called the Famine.

grotty: English slang. Run-down and dirty.

grub: Food.

guard's van: Caboose.

gub: Mouth.

gub, a good dig in: A punch in the mouth.

gullet: Throat.

guinea: Archaic sterling, worth one pound and one shilling.

gumboil: Dental abscess.

gun: A hunting member of a shooting party.

gurrier: Dublin slang. Street urchin.

guttees: Canvas, rubber-soled shoes so called because when they were first introduced the soles were made from *gutta percha*. In the class-bound Ulster society of my youth they were also known as "Plimsolls" by the gentry and "mutton-dummies" by the working class.

guttersnipe: Ruffian; usually preteen.

hairy bear: Woolly caterpillar.

half 'un, wee 'un: Drink of spirits.

half-cut: Drunk.

hand, to take out of: Mock or get a rise from.

handbag: Woman's purse.

hand's turn: Absolute minimum amount of work.

hang about: Wait a minute.

haver: Vacillate.

haverer: One who vacillates.

having me on: Deceiving me.

having none of it: Not allowing.

head staggers, he's taken the: Explanation for making a very stupid decision. Literally, a parasitic disease affecting the brains of sheep and causing them to stagger.

heart of corn: Very good-natured.

heifer: Young cow before her first breeding.

heels of the hunt: When everything has been concluded.

heeltap: Drink slowly so as to avoid having to buy a round.

Henry's: Cockney rhyming slang. Henry Hall's means balls. Henry Hall was a famous band leader of the thirties and forties.

hide nor hair: Not a trace.

highheejin: Very important person, often only in the subject's own mind.

hirpled: Walked awkwardly, favouring a sore leg or back.

hirstle: Chesty wheeze.

hit the spot: Fill the need.

HMS: Abbreviation for His Majesty's Ship.

hobby-horse shite: Literally, sawdust.

hobby-horse shite, your head's full of: You're being stupid.

holdall: Canvas sports bag.

hold your horses: Wait a minute.

hooker: The player in rugby football who is in the centre of the three-man front row in an eight-man scrum (scrimmage) and whose job it is to use his boot to hook the ball into his side's territory.

hooley: Party.

hot flushes: Hot flashes.

houseman: Medical intern.

How's (a)bout ye?: How are you? Or good-day.

humdinger: Something extraordinary.

hump, to take the: To take offence.

hunkers: Haunches.

I'm your man: I agree to and will follow your plan.

in soul, I do: Pronounced "in sowl." Emphatic.

in the doghouse: In someone's bad graces.

in the stable: A drink already paid for, to be poured later.

jabs or jags: Needles. Inoculations or injections.

Jack, Jackeen: Slang terms for a Dubliner used by natives of Ireland from places other than Dublin (who themselves are called culchies by Dubliners).

jam jar: A glass vessel for holding homemade preserves. Mrs. Kinkaid used one- and two-pound sizes.

jar: An alcoholic drink.

jammy: Lucky.

jammy, dead: Incredibly lucky.

jaunting car: An open, high, two-wheeled vehicle. The passenger accommodation was two benches, arranged along either side so the passengers sat with their backs to the cart bed. By the sixties it was rarely seen except in the most rural parts of Ireland or as a tourist attraction.

jigs and reels, between the: To cut a long story short.

keek: Look.

kerb: The border between a footpath (sidewalk) and the road or street.

knackered: Very tired. An allusion to a horse so worn out by work that it is destined for the knacker's yard, where horses are destroyed.

knickers in a twist (or knot): Anxiously upset.

knocking: Having sexual intercourse.

knocking shop: Brothel.

Lambeg drum: Massive bass drum carried on shoulder straps by Orangemen and beaten with two sticks, sometimes until the drummer's wrists bleed.

laughed like a drain (or sieve): Utterly incomprehensible simile describing someone laughing uncontrollably.

length and breadth of it: All the details.

lepp: Leap.

let the hare sit: Leave the thing alone.

liberty bodice: Emancipation bodice. Boneless, sleeveless woman's upper-body undergarment worn to avoid wearing a boned corset.

lift: Elevator; a free ride in a vehicle.

lifted: Arrested by the police.

like the sidewall of a house: Huge (especially when applied to someone's physical build).

liltie: A madman. An Irish whirling dervish.

load of cobblers': A load of rubbish. In Cockney rhyming slang, "cobblers' awls" means balls.

loaf: Head.

looney bin: In the sixties, a residential psychiatric institution was still called a lunatic asylum, which was corrupted to "looney bin."

lorry: Truck.

lough: Pronounced "logh," almost as if clearing the throat. A sea inlet or large inland lake.

lugs: Ears.

lummox: Stupid, clumsy creature.

main: Very.

make a mint: Make a great deal of money.

malarkey: Nonsense.

managing director: CEO.

manky: Tattered and torn.

marmalising: Destroying.

match, not at the: Not playing with a full deck.

me arse: My ass. Rubbish.

medical degrees: In Ireland the degrees awarded after medical school are: M.B., bachelor of medicine; B.Ch., bachelor of chirurgery (surgery); and B.A.O., bachelor of the art of obstetrics. The M.D., doctor of medicine, degree is only awarded after a period of postgraduate study and submission and acceptance of a thesis describing a piece of original research. Specialty diplomas (memberships and fellowships) are awarded after a set residency of several years and the passing of the examinations set by one of a number of Royal Colleges. For example, Professor Dunseath is M.D., F.R.C.S. (Royal College of Surgeons), F.R.C.O.G. (Royal College of Obstetricians and Gynaecologists). These are equivalent to National Board Certification. There are also lesser diplomas awarded after six months' study to GPs who have taken further training. D.R.C.O.G. (Diploma of the R.C.O.G.) is an example.

melodeon: Button accordion.

Melton Mobray pie: Savoury pork-and-bacon pie with a thin layer of aspic between the filling and a buttery pastry casing. Best eaten cold with Branston pickle.

mended, well mended: Recovered from an illness.

messages: Errands.

mickey or Mickey Finn: Originally a drink laced with a drug (usually chloral hydrate) used to incapacitate the victim.

mind: Remember.

mission, no: No chance.

MM: Military Medal. Army award for gallantry given to other ranks. Officers got the Military Cross (MC).

money in the bank: Guaranteed.

moping: Indulging in self-pity.

more power to your wheel: Very good luck to you; encouragement.

mortified: Embarrassed beyond belief.

muffler: A long woolen scarf.

muggy: Hot and humid.

mullet, stunned: To look as stupid or surprised as a mullet, an ugly saltwater fish.

Mullingar heifer, legs like: Cows from Mullingar were said to have "beef to the ankles."

my shout, it's: I'm buying the drinks.

nap: The selection of the day, made by tipsters or racing correspondents, at a horse race. To "go nap" is to take their advice and bet accordingly.

nappies: Diapers.

National Hunt: The body in Ireland and the UK governing steeple-chasing; horse racing over a series of obstacles.

near took the rickets: Had a great shock.

nice one: Congratulations.

nicky tams: Scottish, but used in Ulster. Leather thongs tied above the knee to lift trouser cuffs above the mud.

niggling: *v:* Irritating under the surface. *adj:* Of an amount: meanly small.

nobble: Of a horse: prevent it winning, often by drugging, sometimes by pulling.

no offence (or harm) 'til ye, but: I intend to offer a diametrically opposed opinion.

no dozer: Clever.

no goat's toe, he thinks he's: Not stupid. Has an overinflated sense of his own importance.

no joy: No luck.

nose, on the: A bet placed that will be paid only if the horse wins. See *both ways*.

nose out of joint: Miffed.

no side: No maliciousness.

no spring chicken: Getting on in years.

not as green as you're cabbage looking: More clever than you appear to be.

not at myself: Feeling unwell.

not on: Unacceptable.

not put it past: Would not be surprised if.

och blether: Expression of disappointment or frustration.

Old Nick: The devil.

on side: Has agreed to join in.

on the mend: Getting better from an illness.

Orange Order: Fraternal order of Protestants committed to loyalty to the British crown.

Orange and Green: The colours of Loyalists and Republicans. Used to symbolize the age-old schism in Irish politics.

Osler, Sir William: Canadian-born physician described as the father of modern medicine.

ould goat: Stupid old man, often used very affectionately.

out of kilter: Out of alignment.

oxter: Armpit.

oxter-cog: To carry by supporting under the armpits.

pacamac: Cheap, transparent, plastic raincoat carried in a small bag.

Paddy: Diminutive of Patrick. Generic term for an Irishman, akin to Limey for an Englishman, but not regarded as pejorative by most sensible Irish people and certainly not by me. It is, after all, my name.

Paddy hat: Soft-crowned, narrow-brimmed, Donegal tweed hat.

Paddy's market: A large disorganised crowd.

pan loaf: Loaf of ordinary bread.

pass-remarkable: Prone to making unwarranted observations about other people.

pavement: Sidewalk.

peace, hold one's: Remain silent.

peakèd: Unwell.

peakèd, looking: Looking unwell.

peat (turf): Fuel derived from compressed vegetable matter. Burns with the most evocative scent.

pebble-dash: A method of decorating outside house walls with sea-smoothed pebbles embedded in stucco before it has dried.

peely-wally: Scots. Under the weather; unwell.

pelmet: Valance.

penny bap: A small bun, usually dusted with flour.

petrified: Terrified.

physical jerks: Gymnastics.

piece: Bread and spread (butter, jam, lard, banana, etc.) or a sandwich.

pimple: Zit.

piss artist: Alcoholic.

piss, taking the: Mocking or teasing.

pladdy: Low, seaweed-covered reef usually only exposed at low tide.

poke: Have sex with; a small parcel.

pong: British forces slang for "stink."

pop one's clogs: Die.

poulticed: Pregnant, usually out of wedlock.

powerful: Very.

power of: A great deal of.

praties: Potatoes.

professional titles: In Ireland for historic reasons, GPs and all specialists except surgeons used "Doctor." Trainee surgeons used "Doctor" until they had passed their specialty exams, when they reverted to "Mister." Dentists and veterinarians used "Mister" because their basic degrees were bachelorhoods, not doctorates. "Doctor" was also used by anyone with a doctoral degree (Ph.D., D.Sc., D.D., D.Mus., and the like). Professorial rank was reserved for university departmental heads or endowed personal chairs.

pull the other leg: Stop trying to fool me.

punter: Gambler, particularly on horse races.

pupil: Schoolchild. The term "student" in 1964 was applied only to those attending university, after high school.

purse: A small bag to hold money, usually carried in a woman's handbag.

quare (nor): Ulster pronunciation of queer. Used to mean very or strange. Often succeeded with an added "nor" for emphasis. He's quare nor stupid.

queer someone's pitch: Stand in the way of.

quickening: The first time an expectant mother feels her baby moving.

quid: One pound sterling; a piece of chewing tobacco.

quids in: Everything is all right.

quits: Nothing owing on either side.

randy: Sexually aroused.

randy as an old goat: Very sexually aroused.

raparee: Originally, an unskilled labourer. Now used pejoratively for a ne'er-do-well.

rapscallion: Ne'er-do-well.

raring to go: Eager and fully prepared.

reader: Academic rank equivalent to associate professor.

recimetation: Mispronunciation of "recitation."

registrar, medical: Trainee physician equivalent to a North American medical resident.

reverse the charges: Call collect.

right: Real.

right enough: That's true. Used interrogatively it means, is that true?

rightly: Well enough.

rightly, it will do: It's not perfect but will serve well enough.

rightly, I'm: I'm very well.

RMS: Abbreviation for Royal Mail Ship.

road bowling: A game where a 28-ounce metal ball, or "bullet," is thrown, or "lofted," over a fixed length of road. The contestant with the least number of throws wins.

roast someone: Verbally chastise.

rook: Take money by devious means; a black corvid; a chess piece, also called a castle.

roundabout: Traffic circle. Serves the function of a four-way stop. Vehicles approaching from the right have the right of way.

rubbernecking: Prying into another's business.

ructions: Disturbances.

rug rats: Children.

run-race: Quick trip to, usually on foot.

Saint Stephen's Day: December 26; Boxing Day.

savvy?: *v*: Do you understand? From the French *Savez? adj*: Wise about.

saying no more: The decision is final, or I'll not tell you anymore.

scampi: The Norwegian lobster or Dublin Bay prawn—*Nephrops norvegicus*—a small crustacean like a mini-langoustine, served hot in bread crumbs or deep-fried in a light batter.

script/scrip': Prescription.

scunner, take a scunner at or to: Dislike someone intensely and bear a grudge.

scutch grass: Coarse grass found growing in salty soil.

scuttle, coal: Bucket for containing coal for a fire.

see you?: Make no mistake, it is *you* I'm referring to.

semi: Semidetached house. Duplex.

shank's pony: Your own two feet.

shebang, the whole: Lock, stock, and barrel. Everything.

sheugh: Bog.

shit, to: To defaecate.

shite: Faeces.

shooting brake: Woody.

shooting stick: A single-shafted walking stick with a metal point at one end. At the other end two wide leather handles can be pulled down to form a seat.

short and curlies: Pubic hair.

shout, my or your: Turn to buy the drinks.

shufti: Army slang. A quick look at.

sink a mouthful: Swallow.

Sinn Féin: Literally, ourselves. Pronounced "shin fane." The political party of the Irish Republican movement.

Siobhan: Irish name meaning Joan, pronounced "*shivawn.*" I have omitted the fada (*á*) over the *a*, which lengthens *ah* to *aw*.

sister, nursing: In Irish hospitals nuns at one time filled important nursing roles. They no longer do so except in some Catholic institutions. Their honorific, "Sister," has been retained to signify a senior nursing rank. For example, a ward sister is a charge nurse; a sister tutor is a senior nursing teacher. (Because nursing is now a university course taught by professors of nursing the position of sister tutor is now redundant.)

sixpence: One fortieth of a pound sterling, or about ten cents.

skate: A fish of the ray family. Once common, now endangered.

skinful: Drunk.

skitters: Diarrhoea.

skiver: Corruption of "scurvy." Pejorative. Ne'er-do-well.

skivvy: From "scurvy." Housemaid.

slagging: Can be a verbal chastisement ("She give him a terrible slagging") or a friendly insulting banter.

sláinte (sláinte mHaith): Irish. Pronounced *"slauntuh."* Your health.

slander: Verbal defamation of character as opposed to libel, or written defamation.

sliced pan, best thing since: Presliced, then wrapped, pan loaf (a loaf of bread) was reintroduced after the Second World War. To be better than it was to be the acme of perfection.

slip jig: Traditional dance.

slosh him one: Thump him.

slough about: Pronounced *"sluff."* Laze around.

smacker: Pound sterling; a kiss.

snaps: Photographs.

snotters: Runny nose or boogers.

snowball's chance: Implies, "as much as a snowball's chance in hell." No chance at all.

snowdrop: A small, delicate, white flower. Family: Amaryllidaceae. Genus: *Galanthus.* Blooms in Ulster in February.

soap bag: Sponge bag. Toiletry bag.

sodger: Soldier.

soft hand under a duck: Gentle or very good at.

solicitor: Attorney, but one who would not appear in court, which is done by barristers.

solid citizen: Reliable and trustworthy person.

sore tried by: Very worried by or very irritated by.

sound man: Sensible and trustworthy.

sparks, sparky: Electrician.

spavins: A disease of horses resulting in a swayback.

spill it: Tell us. Comes from gangster movies of the forties, when someone would "spill the beans."

spinster of this parish: On the three Sundays prior to a church wedding, the minister read the banns, the announcement of the impending ceremony, from the pulpit. This was a formal announcement of intent. The single bride-to-be, a spinster, was always referred to in this way.

spondulix: Money.

spunk: True grit. Nerve.

SS: Abbreviation. Steamship.

stays: Whalebone corset.

stewing over: Worrying.

sticking out: Very good.

sticking out a mile: Absolutely the best.

sticking the pace: Hanging in.

sticking the pace rightly: More than merely hanging in.

stiver: The most trifling coin.

stocious: Drunk.

stone: Measure of weight equal to 14 pounds.

stoon: Sudden shooting pain.

stout: A dark beer, usually Guinness or Murphy's.

strip camera: A narrow-lensed camera that exposed film at 55 feet per second, the rate at which horses gallop. Used to record the finish of horse races before digital cameras were invented.

strong weakness: Hangover.

suspender: Garter.

suspender belt: Garterbelt.

sussed out: Figured out.

sweetie: Candy. Also a term of affection.

swindle: Scam.

take a daisy: Relax.

take a gander: Look at.

take in: Hospitals in which there were multiple wards assigned each ward on a rotational basis for a twenty-four-hour period to accept emergencies.

take leave of your senses: Do something incredibly stupid.

take the light from her eyes: Confound or amaze.

take your hurry in your hand: Wait a minute.

talent: Unattached young women.

tall around: Fat.

Taoiseach: Irish, pronounced *"teeshuck."* Prime minister.

targe: Bad-tempered woman with a vitriolic tongue.

taste, a wee: Small amount, not necessarily edible, as in "Put a wee taste of oil on the axle."

ta-ta-ta-ra: Dublin slang. Party.

teetotally: Absolutely.

tenner: Ten-pound note.

Tenniel: Sir John Tenniel, ilustrator of Lewis Carroll's *Alice* books.

terrible: Very.

that's for me to know, you to find out: Mind your own business.

there: Used for accuracy or immediacy. Examples: That there dog (*that*-dog). There now (*now*).

thick: Stupid.

thick as two short planks: Very stupid.

thole: Tolerate or put up with.

thon: That.

thonder, it's at: Over there. Usually indicated by pointing.

thrapple: Throat.

through the wars: Has been sick.

throw off or up: Vomit.

thruppenny bit: Predecimalization coin of the UK and of the Irish Republic before it converted to the euro; worth three pennies.

tickled: In full, "tickled pink." Very pleased.

tic-tac man: Assistant to a bookie, who wears white gloves and by an intricate system of hand signals relays information about changing odds or updated news of a horse's form.

tight as a newt: Drunk.

'til: Until. Can also be used geographically: "I'm going 'til (to) Belfast."

tinker's damn: Worthless item.

tinker's damn, don't give a: Could not care less.

toilet: Washroom; the specific piece of bathroom furniture, complete with a toilet seat.

toty: Small.

toty, wee: Very small.

tousling: Roughing up, verbally or physically.

"tower bird": The cry when a wounded pheasant rockets skyward. It was also the nom de plume of Noel "Tim" Sedgwick, an editor of and contributor to the *Shooting Times*.

townland: A mediaeval geographic unit usually comprising a village and surrounding farms.

tried: Agitated.

tried, to get: Become agitated.

true day: Lovely day.

tuppence: Two pennies; 120th of a pound sterling, or about two and a half cents.

turf accountant: Bookmaker.

up the spout or pipe: Pregnant.

V.C.: Victoria Cross. Highest British award for gallantry, equivalent to the Congressional Medal of Honor. As opposed to all other decorations, which were awarded on class lines (see *MM*), it was open to all ranks. Cast from the bronze of Russian canons used in the Crimean War. It bore the motto "For Valour."

walk out with: Pay court to. See also *coortin'*.

wean: Pronounced "wane." Child.

wee: Small, but in Ulster can be used to modify almost anything without reference to size. A barmaid and old friend greeted me by saying, "Come on in, Pat. Have a wee seat and I'll get you a wee menu, and would you like a wee drink while you're waiting?"

wee buns: Very easy.

wee ways: Near.

Wellington boots, wellies: Knee-high rubber boots patterned on the riding boots worn by the Duke of Wellington.

wet, wee: Alcoholic drink.

whaling away at: Beating.

wheeker: Very good.

wheen: Number of.

wheen, brave: A very large number of.

wheeped: Whistled.

wheest, houl your: Be quiet. Hold (pronounced "*howl*") your tongue.

wheezle: Wheeze in chest.

where to go for corn, did not know: Was completely stumped.

whin: Gorse.

whippet: Small, fast racing dog like a mini-greyhound.

whisky/whiskey: Scotch is "whisky," as is rye. Irish is "whiskey," as are Tennessee and bourbon. Both spellings are derived from the Gaelic *uisce beatha* (water of life). Interestingly, *akuavit* in Scandinavia and *aqua vitae* in Latin mean the same thing.

whore's git: Whore's bastard. Not a term of endearment.

wildfowling: Duck hunting.

willy: Penis.

wind: Intestinal gas.

won't butter any parsnips: Will make absolutely no difference.

worser: As bad as it is possible to get; much more so than worse.

ye: You. Used frequently in Northern Ireland and much more commonly in the Republic (see *yiz* and *youse*).

yiz: Country pronunciation of *youse* (see *youse* below). Ye, yiz, and youse may be used in one sentence.

you girl, you: Emphatic words, usually of encouragement. "Go on you girl, you."

you know: Used extensively as verbal punctuation, usually in circumstances where the listener hasn't the faintest chance of knowing.

you're on: Agreed to, or to indicate acceptance of a wager.

your head's cut (a marley): You are being very stupid; your head is as small and as dense as a child's marble.

your man: Someone who is not present but who has been heard of by others there. "Your man President Obama said . . ." Also, *I'm your man.*

youse: Ulster *you*. Usually plural but can be singular. See *ye* and *yiz.*

zizz: Nap.